a Change of Heart

Sonali Dev's first literary work was a play about mistaken identities performed at her neighborhood Diwali extravaganza in Mumbai. She was eight years old. Despite this early success, Sonali spent the next few decades getting degrees in architecture and writing, migrating across the globe, and starting a family while writing for magazines and websites. With the advent of her first gray hair her mad love for telling stories returned full force.

She lives in the Chicago suburbs with her very patient and often amused husband and two teens who demand both patience and humor, and the world's most perfect dog.

Sonali's novels have been on *Library Journal*, NPR, *Washington Post*, and Kirkus's lists of Best Books of the year. She won the American Library Association's award for best romance 2014, and is a RITA® finalist, RT Reviewer Choice Award Nominee, and winner of the RT Seal of Excellence. She was hailed by NPR.org as a 'stunning debut'.

a Change of Heart

SONALI DEV

HarperCollins *Publishers* India

First published by Kensington Publishing Corp. in New York in 2016

First published in India by
HarperCollins *Publishers* in 2018

Building 10, Tower A, 4th Floor, DLF Cyber City, Phase II,
Gurugram Haryana – 122002, India
www.harpercollins.co.in

2 4 6 8 10 9 7 5 3 1

P-ISBN: 978-93-5302-285-3
E-ISBN: 978-93-5302-286-0

Printed and bound at
MicroPrints India, New Delhi

For Mihir and Annika, because I want you
to believe that every darkness can be overcome.
And because you are the brightness that lights up my world.

1

Nikhil's here and I could just die of happiness. Shit, I shouldn't have said that. Especially not now. Please, Universe, scratch that.

—Dr. Jen Joshi

Nikhil's head felt like someone had squeezed it through a liquidizer. Whiskey burn stung his brain as if he had snorted the stuff instead of pouring it down his gullet. He leaned into the polished brass railing, letting the wind pummel his face. The ship, all twenty-four floors of behemoth decadence, was like the damn Burj Al Arab speeding across the Caribbean. And yet the only way to know they were moving was to watch the waves. His fingers released the glass sitting on the railing and it flew into the night, disappearing long before it hit the inky water.

He imagined hopping on the railing, imagined being that glass. Boom! And it would be over. Finally, there'd be peace.

The sky was starting to ignite at the edges, as though the glass of Jack he'd just tossed into the night had splattered amber flecks across the horizon. It would go up in flames soon. All of it orange and gold when the sun broke through the rim of the ocean. It was time for him to leave. The last thing he needed was the mockery of another breaking dawn.

"Sir, why don't you stay and watch today?" A man leaned on his mop, staring at Nikhil from under his windblown hair, that tentative, guilty look firmly in place. The look people couldn't seem to keep off their faces when they talked to Nikhil—the one that announced, rather loudly, that they were terrified of intruding. Because The Pathetic Dr. Joshi with the giant hole in his heart might break down right before their eyes.

"Very beautiful it is, no?" The man pointed his chin at the burgeoning sunrise that had just pumped Nikhil's lungs full of pain, and waited for a response. But while the blazing pain in Nikhil's heart was functioning at full capacity, the booze incapacitated his tongue. He wanted to react, wanted to have a conversation with the man who was obviously starved for it. He searched for words to say, but he came up empty.

Now there was a word: *empty*.

Still empty after two years.

The deckhand's smiling mouth drooped into a frown. He turned away and started working the spotless floor with his mop. Shit, had he just thought of the man as a deckhand? Jen would have clonked him upside the head for it. Jen would've—

"What's your name?" Conversation was better than the high-definition telecast of memories that kicked off in his brain.

"Gavin." The man looked surprised. "From Goa. In India."

Great. Goa. Jen's favorite place in the whole world.

The steady boat pitched beneath Nikhil's feet. His stomach lurched. The world somersaulted around him. He leaned over the brass railing and tried not to throw up his guts.

He failed. When the heaving stopped, the world was still spinning too fast. He lifted his T-shirt and wiped the foul-smelling puke off his mouth. Gavin from Goa was walking across the deck with a bottle of water in his hand.

Nikhil should have thanked him, should've told him he was fine. Instead he turned toward the stairs. In the light of day he could talk to people, pretend to be alive, but now when the world was as dark as his insides, he couldn't. The stairs dived into the lower deck. He grabbed the railing and stumbled down, landing on his ass on the last step.

The smell of chlorine from the three-tiered pool cut past the smell of regurgitated Jack on his shirt, setting off the churning in his stomach again. He pulled himself up and dragged himself to the elevator, rubbing his face on his shoulder like the snotty, cranky brat he used to be. But no tears came to dilute the unrelenting burn of wanting.

How could it be that he was still here? The sunset, the sunrise, it was all still here when she was gone.

He wanted her back. God. Please. Give her back to me.

"Look what you've done to yourself, Spikey."

His head snapped up. He didn't remember stepping out of the elevator, but he spun around now, his breath loud in the absolute silence. The brightly lit corridor swirled around him. The bloodred carpet, the gold-striped walls, every inch of garish splendor echoed that word.

"Spikey."

There wasn't a soul in sight.

He followed the echoing word across the hallway and around the corner, his racing heart dragging the rest of his body along. He turned the corner, expecting to see nothing. Expecting to chase the sound the way he'd been chasing his dead wife's memories for two years.

A shadow clad in black stood all the way across the corridor. A wisp of dark against the overpowering gold of the walls. Bright red strands cascaded around her face and into her jaw in a razor-sharp edge. Hair he knew better than he knew his own name.

He reached out and leaned into the wall, but the ship continued to seesaw beneath him. She held steady for a moment and then she was gone, melting around the corner.

He sprang after her, running until he was standing in the spot she'd been in. Another long corridor stretched out in front of him. It showed no signs of life, only an endless line of doors connected by endless golden molding, and the endless buzz of the lights overhead.

The walls closed in around him, forcing him to stumble forward. His breath ricocheted against the heavily textured wallpaper.

And then there she was again, a flash of red hair peeking around the corner. He ran at it, at her. But his drunken legs tripped over themselves and he splattered flat on his face, arms and legs splayed like a dead arthropod someone had swatted into the floor.

When he lifted his head she was gone.

His face fell back on the rough, deep pile of the carpet with its polythene smell, and everything went black. Everything except the panacean sound of that name.

Spikey.

Only one person called him that.

Jen, his wife. And she'd been dead for two years.

Nikhil woke up to the sound of drums beating inside his cerebral cortex. And to claws plucking at his spinal cord as if it were a string on the guitar that still hung on the wall of his childhood room in his parents' home.

Pain vibrated down each vertebra, his usual wake-up call. He knew enough not to sit up immediately, because steady as the boat was, his inner boat would pitch and rock like a rabid Jell-O cup until he made it to the toilet and emptied his innards through his mouth and nose. So much for the comfort of morning rituals.

He was in his own bed. Although he didn't remember getting here. He lifted the sheet off his bare chest and rubbed his wife's misspelled name tattooed across his left pec. His running shorts were still in place over his jutting pelvic bones. They had always been prominent after he'd lost his chubby-kid fat in college. But now they were sharp enough to cut through skin. He pressed his hand into the knife-edged rise of bone, the exact place Jen had liked to hold when—

He sat up too fast. Bile jelly-wobbled up his esophagus bringing back everything that had happened before he had passed out in that corridor. The over-deodorized smell of carpet. The flash of red hair. He tried to fight it, but his brain traced back his steps until it hit up against that word.

Spikey.

His wife had taken to calling him that after he'd told her how *Spikey The Dinosaur* had been his favorite TV show in elementary school. He had been a little obsessed with the young stegosaurus who wanted nothing more than for everyone to be happy, who always did the right thing, who had everything a little dinosaur could ask for but was always on the verge of losing it all. Nikhil's mother still had his Spikey toy collection stored in the basement.

When he'd shown it to Jen, she had twirled her fingers in his hair, finding that sensitive spot at the top of his head. *Your hair stands up in spikes just like Spikey, Spikey.*

He scrubbed his hand over the hair he now kept cropped down to a skull trim, over the scar slashing down the back of his head where they had cracked open his skull. Sometimes that sort of thing took your memories. With him it had jackhammered the memories into his brain. And what did you do with memories of your wife having her neck snapped in an alley while they held you down and made you watch what they did to her?

The newly grown hair scraped like a hundred two-sided needles into his palm and his scalp. Jen would have hated his shaved head. Hated it. She had loved his hair. She had loved every stupid thing about him. For the life of him he hadn't known why.

"What is wrong with you?" he'd asked her once.

"Actually, my weakness for men with pathetic self-esteem is my only flaw," she'd told him. She'd been more than a little pissed at him for asking.

He threw the sheets back and pushed his legs off the bed.

Look what you've done to yourself, Spikey.

She had been so real. The hair framing her face, that blasted hair color he'd hated so much. It had been so damn real. Maybe it was time to stop chugging the Jack. The whole point of it was to shut the memories down, not to bring them to life.

He reached out and gripped the nightstand to steady the endless pitching in his stomach. Then yanked his hand back when his fingers landed on two bright white pills on a writing pad. His thumb found its way to his wedding band and went to work, rotating it around his finger at a maddening skip. Around and around.

He knew the slanting scrawl on the pad. The *T* flying off the page; the *g* looping around on itself.

He knew what the note said even before he read it.

Take two aspirin and call me in the morning.

Fuck.

His Jen was back.

2

My husband's G-spot is on his head. There's this point right at his crown under where his hair gets all spiky, and rubbing it makes him totally hard.

—Dr. Jen Joshi

One of these days she'd get used to calling herself Jess. *Just think of it as a role,* he had told her. Of course she thought of it as a role. How else could she possibly do this?

There had been a time when she would have given anything to be someone else, to have a new name, a new history. A fresh slate. Pure again. But there was nothing pure about what she was doing. It was yet another rebirth right into the gutter.

Speaking of gutters, she tried not to think about the smell of vomit in Dr. Nikhil Joshi's room when she had dragged him there last night and left him sprawled on his bed. Maybe pulling off his shirt had been stupid. What if he had woken up? But knowing he was Jen's husband, she just hadn't been able to leave him in soiled clothes. Which was definitely stupid because the sympathy squeezing in her chest was an indulgence she absolutely could not afford.

The good doctor*saab*'s vomit had smelled like the hell he seemed to be trapped in. Booze and bile. Excess and starvation.

His ribs had been so stark against his skin, shades lighter than the burned tan of his forearms and face. The desire to toss his T-shirt into the trash had been strong, but only because she couldn't burn it. Instead she had dumped it on the scattered pile of laundry in the corner of his room, done what she needed to do, and left. Hanging around his kind of pain gouged out all her scabs, and she needed her scabs.

It had been a week. A full week away from her baby. The garish splendor of her shoebox-sized room did nothing to keep it from feeling like a jail cell. All she wanted was to be back in her little flat in Mumbai, with her baby in her arms. Being so far away from him made her feel scattered, as though all of her were parts and pieces floating around without glue. Before this, she'd never left him for so much as a day. Those two days when he'd disappeared, when they'd taken him from her, were something she couldn't think about right now. If she thought about that, she wouldn't be able to get through this.

She picked up her phone. She needed to hear his voice. Calls to Mumbai from the cruise ship were obscenely priced. Good. Because she wasn't the one paying for them. The thought of making the bastard who was paying for the calls pay for something, for anything, gave her a breath of satisfaction.

"Hello, darling." The husky sweetness of Sweetie Raja's voice released some of the tension in her body. Putting people at ease was her flatmate's special gift. She sank into the tiny bunk bed and slipped off her ballet flats, flexing her toes and stretching out her calves. If she wasn't able to dance soon, she was going to explode.

"Hi, Sweetie, is Joy up yet?"

"I'm fine, darling, thank you so much for asking."

"I'm sorry. Everything okay with you?"

He laughed. She could imagine his gorgeous ponytail swaying to his laughter, his kohl-lined eyes sparkling beneath lashes that drove women wild with envy and men wild with confusion.

"You're apologizing? Who are you, and what did you do with my best friend?" he asked, still laughing.

"Ignore me. I'll be my unapologetic bitchy self when I get back. Promise."

The laughter in his voice turned to worry. "Listen to you. You sound exhausted. When was the last time you got some sleep?"

"I'm fine."

Sweetie knew she couldn't talk about it. He hadn't once asked for details. This was why he was her best friend. He was completely at ease around secrets.

"Joy's brushing his teeth. You know you need your strength for the audition next month," he said.

She mumbled something. She knew Sweetie had pulled every string he could to get her the audition with Bollywood's top dance troupe. A dream she could almost touch after working toward it for five years. And here she was a million miles away, where the last thing on her mind was which bloody troupe she danced with.

He called out to Joy. "Joy, Mamma's on the phone, son. Brushing done?"

Her baby's sweet mouth had to be dripping white foam. The bubblegum smell of his toothpaste lumped in her throat. She always made him count ten brushstrokes for each tooth and he did it as though her word were law. Seven-year-olds were supposed to be willful, but it had probably never even occurred to Joy that he could argue with her.

"Mamma?"

With every one of her senses she gathered up his voice. "Hi, Joyboy."

"Ten times on each tooth. I counted." Her sweet, sweet baby.

"You sure?" she said as sternly as she could manage. "Because, you don't—"

"I know, I know, I don't want worms to dig holes in my enalbum."

"Germs, *babu*, not worms."

She heard a soft smack. His palm striking his forehead and a self-conscious cluck. "Yeah, yeah, that."

"Are you taking good care of Sweetie-mamu?"

"I'm trying, but he won't stop drinking so many coffees. I told him you'd be angry if you found out. But . . ." There was a pause, and he lowered his voice to a whisper. "But he told me not to tell you."

She laughed, and the sweet pain in her heart made her whole again. "You keep trying. All we can do is try, remember?"

"Mamma?"

"Yeah, *babu*?"

"I made you something in school. But you don't have to come home soon to see it. Sheila-teacher said she'll keep it carefully for you, okay?"

It took her a moment to respond without letting her voice crack. "Mamma will be home as soon as she can. And you know what?"

"Yes, yes, I know. I know your heart is with me. And yes, yes, I'm taking care of it for you."

"Good, because hearts are important." Her hand went to her chest. The still unfamiliar raised scar pushed into her hand. It was only fair that it still hurt. "I love you, my Joy-baby-boy. Mamma's kissing you and holding you. Can you feel it?"

There was silence on the phone, and she knew he had squeezed his eyes shut, imagining her arms around him. "Did you feel mine?"

"Of course I did. But I didn't hear the kiss."

The smacking of his lips was so loud and clear she soaked up the sound and held on to it.

"I love you most in the world, Mamma."

"Hey!" Sweetie's voice was back on the phone. "What about me?"

"Is he rolling his eyes at you?" she asked, biting her lip.

"Of course he is. And he does it even better than you."

"Thanks, Sweetie." Her teeth dug into her lip. Tears were a luxury she couldn't afford either.

"Thank me by coming home safe."

She made an incoherent sound and let him go. Her safety wasn't the issue. How she wished it was, but it wasn't.

She watched Jen's Nikhil tuck his white uniform shirt into his white pants and walk out of the clinic. He always seemed to move as if an invisible crane were pulling him forward, always against his will.

Why a doctor had to dress like a cruise ship purser she had no idea, but despite the fact that the uniform was ironed and clean, he managed to make it look almost as soiled as his vomit-streaked T-shirt from last night.

For all the effort she had put into preparing herself to come face-to-face with him, seeing him fall flat on his face like a roadside drunkard while trying to chase her down a corridor was the last thing she had expected. Actually, the horrid sadness it set off inside her was the last thing she had expected. Usually, she liked nothing more than to see a man fall flat on his face and get hurt. It was like poetry to her, watching them in pain instead of inflicting it.

She took a deep breath, adjusted the hood of her sweatshirt so it covered her head, and followed him into the elevator, sliding into the back corner behind him. Not that he noticed her. Not that he noticed anything. He seemed to have no idea that there was a world around him and that it was spinning away with or without him.

Even if he did happen to wake up from his stupor, there was no chance in hell that he would recognize her from yesterday. Not with her hair stuffed into a hairband and hidden away under the thick fleece-lined fabric.

She still couldn't believe what hair extensions could do. All her life she had hated her wispy hair. Now that the heavier healthier strands had been tacked on to her head, all she felt was the awful weight of them. But if his dead wife's hair was what it took to get his attention, then that's what it took.

He had been at the clinic since nine in the morning. It was almost seven p.m. now. He hadn't stepped out of the clinic for ten hours, not even to eat lunch. He had the look of someone who had spent a year in a famine-ridden nation. Skin over bone. No quilting of muscle or fat. But unlike those pictures of starving people from famines, there was no hunger in his eyes. There was, in fact, absolutely nothing in his eyes.

The elevator started to move, and the strange tension in her belly heightened. Closed spaces made her jittery, especially when she was trapped in one with a man. The elevator bounced to a halt. Nikhil didn't move.

This was his floor. He was messing up her plan. She cleared her throat. He straightened and dragged himself out.

With a finger on the door-open button, she waited for him to be far enough away that he couldn't reach her before the door closed. Then she yanked back her hood, tugged Jen's hair out of the band, and shook it out so it covered most of her face.

"Spikey . . ." She whispered the word as the door started to slide. It was almost as though she could see the syllables float across the lobby toward him. The instant they struck like a harpoon between his shoulder blades, he spun around. His suddenly alert gaze slammed into her cascading hair and clung to it. Now there was hunger. Crazed, desperate hunger.

He leapt forward. But of course he didn't reach her outstretched hand before the door closed. She had timed her words perfectly.

She stepped out of the elevator on the eighth floor, then slipped quietly into a corridor and then her room. Before long the sound of running feet passed outside the door she was leaning against. The desperate edge to the sound had to be her imagination, the thudding in her heart just adrenaline. With over three thousand rooms on *The Oasis*, there was no way he would find her.

Actively bringing her heartbeat under control, she pulled out her bag from the closet, gripping the rough black canvas with its red stitching so hard her fingers cramped. She hadn't bothered to unpack. If she had her way, she was getting off the ship with Dr. Joshi in a few days, so why bother? Under her neatly folded clothes—black sweats, black jeans, black tanks—there was a zipper that opened the false bottom of the bag. She unzipped it and pulled out a glossy photograph of Joy and pressed it to her heart.

The memory of her baby boy's smell wrapped around her, the sweetness of milk and Bournvita and baby soap all mixed in with his breath and his sweat and his drool. His Joy smell. From that first time they'd laid him on her breast in the hospital he'd grown and changed every day, but that smell of him, that had stayed exactly the same. It was her stamp on him and his on her.

Pressed against the photo, her scar prickled and tightened. The blasted thing had a life of its own and it refused to let her forget it was there. As if she needed a reminder. As if she could ever be the person she had been before she got it.

The sound of footsteps echoed outside her door again. She imagined Nikhil's starved body racing up and down all the corridors on the ship and refused to acknowledge the squeezing in her chest it set off. She could open the door, let him in and tell him everything. But he'd never believe her. She needed him ready. Ripe, and desperate enough to suspend all that he held as true.

Amazingly enough, he had jumped down the rabbit hole rather more easily than she had expected.

You're right, Jen, she thought, *your Spikey does have reverse trust issues.*

Thank heavens for small mercies. She wasn't about to stare a gift horse in the mouth, given that gift horses weren't a problem she'd ever had to deal with.

She gave the photograph one last look, filled her mind with her baby's sweet smile, pulled out the only other thing she had stashed away in the false bottom of the bag, and settled in to read.

3

Nic is going to kill me for doing this to my hair. I just know he is. But I think it might be good for him. It's unhealthy to be this obsessed with your wife's hair.

—Dr. Jen Joshi

Nikhil slammed his fist against the number eight on the wall. He'd forgotten if he had covered the eighth floor already. He no longer knew where the hell he was or how long he'd been running up and down corridors. Or why his brain had waited two years before going kaput. The Jack had to have killed at least half his brain cells by now, but hearing that name, seeing that slide of bright red hair, he knew he wasn't hallucinating. Then there was the aspirin next to his bed. Those little white pills were as real as shit got.

He made his way down the stairs. Groups of people milled around everywhere, dressed as though they were at a wedding. It had to be Formal Night again. He slipped past the crush of bodies, trying to block out the clawing mix of perfume and good cheer.

Take two aspirin and call me in the morning.

It's what Jen had said to him that first time she'd kissed him, and he'd told her he might die if she didn't let him into her room and do it again. She'd leaned into him, pushed her lips into his ear, and said the words: *Take two aspirin and call me in the morning, Dr. Joshi.*

They'd left those words on notes for each other the next morning whenever they stayed up half the night making love. Which was, oh, all the damn time.

Being on mission with Doctors Without Borders was being in the middle of war, and sex in all its life-affirming glory was rampant. The perfect escape. Doctors and nurses and all the workers of the MSF did it like rabbits trying to inherit the earth by repopulating it.

Not him, though. Not until Jen had grabbed him outside her room in Kandahar after they'd ducked under tables and let their clinic be perforated by insurgent bullets and he'd found himself wrapped around the seven-year-old boy he'd been treating for a persistent cough. He'd walked her to her room, and she'd pushed herself against him and stuck her tongue in his mouth with such hunger he would never forget it as long as he lived.

After that . . . after that, his life had never gone back to the way it had been before, and it never would. They had been on the same mission only twice, and every moment they had off, which really was tiny snatches of time interspersed between sawing off limbs and digging out bullets, they had spent digging into each other. In the wretched hell of Sierra Leone and Afghanistan, what could be better than making love to your wife, than listening to her talk, rolling around in her incredible mind, drowning in her laughter, and soaking up her love-drenched moans as she came around you?

He slid his key card into his door and let himself into his room. No warm mirror-work bedspread, no quirky papier mâché eggs with colorful dots and swirls. No pictures made by children tacked on the walls. No matter how frugal, how filthy their surroundings, she had always made their home home.

The clock flashed eight o'clock. Not too early to start drinking. Usually, he'd go running at this time. But dead weights hung from his body. The kind of exhaustion he was feeling belonged to a ninety-year-old, with advanced tuberculosis.

He poured out a glass of Jack and took it to bed. Without removing his shoes he sank onto the mattress and cradled the drink in his lap. His lids grew heavy, but he couldn't give in. The moment his eyes closed, it would all be over. The only way to avoid it was drinking until he was sick to his stomach. Only then did he have a prayer at avoiding the nightmares.

Look what you've done to yourself, Spikey.

He picked up the note from the nightstand.

She'd found him on the deck last night. She'd found him in the elevator today. She was looking for him. Insane and entirely implausible as the idea was, could his wife really be looking for him? He let the thought linger for a few seconds, sucking up the fake relief of it.

Someone was looking for him, all right, someone who had defiled Jen's memory with that word and that hair. Someone who knew what had been so private between them. He'd been too drunk the first time and too lost in his darkness the second time.

For the first time in two years, he put the Jack down without taking a sip and dragged himself to the door. Sitting in his room wasn't going to bring her to him a third time. He stepped out of his room dead sober. The next time she found him he'd be ready.

She had spent a week observing Jen's husband, and he was as predictable as that social schedule they kept displaying all over the ship. Today's Events! (Never terribly different from yesterday's events!)

But suddenly, he seemed to have decided to shake things up because he hadn't shown up on the upper deck yet. All she could do was wait. She pressed herself into the shadows that had hidden her weeklong surveillance.

It was no wonder why he picked this deck for his nightly slow-suicide-by-alcohol missions. It was deathly silent—the only silent bubble in this floating cloud of raucous noise, too high up and isolated for the crowds and too disruptively windy for the peace seekers, all five of them on the ship.

She pulled the hood of her sweatshirt tighter over Jen's hair as it twisted and flipped around her head as if it knew what she was doing and wanted out. She knew the feeling only too well.

Soon enough it would be time to let it out. For now, she curbed it and stole its freedom and reached into the stillness it had taken her ten years of being a dancer to cultivate. Most people didn't realize that dance was as much about the stillness between movement as it was about movement itself. It was about holding your body exactly the way it needed to be held to tell a story. Just like in life, it was the stillness that made all the motion meaningful.

Just as she had done every night that week, she relaxed her muscles one by one and readied herself for the wait. His hand wrapped around her waist before his breathing filled her ear. Fear roared to life in her chest and cut off her breath. His mouth pressed into the hood of her sweatshirt. "Who are you?"

Pain. There was so much pain in that voice. She leeched into it like a bloodsucker until the slamming in her heart calmed and her senses returned. There wasn't a hint of alcohol on his breath today, and that helped her breathe again.

"Does it matter who I am?"

He spun her around and pushed her away. But he kept a handful of her sweatshirt in his fist, as if he was afraid she was going to disappear again.

She met his gaze. His eyes were the darkest brown, like sugar burned past caramelization and hardened to bitter. How had she thought they were empty? Anger and hatred warred with pain, and then there it was, what she needed most, the barest hint of incipient hope.

He pushed her hood back.

The red mass spilled around her face. He let her go so fast the strands licking her face might as well have been flames.

"Why are you doing this?" His voice was the sound of gravel crunching underfoot when you went in search of gravestones.

An unfamiliar urge to touch him pulled at her fingertips. She crushed it against the fabric of her sweatshirt, pulling it tighter around herself. It kept her from covering up her hair. She had to let him look. No matter the pain in his eyes, she had to let him look. What bled from him was not her concern. Bringing him to his senses, that was why she was here. That was all she needed to focus on.

"Jen needs to speak to you."

He stumbled back. Dry rasps of breath pumped from his chest. "How do you know her name? How do you know what she called me?"

"She told me."

His fingers went to his head and fought to grip something but came up empty. He had forgotten how short his hair was. Suddenly, his eyes were empty again, as if he couldn't remember where he was. Who he was.

His fingers splayed helplessly across his skull. "My wife is dead." The words pumped pain back into his empty eyes. Pain and restlessness that turned him into a caged animal that had given up on freedom.

"I know." She struggled to keep her voice even. "I know she's dead."

"Then what the hell are you talking about?"

She swallowed. No matter how many times she'd practiced this, the words stuck in her throat.

He slid his hands to the back of his head and squeezed the nape of his neck. His shoulders started shaking. Something gurgled in his chest. Something that sounded like a laugh but felt nothing like one.

"Shit, you're one of those psychic-ghost-whisperer types. Great." He spun around and started walking away. Then just as suddenly he stopped and turned on her again. "You're sick. You know that. You people are just fucking sick."

"She has unfinished business."

He was on her in a second, his hands on her shoulders, violence in his eyes. She panicked. Age-old terror cramped in her belly. She scrambled back, shaking.

Almost as forcefully as he'd grabbed her, he let her go, as disgusted at her fear as she was. But despite his own pain, he had seen her terror.

Before she could free fall into the whirlpool of her memories, she focused on Jen and forced the words out. "Her killers are roaming free." Thinking about the violence that had killed Jen almost choked her, hitting too close to home. "You're letting those bastards run free. How can you do that?"

This time he turned around and ran to the stairs, desperate to get away from her words. His legs lost purchase, and he almost went flying down the staircase. But he grabbed the railing and righted himself, somehow making it down the steps on the strength of those arms, lean and roped with starved muscle.

She ran after him. "Don't you care?"

He ignored her and kept moving down the isolated deck.

"Jen thinks you care."

He stopped. His fists so tight at his sides, tendons and muscles knotted and jutted against his skin in the harsh lights attempting to illuminate the night.

She had to turn him around.

He started walking again, dragging himself past the neatly arranged deck chairs as empty as his eyes had been. The wind was too high tonight and they had no audience.

She couldn't let an opportunity like this go. She followed him. He was going to turn around. Somehow she just knew he was. He had to.

"I'm not a psychic," she called out. "I swear to you." She knew she had to be patient, give him as much time as he needed to come around. But every minute that ticked by was a minute she shouldn't be here. Please, please turn around.

"I just need five minutes. Please." She was begging. But she'd do so much more. She'd do whatever it took.

He stopped. He turned around. His white shirt billowed in the breeze, curving inward and hollowing out his moonlit form. Well, wasn't the universe just poetic tonight?

She walked up to him, hooking her focus on her own movements, not on the anger on his face. Not the broken trembling in his body. It was just the waves and the ship. The ringing in her ears was just the wind whistling. Empathy, sympathy, generosity were luxuries people like her couldn't afford. *Don't deviate from the script,* she told herself. *Do* not *deviate from the script.*

She planted herself a few feet from him and grounded herself in the moment, mirroring the way his body was rooted to the spot, absolutely frozen. Except his thumb. His thumb worked furiously on the thick gold band on his ring finger, spinning it and spinning it.

"You have five minutes." For all his stillness he was a rock loaded on a catapult, ready to fly out of her hands.

But she had her five minutes.

"I'm not a psychic or a medium. I've never seen a ghost, or any dead person. But . . . but I've been communicating with Jen."

He squeezed his eyes shut and his thumb went crazy on his ring. Other than that he didn't respond.

"She, your wife, she loved you very mu—"

"What do you want? Is it money?" He opened his eyes and looked at her and she felt a little sick.

"I feel like I know her."

"How much do you want?"

The girl with Jen's hair whipping around her face like flames in a storm looked fragile enough for the wind to carry her away, and yet she was clobbering him with her bare hands, uprooting him like the Incredible Hulk going to work on a tree.

She ignored his question the way she was ignoring the windstorm raging around them. Composed. She was so damn composed. No guilt on her face for sucking at his pain, pecking at it like a sharp-beaked vulture.

He'd seen too many of these scavengers on the streets of Mumbai, the villages in Malawi, the lanes of Peshawar. One glimpse of exposed innards and they thought it was their moral right to feed off them because they were starving.

But for what she was making him feel, for even mentioning Jen's name, he was going to make her regret ever finding him. He was going to make sure she never did this to another human being again. It had been so long since he'd felt anything but dead, the sheer volume of his anger made him sway on his feet.

"I told you, I don't want your money. I just need to tell you what Jen—"

"Stop saying her name. Stop fucking saying her name."

"Okay, I won't say her name, but I do need to tell you what she wants you to know."

"Oh and what is that? My bank account number? My debit card PIN maybe?"

"At least hear me out, Nikhil."

"Don't say my name either. You have one minute left. After that you don't say anything to me at all. Ever."

Instead of opening her mouth and parroting the same drivel she'd been laying on him, she unzipped her sweatshirt. It instantly billowed around her, bloating her tiny form. In the floodlit night her cheeks flamed with an almost bruise-like flush.

She looked down at the shirt she was wearing under the sweatshirt and lifted her fingers to the buttons. For one terribly potent second, her hands trembled in place before she took a breath and started unbuttoning her shirt.

What the hell? She'd just tried the "I see dead people" routine on him and now she was going for seduction?

Her fingers clutched the edges of the shirt and started peeling them apart. He was about to turn away. He'd seen enough. But her hands stopped after opening the shirt only a sliver, exposing no more than a mere inch of her sternum.

His eyes locked on that narrow, exposed strip of skin.

She held the fabric in place as the wind tried to pry it apart. The lamp behind him hit her like a spotlight. She lifted her chin, elongating her neck.

His eyes traced the exposed strip of flesh and his dead heart slammed to life in his chest.

Etched into the pale bronze skin was a clean, straight, pink gash starting at the base of her throat and slashing her chest in half right down the center.

"I have your wife's heart," she said so quietly that if the words had been any different he would never have heard them.

A surgical scar.

Holy mother of God.

Jen's heart.

She had his Jen's heart.

He lifted his hand and reached for her. He didn't know why he did it. But Jen's heart was right here, her DNA, her tissue, *her*. Alive and beating.

The girl sucked in a breath and stepped back, moving away from his outstretched hand as though it were a live wire. She pulled her shirt back together and went to work on her buttons. The scar disappeared behind black cotton and trembling fingers.

"I'm sorry." He had no idea why he was apologizing, but she had looked so terrified when he tried to touch her, it just came out.

"I'm sorry," she said at the exact same time, and that accidental crash of words snapped her out of wherever she had gone.

For a few moments, neither one of them moved or spoke.

What could he say to her?

Give it back? Give back that thing beating in your chest. It isn't yours.

"I'm so sorry," she said again. The sympathy in her voice struck a match to the fuse hanging from him. Another blast of rage exploded inside him.

"How do I even know you're telling the truth?"

"I am. My name is Jess Koirala. You can look it up. I was on the national donor registry for five years before I got her heart . . . Jen's heart. It's part of the Government of India medical records."

"No. I mean heart surgery is a physical procedure. It can't—" He had no idea what kind of madness this was, but God, he wanted what she was saying to be true. He wanted it so badly, his entire being vibrated with the effort to break free from a lifetime of medical knowledge. He'd seen it a million times with patients' families. They'd take hope anywhere they found it. They'd dig up a mountain with their bare hands if hope sat at the center of it.

"I'm a physician. This doesn't happen," he said more to himself than to her. A flat line was a flat line. A period. Done. You could scream and pray and pump someone's chest until their ribs splintered beneath your hands. But that door, once slammed shut, was closed forever.

She pressed an unsteady hand to her chest, over the pink slash she'd just flashed at him and then hidden away. "How would I know all the things I know? She tells me things. Intimate things. You went to Scotland for your honeymoon. You were together for four months in Malawi after your wedding and then she left the MSF for a chance to work in Dharavi in Mumbai."

"Anyone could find that out. Anyone could look that up or ask someone we know."

"But how would I know how upset you were about her taking it."

"I was not—"

"Yes, you were. She knew you were, even though you didn't say anything."

He turned away from her, needing to move. Jen was one of the most private people he knew. These weren't things she would share with anyone casually.

* * *

Nikhil walked to the railing and stared out at the ocean. His body remained upright but he looked like she had slid a knife between his ribs.

She knew she had him.

With cruelty she wished she didn't possess, she twisted the knife. "Jen knew you wanted her to wait until you had worked through your posting in Lilongwe. She wished it hadn't happened when you two were fighting about the baby."

He made a pained sound.

Maybe she shouldn't have brought up the baby. But she was desperate. She needed him insensate with pain, unable to think. "Yes. I know about the baby too. The only reason she left when you were angry was because she knew you would come around. She was that confident of your love. And you did come around. You understood."

Something wet hit her face. It wasn't raining, and they were too high up on the ship for surf sprays. But the wind was high enough to carry teardrops. She couldn't think about his tears right now.

"Did you know her in Mumbai?" He spoke without turning around. "You could only know these things if she told them to you."

"She did."

He spun around. "Stop saying that. Stop fucking saying that. Even if you do have her heart. She's dead. Her heart is just a physical organ. There's no way—"

"You think I don't know that? I thought I was going crazy. For months I haven't been able to stop it. But she won't go away. Why would I come all the way here from Mumbai? Why would I make this up?"

He shook his head. "I don't know. But I'm sure you're going to tell me. You want something from me. What is it?"

"You're right. I want you to do what Jen wanted."

"And what would that be?"

"She was—"

"Actually, forget I asked. I can't believe how stupid—No. I'm not getting sucked into this. Just leave me alone."

He turned around and started walking away.

"You have to believe me, Nikhil. Please." She chased past him and pushed her body between him and the elevator lobby, blocking his path.

He met her eyes with absolute, undiluted loathing. “No. I don’t have to believe you. Because what you are saying is nuts.”

“I know it is. But sometimes you just have to have faith. Sometimes you have to leap first to see if your parachute will open.” It was beyond cruel to throw that at him.

Those were the words he’d used to convince Jen to marry him.

All the color drained from his face, one feature at a time, turning his skin sallow under the lights. “How do you—?” He leaned into the elevator button. “Whatever you’re up to, it’s . . . How do you even know that?”

“I told you. Jen told m—”

“Stop it.” He covered his eyes with his hand and it was a relief to not have to look at them. “Please.”

But she had no mercy to give him. “No one else can do this. Jen was working on something. And it’s unfinished. If you don’t help, all the work she did is useless.” She took a breath and fought to steady her voice. “Nikhil, Jen needs you.”

The elevator arrived with a ding, and he limped in. “I think you have that backward.” It was the last thing he said before the elevator doors squeezed him from sight, still unconvinced, leaving her with empty hands. All the weapons in her arsenal used up.

4

Being pregnant is like being ill without a cure. Unless you count bringing a baby into the world as a cure. Nic will never know how terrified I am of that. He believes I'll learn to love being a mom. God, I hope he's right.

—Dr. Jen Joshi

It had been a while since Nikhil had felt smart. But even his sustained and deliberate disconnection from his lifelong nerd status couldn't excuse the asinine direction of his thoughts. "What if she's telling the truth?" he kept thinking.

After starting the day with that, there was only one way the rest of the day could go: down the crapper. Right where he'd thrown up his Jack every night for two years along with a slow supply of his insides.

Evidently, he had also thrown away ten years of medical education and every iota of common sense.

Jess Koirala was either a really good actress or she was one of those metaphysical types who actually believed the crap she was handing out.

But what if it wasn't crap?

And there it was again. He rubbed the stubbly back of his head as though that could erase the stupidity.

No. It *was* crap. But it was impressively well-executed crap. Whatever she was planning, she had pulled it off brilliantly—catching him at the lowest point of his day, or highest, if you were measuring blood alcohol levels. All the disappearing around corners, the trembling fingers, the dark clothes. That hair.

Then there was the scar. He couldn't get that slash of raised skin out of his head. Even though he hadn't touched it, he could feel its pliant thickness against his fingers like a memory he hadn't created yet.

He had to stop this. He might suck at what he did now, but he had been a damn good physician in his past life. Organ transplants transferred no feelings, no memories, no personality traits from donor to recipient. It was just a spare part being installed in a different machine. That's all.

That is all.

So Miss Koirala was up to something.

It was time to find out what it was, and once he did he was going to make her regret ever defiling Jen's memory.

Without giving himself time to think, he yanked open a dresser drawer. Right behind his wallet, tucked at the very back of the drawer, was a plain white business card.

He checked the alarm clock on his nightstand. It was six a.m. Which meant it was still late afternoon in Mumbai. *DCP Rahul Savant,* the card said next to a hand-scrawled number.

Rahul Savant. The cop's name brought on a vivid rush of memories. Jen's body being lifted into the ambulance. The endless line-ups of criminals. Identifying the bastards, but getting absolutely no satisfaction from it, only more anger and the crazed desire to kill them with his bare hands.

The questions that had gone on even after he had put the bastards in prison.

And then that day when DCP Savant had upended his already upended world.

Jen was helping us with an investigation.

He would never forget the look on the cop's face when he had told Nikhil that his wife had lied to him. Kept such a huge secret from him. Put herself in danger. Put their baby in danger. Left him out. Left him.

Jen's murder wasn't a random crime, the bastard had said, looking at Nikhil as though he understood what Nikhil was feeling. *Someone was using Jen's donor registry database to steal organs. She had all the evidence we need to put these bastards away. We need your help finding it. You owe her that.*

Those words had shut everything down, destroyed everything, his anger an inferno so consuming it had burned down who he had been and left behind this charred, smoking mess that he didn't know what to do with.

The bastard had put Jen in danger. He had cost Jen her life because he hadn't done his job and protected her, and he had the gall to tell Nikhil what he owed his wife. Nikhil had told him and his smarmy politician boss to go to hell.

The only way I will ever help you is if you bring my wife back.

The politician had thought Nikhil was kidding. The smile that had split his face had reminded Nikhil of a wound that needed suturing. But Nikhil had meant it. It had felt like the only way anything would ever make sense again. He'd been right because nothing had made sense since then.

Before he could slide the business card back in the drawer, he dialed.

The cop answered on the first ring. "DCP Savant."

Nikhil almost hung up.

"Hello? Who's speaking?"

The bastard didn't have the right to sound this calm. "This is Nikhil Joshi. Calling from America." Technically, they were in Jamaica right now, but he didn't think the cop would care.

"Dr. Joshi?" The cop's voice went from distracted to focused so fast Nikhil might have found it funny, if it hadn't kicked off that sick feeling in the pit of his stomach. "How are you, Doctor*saab?*" The relief in his voice was so acute it was almost as if he'd spent the past two years sitting by the phone, waiting for Nikhil to call.

Two years. It had been two years since Nikhil had told him to go to hell, left India, and stopped answering his incessant phone calls, and he sure as hell was never going back to the country of his parents' birth ever again.

"I'm just peachy. Thanks." Yeah, the party never stopped. "You got a minute?"

"For you? I have all the time you need. Can you hold on for just a minute? Don't hang up, okay?"

Nikhil's finger hovered over the off switch on the phone. He heard some gruff instructions being thrown out. "Okay, I'm back. Thanks for calling. I've been trying to reach you. There's been a theft—"

Nikhil cut him off. "I need some information."

Rahul huffed out a laugh. "Yeah, you and me both." The cop had seemed so angry, so dark and brooding, when Nikhil had last seen him, his laugh, even though it was entirely humorless, scrambled Nikhil's already-inside-out brain.

"You think you could help me?"

"I'm sure we can work something out. What do you need?" Despite having let himself go stupid in the head, Nikhil knew when he was being worked over. The cop was welcome to take his best shot.

"Can you find out who has my wife's heart?"

All the wheeler-dealer went out of the cop's voice. "Excuse me?"

"She was on the donor list. They were able to transplant her organs. Can you find out who got her heart?"

There was another long silence, loaded with the cop's brain working so hard and fast Nikhil almost heard the wires shorting. "May I ask why you want to know?" he asked, finally.

"I'll tell you what, you get back to me with the information and I'll fill you in."

"Sure. This should take me a couple of days. Doctor, listen, it's really critical that I talk to you. Some new information has come up and—"

Nikhil pulled the phone away from his ear. The cop's face when he'd pronounced Jen dead, as if Nikhil had needed the bastard to tell him that, would be an image Nikhil would carry to his grave. And all the lies that had followed after that.

No. He still couldn't do it. Couldn't go back there.

"You know what? I changed my mind. Forget it. Forget I called. Gotta go."

"Dr. Joshi, listen, don't hang up. I'm not saying I won't help. It's just that—"

Nikhil hung up.

His hand reached for the bottle on his nightstand. It was empty. He'd poured the remaining Jack down the sink when he'd thought he needed his wits about him. Now he turned it over and peeked into it like some drunk frat boy. Not a drop in there.

The clock on the nightstand said six-oh-five. Really? Five minutes, that's how long the call had taken? Would time ever stop feeling like an anchor? Heavy. Immovable.

For all his drunken depravity, Nikhil hadn't yet taken a drink in the morning before going to the clinic. If not for the bone-dry bottle, today would have been the day he turned that corner and went down that road.

Jess knew she had to give him time. But it had been two days since Nikhil had left his room. Patience might be her strongest suit, but the longer he took, the longer Joy remained in danger.

That hope she'd seen flicker in Nikhil's eyes, no matter how tiny, had been real. She had played it over and over in her head for two days. Held on to it. Despite his science, despite all the logic of his profession, she knew she hadn't imagined it. The thing about being so entirely without hope was that you recognized it in others.

Yes, he believed he'd given up on hope after he lost Jen, but one gossamer thread of it and the belief that somehow it might lead him to her again—any little piece of her—had trumped everything else. And that, no matter how much it sickened her, was her only hope.

She let herself into the red-and-gold confines of her room. The golden clock across from her told her that it was time. She could set that clock by the timing of the phone call. He was never late.

"Your boy looks really nice in blue. Those gray eyes, oh he's going to be such a lady-killer." No one this evil should have a voice this silky, this harmless. "His daddy must have been one handsome bastard."

"I'm here, I'm taking care of it. There is nothing more I can possibly do right now." She shouldn't have let her voice tremble. Showing fear only gave him more power.

"Ah, I forgot how defensive the daddy issue makes you. What is the big secret? I wonder."

She squeezed the phone between her ear and shoulder and wiped her sweaty palms on her pants. "Dr. Joshi believes me. He's a doctor and I've convinced him." Or she would as soon as she figured out what else to do. "Isn't it time you backed off the threats?"

"Threats? You think these are threats? This is just the reality of our lives. We're two people trying to keep the things that matter to us safe." Well, he was correct about that. She would do anything to keep Joy safe, and if she ever found out what he was protecting, she would destroy it in a second.

He had asked her to call him *Naag*, the cobra. It was perfect; his faceless voice called to mind venomous snakes slithering around abandoned temples. A cobra coiled around her baby and threatening to squeeze. "Such a common cause we have. It's almost as if *Mata*, the divine mother herself, put us in each other's path."

"I told you, he believes me. But he's grieving. I have to be careful."

"*Arrey wah!* Lots of sympathy the good doctor's getting from you. 'Grieving,' very nice," he said in that forked-tongue voice before it turned needle-sharp and stung. "One of the reasons you were chosen was how little you cared for anyone but yourself." Actually he had chosen her because she was from Nepal and Jen was Chinese and some bastards thought that meant they looked alike. "Don't disappoint me, child."

The way he called her "child" and made it sound like "bitch" made her skin crawl.

"Of course I care only for myself."

"And don't forget your son."

She didn't respond. Joy wasn't apart from her. He was her, all of her.

"I can do this," she said instead. "You have to trust me."

"People like us, you and me, since when do we trust anyone? Find a way to get him to stop *grieving*. I'm sure he's in need of some comforting. If you get my meaning." On that note, he let her go. Well, "let her go" might be a bit wishful. He disconnected the phone, but that faceless voice of his continued to vibrate inside her like fear.

He was right. She had no idea what trust even felt like. So why blame him for seeing the truth? Hating him, letting her blood boil, it was the easy way out. All it would do was distract her from getting what she needed from Nikhil.

5

Nikhil was complaining about going to the Mount Mary fair today. He said it was too crowded and he didn't want us to get lost. I told him I was going to keep my hair this color so he could find me if I ever got lost.

His answer? "If you keep it this color, are you sure I'd want to find you?"

Jackass.

—Dr. Jen Joshi

Nikhil clicked "save" on yet another report chronicling his Pepto-Bismol-helmed war on dyspepsia, more commonly known as indigestion, and glanced at the waiting room window. He had first noticed Jess sitting outside the clinic before his first patient came in that morning. Now, almost half a day's worth of patients later, she was still perched on the bench outside the clinic in her Goddess of Darkness costume: black pants, black zip-up hoodie. It's what she had worn every single time he'd seen her. He wanted to storm out there and ask her to leave him alone. Or yank the hood off her head to get another look at the hair.

He turned back to the empty waiting room. His last patient had left half an hour ago, leaving him to fill the unforgiving minutes with absolutely no distance run, to borrow inanely from his mother's favorite Kipling poem. Apparently, everyone on *The Oasis* was out carpe-ing the heck out of every one of their diems, just like the brochures said. But what exactly they were squeezing out of life he couldn't bring himself to see.

And yet, here he was unable to leave after close to two years, overstaying Omar's welcome. Sheik Omar, owner of Golden Gulf Cruises, had gone to the University of Michigan with Nikhil in a different lifetime. They had never been friends, per se. Their interests had been too disparate. But every now and again, Omar had lured Nikhil into his frat parties and Nikhil had returned the favor by luring Omar and his mind-boggling sums of money into supporting whichever campus charity he thought could save the world at that moment.

Almost a decade later, Nikhil had fixed the hole in Omar's son's two-year-old heart. It had been routine surgery, but Omar—who had miraculously transformed into the kind of father Nikhil had so badly wanted to be—had trusted no one but Nikhil to perform it. He had flown Nikhil into Doha from India. At the time, Nikhil still worked at a Hindu Ashram–funded clinic in the Himalayas, before he'd joined the MSF and met Jen. Omar had tried everything to get Nikhil and Jen to move to Qatar and work as his personal physicians. As head of one of the world's largest oil suppliers, Omar had moved as far away as it was possible to move from the partying frat boy Nikhil had gone to college with.

After Jen's death, Omar had come to Mumbai and offered Nikhil the chance to hide out. Nikhil's family had been hounding him to go home to Chicago, but he couldn't. He definitely couldn't go back on mission either, and continuing to live in Jen's flat in Mumbai would have killed him. Omar had given him a choice between being his personal physician and heading up the medical facilities for his cruise line.

For some reason a cruise ship had sounded like the only bearable option. A floating mass of strangers who needed no real fixing. Because really, no matter how fucked up the world was, only the most presumptuous dumbfuck thought he could actually fix any part of it.

Being a waiter at one of the restaurants had sounded like just the thing, but that involved learning a skill and meeting far too many people and Omar had refused to let him clean decks.

For two years Nikhil had done the worst possible job at being a physician on *The Oasis*. With the exception of showing up drunk at the clinic, he had given Omar every reason to fire him. "You are my brother, and you can't fire family," had been Omar's only response.

"What if I kill someone?" Nikhil had asked him.

"You won't."

Thankfully for Omar and his unwarranted faith, ailments resulting from indulging in an excess of food, drink, and sunshine were generally fixable even by a doctor whose hands shook because he was destroying his liver. So here he was, cocooned in the safety of a job he could never be fired from, floating on an ocean so beautiful it underscored every ugliness he had ever witnessed, on an over-decorated, overcrowded monstrosity that highlighted his aloneness with all its familial bonhomie, and he couldn't bring himself to care about any of it.

He poked around at the screen looking for more paperwork, but his eyes drifted back to Jess. Her arms were wrapped around herself and her hood was pulled over that ridiculous red hair Jen and he had fought so hard over. He had loved Jen's hair, her real hair. He could have spent a lifetime watching the jet-black strands catch the light, a black so rich and deep, even the sunlight couldn't insert any gold into it. It shone blacker in the light, as immutable and stubborn as his wife herself.

He had spent every night he got with her with his face buried in it. It was that sleeping by her side, wrapped up in her scent, buried in the comfort of their marriage, that he had missed most when they had been apart.

It was that entangling of spaces with no borders, no separation, skin to skin, existence to existence, that had summarized his too-short marriage. It had been the miraculously healing end to even the hardest day, all-consuming, all-forgiving, like the deep shade of the magnificent oak in his parents' backyard. He had counted on it so completely that the uprooting of it had taken away his entire forest. His everything.

When he'd seen Jen at the airport that last time he visited her in Mumbai, he had walked right past her. She had followed him and tapped his shoulder. He had almost had an aneurysm when he realized that it was her under the punk-rocker-red hair. She had let the local beauty salon in the slum color it, her version of a trust-building exercise to get the girls to come in and get checkups, and it had turned that disastrous red. He had gone completely nuts and refused to let it go.

It's a lesson, Spikey, to teach you to get over things and deal. You hold on too tight.

She'd been right. His completely disproportionate hissy fit had gone on for days.

Then they'd gone to that fair. Their last day together.

The screen in front of him blurred. He squeezed his eyelids together. But, unlike tears, he couldn't squeeze away the blast of pain cramping in his heart.

Of all the things he remembered from that day, his starkest memory was of that ball of panic unfurling in his belly when he couldn't find her in the ocean of people. She was the strongest, most competent person he knew and perfectly capable of taking care of herself. But those minutes of not knowing where she was amid the crush of bodies stretching for miles had been like a flash forward. One of those moments when the universe spins around you and you have no clue what just happened. Just a sense that something did and you missed it and it was important.

He'd seen her hair first. In the unbroken mass of black hair and un-deodorized sweat, the red had flashed at him. He'd been shaking when he pulled her to his chest. She had done what she always did—been overwhelmed by his display of affection and covered it up with amusement.

See? With this hair you'll always be able to find me when you lose me. It can be our beacon.

Holy.

Shit.

"I'll be right back," he shouted to the nurses and rushed out the door.

Jess's only reaction when she saw him jog out of the clinic was the slightest softening of her eyes.

"Come on," he said and headed for the stairs without waiting for her.

She followed him. No protests, no questions. He led her up the stairs, flight after flight. She kept up with him, her steps tracing his as they broke into the sunlight on the main pool deck. The pungent burn of chlorine filled his nostrils. He kept going. They had to dodge people, flashes of bright bikinis and sunglasses and multicolored wraps. Up to the next deck level. Then the next. The number of people thinned as they went higher. Until the sunshine and the wind grew angrier, fighting each other for power over that topmost deck. Until the only ones there to witness it were the two of them.

He grabbed her arm and pressed her against the little cabin room—the only patch of shade on the wide-open deck—and reached for her hood.

She pulled it off before he could touch it.

"Is the hair real?"

She took a breath but her eyes didn't waver. "No." The wind whipped the short strands around her face.

He continued to hold her gaze, but he couldn't get himself to ask the question.

She answered it nonetheless. "Jen knew you'd believe me if I had the hair. That's why I had it done."

He took a step back, needing to pull breath into his lungs.

It made him a fool of gargantuan proportions, but if there was any chance, any chance at all, he had to take it. He had to know. "Can I talk to her?"

Sympathy flared in her eyes, a hot, harsh flash making him sick to his stomach.

"No," she said, shaking her head and spinning that hair around her face. "You can't. I'm sorry."

He lifted his hand and stopped it inches from the flaming strands. The wind teased them to within a breadth of his fingers, but they didn't reach him. "It's amazingly like hers."

Relief swept across her always-calm features, making her look as weary as he felt. "I got it colored at the same place Jen did."

"And where was that?"

She gave a small nod, acknowledging the endless swirl of doubt churning inside him. "Beauty's Beauty Parlor in Dharavi."

He pulled his hand away and rubbed the stubble on his head. He'd forgotten to shave it today. "I hated it." He had been such a jerk about it too.

"I know," she said. "Jen didn't like it much either."

And yet Jen had done no more than be amused by it. He walked to the railing and leaned back into it. She had always been so damn patient with him.

Silence stretched between them, unruffled by the wind so violent everything in its path had to be bolted down.

But silence didn't have the answers he needed. "How does this work? This"—he twirled his finger between them—"her talking to you."

She sagged against the wall behind her. It was the slightest move, but there it was again, the relief she was trying to hide. He hungered for some of his own.

"It's really hard to explain." Her voice was a whisper above the wind. "I feel her inside me. It's not hearing words so much as knowing them. Like a mist of thought sinking into my brain and becoming my own thoughts."

He tried to tamp it down, but the hope that unfurled inside him sped up his breath. He knew he was going to regret this, knew what a pathetic asshole this made him, but there was no backing out now.

"Okay, hit me. What does she want?"

"Jen was working on something," she said quickly, as if sensing how badly he wanted to change his mind. "She was collecting evidence against someone who was stealing organs from undocumented slum dwellers."

His heart started slamming. "Shit. The cop sent you!" He wasn't just a pathetic asshole, he was a pathetic, gullible asshole. Of course Rahul Savant would pull something like this. He was desperate.

He backed away from her, heading for the stairs. Rahul wasn't the only one who was desperate. Nikhil's own desperation had made him crazy. This conversation had gone on too long.

"No one sent me," she called after him. "Certainly not the police. You have to believe me. Her death, they—"

He stopped but couldn't turn around. "I was there. If you know all this you must know that I . . . I watched my wife die. I watched what they did to her."

Her hand rested on his shoulder. But there was no comfort in it. There was no comfort.

"Then how can you let them get away with it?"

He spun around, throwing off her hand. All the scattered scraps of feelings from these past two years balled into rage in his heart. Pure hundred-proof rage. "They already got away with it. Even the bastards who are rotting in jail got away with it. They're alive and she's gone and she's not coming back." He squeezed his eyes shut and tried not to feel another horrible surge of hope. The fucking thing kept leaping up inside him like giant waves, throwing him up then down like an ocean gone mad. Now it slammed him down. "Is she?"

"I'm sorry."

He couldn't believe he had asked the question. What was worse, if Jess had told him that Jen was coming back to talk to him, through her, through the fucking door behind her, he'd have believed that too. Talk about pathetic, gullible asshole.

"The men you put in jail don't matter. They were just low-level hired guns paid to take the blame. Hired by the real criminals she was collecting evidence against."

He lost his center of gravity. The white deck spun under his feet. It's what Rahul had tried to tell him two years ago, what Rahul was probably trying to tell him this morning. And just like those two times it shut his brain down. The burning ball of rage that kept growing inside him wiped out everything except the fact that Jen had lied to him. She had knowingly put herself in danger, knowingly put their baby in danger, and kept him out of a decision that affected her safety, their baby's safety.

They had promised never to lie to each other. It was the basis of their marriage.

"That's not possible." His voice sounded every bit as destroyed as he felt. "It was random. They came out of nowhere." There was no way Jen could have gone walking down that alley if she knew. There was no way this was why she had tried to talk him out of visiting her. But he had needed to see her, needed to touch that tightness in her belly that had changed everything.

He stared down at his hand where he could still feel that tightness, then looked at the stairs he should've taken when he still could and sank down onto the hammered metal step. "Did the cop tell you all that?"

She sank down next to him.

"No. Actually, the police, they might be involved. This thing goes really high up. Jen didn't trust anyone. We can't either."

"Why? If you know all this, you must know why she got involved."

"It was an accident. One of her patients disappeared and she couldn't let it go. She kept searching and they found the body with organs cut out. And then another one of her patients disappeared and then another and she realized that the patients who were disappearing had signed up to be on the organ donor registry she was compiling. After that first one the police couldn't find bodies, but she couldn't let it go. She kept digging and pushing the police to investigate. It started making the people who were behind it uncomfortable and they stopped her," she said, as though killing anyone who stood in your way was just what people did.

He pressed his eyes into his hands, but the visions crashing around in his head only got clearer. Jen had talked so excitedly about how fast the donor database had grown. She had been so proud of what the clinic could achieve with it. But she hadn't said a word about the deaths or the investigation.

"Not only did she document every disappearance, she was trying to track down transplant surgeries across the country without family donors to see where the organs were going. But most importantly she had information on the gang who threatened her." Crimson stained her high cheeks. It was either the sun and the wind or some sort of emotion he couldn't identify.

"Okay, so where did she hide this evidence?"

The color in her cheeks took on the angry redness of bruises, as though someone had slapped her and her skin was gathering up the proof of their violence.

She didn't answer him.

"You don't know?" How stupid did she think he was? She knew all this, but the one thing that only Jen would know, that was the one thing she didn't know. "Do I have 'I'm an ass' tattooed across my forehead? Who sent you? Who do you work for?"

"I told you, I don't work for anyone. This is about Jen. She can't move on until you do this, and she won't leave me alone until you do." For someone who was admitting to being haunted she was so damn calm.

He pushed off the cold metal and stood. "So, you're what, Mother

Teresa?" He started down the stairs like he should have done before she started spewing her lies.

"If I could make her go away, don't you think I would? Don't you think I've tried? But I can't. The only one who can end this is you, Nikhil. I need my life back. Please."

He spun around and faced her, still sitting on that top step, the red hair swirling around her face. "I don't care. I don't care what you need. I don't give a rat's ass about your life."

The rage that flashed in her eyes was so hot it matched his. He was about to turn away again, but she blinked and blanketed it so fast behind such dead calm he was mesmerized by it.

"I'm not asking you to care about me," she said. There was no more bleeding sympathy, just that unearthly calm. "But this is about your wife. You care about her, don't you? Because she happened to believe you would pull out your limbs for her." She waited for him to react, to answer. But if he had any damn answers he wouldn't be here floating on an ocean, wanting nothing more than to be left alone.

Actually, that wasn't all he wanted. But what he did want fell under the category of Fucking Miracle.

And she knew it. She had used it to shovel bullshit down his throat for long enough. He ran down the stairs. But there was no escape. The stairs creaked behind him. "How? How don't you care? How can you listen to what I'm telling you and not want to do anything? How can you stand there and pretend to be broken about her, when—"

He was on her in an instant, his hands on her shoulders. "Pretend? This look like pretense to you? Or can you feel only dead people, but live ones, they're just here for you to mess with. Why don't you go ask Jen how I pretended to love her? Do it now. Conjure her up. Do it," he hissed into her face.

She grabbed the railing with both hands and stuck out her jaw as if she was determined not to be scared. As if *she* was the victim here.

The fragile bones in her shoulders poked into his palms and he let her go. But he didn't step back. "What's she doing right now?

What's she wearing? Let me guess. White robes? Is she transparent? Does she walk through walls and disappear into thin air?"

"I told you it's not like—"

"What about her face? What about her eyes? What does she look like? Like her innards don't fit anymore? Like there's no space inside, because she's a skeleton who can't get any food down her gullet? No, don't look at me like you understand. You don't get to give me that look."

"Nikhil . . ."

"Oh, I'm sorry, you said she floats into you. Becomes one with you. So, will I feel her if I touch you?" He grabbed her again, pulled her into him, her mouth so close he tasted the wetness of it. "If I put my tongue in your mouth will I forget my name? Will I fucking know what—Shit."

She was shaking, her eyes wild with terror. He let her go and she fell back, landing on her butt, and buried her face in her hands. But only for a second. When she looked up the terror she'd let slip was gone, blanketed with that calm again.

But he'd recognized it. Seen it in another set of eyes that would never stop haunting him. He stumbled down the remaining steps. The smell of the sewer in his nose, the grunting of those bastards as they thrust into her ringing in his ears over Jen's screams.

He was back at the blasted railing, back in that alley, his face pressed into mud pooled with his own blood.

He leaned into the ocean, shoving his face into the salty wind. What kind of idiot surrounded himself with this kind of temptation when all he wanted was for this shit to be over?

She squeezed her eyes shut, squeezed every muscle until she stopped shaking. She reminded herself to breathe. It was just a reflex. Just a damn reflex. Nikhil hadn't been trying to hurt her.

This wasn't about her. She tamped down the nausea that clawed up her belly and went to him. She had to finish this. She couldn't back down now.

He stood at the railing, his head bent, his entire body weeping like one of those giant conifers that drooped by the Gandaki River.

He had that same desolation as the mountain town she'd grown up in. As if he had been born for beauty, as if he'd been showered with blessings, and then the tide had turned and no one knew what to do with the devastation, with the ugliness that the storm left behind.

He leaned so far into the railing, she half expected him to let go. "Are you happy now?" he whispered into the ocean. "Is this what you wanted to see?"

No. His pain was unbearable to witness, so sharp it scraped at all the thick skin she'd grown around herself. She shook her head, knowing full well he couldn't see her. His eyes were fixed on the turquoise waves, but she doubted he saw those either.

The vibrant blue swirled around them like an abomination, the harsh brightness highlighting the darkness trapped in their two bodies like a spotlight. Anger and pain, old and new, his and hers, pulling and pushing, multiplying against each other.

Except his pain was pure. It had dignity to it. Her own pain had been ugly, filthier than the deepest gutter.

Despite his defeated stance, he crumbled further. "She used to . . . God . . . She could make me forget my name. She could make me forget everything. I could come home after sawing off a child's limbs and she could make me forget. Do you know what that feels like? To have someone like that?"

No, she didn't. But she knew what never being able to forget felt like. "If I could change things, I would." That much she meant. It was much more than she should have shared, but that much she did mean.

Of course he didn't believe her. He laughed the ugliest laugh and turned around to face her. "Right."

"Yes. I would." She met his eyes and held his stare, angry and suspicious as it was.

"And what about that heart beating inside you?"

She shrugged. "That could have come from someone else."

"So not from my loss but someone else's loss."

"I didn't choose this. It's not like I wanted it to happen. Don't believe me if you don't want to, but I can tell you one thing for sure. What happened to Jen, if I could stop that from happening to anyone, I would do whatever it took to stop it."

6

Maybe I should've told Nic the truth. Maybe I shouldn't have asked him not to come, but sometimes I don't know how to talk to him anymore. The baby thing has made him totally crazy and overprotective. He's nothing like the reasonable man I married.

—Dr. Jen Joshi

It could be the odd, slashed-open feeling of finally being able to talk about Jen, or then maybe it was the expression on Jess's face—like a child determined to have her way despite having no power at all. But Nikhil saw the woman for the first time, past Jen's hair, past his own wretched hope, and he knew she wasn't lying.

In this moment, he would bet his life she actually meant what she said. Her eyes glittered with conviction, the kind of conviction that reminded him of patients after the worst kind of trauma, a vulnerable, bleeding sort of determination that was a silence so powerful, no stringing together of words could match it.

He turned back to the blinding blue of the ocean. The railing reached his waist. Not for the first time, the urge to let go grabbed him. All it would take was releasing his grip, and gravity would take care of the rest.

"Seems like the easiest way out, doesn't it?" Her voice flew around his neck like a noose and yanked him back.

She leaned into the railing beside him, her body adding to the push against the metal keeping his body from escape. The wind picked up whatever perfume she was wearing and swirled it around him. There was something melancholy about the scent, like soporific hemp and meditative incense that made your limbs heavy even as it lightened the weight of the world.

Maybe it was her melancholic air, maybe it was that terror he'd witnessed in her eyes earlier, or maybe it was the fact that every heart transplant patient had glimpsed their own mortality, but he recognized surmounted suffering when he saw it. She had the look of someone who had hiked to the top of the mountain and back, but had lost a limb in the process and wasn't quite sure it had been worth it.

He turned to her. "You sound like you've considered it too." This coward's madness balanced on the edge of a metal railing.

Her breathing stayed steady, but the effort of keeping it steady increased the slightest bit, the way one breathed for a stethoscope. "No. I've never contemplated killing myself. It's a luxury I couldn't afford."

He heard himself laughing again and hated the sound. Luxury? Wasn't it just great that he understood exactly what she meant?

She stuck out her chin again, her stance that of a pugilist bracing herself for impact. "You should try anger instead."

She sounded so much like Jen when he'd first met her. Jen had been so angry at everyone and everything. "I'm going to make this world a better place if it kills me," was her unspoken mantra.

Well, didn't irony suck balls.

But Jen's anger had always been on behalf of other people, against the injustices she loved to go hurtling after. This woman's anger, when she let it out, was an armor. She was protecting only herself. That knowledge only intensified his ache for his wife.

"Anger can help you deal with just about everything." The bitter edge in her voice was a serrated knife against the wound he had let her rip open.

"Oh, I'm plenty angry." It hadn't gotten him through shit. "Jen used to hate that I didn't get angry enough." He'd always told her there was too much anger in the world as it is, and he had never felt the need to add to it.

She should see him now.

"Actually, she was really proud of you for it," Jess said, and paused to gauge if she should go on. "Maybe she was even a little jealous."

He was going to regret this, but he leapt onto that, panting for a scrap like a starving dog. "What else did she . . ." He leaned his head back and let the salty air slap his face. "What else did she say?"

She turned to him, leaning a hip against the railing. He had expected to hear triumph in her voice, but there was only more of that relief and the ubiquitous sympathy. "Where do I start? Your wife thought you were . . . Let me just say, I was shocked to find that you didn't have wings. Or a halo." There was the faintest smile in her voice and he turned to look at it. It was a tight, restrained thing. But he was pretty sure it was a smile. Then it fell away and she looked surprised at what she'd just said.

"Yeah, the bracing ocean breeze took off with the wings and the Caribbean fun-shine has a way of burning through halos. Then there's the alcohol fumes. Those aren't great for halos and wings either."

She looked sad. If she said anything about letting Jen down, he was throwing her overboard.

"She could talk about you forever," she said instead. "She was completely and utterly awestruck by everything about you."

Jen's beautiful, bottomless eyes caressed him. The way she had looked at him, always with disbelief at her own dumb luck at having found him. He'd known exactly how she felt. He had felt it tenfold.

"That wasn't always the case," he said softly, mostly to push past the pain clamping around his throat and because now that he'd talked about her, he couldn't stop. "When Jen first met me, she was just annoyed at everything about me. It was hard work bringing her around."

"And you always knew you had to bring her around?" she said just as softly.

"I knew instantly. I'd always thought I was abnormal because I had never been in love. Then I met her and there could never be anyone else." Jen had thought it was really weird that he was so sure of his feelings after meeting her just once. *It's because it's your first time. It's just the novelty of the thing*, she'd said.

She had slept with him because, well, because she slept with all the new recruits. She'd told him that without the least hesitation, and then she'd been so angry with him because she hadn't wanted to move on. His relief had been extreme.

This couldn't possibly be happening. I mean, this is like Hollywood crap. I don't want to sleep with anyone else, and I can't seem to keep out of your pants, she'd said.

It is a bit demeaning to be wanted just for my body, he'd told her. *But I'm okay with you trying to get it out of your system. Take as long as you need. Maybe it will fix itself.*

It hadn't fixed itself and here he was. "She would be so disappointed in the way I've handled it."

Jess's eyes, which had been studying him with guarded calm, softened again. "Actually, you've handled it exactly the way she was afraid you would. Except for the fact that you haven't gone after the bastards she was trying to catch." She tried to be smooth about it, but her desperation was naked in the determined set of her jaw.

"You can stop working me now. I'm here." And, God help him, he was. Even though he wasn't sure what exactly was going on, and he couldn't decipher what he believed from what he didn't, he knew that he was going to follow this all the way to its end. How could he not?

Instead of looking embarrassed, she shrugged defiantly.

"But I still have questions."

"Sure."

"Why didn't she tell me about the investigation?"

It was a question she had asked herself over and over again. How had Jen not told Nikhil what she was doing? Even if Jen knew Nikhil would try to talk her out of it, she should have told him. He had a right to know.

"Maybe she didn't want to worry you."

"Maybe? Can't you ask her?"

"I can't ask her things. All I have is what she chooses to share."

"You said she knew how dangerous these people were. Did they threaten her?"

She nodded. They had pressed a gun into her belly, into her unborn child, but it hadn't stopped Jen. Unlike Jess, who had learned to sell her soul for far less far too long ago.

Nikhil paled under the blazing sun. The wind whipped the moments of calm he'd mastered from his eyes.

Whatever Jen's reasons for not telling him had been, she'd been wrong. How could she shut him out when she knew he felt this way about her?

Restlessness flapped around him like the T-shirt fluttering around his too-lean body. "Tell me what she said about the baby. How did she feel about becoming a mother?" If she had thought he looked like he was in pain before, this question sucked the life out of him.

It was the one thing about Jen she would never understand. How could anyone not want to be a mother? Her Joy had put her back together. Without Joy she would've been dead years ago. Before him, it was almost as if she hadn't existed. His smile, the devotion in his gray eyes, it gave her existence substance. He filled her in, the way he filled in the black-and-white characters in his coloring books with color, his little tongue pinched between his lips, his soft brow furrowed in concentration.

"She knew how happy you were about the baby."

"I know how *I* felt," he snapped. "I asked how she felt."

Despite how well he thought he knew his wife, despite the fact that Jen had been perfectly honest with him about not being ready for motherhood, he looked desperate for someone to rewrite that part of the story for him. "She's gone," she should've said. "The baby's gone." She needed him to snap out of this, to get him working on what she needed from him. But she couldn't.

"Did she move away because she needed to distance herself from me? From how I was being about the baby?"

"Nikhil, you know why she moved. You know she had always wanted to work in Dharavi because of your family's connection to India."

"I begged her to wait until my rotation was done."

"She would have lost the position. She didn't have the time to wait."

"Because of the baby. She was going to have to take a break and stop doing what she wanted to do because of the baby."

"She just wanted to fit it in before it was time." That wasn't entirely untrue, and Nikhil didn't need to know how terrified Jen had been of losing everything she loved to motherhood.

"The baby wouldn't have changed anything. We could have gone on doing what we wanted to do. A lot of couples manage to do what they love and raise their children just fine."

"Actually, a baby changes everything. But they would have been changes you wanted to make," she said, and instantly regretted it when his sad eyes turned alert.

"You're a mother."

It was the last thing she had expected him to say. The very last thing she needed for him to know.

But he spoke before she could deny it. "How old is she? He?" His entire attention was on her now and she didn't know how to back away from it.

"He's seven. Joy's seven." Shit. She'd told him Joy's real name. Panic unfurled inside her.

"Joy?" he said. "That's beautiful." Of all the things that could have made his voice crack, it was her baby's name that did it.

She couldn't give herself time to process that, to think about Joy. "They knew she was pregnant, Nikhil. They still did this." She attacked his vulnerability instead.

The sound that escaped him ripped through her skin.

"You have to help me find them," she said.

"Yes." He nodded. "Just tell me what she needs me to do."

It took all her strength to not collapse to the deck floor, her relief was so strong.

Then she saw his face and there was no more relief.

It was time to pull out the knife, or to at least stop twisting it. Jen's Nikhil needed respite, and for Jen she'd let him have some.

"Thanks," she said quietly. "It can wait until tomorrow. I think this is enough for one day."

Is this how torturers felt? Weary from their victim's pain. Unable to go on without a break. He wasn't the only one who needed the respite. She needed to regroup. Needed to remind herself why cruelty like this was necessary. Jen would have torn her limb from limb for doing this to him. But she would have understood too. For some reason, Jess knew that no matter how much Jen would have hated her for doing this, she would have done the same thing in her place.

Despite the alarm bells gonging in her head, warning her not to, she couldn't stop herself from reaching out and touching his arm. "It will get better, you know. After a while your body adjusts to the pain and learns how to put it away."

It was true. Pain by its very nature couldn't stay acute. Your threshold for pain grew as pain grew, like a body that kept expanding as you fed it and fed it. How could it not? Whoever decided it was okay to inflict the unthinkable on you had to make sure you lived to experience it. What better way to do that than to keep it right there on the edge of a blade, just bearable enough so you could go on around it?

He pulled his arm away, but didn't argue with her, although it was clear from the way he squeezed his eyes shut that in this moment he couldn't perceive the pain ever lessening, let alone going away. Who knew, maybe he was the one man on earth who really could love one and only one woman until the end of time. People who believed in love did believe in that sort of thing.

Watching him under the Caribbean sun, his body gaunt with pain, his hair shorn off, and eyes that switched from desolation to desperate hope and back again without his permission, all the things Jen had said about him rang true. Watching him like this it was impossible not to believe that he was the miracle Jen believed he was.

Too bad she didn't believe in miracles.

He didn't ask her any more questions. She knew he wanted to. God knew she had answers to them all. But right now she was too weary for questions, for anything more than what she had just done.

He straightened, that alert focus back in his eyes again, and looked like he was going to ask another question after all. "I promise I'll answer all your questions. But not right now. Tomorrow," she said before he could open his mouth.

He shook his head. "I was just going to ask if I could walk you to your room. You look exhausted."

She backed away from him, putting distance between them as fast as she could.

"I'm fine," she said, finding it hard to keep her voice even and kicking herself for it. "You should go get some rest. I'll come find you at the clinic tomorrow."

She spun around and walked away without breaking into a run the way she wanted to.

Once she was in the elevator by herself, she pulled the ultra-fancy phone out of her pocket and punched in the number from memory before typing out a text. *I'm in. Everything on track.*

Then she deleted the text from the Sent folder and deleted the number from the list of calls.

7

I never thought I'd meet two men who threw themselves on top of others when it rained bullets. It's no secret what happened the first time I saw someone do that.

—Dr. Jen Joshi

Rahul Savant often forgot that he had topped the Indian Joint Civil Services Examination. For all the huge deal they made out of the exam, it was just a bunch of questions, and Rahul had never had trouble answering questions, especially the kind that came from books. The real skill, the one no one had found a way to test, was in finding the right questions to ask.

He took a deep breath and raised his arm to knock on the teakwood door that smelled of fresh varnish. This was exactly the kind of moment when he needed to remind himself that he was indeed a top-ranker and that he deserved to be standing here inside the historical Sachivalaya—the South Mumbai office of the state home minister—wearing his Deputy Commissioner of Police uniform as the DCP and not as the minister's protégé. He was well within his rights in asking for what he needed to bring Jen's killers to justice.

He rapped on the wood. But the sharp stab of pain on his always-bruised knuckles did nothing to distract from the shame of having failed Jen.

"Come in." The home minister's unerringly calm voice invited him in, and Rahul opened the door and marched in with more bravado than he felt.

"Exactly on time, as usual." Kirit Patil's kind eyes studied him with their usual generous approval. Instead of dissipating, Rahul's shame intensified.

Kirit shut the leather-bound folder he'd been studying and indicated the chair in front of him. Rahul hadn't opened his mouth yet, but he could tell that Kirit knew he came bearing bad news.

"Still no sign of the diary, sir." He still could not believe that he had allowed such a crucial piece of evidence to go missing. If not for the fact that Kirit had been his mentor ever since Rahul's father took a bullet for Kirit twenty years ago, he might not be standing here addressing the minister at all. He might be opening doors as a security guard outside some fancy hotel.

Kirit shrugged. "It's a closed case, Rahul. If you stop bringing it up, it would be a non-issue. You have to let it go, son."

"Another disappearance was reported yesterday. That's five that we know of this year. I have reason to believe this has to do with Dr. Joshi's investigation." Or what should have been *his* investigation. One he should never have let Jen get so involved in.

"This is ridiculous and you know it. We don't have bodies, no proof that these people exist. We don't even have proof that Jennifer Joshi was even actually collecting any evidence. How do you expect me to sanction an investigation when there is no case? I've let slide the fact that the diary was stolen under your supervision. That's as much as I can do."

Kirit had taken a huge risk keeping such a blunder secret, and he had possibly saved Rahul's job. But Rahul knew better than to thank him again. Kirit didn't need more sniveling gratitude. What he needed was a DCP who did his job.

"I got a call from Dr. Joshi today."

Kirit sat up, raised one questioning brow, and reached for the stainless-steel tumbler sitting on a tray on his desk.

Rahul poured water into the tumbler from the jug and handed it to Kirit. "It was completely out of the blue. Dr. Joshi has been unreachable for close to two years now."

Kirit took a sip and raised his chin, signaling Rahul to continue.

"He wanted to know who had his wife's heart. I tried to tell him about the diary and ask for his help with finding the evidence again. But he didn't give me a chance."

The minister stood. Despite his lean build, the sun shining through the massive windows behind him turned him larger than life. He walked around the desk and put his hand on Rahul's shoulder.

His expression was innately familiar. Kirit's kindness had helped Rahul survive his father's death. Rahul would always carry the weight of Baba bleeding out on his lap after he had taken the bullet meant for the minister at the election rally. But he would never forget that Kirit had refused to flee the scene until the ambulance arrived.

He'd stayed with Rahul through the ordeal at the hospital and held Rahul's hand as he gave fire to his father's pyre. Then he had helped Rahul channel his teenage anger and steered him toward the Civil Services Exam and the police force instead of the limited alternatives available to children like him, if the gangs in the neighborhood hadn't gobbled him up first.

"Rahul, we already have the perpetrators in the Jennifer Joshi murder case in custody. This case is not going to spoil your perfect record. You've already managed to send the black-market organ ring into hiding. These disappearances—you're trying to find a connection where there is none." He leaned his head forward and let his steady gaze calm Rahul. "It's time to let this case go, son. I don't want you to contact Dr. Joshi again. And you cannot let anyone know about the diary being stolen. If the media finds out that evidence has gone missing, I won't be able to protect you any longer. There is only so much I can do."

First, the murderers they had in custody weren't the *real* murderers, not the ones who orchestrated the organ stealing that Jen had unearthed. Not the ones who had threatened Jen and then had her throat snapped in an alley. Second, the deaths hadn't stopped. The department just didn't have the resources to go after disappearances of undocumented slum dwellers, not without Kirit's approval. No, this was far from over.

"Sir, I know that the evidence is still out there. I know Jen's . . . Dr. Joshi's husband has access to the evidence. I don't think the diary being stolen is an accident. I just need a little time to get through to him. He's coming up on the two-year mark. Even the most badly affected victims' families are ready to get back to their lives after two years. I know if I can just talk to him that he can lead us to these monsters."

"You said that when we passed the one-year mark. So far the victim's husband has shown us no sign that he wants to cooperate. We have no case and even if we did we don't have jurisdiction. He's taken himself and all her possessions back to the US. There is nothing more we can do."

"I need clearance to access the donor records."

"It's out of the question."

"Please, sir. I'm begging."

Kirit squeezed his temples. "You know how hard it is for me to refuse you, son. I would give you anything you wanted if I thought it would get us anywhere. I'll tell you what. I've recommended your name to head up the security team for the Commonwealth Games in New Delhi."

"You're transferring me?"

Kirit looked hurt. "No, I'm giving you a promotion and the kind of responsibility anyone else with your seniority would kill for."

"Then don't. I don't deserve it. I haven't earned it."

Kirit patted Rahul's shoulder again. "You deserve so much more. You just have to learn to keep your emotions out of it. If you get my meaning. This business is too dirty to let your heart get involved." He held Rahul's gaze, until he was sure his words had sunk in.

This wasn't about Jen, or how he felt about her. But he was not getting into that with Kirit. Based on Kirit's set face, it seemed like Rahul wasn't getting into anything more with him today.

"Come on, son, let it go. It's over."

But it wasn't over. There were still five people who had disappeared. Jen's donor registry database was still erased without a trace. The diary was still missing from police custody. Nikhil Joshi's dead-man voice was still searching for connections to his wife, a woman Rahul would avenge if it was the last thing he did.

But he had reached a dead end with Kirit and he'd just have to find another way.

Kirit must have seen the resignation in Rahul's face, because he sank into his chair, looking suddenly old and weary. "You're coming home for dinner tonight. Kimi is cooking some fancy foreign food again."

Rahul groaned. "Come on, sir, do I really deserve that?"

Kirit laughed, and Rahul knew that the minister had switched over to doting-father mode. "Why must I be the only one to suffer her experiments?"

"I'll be there." It's not like he could refuse the invitation, even though after his last encounter with Kimi he really needed to stay away from her. He gave Kirit a quick salute and left.

The minister, of all people, should know how much damage the black market did to legitimate organ donor lists. Kimi had, after all, waited years for her heart. For Kimi and for Jen, Rahul couldn't possibly rest until those bastards were off his streets.

8

Today Nic brought me flowers. No big deal. Except it's minus fifteen outside and there are no florists here. His flowers were drawn by Nagma on his prescription pad. He lets her hold it when he examines her amputated leg. He brought me the flowers and pressed them into my hand. Then he cried into my lap. Because she has gangrene.

—Dr. Jen Joshi

Nikhil grabbed hungrily at the scent of freshly washed linen flooding his senses. The feel of long-fingered hands clutched at his skin. Soft strands of the darkest silk pressed into his face. He fought consciousness with everything he was worth. He knew at the other end lay horror—the absence of what wrapped him up right now.

Sure enough, emptiness welcomed him as he broke through to wakefulness. Emptiness and the cold kiss of air against his skin. He had fallen asleep on top of the sheets. His shoes were still on his feet, his overstarched uniform still on his body.

For no reason at all, he thought of the night before when he'd awoken under the sheets. His shoes had been removed, his foul-smelling shirt had been pulled off, and he'd been so out of it he hadn't even noticed.

He turned to the note still sitting on his nightstand and picked it up. The look in Jess's eyes when she'd admitted to coloring her hair flashed in his head. He folded over the piece of paper and slipped it into the drawer. He still couldn't believe what he was choosing to believe.

But he'd never judged a person wrong in his life. His gut had never let him down. Unless an excess of Jack had erased that ability, he knew he'd seen truth in Jess's eyes. Not all of it, because the girl was a clam. How could he not follow this thread she'd handed him? Even though it threatened to unravel the very fabric of him.

He was steady on his feet when he got out of bed. There was a dull ache in his temples. Quite possibly his body's way of rebelling against his sudden forsaking of the Jack. Or maybe his body was thanking him by showing him how much better this was than the usual head pounding he woke up to. He scrubbed his fingers across his forehead. His ring hung loose around his finger. The day Jen had slid it on his finger had smelled of roses. The thick, sweet-smelling garlands hanging from their necks had entangled when he'd broken protocol and kissed her after the priest had finished chanting their vows.

That sweet rose scent, the tang of her sweat, the purifying burn of sandalwood-scented fire—how did one forget a moment wrapped up in those smells? If happiness could fill you up, turn you from the wisp of a sketch into a fully formed sculpture, that moment had been it for him. He had become a life-sized version of who he had played at being. He had been set in stone. You couldn't re-form stone into anything else. Not without crumbling it to dust first.

His thumb found his ring and spun it. Dust. He wanted to be dust.

For the first time since he'd moved into this room, he started his day without his face hanging over the toilet.

He showered and shaved and put himself together with as much care as he had used to assemble Mr. Potato Head as a child. Basically, anything went anywhere. When he stepped out the door he realized that it was only seven in the morning. The clinic wouldn't open for business for another two hours. He headed down anyway.

A woman, thin and tanned and dressed like she was off to brunch with royalty, was waiting outside the clinic door, clutching the elbow of a little boy who was pressing a washcloth to his knee. It was soaked through with blood.

"Doctor?" The woman raised her impressively arched brows at his name tag and waited for an answer to a question Nikhil hadn't heard.

He punched the code into the alarm panel and smiled at the boy.

He had to be no more than five years old. Not only had she made him walk here on that knee, she was using that bracelet-filled hand to keep a safe distance between him and her logo-emblazoned white pants.

Nikhil lifted the child up and carried him into the clinic. He put him in a chair and squatted in front of him. “Do you mind if I take a look?” he asked the boy, trying his best to ignore Mommy-White-Pants.

The boy, like all children, didn’t feel the same way. He looked to his mother for an answer. Then nodded when she nodded.

“Alex was running down the stairs when I told him not to.” She glared at the boy, and his lip trembled in response.

Nikhil lifted the washcloth from the tiny knee and checked out the cut that went clean across the bony kneecap but wasn’t deep enough to warrant stitches. His relief at not having to sew up the child’s knee was ridiculous. But he had a hard enough time suturing adult skin with his shaking fingers, there was no way he was taking a chance on the child’s knee.

If he had needed stitches, Nikhil would have had to call one of the nurse practitioners and face those pity-filled glances that were bandied about when he couldn’t perform the basic procedures he was paid to perform.

“He needs some antiseptic and a bandage and he’ll be good as new. Just make sure he stays off it today.”

“Stay off it?” Mommy Dearest adjusted the rhinestone-studded shades perched atop her head. “But today is a shore-fun day and we’ve purchased our land excursion already.”

Nikhil handed Alex a tissue, but when the boy continued to stare at the gauze Nikhil was pressing to his bleeding knee, Nikhil reached out and wiped the tears off his cheek himself.

“Who’s your friend?” Nikhil pointed at the action figure peeking from the child’s pocket.

The child’s mood lifted. “He’s Tony Stark!”

Of course he was.

Jen had loved Robert Downey, Jr.

Sometimes even more than I love you. But only because he has your hair, Spikey.

"Doc?" She was giving him the "What the hell is wrong with you?" look again. She must have asked him a question that he hadn't heard, again.

Her hand was on the boy's shoulder. Suddenly, she was a model of motherly concern.

Nikhil got up and went to the supply closet and retrieved some gauze and bandages. The boy looked terrified, but he didn't sidle up to his mother or make any effort to draw comfort from her.

Nikhil's own mother was the very embodiment of comfort, her motherliness so over the top she had a way of mothering the heck out of any child who came into her sphere. Maybe it was her or maybe it was all the orphans he'd treated over the years, but despite his awareness that he didn't know this woman at all, the fact that she stood so stiff and tall next to the crumpled boy made him want to break things.

Jen had never wanted to be a mother and she'd always been honest about it. She had believed she would be terrible at it. But he'd watched her treat kids, seen her goof around with them, seen her bleed at their pain. She had been so wrong.

He cut out a piece of tape and handed it to the boy. "You know how Tony presses Arc Reactors into his chest and it makes him Iron Man?" He made a thick pad out of gauze and cut it into a perfect circle like an Arc Reactor. Then he squeezed some antibacterial ointment on it. "Bandages are just like that. When I put it on you'll have a super knee and when I take it off the boo-boo will be gone."

It was a pathetically stretched-out analogy, but the boy smiled. The mother looked at her watch.

"You can even go on your shore-fun excursion." Nikhil dabbed the area with some Betadine.

"Oh, no no. Alex isn't going, it's a grown-up excursion." She winked at Nikhil. "Alex is going to have fun at Camp Camel Caravan, aren't you, Al-bun?"

Al-bun gave a distracted smile, his entire focus on what Nikhil was doing to his knee.

"In that case, his battery pack is going to work even better. Maybe Dr. Nic can come and check up on him after lunch?"

The boy smiled.

"Okay, here it comes." He placed the gauze over the cut and pressed the tape over it. The boy didn't wince. Nikhil patted his head. "No running today. Maybe just video games?"

"For real?" The boy couldn't believe his luck.

"Perfect!" Mommy smiled at her watch.

She was going to make the shore excursion after all. *Yay!*

By the time Nikhil had her sign the paperwork and walked them out, his anger levels were nuclear. She was probably a decent-enough mother. He was fully aware that the sadness and anger overwhelming him had nothing to do with her. All the things he was angry about had nothing to do with her.

What he really needed to do was call his mother. It had been months since he'd seen his parents. They came by and met him in Miami every few months. But he hadn't gone home in two years.

The kind of relationship his mother and Jen had had made him feel like such an outsider sometimes. No matter where in the world Jen was, she had called Aie every week. For the past two years, Aie had diligently continued those weekly calls in the face of his inability to do anything more than answer her most basic questions and then hang up.

Now that he was already at the clinic he should have checked out some charts or taken inventory or something. But he had never been early to work on the ship, so he had no idea what to do with himself.

He'd gone to the clinic in the Himalayas straight out of med school and then into the MSF right after that. In both those positions he had never been faced with a moment that didn't beg to be filled with at least three things that were already past critical. Sitting around in the clinic until it opened was not an option unless he wanted to return to his room and hit the Jack early.

He shut the clinic door behind him and walked to the slatted wooden bench outside.

He could have sworn the bench was empty when he sat down, but when he looked up Jess was sitting next to him.

"Good morning," she said in a tone that sounded as if she were saying, "Take a deep breath, the world is still spinning." Then she held out a brown paper bag and a cup of coffee.

He took the bag from her and peeked inside. It was full of miniature muffins. Lemon poppy seed. The smell kicked off that ever-present nauseated feeling. They used to be one of his favorite things. And practically the only thing Jen ever baked. She had let Aie teach her how to make them and had perfected Aie's recipe to a point of being a gastronomical piece of art. Amazingly, no matter which corner of the world they lived in, poppy seeds were always available. Poppy seeds, of all things, were a universal equalizer. As were lemon, flour, sugar, and butter.

"Morning," he said, curbing the urge to return the bag to her and stuffed a muffin into his mouth. It was like dry sponge. He worked to hold it down, but he was going to need help from the coffee in her hand.

"I wasn't sure how you took your coffee. It's black but I have cream and sugar in the bag."

"Thanks. Black's fine." He took a sip and let the bitter brew wash down the glop and make an unsavory tumble in his belly. "She told you which muffins I like but not how I take my coffee?"

"I told you I can't control what she wants to say." She offered him another muffin, but he shook his head and tried not to bring up the one that was struggling to see daylight again.

"Aren't you going ashore?" he asked, mostly because he couldn't bring himself to respond with, "Why don't we just forget everything else and you tell me every word Jen's ever said to you and then repeat it again."

"No. Are you?" She folded her hands in her lap.

"Nope, I'm working. Clinic opens in an hour." And he never went ashore. Solid land was too much of a reminder of permanent unchangeable things.

She looked confused. "Didn't you just see that little boy?"

So she had been here awhile.

"They just showed up. But it's another hour before the clinic officially opens."

His daily dose of patients would start rolling in soon enough. Tummy aches, sunburns, and bruises, mostly. Every once in a while, someone showed up with something stuck in an aperture where it didn't belong. Cruises made people gluttons, daredevils, and sexual adventurers. All three things made for patients he had no trouble treating.

"Was the little boy okay?" She pointed her chin at the elevator the boy and his mother had taken.

"He's fine. Just a split knee and a mother who almost missed a shore excursion."

Her brows drew together in a frown. "His mother is going ashore? Who's going to stay with him?"

"They have day care on the ship."

Anger sparked in her eyes, and he noticed for the first time that they were brown, an array of shades all flecked together. Her lips pressed together in a livid hiss. "She's leaving him all by himself when he's hurt?"

Nikhil shrugged. "It's just a surface cut."

"Well, on the knee it's just a cut. But he's so little. He's just a—" She cleared her throat, realizing that she'd shown too much, clamped her jaw shut, and arranged her face back into her usual meditative demeanor.

"Who's watching Joy right now? His dad?"

Her spine straightened even more under her blacker-than-black sweatshirt. Other than that, she remained still as a lily pond on a windless night, not a ripple on the surface. But her stillness held no peace. Under all that calm he sensed an earthquake. He latched on to it. He had focused on nothing but himself for, well, for two years. Focusing on someone else was unexpectedly restful.

She surprised him when she answered, an intense surge of emotion rolling under her whisper. "He's staying with a friend." If Nikhil didn't have such an intimate relationship with pain, he might have missed the cold, hard blast of it in her eyes as she said it.

"You miss him."

She pursed her lips as though she were trying not to tell him how stupid he was for stating something so obvious.

"I've never left him alone before." This time, her pain had an aching sweetness to it. A mother missing her baby, the combined force of those motherly memories mothers seemed to store beneath their surface tangible in every breath.

He lifted his hand, meaning to pat hers, to do something comforting, but in the end his hand found its way to his own stubbly head, which he had forgotten to shave again. "You said he's seven?"

She nodded.

"That is very young to be without his mommy." He had meant to commiserate with her, but his words only intensified the pain she was trying so hard to hide.

"It is. I need to go back to him." Her jaw barely moved, but there it was again, that delicate slash of bone holding in an earthquake as it pushed to the surface.

"Please," those eyes said, in lieu of the words she was holding back. "Please help me get back to my baby."

"Do you have any idea where Jen could have hidden the evidence?" Before he could stop himself the words were out, answering her silent plea, and the stab of relief was the last thing he'd expected them to bring.

Jess couldn't believe her ears. She felt like the runaway cart she was on had hit a slope. Yet again Joy had done what she hadn't been able to manage on her own: unfrozen another crack in Nikhil's heart.

The urge to see her baby swelled so large and fast in her heart, she had to wrap her arms around herself to hold it in. She wanted to hold his face in her hands and kiss his butter-soft skin. She sank back into the wooden bench and squeezed herself, crushing the yearning into a ball and pushed it to the bottom of her belly, where it was starting to get crowded with all the crushed-up balls of regret, anger, and unexpectedly overwhelming guilt.

"Where did you put all her things after you . . . after you cleaned out her flat?"

Nikhil's thumb went to work on his ring. Spinning the loose metal band around his bony finger. He had beautiful hands, this man. A surgeon's hands. She was going to need them to dig through Jen's things. But first, she had to help stop them from shaking like that all the time.

Nothing. Nothing came out of him. He sucked in a breath a few times as if he was ready to answer, but then, nothing. His eyes were so raw it was as if he were in a trance. She pushed her voice into his silence. "Is her stuff here on the ship?"

He laughed. "God, no. She would've killed me if I had ever suggested taking a trip on"—he waved his hand around all that red and gold—"on a cruise ship. Nothing of hers is here."

Except him. He'd put Jen's precious belongings in a safe place. Except for what she cherished most.

"What about her Chicago apartment?"

He looked surprised, then angry. Of course he hated when she did that. Hated that she knew these things about Jen. What use was another apology? She pushed away the one that rose to her lips.

His wide, bony shoulders slumped. "No, I didn't move anything there."

He disappeared behind silence again. She waited. He had to burrow out on his own.

For what seemed like an age, he spun his ring around his finger. Maybe it had been too early to heave a sigh of relief. She knew he wanted to believe her, but in asking him to trust her she was asking him to change everything he'd ever believed.

"Did you have a chance to check up on the transplant records?" she asked, trying to sound as if she were asking him if the weather was conducive to walking on the beach.

Her voice dragged Nikhil out of the sinkhole of his memories. Her nonchalance made everything seem mundane. As if these were not the most absurd of conversations. As if believing that your dead wife was communicating with the woman who had her heart was not downright certifiable.

He didn't respond. He shouldn't have hung up on the cop without checking out her story. What if she wasn't who she said she was? Well then, he'd make sure she never walked free to do this again.

Yes, he wanted nothing to do with the criminals his wife had staked her life to apprehend, but this calm-as-a-lotus-pond woman claiming to have his wife's heart, claiming to somehow be able to talk to his wife, he was willing to see her all the way to jail. Did his heroism know no bounds?

"If you need more time to make sure who I am, I can wait. We can talk about this later."

He looked at her upturned face, where her need to go home to her child had just flashed so clear and bright. He searched for a scavenger's deviousness, but found only a strange mix of raw hope and understanding. Something sparked inside his numbness. "What was wrong with it?" He pointed a finger at the center of her chest.

She blinked in surprise. Then did one of her quick recoveries. "Congenital hole in the heart."

"When was it diagnosed?"

"Eight years ago when I—"

"When you were pregnant."

She nodded.

"You still had your baby." Warmth crackled through his numbness, but her gaze went cold. What he had said made her furious.

"As opposed to what?" Her tone didn't alter, but he knew when he was being snapped at.

He reached out and touched her shoulder. "You risked your life for your baby."

She lifted his hand off her shoulder and put it back on the bench next to her. "Actually, my baby saved my life."

For a moment he couldn't look away from her eyes. All those clashing browns coalesced around something so fierce, he felt alive again. But only for the briefest moment. Whatever it was, it flashed by so fast his insides spun. She went icy calm again, drawing back into herself.

His own baby had gone before anyone could save her. But her little heart had kept her mother's beating long enough to save a life.

For hours, for years, for an eternity, neither one of them spoke.

Everything had seemed meaningless for so long, he couldn't ignore that tiniest ember kindling inside him. He couldn't ignore that he wanted to follow where this girl was taking him. Even if he didn't believe her story, he believed something.

He stopped studying the swirls on the thickly carpeted floor and met those perfectly shuttered eyes again. A lock of the violently red hair she had pushed behind a headband and a hood escaped and she shoved it back.

"How will I know what to look for in Jen's things?" he asked.

It took her a moment to absorb what he'd just agreed to. "I'm not sure." Her eyes gave him another flash of hope, asking for things knowing they were impossible. "But I think I'll know when I'm near it."

"Jen will tell you?"

She searched his face, unsure if he was mocking her. Hell if he knew what he was doing.

"Is she here now?"

She nodded. "She's always here. But she's been very quiet since I . . . since I met you. And I know that she'll help us," she said in a small voice.

If anyone could help him right now, it was Jen. That was for sure. "The ship gets back to Miami in two days. It will take me that long to arrange for a doctor to replace me. Will you come to Chicago with me and help me look? All of Jen's stuff is there."

Jess pushed past the floor-to-ceiling glass doors that led into the ship's salon. As if by magic, the red-and-gold splendor transformed into black-and-gold splendor. All that granite and gilding and sheets of falling water put together to affect a soothing mood. The Buddha might have been mistaken in searching for peace amid austerity. There was no austerity here, just a lot of rich people who seemed perfectly at peace thumbing through glossy magazines on plush sofas.

She climbed the black granite steps that led to the reception desk and waited. She couldn't believe they were actually going to disembark the ship today. She was another step closer to going home to Joy.

Part of her had never believed Nikhil would buy her story. If she'd had her doubts before she got here, after she had met Nikhil, it had seemed downright impossible to get through to him, and yet the impossible had happened.

Maybe it was time to move from being a chorus dancer to an actor.

Maybe it had nothing to do with her. Maybe Nikhil had been ready to stop drowning in pain and to move on to the do-something phase. Just his luck that she had caught him at the crest of that vulnerability.

She pulled her headband off and shook out Jen's hair, even as she tried to shake off all that strange, prickling concern and sadness for him that she'd been indulging in. The other choice was guilt. She couldn't afford to let herself feel that either. None of these feelings were worth anything in the face of what she stood to lose.

She was doing what she had to do, what she would do a million times over if needed. But at least she could stop twisting the knife she had slid so ruthlessly into his gut. The hair had done its job. It was time for it to go.

The receptionist at the ship's salon gave her a wide smile. "Welcome to the Well-Spa. How may we help you refresh and replenish today?"

I need to erase the past ten years of my life. "I need to color my hair."

The girl's gaze did a quick sweep of her hair and she looked visibly relieved that the hideous color had seen its last day, then apologetic for having made her relief so obvious.

"Sure," she said, flashing her startlingly white teeth. "It will be five minutes. Please take a seat."

Her phone buzzed just as she settled into the sleek patent-leather sofa that looked incredibly uncomfortable but held her body so perfectly, it was like finding an oasis on *The Oasis.*

It was a text from Sweetie asking her to text him.

Texts from someone asking you to text them were never a good sign. *What's wrong?* she typed out. Then changed it to, *What's the matter?* Not wanting to throw self-fulfilling prophecies into the universe.

Sweetie's text buzzed back in a second. Also not a good sign. It meant he was waiting for her to text. *Those bastards gave Joy a ride home today.*

No.

She knew they were watching him, but the bastard had promised not to touch him.

Is Joy okay?

He recognized the man who took him to the hospital when they took him last time. He thought something was wrong with you again.

The eggs she had eaten for breakfast crawled up her throat.

Can I talk to him?

I told him you were fine, fed him ice cream, and he fell asleep perfectly happy.

If he had worried about her then he had definitely not fallen asleep happy.

I'll have him call you as soon as he wakes up. But, baby, you okay?

I'm fine. I'll make sure it doesn't happen again.

But he knew just as well as she did that they were empty words. The only thing she could make sure of was to hurry this along.

"They're ready for you." The girl from the salon gave her another perfect smile, and Jess followed her across the mood-lit salon that no longer felt peaceful or soothing.

Another girl, just as beautiful, pulled out a chair for Jess. Both girls exchanged a look, taking in her black yoga pants, her black hoodie, her hair—every aspect of her appearance in a fraction of a second. An entire conversation passed between them without a single word being uttered. For a moment it was like being back in the dressing room on a film set. Why was appearance and judgment such a currency between women? Why wasn't it enough that they were no more than their appearance to men? Why did they have to be that to one another?

She sank into the chair and leaned her head back over the sink.

A soft pillow cradled the back of her neck, so different from the sharp-edged sink at Beauty's Beauty Parlor.

"I'm Tiffany." The girl turned on the hand spray and started to work the warm water into Jess's hair. "What kind of color were we thinking?"

Warm water seeped through her hair and tickled her scalp. One of the girls at Beauty's had poured water on her head from a jug while another one had rinsed the color from her hair. The girls had argued about who should do the pouring and who should do the rinsing.

The scene should have been funny, but the fact that she was stealing a dead woman's hair to convince her husband that he wasn't done with the tragedy had sucked all the humor from it.

"Do you want to leave the extensions in?"

She wanted to leave nothing in. She wanted it all gone. The entire ugly mess inside her gone.

"Just the color for now, please." The weight of the hair was a good reminder—of all the things that had to be done before she could go home to Joy, of all the things she could not wish away and that ticked inside her like a time bomb.

The blast of pain in Nikhil's eyes every time they landed on the hair flashed in her head. Maybe she should leave the color in; maybe she needed the pain to hurry things along. But she couldn't do it, couldn't go on witnessing it.

His pain, his anger, every shade of undiluted feeling that passed over his face in those ruthless blasts had taken to bubbling up inside her at the most unpredictable times. Ever since she'd left him last night, an odd fear had gripped her.

It was nothing like her fear when she thought about Joy in a car with those men, his little heart imagining her in trouble. That fear gave her purpose, made her so angry she would do anything. This fear she felt when she saw flashes of Jen's Nikhil emerging from behind his grief was different from any she'd known before, and every time it bloomed in her belly it took her by surprise. It reminded her of that first time she'd felt her baby kicking and not known what it was.

Tiffany held out a board of color swatches. "What looks good?"

"Just a basic dark brown." She just wanted her natural color back. She wanted her life back.

One step at a time. That's what her mother had taught her. The only way to get through life was to look at the ground beneath your feet and take one step, then another. Looking too far down the path was what made you stumble.

9

I glimpsed madness today. Evil so complete has to be insanity.

—Dr. Jen Joshi

Asif Khan had never been inside a beauty parlor. But true leaders did what needed to be done. If saving his empire—Mumbai's most feared gang—meant walking into this flowery-smelling hole where women had hair ripped off their soft parts, he'd do it.

He had to hand it to the bitches. The things they went through to be attractive to men, whom they didn't even seem to like that much. It was hilarious. Then again, life was about doing things you hated for *chutiyas* you hated even more.

He thought he had the fucker by the balls, but the last time he had spoken to him he seemed to be up to something, and Asif hadn't become the biggest bhai in the Mumbai underworld by not staying ten steps ahead of smug *chutiyas*.

This beauty parlor was where that nosy doctor bitch had last been seen before her stubborn neck had been snapped in half so her brain would die but her heart would keep beating. All the ceramic tile–covered walls were lined with pictures of foreign bitches with glossy pouty lips and fluffy hair. Some of them were even showing cleavage. Totally fuckable.

Asif liked foreign *maal*, so spotless and so shameless. He stroked the boobs on the poster and felt his dick thicken in his pants. Not that it took the bastard much to come to life.

He turned to the fat old cow who was cowering behind her counter. Naturally, his dick shriveled.

"Are you the madam of this place?" he asked around the tobacco juicing up his cheek.

She nodded.

"Do you have someone less hideous I can talk to?"

His men guffawed.

"Bhai, look at this!" One of his men had grabbed two pretty young sluts by their arms and dragged them out of a room in the back.

The girls were shaking and sobbing in their tight dresses.

Ah, there was that thickening in his pants again. He licked his lips.

"How can I help you, Bhai?" The fat bitch interrupted his study.

He snapped his fingers in her direction without looking at her and his men moved at her. She squeaked.

"Can't you see Bhai is busy?" He had the best-trained men in the business. Not to mention the most loyal. They would all die for him in a heartbeat. A man didn't rule Dharavi without an army like that.

Which reminded him why he was here. When you sat at the top, ten people waited to topple you over. He turned to the sniveling madam.

"You knew that foreign doctor?"

She looked blank.

"The chinky one." He pulled his eyes into slits and his men guffawed again.

She didn't answer. Asif raised an eyebrow, and Laloo, his right-hand man, grabbed her hair and gave it a hard yank, squeezing another satisfying squeak out of her.

"Jen madam," one of the girls said behind him.

He turned around and waited for his man to drag her closer, then patted her cheek. She was all stacked and tight. He was going to have to pat more than just her cheek. It took one sideways glance at Laloo to get a nod of acknowledgment. Oh yes, his men were well trained indeed. No words were needed.

"Smart girl. Yes, Jen *madam*. How well did you know her?"

"What 'know,' Bhai?" the fat one said behind him. "She was a fancy doctor. She just came in here to help the girls with checkups and all."

"Yes, yes. All these charitable foreign fuckers who show up to clean up our shit and wipe our arses. Did you know her family?"

"She was by herself, Bhai. Husband was somewhere abroad."

Asif was on her in a moment. He slammed her face into the counter. The girls screamed. The fatso sobbed. "Do you know who I am? I didn't become the king of Dharavi by letting dried-up old bitches fuck me."

He pulled her up by her hair and stared into her face. He knew what he looked like. Terror lit up her eyes. "You used to send her husband food when he was here and crying into his sari."

She tried to nod. Her cheek was bleeding. He pressed a finger into the gash and dragged blood up her cheek to her eyelid.

"One more lie and you won't be able to see out of this eye. Who else came here looking for information? The police?"

She nodded.

"Who else?" He must have shouted because the terror in her eyes swelled. His tobacco spittle splattered across her bloodstained face, red mixing with red.

"No one else, Bhai," the hot stuff he was going to fuck later said behind him. He was about to slice one across her face for interrupting him when she said, "But there was a girl who came asking for the same color hair dye we used on Jen madam's hair."

He smiled. Forget waiting for later. This one was turning him on so much he wasn't going to wait.

"Good girl!" he said and swaggered out of Beauty's Beauty Parlor like the king he was. Behind him, his men followed, dragging the screaming bitch with them.

10

I didn't believe that entire "eyes are the window to the soul" thing until I met Nic.

He has this way of looking at you as if he sees you and finds you lacking in nothing. And you believe it. And that lets all sorts of shit out.

—Dr. Jen Joshi

"Are you absolutely certain you cannot find me one single flight from Miami to Chicago? Or from any of the surrounding airports?"

"Yes, sir, I believe that is what I've been trying to tell you for the past twenty minutes." The lady at the airline counter threw another long-suffering glance over her glasses at the line snaking behind Nikhil.

Other airline employees at other counters had been telling him that for the past few hours as well, but she didn't need to know that.

"Sir, this has been the worst blizzard in history to hit the Great Lakes, and no flights are making it into Chicago or into any of the airports within four hours of it. The closest I can get you is Atlanta. But not until tomorrow night. I'm sorry."

He thanked her and she almost collapsed in relief when he finally walked away. She'd suffered enough for the fact that he hadn't watched the news or read the papers recently, and looking out at the sky through the wall of windows, it seemed like all the earth was bathed in sunshine.

He found Jess leaning against a metallic column, the handles of both their bags clutched tightly in her fist. It reminded him of his mother holding on to their bags at a Mumbai railway station on one of his childhood visits to India.

"No one is going to run off with our bags," he said more sharply than he'd intended.

"How do you know that?" she said as if he hadn't just snapped her head off. Her newly colored hair framed her face, which was giving away nothing today. She was in full Goddess of Darkness mode.

He took the bags from her and tossed them on the black leather seats bolted to the floor. This wasn't fucking India. He sank into the empty chair next to the bags and waited for her to join him. "There are no flights into Chicago until the day after tomorrow."

"Are you sure?"

"No. Just a hunch."

She looked away, her blasted stillness untouched. But that chin of hers jutted forward a few millimeters. Yay! A reaction.

"When I asked the travel agent on the cruise ship, she said there were five flights to Chicago from Miami every day."

He sank back in his chair and stretched his legs out as if he were lounging on a beach. Except for the beach ball–sized knots in his belly. "Actually, there are twelve. They're all canceled because Chicago is snowed in." What were the odds of an April snowstorm? But the one thing you could always count on about his hometown was not being able to count on the weather.

She stared out the wall of windows at the spotless sky. "Is there another airline we could try?"

"Oh, I should have thought of that. Wait. I did." Okay, maybe he needed to dial back the snark a little bit. But when he'd braced himself to get off the ship and onto dry land for the first time in two years, being stranded at an airport was the last thing he'd expected.

She looked away in that annoyingly serene way of hers without another word, but the skepticism on her face was as clear as the Miami sky.

"What?" He leaned forward.

She raised an eyebrow and said nothing.

"If there is something you want to say, say it."

He got another supercilious raise of the brow and another whole lot of silence.

"Jess, I asked you a question."

"I'm sorry I didn't hear it."

"If you're accusing me of something, I should at least know what it is."

She lifted her hand and almost patted his hand as if he were a puppy dog who needed to be calmed. But then she put those slender-fingered hands back in her lap, dainty as a fucking ballerina.

"When was the last time you went home?" She might as well have kicked him, right in the center of his chest, with metal spikes.

He felt ten years old again . . . when he'd loved to ask questions but had hated the answers he was given. Why did Hitler hate the Jews? Why did the British divide India? Why did Idi Amin slaughter his people? There were tomes filled with answers—as though just because someone listed reasons, things were supposed to make sense—and he hated every single one of them.

He leaned back in his chair and tried the beach pose again. But the pain in his chest made it impossible. If she said anything about understanding how hard this was, he was leaving her here and going back to the ship. Even if he had to swim to it, given that it had set sail by now.

She said nothing. Just held her body as still as ever.

"Are you suggesting I somehow orchestrated the largest snowstorm in recent history just because I'm a coward?"

She flinched. "You're not a coward."

"Right, I'm an angel with a halo, I forgot."

"It doesn't matter what you are, Nikhil. What matters is—"

"Finding the evidence. I know. Bringing those bastards to justice. I know." She was right, too. He should be burning for redemption. He should be like those action heroes with automatic firearms shooting from both hands, ready to take the world down for justice. Instead, he felt like a slug someone had stepped on.

Her fingers twitched and lifted again. But he was glad she didn't try to comfort him. "Is there a train or a bus we can take?" she asked instead.

He clamped down on all the sarcastic responses that jumped up his throat at once. "I checked. The Greyhound and Amtrak schedule is backed up a few days. That's the bus and train service," he added when she looked confused.

"There has to be something we can do."

His preference would be to swim to *The Oasis*. But that would reinforce her coward theory. "We can wait two days in Miami until a flight becomes available."

She stood, picked up her bag, and slung it over her shoulder.

"You planning to walk there?"

Again no reaction other than the slightest stiffening of that already-ramrod-straight spine. The woman had absolutely no sense of humor.

"I don't know much about America, but I don't think that's possible." Well, he couldn't argue with that. "I'll be back in a few minutes." With that she walked away, her huge black sweatshirt floating around her spear-straight body as it weaved through the milling crowd.

He yanked his duffel off the seat, slung it over his shoulder, and fell in step next to her. They walked past the lines snaking in front of airline counters, dodged wailing babies, running kids, and exhausted people sitting cross-legged on the floor.

He had stepped in throw-up with his favorite sneakers at the Mumbai railway station once when he was ten. Aie had taken them to the bathroom and scrubbed them with her travel-sized Bath & Body Works's soap for so long they'd almost missed their train, but the shoes had continued to stink so bad he'd had to throw them away. Somehow this chaos reminded him of that day. It had to be midwinter break or spring break or something because everyone looked all set to go somewhere, to do something, to somehow make life matter.

Jess walked up to a booth marked INFORMATION. "We need to get to Chicago today and there are no flights available for two days. What can we do?"

The woman behind the counter gave her an entirely blank look. How could you work at an airport and never get that question?

"Have you tried to get a rental?" she asked, speaking very slowly and loudly. The way some assholes spoke to children with disabilities.

Jess had an accent, but her English was remarkably good. Even a little Colonial British, the way his *aie* sounded. Only Aie had an attitude honed from thirty years of being a college professor, so God help anyone who dared to talk to her that way.

Jess didn't seem to notice. "Rental?" She turned to Nikhil and gave the enunciating woman her back and it made him want to high-five her.

"What is she talking about?" she asked when Nikhil didn't answer.

"We could rent a car and drive there." How had he missed that? Oh right. Because he hadn't driven in two years. Didn't know if he even remembered how. And because there was that whole coward thing.

He turned away from her, choosing not to interpret her expression, and forced himself to the rental counter, turning around only once to make sure she was with him.

Miraculously enough, the rental company had one car available. This was explained by the fact that it was a soft-top Jeep. The woman at the rental counter had repeated only about fifteen times how lucky they were to get the one available car. Yes, so lucky that they would have a good ten hours before they started to freeze their asses off in earnest.

At least the car wasn't hard to find in the empty rental lot. It wasn't until he pulled open the door that he realized that Jess had stopped all the way across the lot.

She had gone utterly still.

Not her usual calm-as-a-lily-pond stillness, but an unable-to-breathe, white-as-a-ghost stillness.

He walked back to her. "Jess? What's the matter?"

Her fingers clutched the strap over her shoulder so tightly her knuckles looked like they were going to pop out of their sockets.

"Is that, is that the, is that the car?" She wrapped her arms around the bottom of the bag and hugged it to her chest, then moved it to her hip. He had never seen her fidget before. "How long would we have to be . . ." It took her a few tries, but she managed to swallow. "How long is the drive?"

"Some twenty hours."

Whatever was left of the Mask of Calm shattered. For one long moment her terror flashed before him like a bolt of lightning illuminating the darkest storm.

"Twenty hours in . . . in th . . . that car?" she stuttered and swiped her hand across the sheen of sweat that dotted her lip.

Without meaning to, his voice switched to physician-in-emergency mode. "We'll take breaks. Stop for the night at a motel or something. It won't be twenty hours at a stretch."

"You were right—let's wait and fly out the day after tomorrow."

Her terrified eyes met his, and suddenly, he didn't want to be stuck here with her for two days.

"That'll just delay everything. Don't you want to get back to Joy?"

A cheap shot.

She wrapped her arms around the bag again and struggled to regain the Mask of Calm. Until five minutes ago, he could never have imagined her in a panic. But she was definitely in a full-blown panic now. A live volcano under a snowcapped mountain with all that barely contained smoke hissing out.

He tried to slide the bag off her shoulder, but she didn't let go. He waited for her breathing to even out, then he pulled his own bag over his shoulder and walked back to the car.

She ran to fall in step next to him, her shoulders squared. One mention of Joy and she was going to do this. He felt like the worst kind of shit. This was the last time he'd ever use her son like that.

When he yanked the car door open, she stumbled back as though flames had shot out of the car.

He almost wrapped his arm around her, but she found her balance on her own, set that jaw again, set those shoulders. And even then she couldn't make herself climb in.

The strength of his reaction to her helplessness, to her terror almost knocked him off his feet. He backed away from her. He didn't want to know. He was no longer in the business of fixing people's problems. But he couldn't walk away from what he saw in her eyes.

"Why don't you take a moment? We'll be on the road a long time. Let's use the restroom, pick up some water."

She turned around and disappeared into the rental office so fast, it left him spinning.

* * *

She knew she had to leave the bathroom and get into that car with Nikhil, but she couldn't. Leaning her back against the wall, she clutched her tote to her chest. Her hand traced the rectangular outline she could feel through the fabric bottom of the bag and tried to draw strength from Jen's voice.

Jen would never have understood the abject fear that gripped Jess's belly. Jen always sounded so sure of herself. So strong. Except maybe at the very end. She had to have felt fear then. The kind of fear that was pushing up Jess's throat now—a sense memory so strong it was like reliving the horror. It was horrible to be jealous of the dead, but not having to feel this over and over again would be nice.

"I'm so sorry, Jen," she said into the empty bathroom.

It was her millionth apology and yet it felt like it wasn't enough.

She walked to the sink, hugging her trembling arms around herself, squeezing the sweatshirt that was three sizes too large close to her body. The usual security of her bulky clothing did nothing to comfort her. But it wasn't the clothes. The armor she generally wore under her clothes, over them, seemed to have disintegrated when she saw that car. She felt naked.

How had she let herself lose control so completely in front of Nikhil? How on earth had she let him see her like that? And he'd seen it. He'd seen all the way to the heart of her terror.

"Jess?" he called from outside the door, and followed it up with a quick knock. Bloody hell.

She held her hand in front of her face. It was still shaking.

She leaned into the sink and splashed her face.

"Jess, come on, open the door."

She couldn't answer him, not with her insides still churning like an ocean gone mad. She tried another splash across her face. A hand pressed against her mouth. It's not real. Not real. Hands ripped at her. This was not happening. Another splash. She scrubbed at her lips. All over her, hands and breaths collected and fogged. Sticky cobwebs of memories. She pushed at them, but they only clung tighter and coated her skin.

She stopped struggling. Let herself fall.

"Jess."

That was Nikhil's voice. She focused on it. The crowding, gnawing pressure around her eased. She breathed. Let it slide off.

"Jess, if you don't come out, I'm coming in."

"One moment." She didn't know if the words came out. She cleared her throat and tried again. "Give me one moment." She went to the door.

It swung open just as she went to push it with both hands, and she stumbled forward.

He grabbed her arms. "You okay?" He set her right, then let her go even before her skin registered the shock of the contact.

The door he had pulled open with such force swung back and smacked him, pushing him into her again.

This time she held him up.

"Sorry," they both said together. Their words clashing just as their bodies pulled apart.

"I'm fine," she said, pushing past him to the glass doors, needing to get out of the confined space. How was she ever going to explain this to him?

As soon as the thought entered her head, she realized how ridiculous it was. She didn't need to explain anything to him. He was nothing but an assignment she needed to finish and leave.

She pushed through the glass doors, and the wind hit her face like another splash of water. It was about time she got in that car and got this over with.

11

All you need to fix a torn-up body is a clean scalpel, needle, and twine. Nic doesn't seem to get that our work is done when the incision is sutured. The rest is just self-indulgence.

—Dr. Jen Joshi

When she had pulled herself into the car, she had believed that she could do this. That she could block out being thrown in, being thrown out. That she could block out the box-shaped ceiling so high a man could rear up on his knees with you under him.

No. Don't think about it. Don't. Don't push yourself deeper into the seat either. It only makes it worse. Don't think about it.

Don't. Don't.

The chant hadn't helped. Nikhil's silence hadn't helped. It had to have been hours, but she couldn't get herself to look out the window. Sounds kept lashing at her ears, getting louder and louder. The slash of passing trees and cars whipped against her cheek even though the windows were up.

This time the windows were up.

She refused to tremble.

Refused to feel the pop of her shoulder as it snapped out of its socket or the crunch of bone as she hit the caked earth. Or the torn wetness that burned between her legs as she rolled herself into a ball and waited for the world to end.

The car slid to a halt. A door opened and closed. Someone cursed, hands dug into her arms and shook her. She struggled and tried to get away. Oh God, please make it stop. The scream stuck in her throat. She gagged around the taste of a wet, horribly moist mouth holding her screams in place, pushing them back down her throat. *No. No.*

Hands shook her harder. She struggled harder. Until wetness splashed against her cheeks, against her forehead. She sucked in a breath and opened her eyes.

Nikhil's face was inches from hers. A frown slashed across his forehead. But the hand on her cheek was gentle. She swatted it away and scrambled back in her seat.

He took a step back. "Can you breathe?"

She let a stream of air fill her lungs and looked beyond him at the thick green that stretched out behind him in an endless backdrop. Woods. There were no woods in Calcutta. She was not in Calcutta.

America. She was here in America. Where there were woods, right next to cars zipping past. And there was Jen's Nikhil.

She sat up. "I'm fine. I'm sorry. I fell asleep. It was just a nightmare."

He pushed a bottle of water at her. It was half empty from being poured onto her face. Her sweatshirt was soaked all the way to her shirt. The wetness grounded her. She took the bottle and drank.

"We're turning around. We'll wait for the plane and go the day after tomorrow," he said, watching her drink.

No. She had to get back to Joy. Get this thing over with. "No."

"Well, obviously, you can't handle being inside a car."

She could handle anything. "I can."

"Really?"

She wasn't discussing what she could and could not handle with a man who hadn't been on dry land in two years.

"Yes."

"Your eyes have been squeezed shut ever since you got in."

And your hands have been shaking on the wheel. I'm not pointing that out, am I? "I'm just sleepy, okay?"

"Sleepy. Right. That's the word for it?"

"Yes." *And what was the word for being terrified of going back to your own home?*

He looked annoyed at her monosyllables. But there was no question of getting sucked into talking about what had just happened. Again. This was exactly what she had sworn would never happen. Those bastards would not take her life away.

It had taken her years to stop avoiding getting inside cars, but she had done it. She no longer took rickshaws, or the train, or the bus, even when she could take a cab. She could handle cars just fine. It was just this car, the one that had been her coffin.

Twenty. Hours.

She sat up and stared out at the thick wall of trees behind him. Tiny yellow flowers dotted the grass-covered slope leading to it. Her hometown had been sprinkled with flowers and she had loved picking them for her mother. Aama, whom three years of cancer hadn't broken. *We are copper,* kanchi. *They can bend us and twist us but they can't break us.*

She made herself turn around, eyes wide-open, and took in the dashboard, the steering wheel. Focused on the differences. No leather, there's no leather and it's not black, it's beige, and the back-seat, well, that she wasn't going to look at.

When she looked back at him he was still standing on the gravel, his arms spanning the open car door, one hand resting on the door, the other on the frame. He was boxing her in. But instead of feeling threatened, she felt, well, she didn't feel threatened, and that was something.

She realized with a shock that Nikhil was the only man she'd ever met around whom she didn't feel threatened. Sweetie Raja was her best friend and flatmate, but even him she had been wary of when they had first met, the fact that he cross-dressed as a woman notwithstanding.

Out of nowhere anger swept through her. "I told you, I'm fine. I'll try to stay awake, if that's what you need." Her voice was as cold as she could make it.

He held out his hand. "Just step out for a minute. The fresh air will help you breathe."

She could breathe well enough. But he was a doctor so she might as well take his medical advice. He was giving it away for free, and when did doctors ever do that? She grabbed the car door and stood. For a second his body was inches from hers, then he took a quick step back and wind whooshed between them as a car whizzed by.

The air was fresh and cool and she filled her lungs. Earth and trees and spring and another scent. His sweat. Not stale and rotten-smelling like the Mumbai trains but fresh and clean and filled with life. A complete contradiction to the person it belonged to, who was trapped in death.

"We can still turn around and wait for a flight." His voice was like his smell. Fresh and clear and gentle.

What would delaying this another two days accomplish?

Of all the things she hadn't anticipated, a car was going to ruin everything. This, this travesty on four wheels, the script hadn't covered. She should have known, because when had her life ever followed any kind of plan?

She had already told him she was fine. How many more times did he need to hear it? "Delaying it by two days won't make going home any easier."

He narrowed his eyes. "I wasn't talking about myself."

She shrugged. He opened his mouth, then he too shrugged. Their two shrugs, it was becoming their language.

He walked—no, stormed—to his side, got in the driver's seat, and shut—no, slammed—the door.

She gripped the door hard, took one last gulp of air, with the lingering hint of his fake-alive scent. Then she climbed into the car and slammed her own door shut.

He hit the accelerator, making her stomach somersault. His only response to the sound that escaped her was a quick look at her fingers clutching the seat.

She tried easing her grip and worked on breathing, tried to focus on the world zooming past without shutting her eyes. One step at a time. Everything passes. This would too. If he'd only ease up on the accelerator so her stomach would stop spinning.

He eased up on the accelerator. Her grip on the seat eased. Her relief was so completely out of proportion to the amount of kindness in the act, she wanted to kick herself for how much gratitude flooded through her. She liked him better when he was detached. Liked him even better when he brought out those flashes of mean that he wore like a borrowed shirt. His anger she recognized, understood, found easy to process. Anger in all its forms comforted her.

"Did you and Jen go on many road trips?"

He sucked in a breath so deep it left a vacuum between them. "Why don't you ask her?" He slammed on the accelerator again and her entire focus returned to staying upright, staying calm. Staying in the here and now.

Nikhil's stomach was pumping acid like a ripe colitis infection. It took him hours of speeding before he admitted to himself what had happened. What he had allowed to happen. The numbness that had frozen him off from the world for so long was gone.

In that moment when the woman next to him had folded in on herself, all but screaming without making a sound, her face ghost-white, he had felt panic. Not the memory of panic that had been his constant companion these two years, but panic in real time, panic for what she was going through. Panic and concern and a need to act. He hadn't felt the need to act for so long, it sat like a foreign body wedged between his ribs.

If he hadn't recognized exactly what had been concealed in those silent screams, he might have believed she had fallen asleep and had a nightmare. But being haunted by the ghost of memories that were too graphic to wrestle off when they started wrapping their arms around you like a straitjacket, and closing in strap by strap, was too familiar to him to mistake for anything else.

This stubbornly meditative woman, who shrouded herself in darkness and appeared impossible to touch, was nothing but an eggshell. One that held a torn-up yolk within. The last thing he wanted was to care. But the fact that she sat next to him, so erect, so proud, and swallowed whatever shit had spewed from her past, made him insane with anger.

If Jen was really visiting her, he needed to keep Jen the hell away from whatever sewage of horrors was erupting inside her.

"You ready for a break?" he asked hours too late.

She turned to him. Whatever she was struggling with made it hard for her to twist in her seat. She did it nonetheless.

"I'm fine. You?"

Just for that, he wanted to keep driving. "I'm ready for a break."

The relief in her body was tangible. There was no physical manifestation of it. Her shoulders didn't sag, her face didn't relax. It was in her breathing—it eased. It had been his best skill as a physician. To know what his patients bore when they lacked the tools to articulate it. Jen had worshiped him for it. Her medical skills had been more tangible. She could make surgical magic with the most archaic supplies. Together they had been unstoppable.

He pulled the car into a parking spot so fast he hit the curb. Before he could apologize, Jess slipped out of the car. No surprise. He, on the other hand, wanted nothing more than to stay within the confines of the car, within the comfort of something.

She squeezed her eyes shut and fished her bag out of the backseat as though she were grabbing something from the jaws of a mad dog, slung it over her shoulder, and waited.

What the hell was in that bag? "Leave it in the car. I'll lock it," he said. She was going to break her shoulder, for shit's sake.

Without a word and with only the barest hesitation, she threw the bag in the backseat again, and he felt like such a jerk he wanted to pull it out and carry it for her. He turned away and started for the glum redbrick rest area, her footsteps crunching gravel behind him.

When Nikhil came out of the men's room, Jess was waiting for him. From the look she gave him, he knew she had hurried because she was still mortified about having him drag her out of the restroom the last time. Without a word she headed back to the parking lot and without a word he followed her. But she stopped so abruptly, he almost ran into her and knocked her over. Her body froze in that way he'd seen it do so many times in the short while he'd known her. It reminded him of a dam of ice, seemingly fragile yet strong enough to hold anything in.

He walked past her, resisting the urge to touch her elbow. What the hell had happened to her in a car? He clicked the Jeep open. She started at the sound. It was the barest movement, but he noticed it. Just the way he noticed her eyes sparkling with helplessness when he held the door open. She didn't move.

"Are you hungry?" he asked to distract her, but her stomach groaned so loudly in answer that her embarrassment escaped in a smile. That sudden self-conscious quirking of her lips threw her wide-open for the beat of second.

He slammed the door shut, not ready to let that smile disappear again behind that awful combination of terror and courage.

The glass-and-metal enclosure behind them was lined with vending machines. Before he knew it, he was dislodging every kind of sodium- and sugar-loaded treat from its metal perch. Her eyes followed his plunder of the machines with so much enthusiasm—which for her meant the slightest brightening of the brown in her eyes and the pink in her cheeks—that he kicked himself for having forgotten about food. He filled her hands, then his own, and they dropped down on the grass side by side.

"I'm so sorry we didn't stop to eat. You must be starving."

She was already halfway through a packet of tiny donuts. "I don't think I'm going to be able to answer until it's all gone." She pointed to the stack of packets, her mouth full of donut, and proceeded to rip open and annihilate one after another.

Every once in a while she pushed something into his hand, and he in turn pushed it into his mouth and forced himself to chew and swallow. But only because he didn't want to talk about how he couldn't eat.

She folded each packet neatly into a square and tucked it under her crossed legs as she ate without pause.

"Where do you put it all?" he said without thinking when every crumb was gone.

She tilted her head, a confused frown folding between her brows. "My stomach, usually. You sure you're a doctor?"

"It's a manner of speaking when someone skinny eats a lot."

Her lips quirked. "Really?"

"Oh." She was teasing him? Maybe it was all that sugar. Or maybe it was the fact that he was being a patronizing jerk.

"And I'm not skinny," she said. "At least not for my line of work." As soon as she'd said it she stiffened, because of course she had let that slip without meaning to.

"What's your line of work?"

She waited a beat too long to answer him. "I'm a dancer."

A dancer? That would definitely have been his very last guess. She was far too serious to be a dancer. With all those thorns sticking out of her and her discomfort with attracting attention, how did she ever get on a stage? Not to mention being a heart patient. That had to make it hard.

"You look like I just told you I'm a ghost whisperer or a psychic." Wow, and there it was again, another tiny smile. Sugar and salt were magic on this girl.

"What kind of dance?" Maybe she was a ballet dancer. That whole Goddess of Darkness thing went with ballet, didn't it? He couldn't imagine it being any kind of happy dance.

The smile vanished in another one of those ninja flash moves of which she was master. Instead of answering, her eyes landed on the car and she started collecting the folded-up packets and stuffed them in a garbage can.

"Junk food and generating garbage. Welcome to America!" he said.

"Don't call it junk. It was delicious." She surveyed the grass where they'd been sitting and picked up a chip she had missed. "And yes, I know 'junk' is just a manner of speaking."

Yup. Total patronizing jerk.

She poked the grass to make sure nothing had been left behind, but he had a feeling it was also because she couldn't make herself go back to the car.

"Is it all cars?" he asked.

She looked up at the car and gave the slightest headshake. "No."

That's all the answer he would get.

She started toward the Jeep, shoulders squared for battle, and he had all the answers he needed.

"Will removing the top help?"

She started. "You can do that?"

He was crap at cars and machines, but how hard could it be? He got in the car, pushed around the edges of the soft top, and found a few levers. Fortunately, things popped and unsnapped and he was able to flip back the entire fabric roof covering the front seat. It wasn't the entire top but it was something, and he thanked the engineers at Jeep for not making him look like a fool.

She stood there, frozen, watching the late-afternoon sun flood through the cab. He got out and secured the flap in place and opened the car door for her, mostly to get her to move.

She looked up at him, her incredibly delicate jaw clenched, her eyes filled with something he hadn't seen there before. Something he did not care to define.

He hadn't realized how large her eyes were, their upward sweep unusual. She must be from one of the Northeast Indian states. Her irises were huge. Except you hardly got a look at them when she was holding herself in her meditative stance with her eyes heavily lidded.

They weren't heavily lidded now.

The long column of her throat worked, struggling with what she was trying to say.

"Nikhil?"

His stomach clenched in response to that tentative tone.

"Thank you."

"For what? For starving you?"

He had heard of smiles being sad, but this one bled. And was so damn brave, he couldn't bear it.

"For everything." She touched his shoulder, a whisper of a caress that lasted no more than a second, then she braced herself and sank into the car.

He slammed her door shut and took far too long to make the trip around to the driver's side. His arms and legs felt like water. Like melting ice. He touched his shoulder. "I don't want you to touch me," he wanted to tell her, but they slid back inside the silence that had engulfed them on their drive out of Miami.

It wasn't the same silence as before. The open top meant far too much wind noise for conversation. She closed her eyes against it as they merged onto the freeway, but this time her body didn't go stiff enough to splinter.

Having some food in her system probably helped. The wind-swept silence stretched on, broken only by the flapping of the soft top he'd apparently not secured as well as he'd thought. Just when he was sure sleep had claimed her, her low voice floated through the wind and the flapping. "Jen was right. You are different from any man I've ever met."

Jen.

For the first time in two years, Nikhil had forgotten about his wife. The heavy, painful weight slammed back into his heart—which was hers and hers alone.

His body recognized the pain and restlessness and eased back into it. It wasn't relief exactly, not comfort either, but a feeling of being covered up again after someone had stripped him naked.

Cars whizzed past, flashing at him like the memories he would never be able to let go of. Hour after hour, they slashed through him, punishing him with their clarity.

Next to him, Jess's arms stayed wrapped around herself, her face peaceful in sleep. No, *peace* was too benign a word for her. She was placid, like the upper cool crust of lava. Under it she hid more than he wanted to know. Under it she hid the only thing about her that mattered. Jen's heart.

Jen, whose heart had hungered for life and justice and change. His wife had fixed things. Defeated them. But this impostor she'd chosen to bring into their lives was stone. Lava hardened and frozen so cold it could burn off your limbs.

How can you talk to her? Why her? When I'm still here. He wanted to speak the words into the falling darkness, needed the grief to scrape his throat.

For as long as he had known her, his wife had always known what she wanted. She'd always had a plan. Why had she brought this stranger into his life?

Why, Jen?

She didn't answer.

But that didn't stop him from repeating the question over and over as they flew toward home.

12

I don't think I believe in justice quite as much as Nic does. He believes in it like someone who's only ever known justice. He glimpses evil through windows. He's never in the room with it. Sometimes I hate him for it.

—Dr. Jen Joshi

The one thing Asif hated more than anything else was being threatened.

He was disappointed in the politician *chutiya* for treating him like some common criminal and trying to scare him. A common criminal wouldn't know how to recruit a computer genius away from India's most prestigious engineering college and get him to set up a system that matched up rich people who needed organs with poor people who happened to be lugging them around in their worthless bodies.

Even if the idiot was passed out half the time from not knowing when to stop with the smack. Youngsters these days didn't understand balance. He sank into the spaceship-style chair he had paid for, in front of the desk that was crammed with the millions of rupees' worth of toys he had bought the druggie bastard, and snapped his fingers at the bed where the lump of genius lay unmoving.

It was all the command Laloo needed. His most faithful dog grabbed the boy's skinny, passed-out arse and dragged him to the bathroom.

The sound of water turning on and the boy being shoved under the shower made Asif want to go in there and shove his head into the commode. Look at the house he had given the idiot. If he had stayed in his fancy engineering college, he wouldn't have been able to afford a place like this even after forty years of working his balls off.

Some people had no gratitude.

"Hi, Bhai!" the wet idiot grinned worshipfully at Asif, dragging water across the pure-white marble Asif was paying a minor fortune for.

"You trying to kill yourself on my time?" Asif asked.

"More like killing myself on your dime, Bhai." He chuckled at his own fancy English humor. "You won't let me die, Bhai," he said. "Especially not after you hear what I have for you."

The bastard had never disappointed Asif and he didn't this time. Asif had been right. He was a fucking genius. Seven matches. He had found Asif seven matches.

That doctor bitch had already made Asif rich beyond his dreams with her registry database. With all those details about blood type and plasma and this and that enzyme that she had collected, she had practically handed him a menu card of organs from useless living bodies no one would miss, address and age and all. All he had to do was chop them up and serve them to the clients his druggie pet dog found him using all those computer skills, then put the leftover bodies through a shredder and dump the mess in construction sand. God knows there were more foundations being dug around Mumbai than even he would ever need.

Maybe he was wrong about these foreign bastards who thought they could come feed off India's sewers to assuage their own guilt for being born in mansions. Dr. Joshi had sure as shit changed his life. Like hell was he ever giving up any of it. There were still tens of thousands of names on there. It was his golden goose and he wasn't chopping off its head just because some politician *chutiya* thought he had something on him.

He already knew from the beauty parlor bitch that the politician had some chinky-looking woman dye her hair like Dr. Joshi.

Now, if it were him, he would only make someone dye their hair like someone else if he wanted that person to impersonate the other person. But why impersonate a dead woman? Unless you were trying to convince someone she wasn't dead.

Aha!

But whom would the politician need to convince of that in order to screw Asif Khan over? Only one person would know that for sure. The bitch who'd dyed her hair at Beauty's. She was his key. And there wasn't a lock in the city Asif Khan couldn't open if he wanted to. Finding keys was his favorite pastime.

The wet, grinning fool who was eyeing him for his reward like a hungry dog wasn't the only genius around. Asif threw the bag of goodies on the bed. "There's new syringes in there too. Don't reuse and don't share. Taking care of your family if you die isn't part of the deal."

But the bastard wouldn't die, because Asif never left anything to chance. He never gave him enough to kill him, and if anyone else in the city sold to him they knew that Asif Khan would make sure they didn't live to sell to anyone else.

13

I'm surrounded by medicos—physicians, nurses, techs, all these practitioners of medicine. But we're different from the medicos who don't seek out the mission life. It might seem like this life calls to us because we want to be healers, but maybe we're here because we have the greatest need to find healing.

—Dr. Jen Joshi

Nikhil took the two keys the lady at the motel registration desk was holding out and shoved them into his pocket with a "thank you." When he turned around, Jess was standing just inside the sliding glass doors, the floodlights from the porch behind her illuminating her no-longer-red hair. The brown strands that matched her eyes exactly fell in short wisps around her face and kissed her cheeks. Instead of walking toward her, he walked toward a table arranged with coffee and tea.

She had slept through most of the journey, stirring to wakefulness only as they pulled into the motel parking lot. He had spent the entire drive wondering what he was doing here. On solid ground with a stranger. Headed home after two years.

"Coffee? Tea?" he said over his shoulder, knowing she had joined him in staring at the table. The thick smell of dark-brewed coffee that had been sitting too long assaulted his senses.

"Tea," she said, filing through the tea box. She picked out an orange packet that said *Chai* and held it up. "Do you know if this is any good?"

Such a mundane question. Yet the intimacy of it made his insides burn.

He filled a Styrofoam cup with hot water. "I don't drink tea. My mom always drinks either English Breakfast or Darjeeling. Those are the most like chai. Without spice or ginger."

"Oh, I hate ginger in my chai." She fished out a packet of English Breakfast.

He took it from her, unwrapped it, and dunked the tea bag into hot water and followed it with creamer.

When he looked up she was holding out a cup of coffee. Didn't even have to ask him how he took it or anything.

They exchanged cups and wary looks.

And it was too much.

That simple act was too much.

She took a sip of her tea, studying him over the rim. He couldn't bring his cup to his lips. He tossed it in the trash and extracted a room key from his pocket. "Room two-one-four. Can you find it?"

She gulped down the sip she had just taken. "If I focus really hard." She tried her almost-smile but didn't make it.

Which was just as well because he couldn't do that weird, friendly tête-à-tête thing again.

"I'll see you in the morning then." With nothing more than that he turned around and walked into the night.

He had left his bag in the car. She, of course, had hers strapped across her chest. The motel was located in the middle of the kind of neighborhood motels are often located in. Lots of flashing street signs. Many of the ones here bore the word *adult*.

Just the kind of neighborhood his mother would have freaked out about. Just the kind of neighborhood Jen would have wanted to go exploring in. His hand went to his hair. The weeklong growth scraped his palm.

I love your hair, Spikey.

He pulled his hand away and pushed it into his pocket. His jeans rode low on his hips. All of his clothes were too big. His mother was going to have a fit about it. For a moment he felt the sweet bite of anticipation at seeing his parents, at having Aie chew his head off about something. About anything.

But he knew she wouldn't say a word about it. Not the weight, not the hair, not Jen. She would treat him as if he were made of glass. Of shattered glass held together by sheer chance of pressure and weight. The way she'd done every time she and Baba came down to Miami to see him. *Such a nice ship,* beta. *Such a nice clinic.*

No mention of the fact that he hadn't gone home in two years.

No mention of the woman he had lost two years ago.

Tomorrow he was going to be home, in the house where he had promised his wife a lifetime together the day before their wedding while entering her long and sweet on his childhood bed.

He broke into a run. He hadn't run in three days, hadn't touched a drink in four days. And today he had noticed the shape of another woman's eyes. He felt like someone had gouged out his skin and left his ripped-up flesh to fester.

A car honked at him as he ran across six lanes of traffic. He stuck his hand up and flipped it the bird. Two men stumbled out of a door. He looked up at the sign. BEER AND SPIRITS. That's all he needed to know.

She let herself into the room that opened straight into the night. Nothing but a covered verandah separated the rooms and the parking lot edged with a high, chain-link fence. There wasn't a soul in sight. Even the lobby had been isolated. She felt the strangest sensation in the pit of her stomach when she remembered waking up in the car and then making her way inside the hotel, her eyes searching for Nikhil's stark-white shirt.

He had been standing at the reception desk. Recognition had sparked in his eyes for just one second before disappearing, the Nikhil who had sat with her on the grass while she ate her way through the contents of an entire vending machine, gone. The Nikhil who had dipped a tea bag into her tea had been the Nikhil who had leaned over the railing and looked hungrily at the ocean, longing for the strength to let go, unable to find the strength to hold on.

She thought about him working to remove the top of the car, rolling up the fabric, pinning it back. It wasn't just the skill with which he had quickly and efficiently taken care of it that had struck her. It was the look in his eyes when he had asked her if it would help.

It was the look of someone cleaning up a wound. Singularly focused on making sure she felt no pain. As if the entire world had boiled down to him taking care of what hurt her. The sheer magnitude and purity of the empathy in those eyes, in those words, it was like nothing she'd ever experienced. This man, for all his brokenness, was a healer.

The tiny room was almost fully occupied by a bed. She dumped her bag on the floor, her shoulder cramping with relief. At the far end of the room was a mirror over a sink and a door that led to the bathroom. She stared at the thick hair that still took the place of her own wispy locks, each tacked-on strand a reminder of her actions. It was as if something alien had taken up residence on her head to make sure she didn't forget.

She threw the hair back and shook it out. The motion freed her neck. She rolled it around a few times more, then reached back and lifted the hair into a ponytail and bound it together between her fingers. Her limbs missed movement. She let the hair slip from her grasp and reached up and stretched out her arms. Fingers pointed. Reaching for something. Stretching every muscle. Her other hand trailed from her wrist to her shoulders. Then down her body to her toes. A beat thumped inside her head. *Dadum. Da da dum.* One foot came up. First the heel, then the arch, until only one toe remained on the floor. She dragged it up her calf. *Da dum.* Tracing the curve. Bringing her knee up and up until her leg kicked out. *Da da dum.*

She brought her foot back down. Flipped the other heel up, her heels alternated, her feet following the beat that slammed inside her. One, two, three. One, two, three. Anger surged through her body. Lit her up like a current. Her spine curved over it. Her arms wrapped around it, then flew open as she spun and spun until her blood churned the anger out. Sadness. Then anger, sadness, then anger, her feet pounded it. Kicked at it. *Da da dum. Da da dum. Da da dum.*

Her head rolled forward. Emptying everything out. Shaking it off. The rhythm was all she felt. The rhythm and her breathing. Her breath still carried that scent. Summer and life and sparkling-fresh cleanliness. Fake cleanliness. For all the pain blanketing his skin, wrapped around his limbs, pegged like spikes into his eyes, he still smelled clean. His eyes. God, his eyes. She spun until they disappeared, spinning around her head, but not fast enough to keep up with her. For all that pain, he smelled untouched, un-ravaged. Pure.

More smells came back. Sick, turgid sweat. Alcohol and cigarettes and car freshener. Sick and sweet like overripe mangoes. They had splashed it into her face, splashed it all over her. Just because her flailing hands had tipped it over.

Drink it, whore.

She hadn't opened her mouth and they had flooded her face with it as they pounded. She had tried to scream.

Shut up. Shut. Up.

As if she could have screamed. With hands cutting off her breath. A wet mouth eating up her screams. As if anyone would have heard her. If you were pathetic enough to scream for help, no one was going to help you. That was just the way the world worked. No help for screamers. No alms for beggars. No mercy.

She stopped spinning. In the span of an instant the room stopped spinning around her. She hated that, hated that all the practice spinning had taken the dizziness away. She slammed her hand into the door that led to the bathroom and turned on the shower. Then, without taking off her clothes, she stepped under the burning-hot spray.

Nikhil had really lucked out. Not only was the bar packed with the loudest crowd, but the entire rowdy horde seemed possessed by an insatiable hunger for heavy metal. The scream of the electric guitar tore through all the noise in his head. He slung back what was left in his glass and tapped it for a refill. One more time. Again and again. Until he had lost count. The bartender in his black golf shirt and preppy haircut looked like he'd just finished a full day of classes at the local MBA program. But the way he bobbed up and down as he moved from glass to glass, a splash here, a spray there, the way he kept his eagle eye trained on the dance floor, he could've been in the Secret Service, or the Mafia. Or both at the same time. He was what Jen would have called hardcore.

Hard. Core.

"These guys think they are so hardcore," she would have said. "Imagine putting them on a minefield. They'd run whimpering." She might've leaned into that guy with skull tattoos inked up and down his arm and his neck and asked him if he'd ever seen a baby with half its body blown off.

Yeah. She had loved being a buzzkill, his wife.

His wife.

"Who died?" A woman in a dress so tight he couldn't imagine how she wasn't asphyxiated leaned into the bar and stared at him from beneath some serious quantities of blue eyeshadow.

"Excuse me?"

"You looked so sad, I was just . . . I didn't mean someone had actually died. . . ." She trailed off.

"It's just a manner of speaking," he wanted to say, but she hopped up on the stool next to him and pressed her thigh into his.

"I can make it better."

He laughed into his drink. Like actually laughed until he was choking.

She started to rub his back, looking hurt and alarmed and too many things all at once. She was so young. Definitely too young for her eyes to be this exhausted. Too young to deal with his humorless laughing fit.

"How much?" he asked as the coughing subsided.

She tried to brighten her eyes, even attempted a pout. "Fifty bucks?" She said it as though it were a question. How young *was* she?

He shoved himself off the bar stool. She spun around him; the rest of the bar joined her. He dug into his wallet. There was a wad of cash he'd withdrawn at the airport. He slid a few notes under his empty glass and slipped the rest of the cash into her hands.

Her too-young, too-tired eyes widened. He almost snatched the money back from her. It would make no difference, not the money, not anything. Her life would stay exactly the same with or without his help.

"The bathroom is through there." She pointed across the dance floor and actually batted her eyelashes over those too tired eyes.

"Take the day off. Go home and get some sleep," he said, turning away before the sheen that sprang up in her eyes spilled over.

He stumbled across the spinning bar. Stumbled into the night and into the parking lot.

He had to lean into the cars as he passed them to keep from tasting the pavement.

Cars.

The woman who had his wife's heart hated driving in cars. Had she lost someone in a crash? Had she run someone over? But the way she had pushed him away when he tried to shake her out of her panic. He knew it was nothing that simple. The twin needs to know and not know what it was tore him in half.

He hated wanting to know. Hated that it mattered. He turned onto the road and started walking along the shoulder. The sky was an endless black. The only light in the night came from neon signs and cars zipping by. He swayed on his feet. All it would take was for him to lose his balance and stumble onto the road. Wind slapped his face. He veered toward the road. But escape no longer seemed that easy. Freedom no longer felt close.

14

Maybe this is what they call pregnancy brain, but I had forgotten what it was like to be with Nic. To be loved like that. Or maybe it's the darkness here that made me forget. But Nic is my cocoon. I can burrow into him a listless worm and come out a butterfly every single time.

—Dr. Jen Joshi

The water had been running cold for what felt like hours. She pushed herself off the tub floor and stepped out of the shower. Trying to remove the soaking sweatshirt felt like moving a passed-out body. God knows she'd dragged Sweetie to his bed enough number of times. And Nikhil. When he'd fallen face-first on the cruise-ship carpet.

She wrung out the soaking fabric. Water gushed onto her feet. She kept twisting and squeezing until her wrinkled palms felt like they were being skinned, then tossed the sweatshirt aside and did the same thing with the rest of her clothes. All the black fabric landed in a heap, leaving her inexplicably exhausted. She never felt physical exhaustion. It was her special gift. The only thing her aunt had loved about her. *Strong like a man!*

Even when she had found her way to the Sisters of Mercy in Calcutta after running away, Sister Mary had marveled at how she could carry full buckets of water in both hands and walk up four flights of stairs. Even when Sister Mary had found her that first Junior Artist role where the dancing had involved jumping up and down for hours. Instead of exhaustion she had found exhilaration. Found dance—the only thing that ever exploded through that shut-inside-a-hard-shell feeling.

She slid the bar of soap out of its wrapping, got back under the water, and started to rub her skin with it. On and on and on, until the embossed letters disappeared, until layer by layer the soap itself shrank to a sliver. She washed it all off with ice-cold water, then started over. Going until the soap was gone. Still she didn't feel clean.

Filth sat like a layer on her skin. It had been years since she'd felt like this. Those panic attacks had exposed all she'd buried away, ripped off her scabs. Her hard-earned scabs. No, it wasn't the panic attacks, it was even before that. It was learning what had happened to Jen. The mess in her mind was thanks to what those men had done to Jen, and thanks to the man who had had to watch.

She grabbed a white towel off the rack and started rubbing her skin. Her scar slashed angry red across her chest. So dark it was almost tinged in black. She ran her finger over it. A tight little bump extruded down her chest like a piece of wire embedded in her skin.

We are copper, kanchi.

She tucked the towel around her breasts and stepped out of the bathroom, just as the door to the motel room flew open. Before the scream could escape her lips, Nikhil tripped over her shoes and went flying face-first into the floor.

The shock froze her in place. She stood there staring at him sprawled across the carpet, motionless as a corpse, his hands splayed out over his head, a key card clutched loosely in one fist.

"Nikhil?"

Nothing.

Behind him the door gaped wide-open into the night.

A frog croaked. She heard voices approaching and ran to the door. She lifted his feet out of the way and slammed it shut just before the sound of footsteps passed by.

He lifted his head. "Baby?" His voice was almost a sob.

She walked around his body. Somehow it seemed wrong to be standing upright when he was sprawled at her feet. She went down on her knees next to him.

"Nikhil. It's me—"

"Jen."

"No, it's Jess. What happened to you?"

He laughed and made it sound exactly like another sob. "Jess. Of course. Jess Koirala." He stretched out the two words, using her accent, placing emphasis on the notes the way she did instead of the way he usually did, in his American way.

"I had a question for you." He lifted his face off the carpet again. His face was wet, his words a slurry mess. His bloodshot eyes sought her but couldn't focus. "I just . . . I can't remember what it was." He blinked and it made him look so lost, it reminded her of Joy.

"Can we get you up first?"

He pulled his elbows off the floor and pushed himself up a few inches with his hands. His elbow was bleeding. There was blood on his white shirt. He winced, gave up, and his body slammed back down.

"What happened?" she asked, reaching out and slipping her hands under his shoulders. His body was a sack of bones. Sharp, hard, and not heavy enough for his wide frame.

Again, just that sob-like laugh. She lifted him up to his knees and then up to standing. He stumbled, trying to find purchase with his feet, grabbing on to her arms. The towel loosened around her. As if in slow motion, she felt the tuck she had secured it with come apart and lose its grip around her breasts.

She tried to pull away, torn between grabbing the fabric around herself and letting Nikhil fall back down.

He found his footing and his eyes met hers, scattering her thoughts.

His hands clamped around her arms.

She struggled to push him away. But he wouldn't let her go. His fingers dug into her skin and pressed her arms into her body. Panic welled up inside her, water filling her lungs. No, please, not this.

Some of the fog cleared from his eyes. *Look at me. I'm not going to hurt you.*

His hands weren't ripping her apart. All they were doing was using her arms to hold the towel in place. His eyes locked on hers, as she struggled to calm her heartbeat. Once she had clenched her upper arms against the rough fabric, he let her arms go, grabbed the front of the towel, and tucked it back in place.

The backs of his hands brushed her breasts. A horrible shaking started in her body again. But his mouth wasn't on hers, pushing her screams back down her throat. His eyes weren't crazed, putrid with lust.

They were just sad. Sadder than anything she had ever seen. They anchored her in place, pushing her panic down her throat, not her screams. His eyes. Bloodshot and grief-stricken, and kinder than anything she'd ever seen. They brought her down from the heart of panic and set her back on her feet.

Then tipped her off-balance again, darkening and flickering with something entirely new.

The backs of his fingers pressed against her scar and stroked up and down. The pain in his eyes grew unbearable. His lids came together, his head tilted back, as he traced the raised skin as though absorbing the feel of it and soaking it into his being. There was such agony on his face, she raised her hand to stroke it away.

A moan rose from his lips. If he said his wife's name, the ringing in her ears drowned it out. Her fingers froze inches from his skin. He dropped his head into her shoulder, his own shoulders quaking. The wetness hit her shoulders, streamed down her back, her breasts. Sobs racked him, harsh and relentless. Every part of him shook as shuddering breaths tore from him and slammed against her.

She wrapped her arms around him, but instead of calming him down, it only made him shake more, as though she had added insult to injury by attempting to soothe him. Still she stroked his arms. Just the barest of movements. Knowing in her heart that anything more would be too much.

When his sobs slowed, she pushed him into the bed and sat down next to him, one arm still around him, his face still pressed into the crook of her neck. For long moments she held him like that, his sobs mapping his grief as it ebbed and flowed and set itself free.

"Tell me what to do with him?" she whispered soundlessly to Jen. *Tell me.*

He lifted his head and slid his face into his palms, not meeting her eyes. The wound on his elbow was bleeding again. "You're bleeding. Stay here."

He made no move to acknowledge he had heard her. But it wasn't like he was going anywhere.

She went to the bathroom and noticed that she was still wrapped in a towel. Mortified, she grabbed a pair of yoga pants and another black sweatshirt out of her bag and pulled them on. Then she quickly slid a hand towel off the rack and soaked it with hot water.

When she came back to him, he was sprawled across her bed, eyes closed, body twisted at awkward angles. Every piece askew, as if someone had forced a jigsaw puzzle together even though the pieces didn't fit the way they were supposed to.

Her heart twisted in her chest, mimicking the angles of his body. His feet hung off the bed, two shoes pointing in different directions, one knee going off on one tangent, the other one bent in on itself, his spine caught in the middle of a twist as he'd fallen backward. His face, that heartbreaking, sunken mirror of his soul, was half pressed into the mattress.

She didn't know what to put right first, but leaving him in this mangled mess would mean aching limbs tomorrow. If the alcohol on his breath and his bloodshot eyes were any indication, there was going to be enough pain.

She pulled his elbow out from under his body. The skin had been gouged off. Blood coagulated around gravel and dirt. She pressed the wet towel into the wound as gently as she could and cleaned it out. He didn't even stir. She went back to the sink, washing out the blood and dirt, then coming back and wiping away more. Back and forth she went until finally the wound looked clean. She wished she had some antiseptic, or gauze and tape, but she had nothing. She unzipped her bag and dug through it, looking for something, anything, to wrap around the nasty-looking wound. Back home she always kept Dettol cream and Band-Aids with her.

Joy wasn't a boisterous child by any means, but he still managed to get a scraped knee or elbow every time they went to the park. The clothes in her bag were a sea of black. Pants, jeans, T-shirts, and sweatshirts, neatly ironed and crisply folded, like the layers in a slab of black slate. She dug into the bottom of the bag and found her dance bandanna. She'd worn it to every rehearsal for the past five years. It had been worn and washed so much that it was muslin soft. She folded it diagonally and then rolled it a few times to form a bandage, then bound it around his elbow. Still not a sound, not a movement.

The wet towel sat on the nightstand. Without thinking about it, she reached for it. His face was streaked with dirt. How had he fallen? How had he become such a mess? It was an absurd question. She knew exactly what had happened. And it hadn't been today.

She wiped the wet towel across his cheeks. The grime wiped away easily. Under all that dirt she unearthed surprisingly lovely skin, bronze and gold tones and not a single spot or pore. Even his stubble followed a neat line across his jaw. There were deep creases in his cheeks, where both a smile and a frown brought on dimples. Suddenly, she had an overwhelming urge to know what his smile looked like. Not just the hints he'd thrown her way, but his real smile.

She wiped across his jaw. She hadn't realized how fine boned he was. That sharply angled jaw, the high, wide forehead, those long-lashed eyes of chocolate, every feature was perfectly etched. But somehow she was sure that even if all that wretched grief and anger lifted, it would still be hard to comprehend the beauty of his face, because he wouldn't let you. He would draw you instead with that sharp intelligence and that gentle kindness that had fallen on her unexpectedly and in fleeting bursts like passing showers at the start of a monsoon, but that continued to drench her like raindrops that had soaked too deep.

Having cleaned one side of his face, she pushed at his shoulder to turn him. He went over easily, a shuddering breath his only complaint.

For another long moment his half-clean face captivated her, two faces spliced together. One dirty, one clean. One dark, one bright. Both tinged with pain, but one brought to some semblance of life. She started wiping at the dirty half of his face. This half was grimier, harder to get clean, but in the end she managed to make it halfway decent.

Next came his shoes. The second she slipped them off his feet, he groaned as if he'd been eased out from under a great burden and pulled his knees up, folding himself into a fetal position.

This was how her Joy slept. Elbows to knees, everything pulled in tight.

She'd done enough, more than enough. As a favor to Jen she had taken care of her husband. But to face the task ahead she needed sleep. She tried to push off the bed, but something tugged at her sleeve. Nikhil's hand clutched her sweatshirt. She tried to pry it out of his grip, but he pulled it closer to his chest with such need she could not bring herself to put any kind of force into it.

She slid off the bed, her knees landing on the carpet, and sank back to the floor, her torso leaning against the bed, her head resting on her outstretched arm held in place by her sleeve fisted in his fingers. He took a deep breath, and for a moment the frown between his brows eased. That was the last thing she remembered before she fell into the abyss of exhaustion that had been calling her name.

Nikhil woke to find his wife's hair splayed against his pillow, his face pressed into the heavy silk. He inhaled, breathing her in. She had changed her shampoo. He liked it. A little softer, more floral than her usual, but nice. He stroked his cheek against it and lifted his hand to pull her closer. He clutched air and then cold sheets. There was no body next to him.

He lifted his face and found only her head on the bed. He sprang upright, his heart beating like a drum. He was about to scream, but he saw an arm stretched out next to her head. He followed it and found the rest of her. Life rushed back into his limbs.

She was on the floor, her arm reaching for him. Her face was pressed into the mattress. The familiar aching tenderness rose in his heart but stuttered. Something didn't feel right. It felt like a dream that had lingered into wakefulness.

His hand went to her hair, meaning to lift it off her face, but something held him back. Let her sleep, he told himself. She never gets enough sleep.

She raised her head. A glassy brown gaze met his. An alien gaze.

Jess. Anger surged through him. How dare she be here? Where Jen should have been.

In an instant, the sleep in her eyes cleared. Her brows drew together with concern. "How are you feeling?"

The question was too intimate. Why the hell should he feel anything at all? "I'm just fine. What are you doing in my bed?"

She pulled her arm off the bed and scooted back a little on the carpet. Technically, she wasn't in his bed, but she didn't correct him. She just wrapped her arms around her knees and drew herself in.

He got off the bed. Springing to his feet like that made the room spin. His head felt like someone had placed a bomb inside it and lit the fuse. She was next to him when he opened his eyes, steadying him with one hand and holding out a glass of water with the other.

He wanted to swipe the water from her hand and push her away, but the queasiness cut off any chance of movement. All those mornings on the ship when he had started his day bent over the pot rose up to meet him. He flew to the bathroom and emptied his stomach almost solely through his nose.

She stood behind him but she didn't touch him. Which was just as well, because being touched right now would lead to more gut emptying.

"You shouldn't be here," he said when he was sure speaking wouldn't cause more pressurized vomit to project from him. "Seriously, I don't know what you're trying. But it's not going to happen."

For one stretched-out, suspended moment, she looked as if he had slapped her. But only for one moment. He had the sense that he was seeing her in flashes. That she was two people, one who stood before him and another who flashed at him from behind her.

She took a step toward him and poured the glass of water she was holding into the toilet he had been hugging. Shame, because suddenly a glass of water was exactly what he needed.

"Why are you in my room anyway?"

"I'm not," she said, sticking her chin out until, from his vantage point next to the can, the wings of her jaw seemed as sharp as knives. As sharp as the temper she was letting him see in one of those flashes. "This is not your room, it's mine. You came here last night."

He opened his mouth to speak. She raised a hand to shut him up. The huge sweatshirt lifted around her like a balloon, not exactly ammunition for seduction. "No. I don't want to hear it. I'm going out to get some fresh air. Before I'm back please get out of my room."

With that, she stormed out, slamming the door loud enough to indicate that the temper he'd seen simmering under her frozen-lava façade wasn't his imagination. He tried to stand up, but his body wasn't quite ready to let him off the hook yet. His stomach did another kickass backflip, and air and bile and definitely some of his esophageal lining flew hurtling into the inky-blue water. He was done with the Jack. Definitely done with this particular morning ritual, thank you very much.

He could have sworn he was letting himself into his own room last night, but he must've grabbed the duplicate key to her room. Not surprising at all, given that standing up straight had been a problem. She hadn't chastened him for it, or thrown him out on his butt. All she had done was help him and all he'd done was be a prized jerk.

He pushed himself off the pot and got himself a glass of water. Meeting his own eyes in the mirror was out of the question, but the rest of him was near impossible to recognize. There was a huge splatter of blood and dirt on one side of his shirt. He had broken into a run after leaving the bar and fallen.

He squeezed his throbbing temples. Something tugged at his elbow but he ignored it. The absolute anger blanketed over wounded dignity on Jess's face when she had asked him to get out made another bout of nausea rise inside him. He grabbed his shoes and let himself out of her room. For the first time in a long time, he had the urge to get cleaned up.

15

Something about Rahul reminds me so much of Nic. Everything about them on the outside is different, and yet that part of me that aligns with Nic, that makes me me, that's the part that recognizes Rahul.

—Dr. Jen Joshi

If Rahul knew anything, he knew that when evidence was tampered with, it meant something really nefarious was going on and someone really high up was involved.

"You're right to smell a rat, boss!" Ramesh, his information specialist, said over the phone. He was going to lose his job if anyone found out he was digging through a private hospital's records without authorization. They both were, but this only proved that they had unearthed something. "When I first searched through the organ donor database last week, the records for Dr. Joshi's recipients listed two kidneys and eyes but that's all. Everything but a heart showed up. Which is normal, because heart transplant cases are next to nonexistent. But then I went back to check on something and suddenly there's a heart recipient and there's no record of the database being updated. Someone changed it without knowing I had already looked. If I'd been even a few days late, we wouldn't even know."

Rahul opened the file and read the name on the recipient form for the hundredth time. "So were you able to locate this Jess Koirala?"

Ramesh's voice grew even more excited. The young recruit loved his job in that way only the really young can. Rahul wished there was a way to hold on to that. "Amazingly enough, no one by that name exists in Mumbai. It's almost as though someone came up with that name after making sure it didn't exist and then used it to falsify the record."

"And the address?" All Rahul had asked Ramesh to find was a name so he could call Jen's husband and try again. Not that the good doctor*saab* was taking his calls. But this put a whole new angle on the case.

"The building was torn down six months ago to build a mall. It was a leave-and-license rental property and all the renters were paid off. No forwarding addresses."

"Naturally."

"Exactly! So, boss, the address doesn't exist, and you know what else doesn't exist?"

"Jess Koirala."

"Exactly!"

He thanked Ramesh and left him to continue digging. But he had a feeling they weren't going to find anything more from the hospital records. First, Jen's diary had been stolen from right under his nose, then, the donor registry Jen had worked so hard to build had been erased without a trace, and now someone had tampered with Jen's health records. He'd investigated everyone from the senior-most officers to the newest *hawaldars* on his team, offered immunity if the diary showed up. But it remained gone, Jen's words as lost as the cause and the evidence she had sacrificed her life for, and now every trace of the lease on life she'd given someone was also gone.

Guilt coated his ever-present anger. He had promised to protect her when he'd sent her into the alligator's jaws. Even though it had often felt like her charging ahead while he tried to hold her back. Jen's beautiful eyes sparkled in his head as if she had just smacked him down about something and flounced out of his office.

Do your job, DCP Savant. It should be simple enough.

But it wasn't simple. He was choking on red tape. One of his instructors at the academy had once told him that an IPS officer's success depended on how well he could navigate bureaucracy. With a mentor like Kirit Patil, Rahul hadn't realized how true those words were. Why was it that it took losing things before you recognized the full value of them?

He needed bodies. Without bodies, he couldn't prove that the disappearances in the slum were deaths, let alone murders to carve out organs. And without murders he had no case, and without a case, no funding or authority to investigate. He needed both to go searching for undocumented bodies. But those who didn't exist couldn't disappear.

I have zero patience for anyone who uses "couldn't" as a crutch.

That was how Jen had responded when he'd told her about Kimi and how they couldn't find her a match for years.

Jen had reminded him so much of Kimi. Jen had Kimi's fiery spirit. She had been what he had always known Kimi could be, once they fixed her heart. He had spent all those childhood years watching that spirit triumph every time she struggled for her next breath, every time she struggled to fight off her next fever. For Kimi and Jen, he had no choice but to keep going until he had put away the bastards who were carving up innocents for the cost of their organs.

Maybe he was looking in the wrong place. Maybe the thread to follow was Jess Koirala. All he needed to do was find Jess Koirala or at least find out who had fabricated her and why.

16

Sometimes marriage terrifies me. If I don't keep a piece of me for myself, won't I be just one half of a whole? And if I let that go, what will I have left when there is no us?

—Dr. Jen Joshi

"Where the hell have you been?" Nikhil jumped up from the open stairway he was sitting on. "I've been looking everywhere for you."

Were she a different person she might have believed that he looked worried, but she was nothing if not realistic. He was angry because she had disappeared without telling him. She didn't really care, because he had essentially accused her of trying to seduce him and asked her to get out.

But he had been in hell at the time, so she was going to let it go. Then there was the other little fact, that she had no choice but to let it go. "I'm sorry. I didn't realize how far the pharmacy was."

Now he just looked confused. "What's wrong? Are you not feeling well?" He studied her in that way he had, as though everything but what was wrong with her was immaterial. He was such a doctor, and he wasn't even trying. She refused to let that stupid concern of his make her stupid belly clench again. Refused to let it dig up the memory of his hands on her skin, the back of his fingers pressed into her scar. "I'm fine."

She handed him the bottle of water she was holding and tore open the packet of Alka-Seltzer she had picked up at the pharmacy. Sweetie got the worst headaches when he drank, and this always helped him. She took the bottle back, broke each large pill in half so it would fit and dropped the pieces into the bottle, and pushed it back at him.

He watched the water fizz and bubble with eyes so tortured she might as well have offered to suck his soul from him.

"I'm not a doctor, but I do know you have to drink it before the fizz is gone. Otherwise it won't work."

He touched the bottle, but he didn't take it from her. "Actually, the fizz makes no difference to the efficacy. The fizz just helps it dissolve without a spoon."

She tried not to roll her eyes, and failed. His eyebrows lifted the slightest bit and the hint of something like amusement dented his cheek.

She pushed the bottle into his hand. "Drink."

He did, his throat working as he drank. His stubble dithered off and disappeared down his jaw and down his neck. The tendons on his neck were long and lean, just like the rest of him.

"You didn't have to do this," he said when he was done.

Without responding, she reached into her pocket and pulled out a bag of lemon drops. "These are supposed to help with hangovers too."

"Why are you doing this?" He looked at the candy, that same tortured look on his face again, as if what she was offering was so much more than just the candy.

"We have to get on the road. We need to get to her things."

"Jen, her name is Jen."

"I know what her name is, Nikhil. And her name *was* Jen, since we are getting technical. And before you go making all sorts of assumptions again, the only thing I want out of this. The. Only. Thing." She gave him her hardest look. She wanted no doubt in his mind about this. "Is to find that evidence, and then I need to get back home." To her baby.

He brought his hand to his hair, once more finding nothing to grip. "I'm sorry. I shouldn't have said that." He met her eyes. "In fact, I shouldn't have said any of that stuff I said before."

Yes, he shouldn't have. "And just so you know, when I told you I was a dancer, I don't know what you understood it to mean, but I'm a chorus dancer. A backup dancer in films. I . . . I dance only for the camera . . . as part of a dance troupe . . . not . . ."

He tilted his head to one side, a curious frown folding between his brows. "Why are you telling me this?"

"I'm not a bar dancer, not, not that kind of . . ."

"What the hell are you talking about?"

You're a whore. With a whore's body. This is what whores get.

She pushed away the leering faces in her head and raised her hand to stop his words. "I was not trying to get in your, in your . . . I have no interest in . . . Are you smiling?"

Sad as his eyes were, he was definitely smiling. Heaven help her, those dents in his cheeks, they were by no means little. They stripped away everything harsh in his face and transformed it. She stepped away from him, trying to get away from what that smile did to him.

"You can't even say the words. How could I, how could anyone ever think of you that way?" He looked incredulous. More than anything he could have said, even more than that smile, his incredulity pooled in her chest, wet and hot.

"Hey." He lifted his hand but stopped it inches from her cheek and then dug it back into his pocket. "The way I behaved last night. It had nothing to do with you. That was just . . . I was just . . ."

She wasn't the only one who couldn't speak her past.

She shook the bag of lemon drops at him. "Lemon drops are great for headaches."

"Is that your medical opinion?"

"No, that's my mummy opinion."

He bowed his head and gave her the last word, taking the bag from her and popping one into his mouth.

"You don't have to take care of me, you know."

"I don't carry debt well. You took care of me yesterday; now we're even."

"Actually, you took care of me last night, so you're plus one."

Apparently, she wasn't the only one who didn't carry debt well.

He had lied. He hadn't been looking for her everywhere when she walked to the pharmacy. The car he unlocked and threw his bag into was small and red with two doors. Not the monstrosity they had driven yesterday.

When he held the door open for her, she just stood there, sure she'd collapse to the floor if she moved.

"It's going to get pretty cold as we head north. You don't want to drive in an open car." He left the door ajar for her, got into the driver's seat, and started the car, forcing her to move.

They sank into their seats and back into silence. He burrowed back under the shell that had been snapping on and off him so fast and relentlessly it was making her head spin. It was just as well. Because no matter how much she told herself she could do this, do anything she needed to do, in this moment, she could not open her mouth without breaking down. Not even to thank him.

This is not how she had expected to feel when they left the motel and its decrepit surroundings behind. She didn't know how she knew they were decrepit. There was none of the obvious decay of such places back home, but something about it couldn't hide the fact that money and privilege didn't reside here. Or maybe her heart just recognized beaten-down and forsaken things.

For all his silence, Nikhil's hands were a little steadier on the steering wheel today. He'd had nothing more than another mug of black coffee for breakfast. She had no idea how he survived. Apart from those poppy-seed muffins, which smelled like old ink from her uncle's table, and a few morsels from the junk food stash, she had never seen him eat.

Instead of filling his stomach, she had actually watched him empty it out a few times.

She remembered the feeling only too well. She had thrown up everything she ate for so long after what those bastards did to her, she hadn't realized that she was pregnant until she was six months along. "It's too late to get rid of the baby," the doctor had told her with such regret that she had changed doctors. How could she let a doctor who thought of her baby that way bring him into the world?

Another pang of longing to hold Joy hit her. Between the memory of Joy's voice from when she'd called him this morning—trying so hard not to let her see how badly he wanted her to come home—and this car they were driving in, it was time for her to shut down all the rawness she was allowing herself.

The only blessing was Nikhil's silence next to her.

She tried to shut out all thought, focus on her breath, and center herself. But today, she couldn't manage it. The longer they drove in silence, the harder it became. Between a past she couldn't seem to put away, a present she couldn't control, and a future she couldn't avoid, she couldn't shut her mind down. She wanted to shake Jen for all the things she had said. She wanted to kill Nikhil for living up to each one of those things.

"How's your head?" she asked, resisting the urge to twist her fingers together.

He shrugged. She gripped her hands together and tried to accept that his silence was going to be impenetrable.

"What happened to you?" he asked, just as she was easing back into the silence again.

"I knew you'd had too much to drink, so I asked the receptionist where I could find some Alka-Seltzer and the place was two miles away."

He threw her an unsure look, trying to gauge whether she had really misunderstood his question, and decided she knew exactly what he'd been asking. He let it go, nonetheless. "So this car helps, then?"

This time she shrugged.

"Does it help to talk?"

She should have said no and shut him down, but she couldn't. "I wouldn't know."

"Want to try?"

She didn't respond.

"Tell me about Joy."

Despite herself she smiled. "What do you want to know about him?"

"I don't know. What's he like? Is he a handful?"

She almost laughed at that. "No, quite the opposite actually. He carries the weight of the world on his shoulders."

"He's a lot like his mother then."

"Oh no, he's nothing like me. He's affectionate, full of love. He's a cuddler; he loves to be held. It's really hard to be sad around him. He's also incredibly funny and wise."

"And this is your seven-year-old we're talking about, not his dad, right?"

Her gut clenched.

She usually told people Joy's father was dead. That he had died in a car accident in Calcutta. Which is why she had moved to Mumbai. She usually enjoyed filling in the details of his death in colorful and gory detail, at least in her own head.

"Hey, I'm sorry. I was making a joke, or trying to make one."

"I know."

"So, tell me more about Joy."

"Think of the most perfect little boy you can imagine. Sometimes I think he's more perfect than any child should feel the need to be. He's caring and kind and sees beauty in everything." She wrapped her arms around herself and imagined his body melting into her, his baby breath collecting on her neck. "Even the smallest little things, like a twin pod in an orange, or a centipede crawling on our floor, the smallest little thing just excites him so much he almost explodes with it.

"We had a sparrow lay three eggs behind the railing in our balcony earlier this year. Every single day for a week, he would run home from school and run to the balcony to see if they had hatched. And once Raja . . . he, umm . . . lives with us, told Joy that the eggs were close to hatching, Joy just refused to leave the balcony.

"He spent every moment out of school there. He ate there, did his homework there, basically he'd just stare and stare at the sparrow sitting on her eggs until he fell asleep right there. One day he looks up at me and says, 'Mamma, isn't it funny, that I sit and sit on your lap, and the mama bird sits and sits on her babies?'" She smiled at the memory. "I had to carry him to bed after he fell—"

She stopped short, and the strangest jolt sparked through her heart. Nikhil was smiling. Not the halfhearted, I-think-it-might-be-a-smile kind of smile, but a wide, flat-out smile.

By all that was holy, how on earth had she forgotten what those dimples could do to his face? Two full-fledged whirlpools dug deep into his stubbly cheeks and his eyes crinkled and shone.

"And?"

"And what?"

"And what happened when the eggs hatched? Did he get to watch?"

She swallowed. "Yes. First thing in the morning when he was

brushing his teeth. He pulled me out of the kitchen, dragged Raja out of bed, he didn't want anyone to miss it. We were both late for work that day, and I think he missed the first half of school."

"That's amazing." He was still smiling and it was like watching the sun break through clouds in bright, sharp columns of light. "That you let him miss school for that."

"Heaven help me, can you imagine if he had missed it? I had a good mind to crack the eggs myself at one point and let the baby birds out. I swear I lived in fear of it happening while he was at school that week."

"I don't think Aie—that's what I call my mom—ever let me miss school. I think I had perfect attendance almost all twelve years."

"You never got sick as a child?"

"Well, I would have had to be in the hospital or in a coma for Aie to let me stay home from school. Even then she would have rolled my bed into the classroom if she could. Education for my parents is like a religion. My mother is a teacher, and I mean she doesn't just teach, she has the genetic composition of an educator, you know what I mean?" He raised an eyebrow at her. "What?"

She found her hand pressed to her mouth. "Mine too. My mother was a teacher too."

"Great, so you're familiar with the Homework Before You Get to Breathe theory of parenting."

She giggled. Nikhil could never have imagined such a thing, but it sounded so natural on her he wondered why he was so surprised by it. That light that had engulfed her when she talked about her son lit her up from the inside.

"And the All the Teachers Have a Direct Line to Your Mother curse," she said.

"Did she teach in your school?"

"Yes, yours?"

"No. She taught college, so technically she's a professor, but some of my teachers had taken her classes in college, and let's just say it's not every child's dream."

"You sound very close to your mother."

"Really? I was going for terrorized by her."

She giggled again. "She sounds like a wonderful mother. Are you an only child?"

"Technically."

"Technically? So, you're an only child but with siblings?"

"I am an only child, but my parents practically raised my cousin—my mother's brother's daughter. She went to school in India and spent summers with us. So, she's more a sibling than a cousin, and my dad's sister's son also spent his summers with us. I know it's confusing."

"It's not confusing at all. Your childhood sounds beautiful."

The Joshi household had been a zoo sometimes, always overrun with friends and relatives. But she was right. "It was pretty amazing. If you're not big on privacy. Our house was always filled with guests."

Suddenly, he wanted to turn around. He couldn't go home. Then he wanted to go home so badly, his foot pressed into the accelerator.

"What about your mother?" he asked, mostly to step off the see-saw he found himself on.

"Aama—that's what I call my mother—taught English at the school in the city." Ah, an English teacher's daughter; that explained the impeccable English. "But we moved to the village after my father died when I was seven. At the village school she taught everything. Even after she got sick and couldn't leave home, she tutored any child who needed help at our home. And she did it until her very last day."

"What happened?"

"Cancer. Lung."

"I'm sorry."

"It's okay, it's been a very long time," she said, although she looked too young for anything to have been a very long time. He wanted to ask her how old she was, but what came out of his mouth was completely unexpected. "So how did your husband, Raja, you said, agree to let you leave your son and go chasing after a complete stranger by yourself?"

Evidently it was the wrong thing to say, because the veil that was never too far away slipped over her face like liquid rock and solidified. It was as though the past few minutes had never happened.

"Raja's not Joy's dad." And then, just to make sure he understood that he had stepped on one of her land mines, she asked, "When was the last time you went home?"

The silence stretched out for a few moments, and she tucked her hands under her legs, sitting on them.

"I haven't gone home since my cousins' wedding," he said. "A little more than two years."

He must have sounded the way he felt, because her tone softened again. "I'm sorry I didn't give you more time."

Another sad silence followed.

"Did Jen say anything about where the evidence might be hidden?" he asked her, because really, it was the point of this entire excursion, wasn't it? "Do you have any idea what it is?"

Her eyes were back in fully guarded mode when he threw her a quick glance. "All she said was that you would destroy everything from your life together but you would never destroy the thing in which it was hidden."

That did nothing to narrow it down. He couldn't imagine going through Jen's stuff, ever. As for throwing away any of her stuff, it was unthinkable.

"So where are her things?" she asked when he didn't respond.

"Most of it is in my parents' home."

"So are we going to your parents' house?"

"Yes. Why does that surprise you?"

"I thought Americans didn't live in their parents' house once they were adults."

"Well, I never bought my own place because I never lived in the country for too long after med school." And once he'd met Jen, her apartment had become their home.

They talked like that. Jumping over each other's land mines, skirting topics and details that were too painful and skimming over the ones that were more bearable until they found their safe places.

Nikhil told her about med school and being a doctor's son. She told him about Joy. Of all the things they could talk about, her son, Joy, seemed their safest haven.

17

Rahul says it's not possible to run an illegal organs racket without having someone really high up involved. I know there's someone on my staff who's leaking my donor registry to them. How else are they finding the matches?

—Dr. Jen Joshi

"Just find the bastard's daughter and kill her." Asif had had enough. He hadn't worked his way up the ranks of the gang to have some useless politician hold a sword over his head. It wasn't just his hands that were bloodstained. His vision dripped blood. The red haze through which he saw the world had become thicker and redder with every passing year, and fuck if now, when he was king of his world, he would let someone finger his arse.

"Bhai—" Laloo was the only one of his men who would dare to interrupt his thoughts. When he didn't lift his *ghoda* and blow the *chutiya*'s head off, he took it as permission to keep talking. "Bhai, she's the only leverage we have. We kill her, we have nothing to hold over the bastard's head."

He looked smug, as if Asif Khan, whose very name loosened people's bowels until they were shitting their insides, needed some idiot to point out the most basic shit. He lifted his gun and pointed it at Laloo's head.

"Sorry, Bhai. Of course you already thought of that. Bhai thinks of everything." He was trying not to look scared. Even his number-one commander believed that he was crazy enough to blow his brains out. This was power. His *chutiya* uncle should see him now.

Asif started to laugh. Not because he was crazy, the way he let his men believe he was, but because the memory of sticking a Diwali bomb up his uncle's arse and blowing it up before drowning him in a commode filled with his shit still made him collapse with laughter every single time.

"You're not the only one who can stick your junk up someone's arse, *chutiya*. How does it feel now?" he had asked, and his uncle had pissed right there on his bathroom floor, with his wife and children watching. It was the last thing any of them had seen him do.

"Three minutes. You have three minutes to find an alternative to killing the politician's daughter," he said to Laloo, smiling at coming up with that number. Why did people always go with five minutes, ten minutes? Bastards, so predictable! He started to count down. "Tick, tick. Tick, tick . . ."

"K . . . K . . ." Laloo stuttered

"What are you, Shah Rukh Khan from *Darr*? K . . . K . . . Kiran . . ."

"Kidnap, Bhai, kidnap! We kidnap the girl."

He clicked off the *ghoda*'s safety and placed the muzzle on Laloo's crotch. He started sobbing like a bitch. "You think that wasn't the first idea that popped into my head?"

He looked at the man's pants. They were dry. He fucking needed to see someone wet their pants really soon. Life was getting too damn serious.

Satisfying though the idea of killing the politician's fancy daughter was, Asif needed her to find the girl with the doctor's red hair. She was the one he needed to figure out what the bastard was up to. So he could stop him once and for all. She was his key and the bastard's daughter was his only path to her.

"Follow the bastard's daughter. Every moment. I want to know how she breathes, who she fucks, what her daddy does to protect her fancy arse."

It was a good thing people had children. It was the best leverage in the world.

18

Why do people assume that making a baby from your own DNA automatically creates a connection? I've never felt the need to meet my birth parents.

—Dr. Jen Joshi

Nikhil's shoulders had been getting progressively higher and tighter ever since they had entered what seemed to be Antarctica, but with flyovers. The streets were edged with banks of blackened snow like flesh peeled back from knife slashes across endless white skin.

By the time the fields gave way to neighborhoods and their car turned into a wooded street and rolled to a stop in front of the biggest house she had ever seen, he looked stiff enough to snap. She followed his eyes to the house. A perfectly round moon shone large and low in the sky, throwing a milky glow over the snow-blanketed roof.

A blanket seemed to have fallen over his face too, turning it almost as dark as it had been when she had first seen him. But somehow without the smell of vomit and the drunken haze it didn't have quite the same level of devastation. He turned and caught her watching him, but his eyes stayed flat, every hint of that elusive twinkle gone from the deep chocolate. The spots in his cheeks, where those transformative whirlpools reclaimed and trapped laughter in flashes, were also flat.

Thanks to Jen, Jess had felt like she knew him even before she met him, but these past days had erased Jen's words and replaced them with reality, and the reality of him was like nothing she could have imagined.

She had never had a friend, never shared anything about herself with anyone. Truth be told, no one had ever shared any part of their life with her either. She hadn't allowed it. Sweetie Raja was her best friend. She would do anything for him, but he was almost as private as she was. On the days when he happened to be home for dinner, they talked about their day and listened avidly to Joy's stories. But she knew nothing of his past, his childhood. One look at his face didn't carry the entire impact of his current mood.

"Ready?" Nikhil asked.

"Yes," she responded, fully aware that the question wasn't targeted toward her. "Did you want me to wait in the car?"

It seemed far too intrusive, far too intimate, to be part of a reunion so painful. He waited to answer. Maybe he needed time to think, or maybe he hadn't heard her. But he was no longer looking at her. His eyes caught something in the rearview mirror and he twisted around so fast she started.

"Holy shit."

"What?" She followed his gaze to a huge red truck parked next to a brick mailbox.

His hand went to his scalp, gripping helplessly at the stubble that was fast turning into a crew cut. "Vic and Ria are here." There was panic in his voice.

She had no idea what he was talking about.

"My cousins. Remember I was telling you about them," he said, without taking his eyes off the car. "They're here. Shit."

Before she could respond, the front door of the house flew open. "Hello?" A tall man stepped out of the front door causing several lights to flash on all around them and flood the night.

The stark panic in Nikhil's eyes flared. The man walked toward the car, slowly at first, then he broke into a run. "Nic?" He reached the car and peered into the window. An incredible array of emotions crashed across his face.

He yanked the door open and bodily lifted Nikhil out of the car. "Nic? What the fuck are you doing here?" He pulled him close. Pushed him away, looked at him to make sure it was really him, and then squashed him into another bone-crushing hug as Nikhil barely kept up.

"Ria!" he hollered over his shoulder.

An older woman, who had Nikhil's exact face, only softer and prettier, appeared in the doorway. "Stop shouting. Your wife is otherwise occupied right n—" The woman's eyes landed on the two men locked in an embrace and her hand flew to her mouth.

"Nikhil?" Her voice cracked. The two men separated and turned to her. Nikhil's cousin lifted his shoulder and wiped his face against his shirt.

Nikhil took two steps toward the woman and she broke into a run, stopping only when she was inches from him. She touched his face and then she pulled him so close, so hard, that even from inside the car Jess's chest tightened with the force of it. It was a scuffle of searching and engulfing and absorbing. It took Nikhil a moment, but when he wrapped his arms around her, the force of his response lifted her off her feet.

She pulled away, the harsh lights catching the wetness on her cheeks as she held his face. "My baby, you're home."

An older man came through the door next, stopped short when he saw Nikhil, grabbed him out of his mother's arms, and pulled him to his chest. Nikhil's cousin hollered his wife's name again. She ran out, one hand clasped under the huge stomach that preceded her. "Viky! Why are you yelling like a madman?"

Her husband ran to her. "Ria, slow down." He grasped her shoulders and turned her around to face Nikhil.

Like the rest of them, one look at Nikhil and an explosion of emotions filled her face. Nikhil turned to her. But before she could hug him, he stepped back, his entire body going utterly still.

Every one of them went still. So still, in fact, a ghost might as well have descended in their midst.

"You're pregnant," he said, his voice so strained, Jess's heart turned over.

The family, who had attacked him with such fierce affection, drew back as one.

Nikhil looked from one to the other. "And no one bothered to tell me?"

The male cousin spoke first. "Can we take this inside? It's freezing and Ria needs to be inside."

"Why? Is something wrong with the pregnancy?" Nikhil's voice switched seamlessly from anger to worry.

"I'm fine, everything is okay. Can we go inside, please?" The pregnant woman spoke and the smile she forced onto her face made Jess's heartbeat speed up. Bloody hell. She knew that smile. She knew this woman. It was that actress, Ria Parkar. Oh God. She had danced behind the woman in three films. Jess tugged her hood over her head and sank deeper into the shadows.

Nikhil turned to the car and found her eyes in the darkness. His eyes were more vulnerable, more naked, than she'd ever seen them. His pain more exposed to her than it had ever been before. She held his stare, wishing she could pull him back into the car and drive back in time.

"Is there someone else in the car?" someone asked.

"Nikhil, who's with you?"

Nikhil strode back to the car, clinging to her gaze like a drowning man, and opened her door.

"I'm sorry," he said in a soft voice. "Are you okay?"

"I'm fine," she said, realizing for the first time that he always asked her that when he himself wasn't okay.

He stepped back to let her out. His family flanked him like troops bringing up the rear. They studied her as if she had just stepped off a spaceship with more limbs than they had expected and she was about to abduct their precious child.

"I think you've done the impossible and made my family speechless." He smiled his halfhearted smile, leaving his cheeks heartbreakingly unchanged.

"That she has," the older man, who had to be Nikhil's father, said, placing a hand on his son's shoulder. "But that's no reason to be rude. Aren't you going to introduce us?" He said it in a kindly enough manner, but there was no missing the reprimand.

"This is my friend Jess," Nikhil said without taking his eyes off her.

A gasp rose behind him. "Nikhil!" one of the women said.

He closed his eyes and drew a breath. "I said Jess." He stressed the *s* in the name she had been given. Possibly for this very reason.

Ria Parkar's husband pushed Nikhil out of the way and stuck his hand out at Jess. "Hi, Jess. Is that short for Jessica?"

She put her hand in his and let him give it a shake. "No."

Nikhil looked sallow under all those lights.

"I'm Vikram. It's nice to meet you." Vikram gave her an open if quick smile and turned to the rest of the family. "This is Nic's dad, Dr. Vijay Joshi. That's his mom, Uma, and that's my wife, Ria, who needs to be inside."

He pulled Jess out of the car and pushed her and Nikhil toward the house. "We'll do the rest inside." His eyes went to his wife. "Please. Nic, help me out here, man. She won't go in if you don't." He walked around the car, leaned into the driver's side, and popped open the hood.

Nikhil placed one hand on the small of Jess's back. It was an unconscious move and so unexpected she should have started. Instead, it felt so essential to this moment that she let her body adjust to the weight of it and tried not to notice that she felt it, well, everywhere.

As did the other two women, if the quick widening of their eyes was any indication. Their gazes hitched on his hand and quickly met. A silent something passed between them. A something Jess had no interest in interpreting.

They headed back to the house.

"Please let me get that," she said as Vikram lifted her duffel bag over his shoulder.

Nikhil's hand pressed against her back and nudged her along. "He's not going to run off with it. I promise."

Nikhil couldn't believe he was hiding in the bathroom of his parents' house again. All those times he'd been in trouble—a B in Spanish (his only B ever), last place in cross-country (his only ranking in any sport ever)—this is where he had come. His Simmering Pot, Ria called it.

He straightened up, his jeans still in place, and stared up at the ceiling. He was home after two years. Two years that seemed like two decades and he felt nothing. Even as he had walked into the house, his entire being had been encased in paralytic numbness.

He had felt nothing except the need to keep holding on to the complete stranger he had brought home. He hadn't been able to lift his hand off her ramrod-straight back. Something about the connection had kept him standing.

She hated being touched. He knew that. But somewhere along the way she had stopped drawing away from his touch, and she hadn't drawn away from it while surrounded by his family. His family, on the other hand, had drawn away from him. Shut him out.

They had kept Ria's pregnancy from him. How could they have done that?

Not so long ago he would have been the first to know.

Ria would have called him first, before she called anyone else. She always called him first about everything, and he would have assured her that she'd make a great mother despite all her neurotic worrying. Vic would have come to him too, madly excited but also worried as hell. Then Aie would have called him with her twenty pointed questions and done her reading-between-the-lines thing. Then his dad and he would have discussed every medical contingency, their private language of putting each other at ease.

That had been his role in the family. He had been the fulcrum. Until Jen. After Jen had come into his life she had taken on that role. She never took a problem too seriously, never thought anything was the end of the world. To her, every problem came with a solution and every happiness was deserved. Jen would have talked all of them down off their collective ledge, then she would have handed him the phone and let him cheer everyone up. Afterward, they would have celebrated the good news the way they celebrated everything. With a good Malbec and sex.

Except their own baby, who had gone uncelebrated to the very end.

He forced his mind back to the deep-green wall in front of him. To the people one floor below. The foundation on which his life had always stood.

They had shut him out.

Yes, they had all visited the ship and called regularly. But the thing that changed everything was the thing they had withheld from him. Apparently, he wasn't the only one who had been going through the motions. He wasn't the only one who had spoken but not said a thing.

Even now, standing in his childhood home, he wasn't really here. It was as if none of this was happening. As if that door didn't open into his room. As if that attic bed with the ladder leading up to it was not the place where Jen and he had made incredibly tender love the afternoon before their wedding while a houseful of wedding guests decorated the house with Christmas lights.

"Nic, you need help in there?" Of course Vic was the one who had finally come up to check on him.

"I think I can wipe my own ass, thanks," he said, but he got up and opened the door and stared into his cousin's face.

"That's a huge relief." His cousin's cocky grin barely concealed all that brotherly concern.

"You're looking good," Nikhil said. "Congratulations."

"Thanks. Listen, man, I'm sorry we didn't tell you. You know how complicated Ria's—"

"Where's Jess?"

Vic answered him with a raised eyebrow—a look Nikhil ignored and headed down the stairs without waiting for an answer.

Jess was sitting on a sofa chair, a cup clutched in her hands, her tiny body tucked into itself, trying even harder than usual to disappear into her surroundings.

His parents and Ria sat all the way on the other side of the room, gaping up at him.

He walked straight to Jess. "I thought you were upstairs getting settled in. Aie, which room can she have?"

He was such an ass to have gone off without making sure she was taken care of. But running away when things got overwhelming had become too easy.

"Both my room and Ria's room are empty," Vic said. "Ria's not supposed to go up and down stairs so we're in the den."

Nikhil turned to his mother. "She can have Ria's room, right?" His mother nodded, but he didn't miss the slight widening of her eyes.

Ria's room and his were interconnected through that bathroom he'd just been hiding in. He would bet his arm every single person in this room had processed that thought just now. Except for Jess, who looked like she always did, pristine and unruffled. Except there were cracks and he hated seeing them.

Nikhil took the cup from Jess's hands. The familiar aroma of his ma's ginger chai wafted up his nose. He put the still full cup of tea down on the coffee table and held out his hand. "Let me show you to your room."

She stood without taking his hand, her arms wrapped tightly around herself, and threw a tentative look at his mother. The look would usually have broken Aie's heart, but Aie's face remained a detached mask.

"Aie, I'm going to show Jess to Ria's room." He knew his tone had to kill his mother.

"Of course." There was no detachment in Aie's eyes when she looked at him. "When was the last time you ate?" she asked him, her aie-voice so raw, he wanted to go to her, but he couldn't make himself.

They hadn't eaten anything all day. Yet again, he had forgotten all about food, and about the fact that there was another person with him who needed to eat. The only thing she'd had since breakfast was that ginger tea that she hated so much.

"We need to shower," he said and another wave of discomfort washed across the room.

Jess's cheeks colored, and he swallowed his retort about the two of them not showering together.

"But we are starving," he said instead.

As expected, the mention of anyone starving in her home swung Aie into action. She pushed them out of the room. "We were about to sit down to dinner. Go get showered quickly before the food goes cold."

19

One of my earliest memories is of my mom picking me up from the orphanage. I was five, but I can still taste the desperation with which I wanted to be liked. The only other time I've ever felt that is when I met Nikhil's aie.

—Dr. Jen Joshi

Jess felt like she was stealing when she touched the soap, the shampoo. She felt like a downright thief when she turned on the water. Nikhil had handed her a towel, shown her where everything was and how it worked. As usual he seemed far too focused on her discomfort. It seemed like the only thing that made his own discomfort bearable.

And she had it to offer up in droves.

There were many ways of being a whore. Being paid to use your body was just one form of it. Sometimes you provided a place for someone to shove their sexual hunger into and then took money for it, and sometimes you provided your own pain for them to shove their pain into, and you took your payment for that.

Basically, you fed one need to feed another. She should've been more comfortable with the barter. If she understood anything she understood the transactional nature of life.

But Nikhil's discomfort at coming home had unhinged something inside her. It didn't sit right no matter how she tried to rationalize it.

It was obvious how close this family had always been. But no one seemed to know what to do with one another right now. It was so painful to witness that she almost wished she hadn't been the one to force Nikhil back into what he obviously was not ready for. Almost.

There was also the other half of that truth. Someone had to bring him back here, where there were people who would heal him, and being that person alleviated some of the unforgivable evil in her actions. She chose that option. It was the only option that made it bearable and she chose it.

Already, Nikhil wasn't the same man she'd found trying to drink himself to death on *The Oasis*. The signs of him edging back toward life were obvious, and now that she had brought him back to the care of his family, she refused to feel guilty about making him help her get back to her own.

She was here. The evidence was here. This nightmare had to have an end.

Once she handed the evidence over to Naag, the deal was that she would get out of the picture. He had promised he would never contact her again. Not that she had any leverage to make sure he kept his promise. People with power were the ones with all the leverage. They were the ones who always won. The only chance at survival someone like her had was to give them what they wanted and disappear, just like she had before.

There was the little problem of her having told Nikhil what she did and Joy's real name. Huge mistakes. But there were thousands of dancers in Bollywood. Without her real name he had no chance of finding her before she disappeared. Then there was that little detail: Why on earth would he ever want to look for her? Especially if she did her job right.

She toweled herself dry with the ridiculously lush towel and got dressed. Despite the thick sweatshirt she pulled over her tank top she felt utterly naked. One of these days that horrible exposed feeling was going to go away. It would just lift off her shoulders the way it did when she danced and stay off.

She checked her phone. No call from Naag, who was surprisingly giving her enough time to do her job as she'd requested. There was a missed call from Sweetie. She quickly called back.

"Is everything all right?"

"Of course it is." She could tell from Sweetie's voice that she had woken him up.

"I'm sorry I lost track of time. I saw a missed call. They didn't take Joy again, did they?" She had tried to get Naag to promise to leave Joy alone, but he'd laughed. He'd been amused that she thought she could make any demands.

"No, they haven't. I've been with him every time he leaves the house. I've even been visiting his school as much as I can."

"And they've been there?"

"Every moment. Baby, I'm sorry. I'm doing all I can."

"I know you are. Thank you. Is he awake?"

"At six-thirty in the morning, on a Saturday?" She heard the smile in his voice and reminded herself that he wouldn't be smiling if things weren't under control.

"Was he the one who called me?"

"Must've been, because it wasn't me." Sweetie's love for her baby was clear in Sweetie's voice, and she focused on it. It was the only way she could leave Joy with him for so very long.

"You know him, he didn't want to let me know he was missing you, so he must've called. He's doing fine. You have to trust me."

She waited until she could speak without choking up. "Of course I trust you."

Joy would never throw a tantrum or ask about her, because he wouldn't want to upset Sweetie. That he felt the need to be so careful was a stain on her heart, her greatest failure.

"I'll have your baby call you as soon as he wakes up, okay?"

"Thanks, Sweetie. I can never repay you. You know that, right?" There was so much she could never repay him for. This was just a drop in the ocean. If he hadn't offered to rent her a room in his flat when she had first come to Mumbai, she didn't know what would have happened to her.

"*Oy*, what's this? I'm getting emotion out of you? Next thing I know, you're going to be sobbing on the phone."

No joking. She was this close to just that.

"How have you been? How's Armaan?"

"Don't mention that jerk to me. I don't want to talk about him, or talk to him ever again." This didn't surprise her at all. Sweetie and his boyfriend were perpetually on the off-again-on-again roller coaster. They'd been together for ten years, but Armaan, who fancied himself TV's biggest star, was still firmly inside the closet.

Given that he had a wife and three kids who were the very poster of the wholesome Indian family, he was never, ever coming out of it. That was never going to change.

Sweetie didn't expect it to either. Mumbai could handle an openly transsexual person who mocked himself on screen to give them a good laugh, but bringing a public homosexual relationship with a married man into the mix was asking for far too much. To Armaan's credit, when he wasn't being a jerk, he made Sweetie happy. For that alone, Jess would forgive him all his obnoxiousness.

"This has to do with you needing all this time for Joy, doesn't it?"

"See, baby, you should go out with him, you get him so well."

"I'm sorry, Sweetie. It won't be much longer, I promise."

"Shut up. I really don't need you getting all senti with me. I would do anything for Joy, and it hurts me when you act like I'm doing you some big favor. I love Joy. So don't insult me, please. I get enough of that shit from that man. He has been driving me half insane with his bull. I mean, excuse me, but if I'm okay with sharing him with his family then why can't he be okay with me taking care of my family? I mean, the man is fifty years old, he needs to grow up, for God's sake."

She let him vent for a while longer before letting him go. Focusing on Sweetie's problems was relaxing and she indulged for a bit, not missing the irony she was living. All the distraction in the world wasn't going to save her from going down and facing the frosty awkwardness of Nikhil's family. In the end, your demons were more loyal than any friend. They were always there waiting with open arms.

She made her way down the stairs, the carpet sinking like pillows beneath her feet, the polished banister sliding smooth beneath her fingers. The house was so large she wouldn't have known where to go if it weren't for Nikhil's voice echoing from the kitchen. His tone was like dry tarp around wet pain, jarringly detached.

That tone made her grind to a halt outside the room.

"I met her on the ship, Aie. What more do you want to know?"

"*Arrey*, what kind of question is that? You just bring someone home—no call, no nothing, and I'm not even supposed to ask who she is? How are we supposed to behave with her?"

"The way you behave with all my friends."

"So she's a friend?" This was from Ria Parkar.

"Of course she's a friend. Ria, why don't you start, I'm sure Jess won't mind." This had to be Vikram, given the worshipful note in his voice.

"Yes, Ria, *beta,* I think it's time you ate and got some rest." Nikhil's mother sounded nothing like she had a minute ago. Ms. Film Star seemed to be everyone's pet around here.

"I ate an hour ago. I swear if you two don't get off my back, I'm not eating at all." A spoiled pet, apparently.

Jess forced herself into the kitchen "Sorry, I didn't mean to keep everyone waiting."

The family turned to her as one, assessing her across the table piled with food that smelled so good she prayed her starving belly didn't decide to make itself heard.

Nikhil pulled out the chair next to him. All those gazes switched their focus to him. She wished he'd stop doing things like that, wished she didn't know why he was doing it.

"Thanks." The quickest way to get everyone to look away was to sit down.

Nikhil picked up her plate and started spooning rice onto it, watching her for a "when." She nodded before the mound grew embarrassingly high. Now that she could smell food, her stomach was all but crawling up her gullet for it.

Nikhil's mother fussed over Ria Parkar's plate, eliciting a long-suffering sigh. The star caught Jess staring and a detached mask descended across her face. No wonder they called her The Ice Princess in Bollywood. Not even a flicker of recognition crossed her eyes. Jess had nothing to worry about. Since when did stars like Ria Parkar start noticing chorus dancers like her, no matter how many films they'd danced in together?

"Please start, Jess," Nikhil's father said kindly. No marks for guessing whose personality Nikhil had inherited.

Nikhil's hand hovered over his plate like an airplane struggling to land in turbulent weather. He stared at the food, seeing neither the roti, nor the dal, nor the red-gravied chicken that was making Jess dizzy with wanting.

This was exactly how he had been with the muffins. He hadn't been able to touch them until she had thrust them into his hand.

"Nikhil, could you pass me a roti, please?" she said before anyone noticed.

He looked up at her, lost. It took him a second to process what she had said and reach for the rotis.

"I need only half, if that's okay."

He tore one round roti in half and handed it to her.

Now that he was holding one half of it, he broke off a piece, dipped it in the dal, and put it in his mouth.

She exhaled the breath she'd been holding and mirrored his actions.

They ate in silence. Their silence intertwining with the silence at the table, but not merging with it. He kept it apart, his eyes straying to her every now and again and avoiding everyone else he should've been looking at. After the welcome they'd given him earlier, the quiet felt malignant.

"I hope the food is all right." His mother's voice was such a relief, Jess almost choked in her hurry to answer.

"It's delicious." It really was. Even if this hadn't been their first real meal in two days, it would have been some of the best food she'd ever tasted.

A hint of a smile lifted his mother's lips, transforming her face, transforming the room, even as her brows drew together. "Really? It's not too bland?"

It's exactly what Aama would've asked. "Not at all, it's perfect."

She slid a quick glance at her son. "Thanks. Nikhil likes his food spicy. But I had no idea . . . I wasn't . . . Nikhil, *beta*, do you want some chutney?"

"No, Aie. Really. It's great."

"Actually, spicy food bothers Ria these days, so . . ." She blinked as if she'd made another wrong turn down another forbidden path.

It was so heartbreaking, Jess turned to Ria Parkar. "How far along are you?"

The silence in the room turned positively explosive. How had she forgotten that Ms. Parkar's pregnancy was the live bomb not to be touched?

Everyone shifted. Then froze. No one seemed able to breathe. Each individual awkwardness mixed in the air like a discordant orchestra.

Instead of an answer she got a look of utter loathing from the star.

"Yes, Ria, how far along are you? Or can't you tell me because I won't be able to handle it?" Nic said.

His mother groaned.

"Nic, come on," Vikram said.

Nikhil narrowed his eyes at Jess in response to the look she threw him.

All those gazes loaded with anger and hurt ricocheted around the room like little torpedoes. If she'd known her question would tip the dominos of all the things Nikhil was feeling, naturally, she wouldn't have asked it. Entitled princesses like Ria Parkar could take their guilt trips somewhere else. Her quota was full, thank you very much.

"When was I supposed to tell you, Nikhil?" Ria said, turning to Nikhil, her voice quiet and hurt and entirely devoid of the anger she had just flashed at Jess. "It's not like you answered my calls. I haven't had a real conversation with you in two years."

"Is there any yogurt in the fridge?" Vikram asked. "This okra is a little spicy."

"I'll get it." Nikhil stood. "I think I'm done."

"Sit down, Nic, and finish the food your mother cooked." Nikhil's father didn't raise his voice, but Jess would have been shocked if anyone had dared to argue with him.

Nikhil sat back down. "By the way, you know how you were asking me how I know Jess? Well, she—"

"I knew Jen. In Mumbai." Jess cut him off, her heartbeat suddenly haywire.

His eyes narrowed again, but he didn't contradict her. There was no question of letting him tell his family about the heart. With The Great Wall of Family staring down at her, she had no doubt they'd strip down every word of her story, maybe even knife her in the night if they thought they could take Jen's heart back.

"You're her friend?" his mother asked just as Ria said, "She never mentioned you."

Nikhil stood again. "Seriously, I'm not hungry. I just drove twenty hours. All I need is a little sleep. We can catch up with the inquisition tomorrow." With that he was gone.

And she was still here.

She felt her cheeks heat, but she was too embarrassed to touch them. Her hands turned cold over her still-full plate. Suspended animation. That's what this was. With her heartbeat as the background score.

"Jess."

She spun around at the sound of Nikhil's voice.

"You're done too, aren't you?" Once again he held out his hand.

No one suspected how badly he did not want her to take it.

She didn't.

But she did follow him out. Right after she had thanked his mother for the meal and seen a mother's pain in her eyes.

20

People think secrets are about lies, or shame. But what secrets are really about is fear.

—Dr. Jen Joshi

Nikhil had been sitting on the floor of his childhood bedroom for over an hour now, but he could not bring himself to climb the ladder to his bed. If he didn't leave the room right now, he was going to go down to his father's bar and empty a bottle of Jack down his throat.

He slid open the door to the Jack and Jill bath he had shared with Ria and stepped inside. Now it was Jess on the other side of the door in Ria's room. Probably fast asleep.

The door to her side slid open.

She froze in place, her eyes wide with horror. Her arms went around herself, struggling to hide not her usual humongous sweatshirt but a fitted tank top that came down to her underwear and skimmed the most spectacular pair of legs he had ever laid eyes on.

She cleared her throat. His head snapped up and he caught the flaming blush on her cheeks before he spun around and looked away.

Idiot. Idiot.

"I'm sorry," he said, the image of her knees pushing self-consciously together burning a hole in his head.

He heard the door slide shut behind him and then some quick muffled movements he was far too aware of.

When the door slid back open he didn't turn around. "I had no idea you were still up."

"I couldn't sleep," she said from behind him, then added more softly, "You can turn around now."

When he did she was exactly the way he had always seen her. Huge black sweatshirt, loose sweatpants. All that ridiculously beautiful skin over ridiculously beautiful muscle he should never have witnessed, put away. He really should never have set eyes on it, because now he couldn't un-see it.

The Goddess of Darkness without her darkness.

Her hair was tucked into her sweatshirt, a sign of how quickly she'd pulled her clothes back on. He wanted to flip it out, set her straight. Now that her hair was brown he couldn't seem to remember how it had looked red.

"I couldn't sleep either," he said, sounding every bit like the pathetic bastard he was.

Her eyes remained undisturbed, no accusation, no judgment, no sympathy. Just a whole lot of knowing. Someday this girl would tell him how she knew pain so well. How she handled it with so much grace when it turned every other person he knew into cringing strangers.

He walked up to her. She looked startled, her flush going crazy and painting itself into two streaks across her cheeks the way it had a habit of doing. He reached around her. "Both our rooms open into this bathroom." He slid the door in place and flipped and then undid the lock. "Remember to lock both the doors when you're in here, okay?"

He stepped back and she exhaled. "I've never seen a bathroom like this." She turned her flaming face away and looked around the marble-and-travertine room with the Jacuzzi in one corner that probably had never, ever been used and the huge Ficus tree that reached for the skylight. He still remembered it as a tiny sapling his dad had let him pick up at Home Depot when they'd gone out to buy a lightbulb.

The space was so familiar he had stopped noticing the details. Now he saw them through her eyes. The huge skylight, the heavy wood-framed mirror. He had no idea if she meant the two doors or the decadence of the bathroom itself.

"Why would a bathroom have two doors like this?" she asked.

"It's called Jack and Jill."

"Jack and Jill? Like the nursery rhyme?" She smiled a confused smile that turned her young and full of wonder. His heart did the tiniest little stutter.

Before he could stop it, that image of her in her underwear flashed in his mind. He backed up all the way to the other end of the room. "I have no idea where that name came from. But it allows two bedrooms in the house to have attached bathrooms."

She slid the door open a crack and left it like that. The smile on her face widened the slightest bit. "What is it with us and bathroom doors?"

He had to smile in response.

"So you and Ria Parkar shared this bathroom growing up?" She seemed to have connected his family's reaction to him announcing that she would be staying in Ria's room to the adjoining doors.

He nodded and looked back at Ria's door. "I smashed Ria's fingers in there once."

"Ouch." She pressed her own fingers together.

"Yup. Slammed the door shut without realizing her hand was in there. She always puts the 'without realizing' in air quotes when she tells the story. We spent a lot of time in here talking and torturing each other."

"I can't imagine you torturing anyone," she said, and then looked away, embarrassed, her fingers twisting together.

He walked over to the Jacuzzi and sat down on the marble steps and patted the stone next to him, inviting her to sit down. Neither one of them seemed sleepy. She didn't move.

"It was easy to torture Ria. She's very proper, and she had to have everything in its place. So I used to move all her stuff around. I thought I was just teasing. But of course I was acting out. I just didn't realize it until much later. Ria kind of took over my parents' attention when she came down for the summers. Then when she was gone, I missed her terribly. You know, your typical sibling shit."

He liked that she got that Ria wasn't just his cousin. It wasn't usually this simple to explain it.

"You didn't tell me your cousin was Ria Parkar." She said Ria's name with a mix of bitterness and awe.

"You know her?"

"You know someone who doesn't know her?"

He found himself smiling again. She was in quite a mood today.

"So the two of them, Ria Parkar and her husband, they're both your cousins? So they've known each other a long time."

"Pretty much their whole life. They were separated for a good ten years. They got back together at our wedding." He slid her a glance, but the mention of his wedding didn't throw her into a panic, like it did everyone else.

"That sounds very film-y." She gave him a small smile. One that had everything to do with what they were talking about and nothing to do with the fact that he had dared to mention his past.

He got up and reached out. Grabbing her wrist, he pulled her down next to him.

She sat, but she tugged her arm back and folded her hands in her lap before giving him a curious look. "What?"

"Thanks."

She blinked up at him. "For?"

"For being so cool with me talking about Jen. Everyone else freaks out every time I mention her name. It's not like just because she's gone, she's disappeared, you know?" Because she hadn't. She was still with him. Inside him. He would never, could never, let her go.

"I think." She stopped and studied him in that way she had, as if she were dipping a toe in unpredictable waters.

"What?"

"Maybe everyone's just being sensitive to your feelings."

"But I need to talk about her."

"I know."

How? How did she know exactly what he needed? How was he here? Sitting in his childhood bathroom, off the ship, sober, having a conversation. Things that had seemed impossible just a week ago.

"Have you? Has Jen, you know, spoken to you since—"

The softness in her eyes hardened just a tiny bit. "No. It hasn't happened since I met you." Her intertwined fingers clasped and released. "I'm sorry," she said, meeting his eyes.

He looked away and took in the details of the bathroom he'd stopped noticing decades ago. Fresh towels, a glass with a full tube of toothpaste, candles. How his mother managed to keep the bathroom from looking as if it had not been used for years he didn't know. But there was still life in it. It felt warm and lived in.

"Why do you think that is?" He must've been silent for a long time, because she looked a little lost when he spoke. "Why do you think she stopped speaking to you after we met?"

She tucked a short spike of hair that fell over her cheek behind her ear and he wondered for the umpteenth time why he had chosen to believe her. Her face had looked so young a few moments ago. Now lines of worry strained it as if his question had aged her in the span of minutes.

"I don't know. Maybe she's said all she needs to say. Maybe this is what she needed, for us to take care of things." Her eyes were fully hard now. They could have belonged to anyone, even a stranger off the street, and he knew what she was going to say next. "We need to find the evidence."

"You said it's in something I wouldn't throw away."

Hell if that didn't leave things wide open. With Jen everything had been special. That was the problem with being two people who took themselves too seriously. All they owned was meaningful. They hadn't had time to be frivolous. To collect the mundane things other couples spent lifetimes gathering. With them, every little cup in their kitchen, every piece of clothing they wore, it had a story behind it. Every conversation, every moment, it had meant something.

He rubbed his thumb on his ring. The cool roll of metal skidded across his skin, in time with his heartbeat.

"Are all her things here? In this house?"

"I'm not sure. Ria and Vic packed and shipped everything." Just the thought of their life together in boxes made him implode back into himself.

"They must've been really close to Jen for you to let them touch her things."

Let them? He hadn't even thought about it. Vic had saved his ass and done it for him. If anyone had the right to her stuff it was Vic and Ria. "They were like this." He crossed his fingers the way you did when you were praying for luck. "Ria and she were like sisters. Vic walked her down the aisle at our wedding. Aie and Baba— Didn't she ever talk about them?"

With nothing more than a quick widening of her carefully distant eyes, she shook her head. "Barely. She mostly talked only about you."

The ring spun beneath his thumb. "She loved our family." And his family had loved her.

They had been through hell these past two years too. He hadn't spent a moment thinking about them. He thought about his mother's face when he had left the dinner table last night without touching the food. His parents had lost two children, not one.

"At dinner . . ." He squeezed his temples and met her placid, knowing eyes. "Food . . . I can't taste it."

Her eyes didn't flinch. "I know."

How? How do you know? But the words stuck in his throat.

"It goes away." She cleared her throat as though her words too were stuck, but unlike him she was strong enough to push past it. The delicate tendons in her neck stood out in deference to her strength. "You just have to take one bite. Then another. And it comes back. Your body . . . it will ease up on the reactions. But you have to help it. You have to force yourself to put it in your mouth, force yourself to taste it."

Whatever it was she was remembering, it darkened her eyes, turning those huge irises almost opaque. If pain had a color, that flat caramel was it. "And the way your mother cooks, it won't take much. Really."

He had been such a selfish bastard. "I pulled you away before you finished dinner last night. You must be hungry."

Maybe that's why she couldn't sleep, Einstein.

He stood and didn't bother to put his hand out. He knew she wouldn't take it. He took her arm and pulled her up. "Let's get something to eat."

"Really? Now? But won't we disturb everyone?"

He had a vision of Aie in her kitchen. "You know what? I'm willing to bet money on something. I'll bet my mother has left food out for us."

They tiptoed down the stairs and stopped short as they entered the kitchen.

Nikhil had never felt so small in his life.

Two plates filled with food sat on the dining table covered in plastic wrap. Two small serving bowls, also covered with wrap, sat in the middle of the table.

Nikhil could see his mother filling the plates for them, moving through the spotless, lived-in kitchen that embodied everything his childhood had been, her movements purposeful and so very familiar, warmth rose in his heart.

He unwrapped the plates. Rice, rotis, vegetables, and lentils were arranged in neat mounds. He unwrapped the bowls, chicken curry in one and sweet *kheer* in the other. She hadn't served the chicken because she didn't know if Jess ate meat.

Nikhil stole a glance at Jess. She looked as if someone had pulled her into a hug too tight and she couldn't breathe.

He picked up a plate, heated it in the microwave, and set it in front of her. She sat down. No words.

He heated the second plate for himself, then sat down across the table from her.

You have to force yourself to put it in your mouth, force yourself to taste it.

She was eating, her entire focus on the food, an almost desperate hunger in her chewing. He broke off a piece of roti, scooped up some vegetables, and put it in his mouth. He closed his eyes, forcing himself to taste the flavors Aie had worked so hard and so long to perfect. Recognition tapped at his taste buds. The slightest little nudges. His usual gag reflex threatened, but he pushed it back.

For the first time in two years, he ate. Really ate.

It wasn't until all the food was gone that he realized his face was wet with tears.

21

The bastard held a gun to my belly today. He doesn't even know there's a baby in there and he threatened it. And the terror was so bad I considered walking away from everything, considered letting him get away with it all. How can Nikhil want to bring a baby into this shithole we call a world?

—Dr. Jen Joshi

It was the strangest feeling, sleeping in Nikhil's bed. Especially since it involved going up a ladder. It was every little boy's dream bed. Her Joy would've been so excited he wouldn't even have been able to fall asleep. She stared up at the clouds painted on the ceiling above her. What kind of people had lives so orderly their home was like a Karan Johar movie set?

No surprise that he had asked her to switch rooms with him last night. Who could stand to have memories this warm turn to pain?

Her phone vibrated. She pulled it to her ear.

"Mamma?"

She rolled onto her side and pressed the phone to her ear. "Joy-boy. I called earlier. You were sleeping."

"Sorry, Mamma. I was dreaming about you."

"Really? That's crazy because I was just dreaming about you too."

"What happened in yours?"

"You first, *babu*."

"I dreamed," he said, sniffing, "that you were home."

"You know what? I don't think that was just a dream. I was sleeping too just before I called, and guess what I was doing in my dream?"

There was a delighted gasp. "What, Mamma?"

"I was with you."

Another gasp. So much wonder in the sound. She could see his face. Eyes wide, delighted. All that trust.

"I was holding you close. Pulling you against my heart."

"And I was holding your ear."

"Of course." She smiled deep in her heart. What was it with Joy and her ears? As a baby, he hadn't been able to fall asleep without his chubby little hand clutching her ear. She pushed her hair behind her ear and rubbed the outer rim, where the sensation of his fingers was imprinted.

"And my leg was thrown over your tummy."

She wanted that leg over her tummy so badly, her chest hurt.

"Mamma will be home soon, *babu*. Can you be good just a little bit longer?"

He was silent but she knew he had nodded.

"And I promise I'll come see you in my dreams, so look for me, okay?"

There was such an ache in her chest when she turned the phone off, she didn't know what to do with it. She wanted to dance until her heart felt nothing more than her heartbeat. Until her calves cramped. But somehow the bright boyish room didn't seem the right place to break into a solo, spinning and spinning until the world became bearable. She needed to get out of the room. Needed, in fact, to get out of this house entirely. This ache would not stop until she was back home with her baby pressed against her chest.

She sat up and looked down at the wall full of books, the TV the size of a theater, and photos in wide, matted frames covering every wall. She went down the ladder and peered at a picture of three kids who had to be Ria Parkar, Vikram, and Nikhil sitting on the branch of a tree, their feet dangling over a river, their eyes sparkling with laughter. Vikram and Nikhil sat on either side of Ria, who was completely unaware of the bunny ears they were holding up behind her. Vikram had no shirt on, and even as an adolescent he was as self-possessed as a model. Ria was as long-limbed and beautiful as ever in shorts over a swimsuit. But it was Nikhil's smile that filled up the picture. Two deep dimples digging into cheeks so huge they almost ate up his eyes. Huge teeth covered in braces. His swim shirt rolled up beneath a round belly that popped out from under it.

Nic had been a chubby child? She could never have guessed from the way he looked now. Something about that picture with two models of perfect beauty flanking him made her heart hurt. His child's face was so stoic it was as though he were determined to be happy, to be more than he thought he was. It reminded her so much of Joy, she pressed a hand into her heart to stop the ache. The rest of the pictures were just as happy, a sun-soaked childhood for a child who knew exactly how blessed he was.

Then there were his pictures with Jen. Not artistic black-and-white portraits like the childhood ones, but snapshots that froze moments in the middle of living. In these pictures, Nikhil looked like a *National Geographic* photographer. At once rugged and intellectual, stubbly cheeked and touched by the wind and the sun. With a backpack and cargo shorts and unkempt spiky hair. Those kind, intelligent eyes, so hopeful, so complete, even when he was pulling some sort of silly face. Then there was a picture of his wedding, where he looked like exactly the Nikhil he was born to be.

"Hi," he said behind her and she turned.

Tortured eyes met hers. "Did you sleep?"

She nodded. No point in asking him if he had. She could see the answer on his face.

His eyes hitched on his wedding picture. Someone should have removed at least that one.

"Aie would have removed them if we hadn't surprised her." He sniffed the air. "Do you smell that? She's cooking breakfast. Do you like *pohey*? We should go now if you want some before Vic siphons off the entire thing. That guy can eat unearthly amounts of food."

"From what I've seen, your *aie* will make sure there's enough for you."

"For us," he said and held out his hand.

It had been so long since anyone had filled a plate of food for her she had forgotten what it felt like. Before her *aama* got sick she had done it every day, stood over her shoulder and spooned the dal and vegetables and rice onto her plate. After Aama got sick, it's how she had known if Aama was having a good day. If she came home from school and found a plate filled for her on the desk in their room she knew Aama had been able to get out of bed. Then a time had come when it had been Jess's turn to hide food away so Aama had some, to force her to take another bite, just one more bite so she could have her for a little while longer.

After Aama, no one had ever filled a plate for her or cared if she ate. Until last night.

Nikhil had popped the plate into the microwave and placed it in front of her with such ease. Now here he was holding out his hand to her with such ease.

Then again, maybe it wasn't easy, maybe it took all his courage to do it.

She wasn't brave enough to take his hand. "I need to get cleaned up. You go on."

He was gone so quickly she wasn't sure if it was relief or disappointment that flooded through her.

"It's out of the question," Nikhil heard Ria say as he came down the stairs. "You have to talk to the aunties. I'm really not doing it."

Aie was about to respond when he entered the kitchen. Her mouth snapped shut and she gaped at him as if he had caught her going through his stuff. God knows he was familiar enough with that look.

"Morning," he said, ignoring the guilt on her face.

Vic yanked his arms from around Ria. He had been standing behind her with his arms wrapped around her, his palms splayed on her belly, his chin resting on the top of her head. A pose Nikhil had seen the two of them in a million times, minus the hands on pregnant belly, of course. Now here Vic was, pulling his hands off his wife as if it were some sort of sin to touch her.

Before Vic's arms slid off, Nikhil caught his thumb stroking the bump. Caressing his baby. The memory of the tautness of Jen's barely swollen belly tingled on his fingers.

"Coffee?" Vic said and turned to the coffeemaker without waiting for an answer.

"Morning, *beta*." Aie tried to smile at him, but there was so much sadness in her face it just came out a worried frown. "Did you slee—"

"I slept." He met her eyes, lying. "The food was delicious. Thank you."

For a moment she looked like she was going to cry, but then she was her stoic self again. "Your friend has good manners." She placed both hands on his cheeks, pulled him to her, and dropped a kiss on his forehead, her fingers tight with the restraint of not doing more. "The dishes were all washed and put away."

"Oh, and I couldn't have been the one who cleaned up?"

Great, so that's what it took to get them to break into chuckles.

"Really? I can clean up when I want to. I am not that much of a pig."

More chuckles.

"Of course you're not a pig." This from his pregnant cousin, who had always been the master of the eye roll. She didn't disappoint. "Pigs are actually quite clean," she said with all the sincerity of a bossy sister.

He narrowed his eyes at her and everyone relaxed a little bit.

"It's a myth that they dirty their surroundings," Vic added, sliding the coffee cup across the island to Nikhil.

Ria intercepted the cup and took a quick sip. "It's just one sip." She threw a warning glare at Vic. "Don't you dare start."

"Why don't you just drink an entire cup?"

"Because I want only one sip, Viky, and one sip is not going to hurt the . . . It's not going to hurt anyone."

"When I was pregnant, we had no idea we weren't supposed to drink caffeine. I drank my chai every day," his mother said.

"And look what happened," both Ria and Vic said together and then grinned as if they had achieved Laurel and Hardy's perfect comic timing.

The grins lasted for precisely two seconds.

"It's okay to smile in my presence, you know," he wanted to say. Instead he took his cup to the dining table. "Baba's at work already?" He turned away from Ria's and Vic's guilty faces and faced his *aie*.

"Of course." She brought a plate of spiced flaky rice to the table and set it in front of him. "Did you want to wait for your friend for breakfast?" She nudged the plate of rice toward him.

"She'll be down soon."

All three of them were studying him. He put a spoonful of the fluffy rice in his mouth, and instead of answering the questions in their eyes he turned to Vic and said, "I need to get to Jen's stuff."

Vic froze.

His mother slumped against a chair.

Ria clutched her stomach.

Nikhil ignored the stricken faces of the women he loved so much and kept his focus on Vic. "The things you had shipped from Mumbai. Are they here?"

Vic allowed the muscle in his jaw one twitch. "Some are here in the basement. I started to move them to your apartment, but then I wasn't sure what you wanted to do so I stopped."

Nikhil took another bite of the spicy yellow rice flakes dotted with fresh green peas. *Take one bite. Then another.* "Thanks. Jess and I were going to go through the stuff in the basement today."

Another chorus of indrawn breaths.

Ria and his mother both opened their mouths, then shut them again and looked at each other. A silent message passed between them. Except it wasn't silent at all.

"Say what you want to say," he almost said. But he couldn't bring himself to say it because he wasn't sure he wanted to hear what they were thinking.

"Anything specific you're looking to find?" his mother asked over her cup of tea. Another gesture so familiar, he hated it. And loved it. This was her nonchalant pose, her nonchalant tone. When she was dying of curiosity but didn't want to put him on guard. *So have you asked anyone to the homecoming dance? Do you feel ready for the test?*

Always no to the first one. Always yes to the second.

The spoon shook in his hand. He put it down. *Oh, I'm just going to be looking for the thing she killed herself for.* How did you tell your mother something like that?

"Are you planning to get rid of things?" she pushed, surprising him.

"Of course not."

"If you want, we can take care of it," Vic interjected.

"No. I got it."

"Do you need help? I can—" Vic said again.

"I said no." It came out much harsher than Nikhil had intended. "Thanks. Seriously, I got it, Vic," he said much more calmly.

Ria looked like Nikhil had slapped Vikram. It pissed him off so bad he gripped the table to keep from pushing the chair back and leaving the kitchen. He couldn't remember the last time he'd experienced the all-too-familiar feeling of being left out of their tight little circle of two. It had been the bane of his childhood. Although, until this moment, he'd never admitted it to anyone, not even to himself.

"I need to do this myself," he said to Ria.

"But you aren't doing it yourself," she said.

"Yeah. I hadn't noticed that. Thanks for pointing it out."

Ria looked at her toes. Vic walked to her but he didn't touch her, his arms reaching for her then backing off like some guilty thief having a bout of conscience.

"You can touch her, you know. Even if I'm in the room, you can touch your wife."

Vic's head snapped up. He closed his eyes, pushed back whatever retort he was suppressing this time, and said nothing. Vic, who never had a problem kicking his ass about the smallest thing, said nothing. Just looked at him with all that damn sympathy.

"It won't kill me if I see the two of you touching each other," he said, feeling like a drunk trying to start a fight in a bar.

"Nikhil, please." Usually, his mother would have snapped his head off for being such a brat; now she couldn't even admonish him without more of that damn sympathy. This time he did push away from the table. Hard. The screech of chair against tile jolted through all that awkward silence and spotlighted it like a subwoofer on steroids.

"I'm sorry—I didn't realize that's what I was doing." Vic dug his hands into his pockets, the blasted sympathy still dripping from his face. Dripping from all their faces and bouncing off the tile, the walls, the granite, the fucking recessed lights cramming the ceiling with myriad sources of fake brightness.

"We are your family, Nic." Well, wasn't Ria the master of stating the obvious today.

"Is that why I was the last to find out about the baby?"

"I told you I tried to call you. You wouldn't take my calls."

"You left me messages. You could have let me know I was going to be an uncle."

"It was complicated. You know we never expected to have children. I still have no idea how it happened. You know it wasn't something I was prepared for. We weren't even sure we were going to go through with the pregnancy, Nikhil."

There was a gasp from the doorway.

Nikhil spun around to catch Jess with her hand pressed to her mouth, horror widening her eyes. It was a real pain how silently she moved.

"Jess, hi," he said, but she didn't seem to hear him.

Her eyes, her entire being, in fact, was focused on Ria with such loathing, Ria actually pressed back into her chair.

Okay. What the hell?

He tried again. "Come on in. You want some breakfast?"

Her hands were tight fists. She turned around and looked at the arched kitchen entrance she'd just come through, then back again at him, as lost as a doe on a freeway.

"Breakfast?" he repeated.

"Sorry. I'm . . . I'll be right back." She backed out of the room, not stumbling but looking as though she had.

He followed her.

Instead of going back up the stairs, she opened the front door and stepped out. He grabbed the heavy wooden door before it slammed in his face and followed her into the blast of sunshine. His hometown had just done one of its spectacular weather backflips and flown from a blizzard and landed on a bright spring day. Everything was melting fast and furious, turning the driveway, the sidewalk, the road into impossible-to-navigate, gushing rivulets. A perfect reflection of the Joshi household.

He found his hand holding her arm. It was so tiny under the thick fabric. She yanked it from him and stepped away, pressing a hand into one of the high pillars that held up the porch, her entire body sagging into the support. Her feet were bare on the wet concrete. He had the urge to scoop her up in his arms, to take those feet off the ice-cold water.

He had never wanted to scoop anyone but his wife up in his arms. He half twisted away from her, needing to go back inside, but the door clicked shut behind him. Jess spun around and met his gaze, her eyes tortured beyond anything he had ever seen.

"What's wrong with you?" he said, trying to snap her out of wherever she was lost. But maybe he didn't want to know the answer. His hand reached for the doorknob behind him.

"Was she talking about dropping that baby? How could she do that so calmly? What kind of person is that?"

Anger popped inside his head. Hot. So hot. So large. It was like all his previous anger was tiny paper boats in the face of its wave. "You don't know anything about Ria, Jess." He could not believe the look in her eyes, her anger matching his own. "It's complicated."

"Complicated? What's complicated? There's a mother and a father and they have everything in the world. What more does a child need?"

"Ria has health concerns. There's severe genetic mental illness in her family. She could get very sick over her pregnancy." They could lose Ria. Suddenly, he wanted to go back in and make sure she was okay.

"Yes, Ria Parkar's life does seem so very hard. What is it with you people acting like a child is some sort of inconvenience?"

"We people?" Blood pounded in his ears. "Jen didn't not want a baby because it was inconvenient."

Jess drew back. Guilt nudged out the anger on her face. "I'm sorry. That's not what I meant."

It's exactly what she had meant. "Who died and gave you the right to judge people?" He was sick of her righteous self-pity, her know-it-all indignation. "You're here chasing a problem that's not even your business. Shaking things up. Abandoning your own child. Leaving him with a man who's not even his father, and you want to throw judgment around?"

If her eyes had looked tortured before, now her entire body seemed to fold over with pain, and because he was a vulture he fed on it. As long as the pain was outside of himself, that's all that mattered. "Where's his father anyway? How is it you never talk about him?"

She wrapped her arms around herself. The pain hardened and peaked in her eyes before she blacked it out. He wanted to yank her arms apart, wanted to bring the pain back, so he could be the one to take it away. "I'm sorry," he said, disturbing the silence that sprang up between them like unbridgeable distance.

"No. You're right," she said, fully back in her yogic mode, measured and distant, making sure everything was about him again. Eager to give him whatever he wanted. Eager to get this over with. "I had no right to judge her. I'm sorry." She had withdrawing into herself down to an art, and she wielded her skill without mercy. It was as though she were a snail and all the air between them crisp, hard shell.

"Don't," he wanted to say. "Not you too." He was sick of everyone tiptoeing around him. The fact that she had never done it had kept him sane the past week, and the idea of losing it kicked him off-center. He spun away from her, his face inches from the closed door, and breathed until his heartbeat slowed. Despite the sunshine, the cold from the wet concrete was seeping through to his slippered feet. Her bare feet had to be freezing.

"Let's go inside," he said without turning around.

For a long time she didn't answer, but he knew she had moved closer behind him. "Can we look for it, Nikhil? Please," she said, her voice even, safe and sound in that shell he wanted so badly to grow around himself too. "Please. I need to get back home." Her tone was raw and he knew she was thinking about her baby. It was the only time desperation leaked past her armor. He would have done anything to take the words he'd said before back.

He turned around. "Is Joy okay?" he asked as though it was apology enough.

As if she weren't already buried inside that sweatshirt, her head fell forward, her chin dug into her chest, her fingers squeezed her arms. "He's fine." For all her rolling up into a ball, her voice was as fierce as a tigress. "But I'm here. He doesn't know why his mother has to leave him alone for so long."

His hand itched to slip the hair flopping onto her face behind her ear, to smooth away those thorns that prickled from her skin. He dug his fists into his pockets.

"Most of her things are here. In the basement. We can go down and start looking." They had to get this over with. It was about time for her to get back to her child. It was about damn time.

22

I could destroy the registry. But Rahul thinks it's the only way to prove that the organs are being stolen. Plus, the registry is saving lives too. I'm holding the blade of a double-edged sword and I can't let it go. If I don't end this soon, I'll lose more than my fingers.

—Dr. Jen Joshi

With the Jess Koirala trail leading to nothing but dead ends and Nikhil Joshi not taking his calls, Rahul's only hope was to be able to convince the home minister to sanction a trip to visit the good doctor*saab* in America.

"You want a foreign trip? I'll put you on the Interpol exchange list. Why America? Europe is so much more beautiful. How about Switzerland—it's where all our movies used to be shot in my day." The minister hardly ever spoke of his days as one of Bollywood's first superstars.

He had once told Rahul that it made people take him less seriously as a leader and that his Entertainment phase was behind him. This was his Service phase. But they were in the minister's home and he was always a different person in his home, especially around his daughter. No matter what his phase, Kirit put his family above everything else.

"Or maybe South America. These days those Brazilian beaches are all the rage. You can go there. I'll take care of it," the minister said, dipping his fingers into the finger bowl the bearer had just placed in front of him. He rinsed his fingers and wiped them on the towel the servant held out.

"Papa, I don't think Rahul is asking for the charitable donation of a vacation for himself. Are you even listening to what he's saying?" Kimi glared at her father with those huge eyes, and Rahul didn't bother to glare at Kimi because he knew how useless it was. He didn't need her help. Not that that had ever stopped her.

All Rahul had wanted to do today was take a few moments to talk to Kirit privately and leave. But she had found them talking and insisted he stay for dinner, undoubtedly to prove to him that they could still be friends after he'd pushed her away. Naturally, her mother had excused herself from dinner, as she always did when Kimi forced Rahul to eat with them.

Her father frowned at her, the way he always frowned at her, with the fondness of one scolding a precious and infallible pet. "Kimaya, *beta*, I would never assume Rahul was asking for a donation. You know I don't consider anything I've done for him charity. But you're the one who keeps reprimanding me for working him too hard, and now here I am trying to make sure he gets some time off and you're making me look bad."

She colored. Not in an admonished sort of way, but the way she always reddened when her family called attention to the difference in their social class and it made her fume. Not that her denying it changed the fact that he had been a servant in their home. Just one of the many reasons why what she wanted was impossible. They didn't stand a chance in hell.

He cut her off before she jumped on her soapbox and went to war over him once again.

"We found parts of a dismembered body at a construction site, sir. The eyes were carved out. It's time to open up an investigation. I have no doubt this is related to the Jennifer Joshi case."

"Rahul! Can we please maintain the sanctity of this dinner table? You know Kimaya's mother hates business talk at dinner, and you know she's the home minister within these walls, so even though she's not here right now her ears are everywhere." He looked at one of the servants and smiled, but Rahul knew his smiles and he knew he had pushed too hard. "At least wait for the ladies to retire."

Kimaya was the only lady at the table. And she was the least retiring person Rahul knew in all the world.

"I'm not *retiring*, Papa. I have a movie premiere after-party to cover." She typed furiously into her phone before glaring at her father again. "And I've had my heart replaced. I'm hardly queasy about organs."

"You're going out at this hour again? Rahul will go with you."

She stood. "No, he won't. He's not my bodyguard. He's the Divisional Head of the Crime Branch, who needs you to help him do his job."

Rahul took a breath, and stood. "I'll follow her, sir."

His phone beeped. Naturally, it was a text from Kimi. Actually, it was three texts:

Not

My

Bodyguard

She threw him a look so fiery it was almost as though things were normal between them again, and walked out the front door before the doorman rushed to open it.

He followed her out and responded to her text. *I know. But please stop trying to be mine.* Great, now he was being just as juvenile as her and texting instead of talking like they used to.

His phone beeped again, because even lying on her deathbed for years, the girl had never let anyone else have the last word.

Fine. Then stop trying to get his approval on everything. It's your case, not his.

She drove off. He straddled his Enfield Bullet.

Another text from her.

He shouldn't have read it. But of course he did.

Your. Case. And if you follow me, I'm crashing my car.

23

There are two kinds of people in the world. Those who knew growing up that their parents loved them and believed it, and those who wished they knew what that feels like.

—Dr. Jen Joshi

Nikhil didn't actually drag her down the stairs to the basement, but it definitely felt like that. He stormed down as though he was too afraid to stop, too afraid to look at the framed artwork covering the walls. Not paintings by artists, but the kind of drawings young children made. Flowers and footballs, and kittens drawn with two circles and a spiraling tail. Crayons and finger paints lined with felt-tipped pens. The thick, matted frames made them look like art gallery prints. But what they framed was undoubtedly innocence.

She raced to keep up. Suddenly, he stopped as if he had run into a glass wall. Maybe she shouldn't have been so good at stopping in the middle of motion. Maybe she should have run into him and pushed him through the wall he'd hit. Because he looked like he couldn't get through it for anything.

Next to them was a picture of a purple dinosaur with spikes on his head. "This one is yours," she said, unable to make it a question.

He didn't respond. She walked around him and took a step down.

"That's Spikey," he said in a voice that made her regret calling his attention to the picture. "I think it's from second or third grade. It was the first year Ria and Vic spent the summer here," he said from behind her, not following her down as she'd hoped.

But he was talking. She turned around to face him. "How was that?" she asked and took a backward step down.

"What? Having them stay with us for the summer? It was great. Why wouldn't it be?" He looked at her as if she had accused him of something horrible, but he still didn't follow her down. Her heart twisted under the roped scar. She wanted to touch it. But now was not the time to call his attention to it.

What she needed to do was keep his mind far away from what they were about to do. "Sometimes children don't like having people take over their space." She reached for his hand, meaning to tug him along.

But as soon as she touched him, he grabbed her hand and clutched it hard, as if it could keep him from drowning. "Is Joy possessive about you?"

"No. I wasn't talking about Joy. I grew up in my uncle's house too. My mother and I moved there after my father died and we had nowhere else to stay." Bringing up her pathetic childhood here, in this altar to everything a childhood should be, made shame well up inside her.

But his eyes softened, and his focus shifted outward to her. "They weren't nice to you, your cousins?" His eyes skimmed the pictures then met hers, gathering all that was different about their childhoods into that one intuitive glance.

She took a step down and tugged his hand, forcing him down the last remaining steps. When they reached the bottom, she tried to withdraw her hand, but he resisted and she couldn't force it.

"It's not like they weren't nice. There just wasn't enough space in the house." And never enough food. They had been like a bunch of mongrels fighting for the same scrap.

She had hated fighting for food, hated it so much she had stopped fighting after a while and her appetite had slowly disappeared. At least while Aama was alive, she had insisted on hiding some food away for her and making sure she ate. But once Aama was gone, her aunt had praised her lack of appetite as if it were her greatest virtue.

This time he tugged her hand to get her to move, pulling her away from the memories, and he led her past a large living room. He didn't seem to notice anything, not the white leather couches, not the TV that covered an entire wall.

"How old were you?" he said, stopping outside a door as if a flesh-eating python lived inside. No marks for guessing they had finally reached their destination. "When your father died."

"Six, and fourteen when my mother died."

"I'm sorry," he said turning to her. "That's terribly young."

His eyes were so kind, she wanted to tell him it was all right. But having someone squeeze her hand and acknowledge what no one had ever acknowledged stole her words and all she could do was soak it up.

He twisted the knob with his free hand and pushed the door open. It was a storage room of some sort, with boxes and bins lined up from floor to ceiling on wooden shelves. They stepped into the room together.

"What about your aunt and uncle? Didn't they correct your cousins when they treated you badly?"

She laughed and he looked at her with such sadness, her bitter-as-bile laughter died in her throat. If the idea of her aunt and uncle not correcting their girls made him this sad, what would he say if he knew her uncle had sold her to the first man who offered to take her off his hands? And her aunt had actually sat her down and explained how it was her duty to help her younger cousins by "marrying" the man her uncle had found for her.

Could two people be from more different worlds?

"Why is that funny?" he asked.

"Not funny." No, funny wasn't the only reason you had to laugh at life. "Which of these are your boxes?"

His gaze swept the room. His eyes hitched on two yellow suitcases pushed against the far wall and finally he let her hand go.

"So how old were you when Ria Parkar came to stay?" she asked, knowing she had to keep him talking.

"Eight. She didn't speak for weeks when she first got here." He walked to the suitcases and went down on his knees next to one. "My parents spent every waking moment with her. I tried to be friendly, but all she did was cry. I remember being so annoyed with her."

Jess squatted down next to him.

"I didn't recognize it then, but it was the worst case of jealousy ever." He laid the suitcase down flat.

She followed his gaze. JEN + NIC. The words were emblazoned in shimmering metallic red across the bright yellow plastic.

"It's nail polish." His fingers skated the air over the letters, a horribly sad half smile on his lips. "Then Vic came to stay. Vic was my best friend. My way-cooler best friend. I was this fat, uncoordinated kid. Vic was athletic and funny, and he was just so blasé about it. Always acted as if I was exactly like him, not the ungainly nerd everyone else saw." He pulled his hand away from the letters he'd been trying to touch. "If Ria had taken my parents' attention, she completely mesmerized Vic." He snapped his fingers. "Just like that, our little team of Vic and Nic was gone. Of course I reacted like a total brat."

He turned back to the red nail polish and this time his hands touched the sparkly names and stroked them.

"What did you do?" she prodded, her need to keep his mind away from that bag and on less painful memories overwhelming her.

He looked at her gratefully and went on. "We were riding our bikes in the park behind the house one day. I knew of this low-hanging branch that shot across the bike path. I stopped my bike and walked it around the branch, but before I could warn Ria she came up behind me. I knew she was behind me. I could've shouted out to her, but I didn't."

"What happened?"

"I can still hear the crack when the branch hit her head." He pressed two fingers into the top of his head. "It was so loud I was sure she had cracked her skull and died." The memory shone so clearly on his face it was like seeing the horror on his eight-year-old face.

"I still remember praying as I raced home on my bike while Vic sat with her as she bled onto his lap. The ambulance, my parents, I remember everyone arriving in a haze. I never stopped praying. I felt sure she was going to die. It was like this cold, tight fist around my throat. I couldn't leave her. Vic and I sat outside her hospital room as the adults took care of things. I swore I'd never, ever hurt anyone again. I swore. I promised if she came out of that okay, I would never be jealous again, never get angry again.

"When she finally got out of bed two days later, that's when I cried."

His hands shook on the number lock. He rolled the numbers. "Baba found me crying on the deck steps." He snapped the lock open. "You know what he said to me?"

She shook her head, although he wasn't looking at her.

"He said, 'Nothing will ever change how much your *aie* and I love you. You know that, right?' I remember knowing with absolute certainty that I was a fraud. That as soon as he found out the truth about what I had done, he'd know it."

"And you told him, didn't you?" she said as he clutched the suitcase.

"I told him I knew . . . I knew about the branch and that I could have stopped Ria from getting hurt and I didn't." Nikhil lifted the lid off the suitcase, but he didn't open it up all the way. "Baba asked me if I had taken her on that path on purpose."

"Of course you hadn't." Her heart was beating hard. She wished he hadn't let her hand go.

He shook his head. "I didn't know we were going to take that path, and I didn't remember about the branch until I was almost under it. That's when Baba told me about why Ria had come to stay with us. He told me that she'd been hurt, that she didn't have anywhere else to go when her boarding school closed for the summer.

"I remember the horror of thinking about Ria with no home. I remember asking him, 'Can't this be her home? Can't we be her family?' 'We are.' That's what he said." And with that Nikhil threw the suitcase open.

24

I identified another two bodies today. Two sisters I'd talked into getting on the registry. I remember every word they said to me, how they bickered with each other. Why do dead people live on forever? Dying should erase life, not leak into it as memories.

—Dr. Jen Joshi

Shimmering silk and intricately embroidered gold spilled from the bag as Nikhil threw it open. Just his luck that the first thing staring at him when he opened it was Jen's wedding sari. Jade. That's what she had called the color. It was Ria's word, of course. The only way Jen would ever use *jade* for a color was if it identified a radiology dye. And yet on their wedding day she had looked as elegant, as beautiful, as impeccably put together as the most fastidious fashionista.

He squeezed his eyes shut. Jen walking up the aisle to him as he waited for her under an altar of lilies, running those last few steps—it was a vision he was going to carry to his dying day. It would always be as fresh, as real, as the moment it happened.

The silk slid between his fingers, every one of his senses searching for her beneath it. He'd peeled it off her body fast, too fast, mindless in his hurry to get to her. Her skin. Her smell. She had smelled like a drug. She had *been* a drug. Familiar, irresistible, sparking unfathomable hunger, bringing incomparable numbing peace. His tough, take-on-the-world wife had been his drug. She was *charas* to his *charsi*. Weed to his pothead.

What kind of idiot smiled now? Here. Where his dead wife was all around him. In boxes and bags and lifeless saris. But he'd just called her "weed" and it was hilarious. And she would have thought so too.

He let the sari go. How could you want something so badly and be so very tired of it all at once?

"Nikhil?" The soft hand on his shoulder wasn't her, he knew it wasn't. And yet it kept him from folding over and throwing up the grief that consumed him.

"Sometimes I feel like this isn't happening. That I'll wake up and she'll be here and all of this will have been a nightmare."

"I know."

"How? How could you possibly know what this feels like?" Even as he said it he was certain she knew what it was to be altered by loss. "Was it Joy's dad? Was he someone you loved?"

That trademark blast of pain, which he'd grown to recognize, flickered across her face and was gone. "Will it be easier if I went through the bags?" she said with a gentleness that turned her into someone entirely different from that yogic Goddess of Darkness she wore so well.

He let go of the sari he was gripping. "No." He had to do this himself.

He started filing through the saris. Shoving away the images of Jen in each one of them. The midnight-blue, in which Ria had first taught her how to wear a sari. The shimmering burgundy she had carried with the confidence of a princess at their reception. The black-and-gold, in which he had twirled and twirled her as they danced at Ria and Vic's wedding. When she'd told him she was pregnant.

When she'd told him she didn't want to be.

But she had learned to want it, for him. *Because she's yours, Spikey.*

"She's ours," he'd told her, and she'd repeated it in wonder. *Because she's ours.*

Their little girl.

Under all the saris was the jewelry. Coordinated sets of necklaces and earrings and bracelets Aie had bought for her daughter-in-law even before Nikhil had met Jen. Nothing made Jen cry, but having his mother slip his grandmother's gold bracelets onto her wrists at the engagement ceremony had made tears stream down her cheeks.

She would have slipped those bracelets on their little girl's wrists at her wedding.

"I wouldn't get rid of any of this stuff," he said, turning to Jess's hopeful eyes. "But there's nothing in here that looks like any kind of storage device would fit in it."

He opened a red velvet–lined box, removed the bracelets, and pulled at the lining, tearing it off, trying not to let the ripping sound bring satisfaction. There was nothing there. He put it aside and started on the rest of the jewelry boxes. Ripping and ripping.

But he found nothing. Jess put each box back together when he was done tearing it up. Folding the velvet lining and pushing it in place until it looked like it had never come apart.

Nothing. The bag held nothing but the remnants of his life with Jen.

Opening it had been hard enough. Putting it away—the lingering smells, the fresh-as-a-flesh-wound feel of the memories—was impossible.

Jess pulled the bag away from him and put everything back in place, her movements quick and efficient and soundless. She snapped it shut, her jaw so tight her lips all but disappeared. Her hands hesitated a second before she moved the other bright yellow bag toward him.

The same bright red nail-polish letters emblazoned this one too.

Given how much they traveled, Jen had believed the best way to spot their bags on baggage claim belts was to buy the brightest color. But on their first flight into Heathrow it had been clear that all travelers basically had the same idea.

Jen had bought red nail polish at the airport and painted their names on. Actually, she had done one and he had done the other. The closest he had ever come to carving his name into a tree for a girl.

She had laughed at him about that. *What kind of man marries the only girl he's ever fallen for? You have to have someone break your heart before you find your soul mate. You're so unromantic, Spikey.*

Or too darned romantic. Depending on how you looked at it.

He threw the second bag open.

This one was chockfull of what looked like crushed-up newspaper balls. He picked one up. Wrapped in the newspaper was a cup. They never moved with this stuff. They always gave it away to their local friends or people they had worked with. Then they bought all of it again at their next posting. But Vic or Ria, whoever had packed up the stuff, had wrapped each piece. Baggage gathered on Jen's behalf when she had fought so hard not to collect any on her own.

"It's not in this one," he said and turned to the boxes.

He ripped one open before his brain kicked in. Books, clothes, bedding. More smells and sights. More *them*.

Coffins. These weren't boxes. They were cardboard coffins. Body parts of their marriage, chopped up by a killer and disposed of in garbage bags. Mangled and maimed and entirely unrecognizable. Not a trace of the beautiful body that was gone.

"How do you deal with it?" he asked when they had spent God knows how many hours, lifetimes, trudging through the Dumpster of severed limbs and he found in his hands a picture of himself with his head on Jen's lap. A selfie she had taken and then printed to take with her when she left for Mumbai.

"Deal with what?" Jess had been silent for so long the sound of her voice was like breaking through the surface of water and filling his lungs with air.

"With whatever it was that happened to you." His own voice came from miles away. They were solidified distance. Each particle vibrating between them its full-blown self.

"That depends," she said, her hands working methodically on wrapping up and putting away everything he had pulled apart.

"On what?"

"On what you mean by dealing with it."

"How do you fucking go on?"

"As opposed to what?"

He pushed himself off the floor and stood, her eyes following him like floodlit probes, demanding to be answered.

He flipped the mirror on her. "Didn't you ever consider it? The alternative?"

She looked away, going back to folding and wrapping, the precise care in her actions falling on his frayed senses, soothing one moment, gouging the next, an unperturbed glance her only reaction to the hideous question that had just come out of his mouth.

"I had Joy. How could I?"

And he had nothing. But it sounded too weak, too selfish to say it.

Her hands stilled. "There's a difference between considering it and doing it." Her words were empty, but her eyes, they filled them in. "It's okay to consider it, Nikhil. If that gets you through. It's okay to do whatever you have to do to make it through the hours."

That was the problem. Making it through the hours.

"Look at you," she said. "You just went through all these boxes and you're still here. You're going on."

"I'm really not. This isn't going on. I can't even get out of bed in the morning."

"But you do get out of bed every morning."

"But I don't want to. All of this—it doesn't feel like my life. It doesn't even feel like life. I don't feel alive."

The pain in his eyes was so raw she wanted to run from it. Instead she made herself stand and face him. People with healed injuries claimed forgotten pain returned when they heard someone else talk about their pain. Muscles and nerves had memory and the reminder resurrected those memories. Jen had already brought all her suppressed memories back to life. Now here was the pain in Nikhil's eyes to give those memories bulk and blow them up like an inflatable raft.

"You're right. You don't feel alive. You feel trapped in what happened. Like you're still in the middle of it. Like it's still happening. Like it will never stop. But the feeling passes, in flashes at first, then for longer and longer stretches of time. You live in those stretches of time. That's all I can tell you."

He reached for her then and the shock of it jolted through her. She had been wrong; his pain wasn't like hers. His tragedy was completely different from her own. He needed to touch someone, needed to feel something real in his hands. Something alive. His arms circled her waist, his head found its way to her shoulder. "Tell me something she told you. Tell me what she wanted. How she sounded. Tell me where she is."

"I told you I don't . . ." Her hand went to his shoulder. She patted it tentatively, trying not to think about it. Trying not to think about the fact that he was a man, and that his hands were around her. Somehow it was different this time. He wasn't half unconscious with alcohol. "Jen wanted you to be happy. She worried that if something happened to her, that you would not be okay. She wanted more than anything for you to continue to be who you are. To never lose your faith. She knew you would find it again. Find your way. Even if you got lost for a while, she knew you would find your way in the end."

He started to shake in her arms, a subtle, unwilling trembling. A kite fluttering to break free as you tried to hold it in place against the wind.

For long moments the shaking went on, him struggling to hold it in and failing. The need to soothe him was a wave and it took her down. She stroked his shoulders, his hair. She couldn't not hold him, couldn't not speak words she knew he needed to hear, as, body and soul, he fell into his pain.

When he finally pulled away, his eyes were bloodshot, but unlike the last time he'd cried in her arms, there was courage there.

He cupped her cheek. "Do you mind going up by yourself? I need a moment."

"Of course." She should have run up, run away from him and his brave, hurt-soaked eyes. But she stood there a moment watching him before turning around and slipping out the door.

"Jess," he said when she was halfway to the stairs. He was leaning on the door frame.

"Yes?"

"Thank you."

25

More than anything, it's what you're afraid of that defines who you are. Most people are afraid of losing something—their life, people they love, things they own. Nikhil and I? We're terrified of amounting to nothing. Of being powerless against the things we want to change.

—Dr. Jen Joshi

She heard voices coming from the kitchen and couldn't bring herself to go in. But she couldn't go back down either. He wasn't the only one who needed a moment. The feel of his hair was imprinted on her palms. A strange bundle of knots was lodged in her chest, and she tried to untangle it and find the triumph she should've been feeling.

This was a huge step after all. It was why she was here. She pulled out her phone and typed out the words *Search begun.*

Almost immediately he responded with his Naag strike. *About time. And?*

And we'll find it.

Tell your roommate he doesn't have to pick up and drop Joy off at school. My men will take care of it.

She pressed back into the wall. She was going to throw up.

If you go anywhere near him, I'll go tell Nikhil what you're up to right now. Her thumb hovered over the send button. Why would Nikhil care? She deleted the juvenile words.

I am in his house. He trusts me. If you pressure me like this I can't work. One more week. Then she typed the hardest word. *Please.*

OK, but after that I'll have to do more than just drive him back and forth from school. One of my men enjoys slapping children around.

Nausea squeezed up her throat. But he wasn't done.

Oh, and I was talking to some old friends from Calcutta and trying to find out about Joy's father. Her knees buckled.

He's dead.

That's what you say. I'm sure Joy will appreciate someone filling him in on his "dead" father.

I know where the evidence is. I'm taking Nikhil there tomorrow.

Much better.

Her hand was shaking when she erased the messages. *Please, Jen, give me a clue. Give me something.*

But Jen had helped her as much as she could. It was all up to her now. Watching Nikhil go through the remnants of his marriage had made her feel like someone had peeled off her scabs and left her perennially ripe wounds exposed. Despite her lecturing Nikhil about moving on and getting through the pain one step at a time, all she wanted was to shove past it for him.

And no, it wasn't because she couldn't bear to see him in pain, but because running out of time meant losing everything.

For all the relief of having dragged Nikhil away from the absolute darkness he'd been trapped inside, she was here to steal from him. She wasn't a complete idiot. She knew exactly why she'd been able to get this far. He sensed her brokenness, recognized it, unlike everyone else who never saw beyond the frozen exterior. At first she'd thought that was the reason he leaned on her, because her brokenness made his own less daunting. It was why he focused on her pain every time he needed to deal with his own. But that wasn't all it was. Truth was, he was someone who couldn't walk away from broken things without trying to fix them.

Luck had been on Naag's side when he had picked her out on set because of her Nepalese features and then found out that she was a single mother. Such an easy target.

The fact that she came with the horrors of her past was entirely coincidental. Without those she would never have been able to get through to Nikhil. Who would have thought a time would come when she would have to be grateful for what had happened to her?

In the kitchen, Ria Parkar was still talking to Nikhil's mother in hushed tones, and there was no way to get out of the basement without passing through the kitchen. Those two were the last people on earth she wanted to face right now. The looks they had thrown her when they'd heard she was going to be with Nikhil when he went through Jen's things still stabbed at her skin like needles.

Not that she blamed them. They had good instincts to know that she was after something. Only, contrary to what they believed, it wasn't Nikhil.

"We have to cancel, Uma Atya," Ria Parkar said. "Nikhil can't handle it. There is no way I'm having a baby shower with Nikhil in the house. You know what that baby meant to him."

"We can't not have the ceremony," Nikhil's mother's voice said after a long pause. She sounded like she was crying. "We have to do the *aarti* blessings and I have to make the cravings feast. This baby is a miracle, *beta.* We can't let her come into the world with no celebration. It's inauspicious. It's not what Jen would have wanted."

"Do you know his plans? Maybe we can wait."

"He's spoken all of two lines to me." Nikhil's mother sounded so sad, Jess's heart did that horrible squeeze again. "But I hope he's not leaving soon. I don't know what I would do if he took off again."

"Viky can talk to him and find out. If he's going back to the ship, can't we do it then? I don't want him to leave either, Uma Atya, but I can't do that to him. As it is, this feels wrong."

Uma gasped. "Don't say that. How can it be wrong that you have this gift?"

"Nikhil and Jen." Now Ria seemed to be struggling with tears. "They were the ones who should have been here. We should have planned Jen's *dohal jevan,* not mine." For a moment the resentment Jess felt toward the woman eased.

"But we can't wait. It's the ninth month."

"What are you doing?" Nikhil's voice floated up the stairs behind Jess.

She spun around and ran down the steps before he made it all the way up. "I was coming back to see how you were."

"I'm fine," he said, only one step below her, his eyes level with hers. The red-rimmed exhaustion in them made a strange restlessness churn inside her.

A normal person would be able to say something, maybe stroke his cheek, do something to soothe him. She just stood there looking in his pain-ripe eyes.

He was the one who reached up and touched her face, flipping the world on its head by soothing her. "I couldn't have done this without you. Thanks."

She took two steps up. "You thanked me already."

"I'm sorry, that was horrible of me." His lips quirked the slightest bit, but the pain in his eyes didn't budge.

She should smile back, say something to lighten the moment, to acknowledge how brave he was. She backed up another step, trying to get away from all that gratitude and courage.

The door above them flew open, and she spun around and lost her balance, fumbling for the railing as she fell backward. Her back slammed against Nikhil. His arms wrapped around her. His body kept them both from toppling over and landing on their bums. A shock of heat flushed through her, the push of his thighs registering against her bottom, the press of his forearms finding the undersides of her breasts.

Nikhil's mother and Ria Parker gaped at them as though they'd been caught holding each other naked. Behind her Nikhil started to shake, his shoulders vibrating against hers. She spun around in his arms to find him laughing. Of all things.

"You should have seen your face when the door opened," he told her. "Aie, one of these days you'll learn to knock."

She turned to Nikhil's mother's half-frowning, half-smiling face. "Are you all right?" she asked Jess and then shook her head at Nikhil. "Nikhil has this horrible habit of laughing at the most inappropriate times."

For one second, the three of them smiled at one another as if it were just another day.

"She's right," he said through the laughter that wiped him clean. "It's a horrible habit." But his arms were still around her, gentler than any touch she'd ever experienced, and she couldn't respond to his smile.

She pushed him away and he set her straight, his hands slipping off her waist carefully. Completely clinical. He didn't even seem to suspect the fire that burned where his thigh had touched hers, where her back had molded into his chest.

In a flash the heat was gone. Shame and panic doused everything that had just bubbled up inside her, and it left the feel of other hands in its wake.

Hands that tore at her. No. Don't fall into that darkness. Not now. She tried to step away, but was trapped between Nikhil's body and his mother's. Don't start shaking. Don't dare start shaking.

Nikhil's mother stepped back quickly. "I'm sorry, I didn't mean to startle you, *beta*."

The gentleness in her voice made Jess want to start shaking even more. "No. Please, it's not your fault. I just lost my balance."

She knew Nikhil was watching her, but she couldn't look at him. The stairway was too narrow, and the walls started to close around her. She would not faint. God, please don't let her faint.

"Aie, let's go up. You two look pretty scary glowering down at us like that. It's a good thing I was standing right here, because she could have hurt herself if she'd fallen." All the levity was gone from him now.

"Nikhil, please. I'm fine."

Ria pushed through the door and Nikhil's mother followed her into the kitchen. "I was just going to bring down some coffee. Unless, Jess, you prefer chai?" she said, the bright kitchen lighting her up from behind.

Jess was about to say no when Nikhil walked past her. "She prefers chai. But she doesn't like ginger in hers. I'll just make her a cup." He picked up a stainless-steel kettle and held it under the faucet.

"You don't like ginger in your chai? What kind of person doesn't like ginger in their chai?" his mother asked, placing the softest hand on her shoulder, that touch taking away all the panic from before.

"Don't let her scare you," Nikhil said, when the kettle was on the stove. "Admonishing you is how she shows affection."

Ria Parkar and Nikhil exchanged commiserating glances as Ria arranged some biscuits on a plate. "Nikhil, I think you should sit down, because guess what Uma Atya made?"

Nikhil stuck his nose up and sniffed the air like a dog. His hand reached for the lid on a pot sitting on the countertop.

His mother smacked his hand. "It's not a guess if you look!"

"Oh, you think I can't smell your carrot *halwa* now?" He lifted the lid off the pot, stuck a finger into the bright orange dessert, and popped a fingerful into his mouth. His eyes fluttered shut. "Wow, Aie!" He was about to stick those fingers, which had just come out of his mouth, back in when Ria Parkar shook a spoon in his face and jabbed it into the *halwa*. The woman did have some redeeming qualities after all.

He used it to scoop a heaped spoonful of it into his mouth.

Before he could dunk his spoon back in the *halwa*, Ria slid a plate at him and used a different spoon to serve him some. A smile played around Nikhil's mouth.

His mother put some on another plate and handed it to Jess. "How about you at least offer it to your friend first? I would ask where your manners are, but you just stuck your fingers in a serving bowl." She patted Jess's cheek. "Eat, *beta*. Do you like sweets?"

She had loved sweets as a child. Hungered for them even, but she'd rarely had any. Now she just felt strange eating them.

Nikhil held her gaze. "Seriously, I think wars might be fought if someone discovered Aie's carrot *halwa*." He pointed to her plate with his spoon and put another spoonful in his mouth.

She followed his unspoken advice and tried some.

Holy. Lord. Above!

Nikhil threw her a smug grin. Ria grabbed a spoon and dug into Nikhil's plate. Nikhil's *aie* sank into a chair with a satisfied smile.

For a few moments they just ate. There could be nothing else when there was this, this crazy assault of sweet, buttery flavor on your tongue. No wonder Jen had loved it so much.

Everyone around her froze.

Please, God, don't let her have spoken that out loud.

"How did you know Je—did you know her well?" Ria's voice was strained, and her eyes darted to Nikhil, who had stopped eating. "Did you work with her?"

"Jess has Jen's—" Nikhil's flat words never had the chance to make it out of his mouth.

She cut him off. "Yes, I knew her well. It was for a very short time, but I did know her well." She looked at Nikhil, silently pleading with him to not tell them about the heart. They absolutely could not find out.

"Did you work at the clinic with her?" Ria said, studying her. "Actually, you look familiar. Have we met?"

Fantastic. Perfect timing for the star's memory to kick in.

Nikhil raised an eyebrow at her, every trace of laughter gone from his eyes. His quicksilver mood swinging all the way back to the darkest dark. Fortunately, he held his silence, taking his time to chew the dessert he suddenly didn't seem to want anymore. It was clear he wasn't going to say anything about the heart. But he wasn't about to help her either.

It was a good thing she had enough practice doing just fine without help. "I never had a chance to meet any of you because we knew each other for too short a time."

"Really? Jen usually took so long to make friends," Ria said, still watching her like a hawk.

"It surprised me too. It was really unusual how we connected."

Nikhil narrowed his eyes at her. It was the slightest move, but of course his cousin caught it. Weren't pregnant women supposed to get all fuzzy in the head? This one was as sharp as a crow's beak.

She used it to peck some more. "How did you meet Nikhil? Did Jen introduce the two of you?" Well, at least she was no longer having trouble saying Jen's name in Nikhil's presence.

"You're full of questions today, Ria." So he did decide to help her out after all. "Jess found me on the cruise ship." Or to throw her under a speeding cruise ship.

"Found you? She just happened to be on the same cruise ship as you?"

Nikhil didn't look like he was going to answer, so she did. "Actually, I went there looking for him. I wanted to make sure he was okay. It's what Jen wanted."

"Jen asked *you* to take care of him?" Ria's eyes went all wide with hurt, but the way she said the word *you*, as though no one in their right mind could possibly put someone like her above The Ice Princess, made it impossible for Jess to conjure up any sympathy for the star.

So she wasn't born with a silver spoon in her perfectly etched mouth, but she was the one who had dragged Nikhil off the ship. *He's been on that cruise ship for two years. I didn't see anyone else board-*

ing the ship to bring him home. She wanted to say the words so badly she had to clench her jaw to keep from saying them.

Nikhil's suddenly furious gaze was filled with warning.

Not that she needed the warning. She couldn't go up against Princess Ria and win. She knew that.

"I'd still be on the cruise ship if Jess hadn't shown up," he said, jabbing the carrot *halwa* with his spoon.

"You asked us not to come," Ria Parkar said, throwing another loaded glare at Jess. But when she looked at Nikhil her eyes were sad again.

He pushed away the bowl of *halwa*. "So I did," he said in a tone so sad, there was no way to respond to it. And just like that they were back to where they had started.

26

What happens if one of us dies? It's possible. Look how we live. I wonder which one of us would handle it better. Actually, I don't. Nic would be a disaster.

—Dr. Jen Joshi

She slipped out of the kitchen and headed for the stairs, leaving the family to the sadness she had no place in. It marked her indelibly as the outsider she was.

But she couldn't go back to that room that was every little boy's dream and which reminded her too much of her little boy and the fact that she had failed to protect him. She let herself out the front door. Almost all the snow was gone, leaving behind endless wetness. Instead of the sharp bite of cold, there was a gentle chill in the air that smelled like winter but felt like spring, and it brought back a million memories from her childhood.

The scrape of wool against chapped skin, the slap of icy wind on her cheeks. It had been a million years since she'd felt anything but the Mumbai heat, sticky as a blanket of steam that wrapped around you and didn't ease up for anything. This cold scraped at her and soothed her all at once.

She spread out her arms and embraced it, wanting to spin and spin in it until time turned back. She wanted to scream at the sky. Wanted to go back in there and shout into Nikhil's face, into his smug cousin's face. Wanted to tell them to just stop it and hold each other. To be the family they were. But she couldn't remember the last time she'd let anything inside her loose or said what she wanted to say.

There was this tree at the edge of the river in her village that she had loved jumping off. What she loved most about it was that moment when she threw herself into the air. She would squeeze her eyes shut and imagine that the river had suddenly dried up. That false moment of terror had sent a heady flare of adrenaline through her. But that deep knowing that the water would be there to keep her from breaking her bones was what she had really loved most. That welcome slap of water so dependable it reinforced her own existence. She no longer knew what that felt like.

The carpet of grass beneath her feet was waterlogged. It sloshed around her ankles, making her glad that she had left her shoes in the house. She had walked through snow in handmade shoes as a child. Her feet ate up the wet cold, hungrily consuming the sense memories as she put distance between herself and new memories she knew she shouldn't be making.

No matter how much she hid from it, her mind kept reaching for how necessary Nikhil had made her feel in that basement. The warmth of his arms around her sat heavy on her skin. She rubbed her arms to erase it, to embrace it. But it had felt so good. He had felt so good. His trust had felt so good. Then there was that other feeling. The one that had made her belly clench as his body pressed against hers and his arms wrapped around her to keep her from falling.

She waited for the panic to follow, for her memories to rip away the warm, safe haven of that fleeting feeling.

There was no panic.

Knowing it was Nikhil took away the panic.

That's what made him dangerous. She didn't want these feelings. Not knowing was so much better than being handed this list of everything your life was missing.

One: This is how it feels to have someone make you tea without even thinking about it.

Two: This is what it's like to have someone leave food out for you, even if you're an afterthought.

It made you start wondering what it would be like to feel those things for real, for life.

A pang of longing for her mother sliced through her. She spun around and looked at the huge house. Big enough for ten families, and her aama had died in a seven-foot-by-seven-foot room with a crumbling cement floor and peeling walls, the lime dust from the whitewash hurrying up the degeneration of her malignant lungs.

She wanted to pick up a rock and hurl it at the house. Its solid serenity against the bright sky an abomination of the memory of the house that had chewed up her mother and then spit her out like the red *katha*-stained tobacco her uncle had loved to squirt into walls after it had served its purpose. Its warm coziness an abomination of the house that had raped her childhood out of her.

If you let me touch those, I'll give you my wife's old wool coat. The shopkeeper who owned the shanty grocer's shop at the end of her lane had begun eying her chest long before her breasts had started to bud. He'd repeated some form of that offer every time she passed by shivering in the cold. His eyes doing the job when there were other customers present and his mouth couldn't.

The memory of him stroking his thing through his pants every time her aunt sent her to pick up eggs and bread still made her sick to her stomach. Even as far back as eight years old, she remembered it tenting his pants as he tried to stroke her hand while slipping her the bags. She had learned to stop crying before she got home. The only thing more shameful than ignored tears was exposing your sick mother to more pain.

When she turned fourteen and her breasts became impossible to squish into the cotton inners her mother sewed for her, he had become more and more insistent. Until one day he'd come around the display of orange candies and biscuits and tried to push her into the corrugated iron sheets that held up the rusted roof of his shanty store.

She had kneed him. With so much force, spittle had flown from his mouth as he went down. It had been stained with blood from him biting down on his own tongue. She wished he'd bitten it off and choked on it. She had wanted to go on kicking him. Instead, she'd spit on him as he lay writhing in the ditch sobbing over his smashed balls.

"If you touch me again, I'll find you and cut off your stick in your sleep," she'd hissed at him.

Back then she'd still known how to say what she felt. She'd still felt like she could fight. *We are copper,* kanchi. *We bend but they can't break us.*

She hadn't known then quite how much they could bend you. Aama had been wrong. If they bent you enough, no matter how strong your copper, you broke.

The hill rose, she crested it, and came upon the most beautiful sight. A huge tree at the edge of a river. Once she'd seen the water she heard it. She walked to the water's edge and sat down on the bank. The swollen river raged with the force of melting ice. Looking around to make sure she was alone, she rolled up her sweatpants and slipped her feet in. This was like the ice-water footbaths she needed when she danced too long, but with a live, healing current. The icy sting felt sinfully good.

All the feeling was gone from her feet when he spoke behind her.

"I'm sorry."

The sorrys were starting to fall too thick between them. She didn't even know what he was apologizing for this time. He squatted down next to her.

"Why did you leave?"

She shouldn't answer. Already she had allowed herself to get sucked into this far more than she should have. "I wasn't needed there."

The look he gave her broke her heart.

He needed her. He hated needing her.

"Why is it so hard for you, being in a room with them?" He was in the mood to push. She could tell.

She considered slipping into the water. Letting the swollen current take her away.

"Why is it so hard for you, sharing how much you're hurting with them?"

The hurt in his eyes shoved her back in time to when she'd first found him. He opened his mouth, shut it again, and sprang up.

From the periphery of her vision, she saw his feet spin around and walk away. But she refused to turn toward him.

She hadn't meant to push him away like that, but she couldn't go after him either. This is what you got when you hurt each other because you needed distraction from your own pain.

His feet reappeared next to her, bare this time.

They were long-toed and pale, the nails neatly trimmed. Something hot and helpless squeezed inside her. She was used to seeing him vulnerable. He had never bothered to hide the depth of his grief from her. But the sight of his feet, his toes tucked into the grass, ripped her heart out.

He lowered himself next to her again and put his feet in the water. Not bothering to roll up his jeans. "They're still hurting too," he said without looking at her. "And I can't add to that. I don't want them to be stuck in hell."

Like him. But he didn't say that.

He couldn't see it yet, but the two days around his family had been really good for him. It had helped the man he was behind the man he'd become to find his feet.

The strangest thought struck her.

Whatever Ria Parkar and his mother had been planning, their version of the baby shower, Ria was convinced he wouldn't be able to handle it. But it might just be exactly what he needed.

"Can I ask you something?"

"It's never a good sign when people ask you that before they ask you a question."

Despite herself, her lips pushed up on one side. "You're right. This is your warning: It's a hard question."

He didn't look away, just waited.

"How do you feel about your cousin's pregnancy?"

His pause was slight, but she couldn't tell if that was surprise or deliberate thought to find the right answer. "What do you mean, how do I feel? Ria is healthy and I'm thrilled to bits she and Vic are going to be parents."

"No, I mean the fact that she didn't tell you about it. Why are you so angry about that?"

He studied their rippling feet beneath the racing water. "I don't know. I guess I do understand why they didn't tell me. Jen's pregnancy was the last conversation we had before she died. Why are you asking me this?"

"No reason, it just seemed to create such an undercurrent between you and Ria Parkar."

"I told you Ria and I were raised like siblings, so, like all siblings, our relationship is all about undercurrents."

"So she lives here?" She tilted her chin toward the house. "With your parents? She and Vikram?"

"No, they have a home in Mumbai and in San Francisco, and they spend part of the year at each place and then travel for Vic's work." His brows drew together. "I wonder what Ria and Vic are doing here," he said absently.

Suddenly, his eyes narrowed and his focus sharpened—his patented I'm-studying-you look.

She pulled her feet out of the water and wiggled her toes to bring back the feeling in them.

"What?" he asked, not looking away from her face.

"What?"

"You know something I don't."

"That would be many, many things. Which one are you talking about?" She focused harder on her toes. She'd left them in the freezing water too long the way she always did when it felt so good.

His finger crooked under her chin and turned her face to him, his eyes sparkling with such amusement for a moment she forgot what they were talking about. "I can see it written all over your face."

Warmth kissed her cheeks and spread. "I'd better go wash my face then," she said, pulling away to smack her forehead. "That was a manner of speaking, wasn't it?" She blinked up at him.

"Very funny." He didn't smile, but he was amused, she knew it.

"Thanks," she said, needing desperately to set that amusement free, to have it tease those dimples out of his cheeks. "It's not bad for what I had to work with."

"Stop deflecting. I'm not that stupid."

"Oh, you're not stupid at all. Your mother was telling me you skipped two grades and you had perfect SET scores."

"Still deflecting. But it's SAT and, FYI, Vic had the perfect SAT score, not me. I was one point short on the ACT and three points short on the SAT."

She clucked her tongue. "How sad. Seems like the story of everyone's life around here. Keeping Up With Vikram."

Nic had the craziest urge to smile. Who would have thought the Goddess of Darkness could tease him like this. How had he ever even thought of her as that? There was no darkness in her when she was like this.

"Are you going to stop deflecting and tell me why Ria and Vic are here? And why you didn't tell me before that you knew?"

"First, how would I know why they are here? Second, even if I did, when did I ever agree to share everything with you? And you're throwing stones from a glass house."

Her usually placid eyes did that soft blaze again with that amalgam of hope and spunk and something else he didn't want to name. Suddenly, he didn't feel like smiling anymore. "I'm letting you look at the carcass of my marriage, for God's sake. What have I hidden from you?"

She wasn't smiling anymore either, but she didn't withdraw into her shell, and the relief of it was a sucker punch to his gut. "For starters, you said all the boxes were here."

He hadn't expected that, and it must've shown on his face because she looked like she wanted to scream "Aha!" at him, the way they did in old sleuth movies when they figured out who the killer was. Suddenly, he wanted to smile again.

"I was going to tell you," he said, refusing to sound sheepish.

"I'm sure you were."

She was still teasing him, but there was a razor edge to it. Her eyes challenged him to back off. Nothing soft about their interaction anymore. "You know what. You're right. There's no deal between us for sharing things."

"So that's it?" She tucked her feet under her. Not looking disappointed, not looking afraid either. This strange, pushy side of her making it impossible for him to withdraw from her. "There are more boxes, you know where they are, and all I get is that." She pointed at him with her entire hand. Palm up.

He put his hand on hers. "No." No, he couldn't give her just that.

She blushed and tried to pull her hand out of his. He tightened his fingers around her hand, it was soft and warm. "No, that's not it. I'm making that deal with you now, for 'sharing things.'"

Her blush flamed, all the playful teasing, all the inability to play, all of it melding. Whatever raged inside her, beneath that cool exterior, pushed to the surface. She closed her eyes.

He pushed their joined hands under her chin, and turned her face up to his again.

It took her a few moments, but she opened her eyes and everything was back in place. Her shields locked and loaded and in place.

"I'll go first," he said, wanting to tear those shields away again. Needing to tear them away. "Jen owned a condo in the city. Vic moved some of the boxes there."

She held her silence, but obviously she knew about the condo.

"We'll drive to the city tomorrow and look through the stuff." Amazing how he was still sitting up after saying those words. "Your turn."

She yanked her hand out of his. "We should go back inside." She stood and turned to the house.

"Why are Ria and Vic here?"

"Why don't you ask them?"

He had to smile. "Okay," he said, standing up to follow her.

She looked suspicious. Throwing her was fun.

"Okay, let's go inside now?" she asked hopefully.

He had to laugh. "No. Okay, I'm going to have to figure this out on my own. But let the record indicate that I kept my end of the bargain and you didn't."

"It's not really a bargain. You made it. I never agreed to it."

"So I tell you everything and you do what?"

"Listen without judgment?"

He laughed some more, and her eyes hitched on his laughing face before she looked away. "Okay, I'll just have to figure it out myself then." He studied her. The unexpected playfulness inside her was a rush of relief and he filled his lungs with it.

She kept her face noncommittal, or tried to, and started toward the house.

"But they are here for a reason?" he pushed, running past her and turning to keep on looking.

She gave him nothing. Just looked bored and kept walking.

Okay, so he did have to figure this out on his own. "It has to do with the pregnancy if they haven't told me what it is," he said.

She stared out at the house and looked like she was going to start humming.

"It's not her health," he went on, "because Vic wouldn't lie to me about that."

She started humming. It was quite nice actually.

"That's lovely. I had no idea you could sing."

She blushed. "Thank you." She didn't go back to humming.

"Oh." He'd heard Ria tell Aie that they wanted to cancel something. Bingo. "They're here for her baby shower, aren't they?"

She looked so surprised he laughed. "My mother did tell you how smart I was."

She narrowed her eyes at him again, but she looked so impressed it made the strangest thing happen inside him. He was pretty sure the thing was called smugness.

"I'm fine about it," he said, holding her gaze. "Look at me. I'm not breaking down. Of course Ria should have a baby shower."

Her eyes got serious. He shrugged. She had dragged him back home. If not for her, he might have missed this. Him becoming an uncle.

"Thank you," he said again and the gratitude felt good inside him.

27

Sometimes I'm amazed at the bread crumbs we scatter through life like the little trinkets the Goddess Sita had used to leave a trail so she could be found. There really should be no way to ever get away with anything. And yet, crimes go unpunished every day.

—Dr. Jen Joshi

"Bastard, you never told me what *maal* your daughter was. Totally fuckable, like." Asif rarely needed to make an effort to be a bigger *chutiya* than he was, but this bastard was definitely deserving of the effort.

Instead of losing it the man laughed. By God, was there a greater *chutiya* in the world than an Indian politician?

"You think this is funny?"

He didn't stop chuckling. "What's funny is how yellow your pants are getting right now, Asif Khan. You know you've lost. Pack up your bags and go hide in Dubai or something. Your brothers there can deal with you. We're trying to get the garbage off our streets here in this country."

Asif squeezed the *ghoda* he was holding—the real stuff, Smith & Wesson, not the local handmade garbage the rest of the gangs had come down to—and watched the bitch through the darkened windows of his car. She looked just like her *chutiya* father. She was thrusting a mike at the drunk-looking TV star, who was trying to get away from her and the rest of the mob of journalists. Apparently, he was fucking someone other than his wife. That was news, why?

The bastard was playing up his shame for the cameras like the TV-serial star he was. You had to love actors. Asif would bet both his balls that he was taking that ashamed face straight to his girlfriend (or boyfriend, if the rumors were true) to have her (or him) blow off the stress of all those mikes shoved in his face.

"As long as big-shit garbage like you is sitting in parliament, minister*saab*, small garbage like me isn't going anywhere."

"Fun as it is to chat politics with you, I have better things to do with my life. So unless you have anything more—"

"I have an order for seven kidneys going to Sharjah. Make sure your police dogs stay off it."

"Seven! Are you out of your mind? Saving your pea-sized dick with one or two was difficult enough. Even if I were still playing this game with you, I could never cover up that many. I've already told you, it's over. I'm not risking my job for you anymore. I'm finished."

Sure, and Shah Rukh Khan was Asif's bitch. "You should have thought about that before you paid me five crores to kill that doctor bitch and get your daughter her heart." It had been a sign from God, finding out that the nosy doctor bitch was a match for the minister's daughter. And he'd found that out from her own donor registry. It was hilarious, really. He had been meaning to get rid of her anyway because of all her digging around. But getting to use her to trap the home minister and blackmail him for the rest of his life could only be divine intervention. Good thing he had fed a thousand starving beggars outside the Haji Ali mosque for it.

"I did not pay you to kill anyone. You told me you knew how to get the heart. You tricked me. My daughter was dying, you bastard. You used my desperation to trap me." Oh, now the *chutiya* was breaking down?

"So, you thought what? That I went to the heavenly concubines and requested a heart for your daughter from their freezer in heaven? You knew exactly where the heart was coming from. Or was it okay to kill some undocumented refugee for it, but not some fancy, noisy doctor?" Seriously, rich people were the sewage of the earth. Even he felt like a saint compared to them. "You better make this happen or your voting public and adoring fans are going to find out exactly what kind of dog you really are on top of your precious daughter dying." And wouldn't that be poetic justice?

"Asif, are you deaf? I said it's over. I have everything I need to get you the death sentence. If I were you, I'd listen and disappear while there's still time."

Why did these guys continue to think Asif Khan was stupid? If the bastard had anything incriminating, Asif would already be inside the slammer. "Listen, *chutiye*, if I get the death sentence, I'm taking you down with me. You can be my bitch in prison while your government feeds me biryani for twenty years before they gather the balls to execute me."

"Or we could both back away from this and stay out of prison."

Asif lifted his *ghoda* and pointed it straight at the man's daughter across the street. She looked even more fuckable through the cross-hairs. "So you color some bitch's hair and send her after that doctor bitch's husband and you think I'm going to chop off my dick and hand it to you?"

That earned him a stunned pause, and he knew his boot had found the bastard's balls. He lowered the gun. No, when the time came, he had plans for the daughter. She was going to swallow his load once for each time her father had fucked with him.

"I have no idea what you're talking about." But the bastard knew exactly what he was talking about. Asif hadn't become the Bhai he was without knowing how to read these entitled *chutiyas* like those books they kept waving around and mistaking for brains.

"Seven kidneys," he said.

"Or I hand over what I have, you hand over what you have, and we walk away from this like intelligent men."

Not a bad idea. "Sure. Where's the bitch with the colored hair? In America with the doctor's husband? What do you have on her?"

The politician laughed, but Asif had watched enough of his movies to know when he was acting. "You have a very good imagination, Asif Khan, maybe you should join Bollywood. I can put in a good word."

"Is that where you found her? Is she an actress?"

"Whoever she is, she's already made sure your days of stealing lives are over."

"Now, now, minister*saab,* I know you want that to be true, so you'd better get her to hurry. Because seven kidneys are moving next month." And with that he tired of the game and hung up.

Across the street the bastard's daughter got in her fancy Mercedes-Benz. The black Pajero that had been tailing her followed faithfully. His man put the car in gear and joined the caravan. It was only a matter of time before he found the bitch the minister had sent to screw over the doctor's husband.

28

I think I'm in love.
With my boyfriend's mother.

—Dr. Jen Joshi

Maybe Jess shouldn't have agreed when Nikhil's mother asked her to join Ria Parkar and her in making sweets for the cravings feast. But Nikhil had embraced the idea of the feast with such courage, she couldn't shove him back into hell by forcing him to Jen's home in the city so soon after all that joy and lightness had emanated from him. The stronger he was, the faster they would get through the nightmare. She had been right; the baby shower preparations were exactly what he needed.

She finished wiping her hands in the powder room and hung the towel back on its shiny chrome ring. Her phone buzzed in her pocket. A text from Naag. Yet another reminder of why she was here. As if she could forget.

What if she did forget? What if they didn't find the evidence? What if they did? Was there even a way out of this?

Another text. *I met an old friend of yours from Calcutta. She doesn't remember you having a husband.*

Before she knew it, she was dialing Sweetie.

"I want you to take Joy and run away to somewhere safe."

"Hello? Babes, are you okay?"

"Just for a little while. Just until I know what to do. Your sister lives in London. It should be pretty safe there, right?"

"You know I'll do whatever it takes to keep Joy safe," he said in his most calming voice. She had heard him use it on his hothead

Armaan a million times. He'd never had to use it on her. "Just let me know what you need and I'll call Didi and arrange things."

But what if Naag found out what she was planning?

One of my men loves slapping children around.

What had she done? Why had she called Sweetie? When she knew escape wasn't possible. His men were watching Joy every day. Even if he disappeared, they still knew where to find her. Leaving Joy without a mother was only a little bit better than leaving her without Joy.

"No. Don't do anything yet. I'm sorry. I just lost my mind for a bit." She took a breath. "Just tell Joy not to be afraid."

"Your baby boy is a superhero, babes. We should all learn how not to be afraid from him."

This was true. She thanked Sweetie for reminding her and ended the call. Something told her she'd just made a huge mistake by calling Sweetie. But for those few minutes when she had imagined him disappearing with Joy to safety, the massive weight on her shoulders had eased. It had been a self-indulgent escape to act without thinking like that.

That text had shoved her off her feet. The one thing she knew for sure was that she would die, she would kill, to keep Joy from ever finding out where he came from. She deleted the text and shoved the phone into her pocket. She needed to get Nikhil to the city. But first she needed to regain control before going back into that kitchen. Because all she would find there was more self-indulgent escape standing in her way.

"She seems really nice," Vic said, taking another sip of his beer. It was all kinds of weird, and still somehow nice, to be standing in his parents' kitchen with Vic, drinking beer and watching Ria and Aie bicker over cooking. Except Jess was there with them, looking so uncomfortable he had a good mind to pull her away.

"And she's definitely easy on the eyes." Vic studied him as though they were teenagers again and he was trying to figure out if Nic had a crush on someone.

Nikhil gripped his chest and gave him a shocked look. "Since when did you think any woman was beautiful? I thought that never happened on Planet Ria."

"Don't be ridiculous—no one's as beautiful as Ria." As soon as Vic had said it he looked so guilty Nic wanted to punch him in the face.

At least Ria, Aie, and Baba were out there with their damned worry. He could almost see the reel of his life with Jen run in their heads when they talked to him.

But Vic tried to act like everything was cool, except he couldn't touch Ria, or talk about the baby he had so badly wanted. Now he studied his beer to keep from looking at his wife, lest it make Nikhil break down.

Vic was also completely wrong about Jess. She wasn't merely easy on the eyes, she was beautiful. Or maybe *beautiful* was too insipid a word for her.

There was something otherworldly about her. Especially standing under those pendant lights over the kitchen island, her hair all shiny around her luminous face, she looked like one of those watercolors his mother loved so much, translucent, ethereal, all that lightness of color and stroke essential to capture the tentative pout of her mouth, the exact crystalline caramel of her eyes. How had he missed those pinprick dimples that dipped at the corners of her mouth and made her look like she wasn't quite ready to face the world? Except there was no innocence there. Only a fractured awareness of a world that destroyed innocence.

She turned and looked at him, possibly sensing his study. Red collected in the high curve of her cheeks as though an invisible artist brushed it across her face as he watched. Her eyes, however, remained as controlled as ever. What would it take for those eyes to flood with emotion, with joy, with anger, with anything at all that didn't flash by in a second?

Her chin went up and he realized he was frowning at her.

"You have a child?" Aie said, giving Jess a rare look of open-mouthed incomprehension.

Ria's hands stilled on the dough she was shaping into balls. She turned to Jess as though seeing her for the first time.

He knew Jess was eager to head to Jen's condo, but she had said yes when Aie had asked if she wanted to help her make *karanjis.* It was his favorite food on earth, and now he loved it even more, because, well, because there was that coward thing.

Apparently, along with teaching Ria and Jess how to make *karanjis,* Aie was carrying out a stealth information-gathering mission on the side.

"Yes," Jess said, and smiled at Aie, her eagerness to please naked on her face. The pinprick dimples that dug into her cheeks at the two edges of her mouth danced in and out of sight.

Aie's eyes warmed. "But you look like a child yourself."

"I was eighteen when I had him."

That information was met with silence. But it didn't disturb her. As usual, talking about Joy seemed to make her ready to take on the world.

"And his dad?"

"Aie!" he said, glaring at his mother. "Please!"

Naturally, Jess looked calm as ever. But all the warmth was gone from her eyes.

"No, that's okay. Really." She gave him a small smile and turned back to the dough she was rolling into small round sheets the way Aie had just shown her. "I don't have a husband," she said in a voice as serene as her face. "He died before Joy was born."

Shock and guilt cartwheeled across Aie's face.

Ria placed a hand on Jess's shoulder; she looked shaken, all her usual self-possession gone. "Was it hard?" she asked. "Having him by yourself?"

Jess examined the dough circle in front of her, but it was the question she was studying with care.

"Not at all," she said, finally looking up at Ria. "Joy made it easy. Actually, he made it possible for me to go on. The last thing I ever expected to be was a mother. The last thing I ever imagined knowing how to do was raise a child. Especially when I didn't have a single thing to give him. But he needed nothing but me. And I . . . I had everything I needed when I had him." Suddenly, she looked embarrassed, her signature look that said she had given away too much.

Ria looked like someone had kicked her. Her hand was wrapped around her belly and she wouldn't meet anyone's eyes. Vic went to her and rubbed her shoulders and she leaned into him, both of them forgetting that Nikhil was in the room.

Emotions bubbled up in Jess's eyes too, but she blanketed them before he could name them.

"Am I doing it right?" she asked Aie.

"Oh *beta*, you're doing it perfectly." Aie put a spoonful of sweetened coconut filling into the pastry Jess had rolled out and folded it over. "I'm so sorry. And you were just eighteen?"

"That filling looks delicious. I managed. He is a very easy baby."

"It's coconuts, jaggery, and cashew nuts, what's not to be delicious? Here." Aie held up a spoonful to Jess's mouth and Jess took a bite. "Do you at least have help back in Mumbai? Your parents?"

Jess's eyes fluttered shut as though flavors were exploding in her mouth. No surprise there: Aie's *karanjis* were the most delicious things in the world. Pleasure warred against the pain Aie was unintentionally inflicting.

"This is amazing. No, my parents passed away when I was younger. I'm an orphan," she said through a mouthful.

"Not too sweet?" Aie asked.

Jess shook her head fervently. "It's not too anything." The sincerity in her eyes made it hard for him to breathe.

"The trick with desserts is the sweetness. They can't be too sweet. That kills it, and then if they aren't sweet enough, that's even worse. My Nic was very easy too. He's always been an easy boy."

"Did you just tell her I'm easy, Aie? Really?"

Jess would never get used to listening to that smile in Nikhil's voice. The one that said he was sharing an inside joke and he had no doubt you found it just as funny as he did. The sound of that smile made both Ria Parkar's and his *aie*'s faces light up.

She would also never get used to him standing this close to her. He reached over her shoulder and stuck a finger in the filling.

"Nikhil!" This from Ria Parkar, who thrust her ever-ready spoon into his hand and actually smiled at Jess. Not her usual frosty smile, but an open and kind one. The type of smile Jess had seen her smile at her family but never at her.

Nikhil's mother picked up the pastry she'd just folded into a neat little *D* shape and trimmed its edge with a serrated cutter. "Ta da!" she said, holding it up, "our *karanji* is ready to be fried!"

Jess and Ria followed her lead, rolling out and stuffing the dough, and soon the large steel tray was lined with concentric half-moons ready to be fried. Jess had loved working in the kitchen with Aama. Loved all the little tricks Aama loved to teach her as they went along, like adding a pinch of sugar to anything spicy to pull out the flavor. Having Aama share the kitchen with her had made her feel all grown up, like a sister, an equal, an accomplice.

"You're a natural." Nikhil's *aie* threw an appreciative glance at her handiwork, and it pleased her far too much. "Jen hated to cook. But she did love *karanjis*."

"She didn't hate to cook," Jess said, focusing so hard on getting it right that she forgot to think about what she was saying. "She was just afraid of being bad at anything."

The kitchen went silent, as if she had hit a mute button and all the sound they had been drowning out suddenly found voice. The ticking of the clock, the buzz of the lights, the hum of the refrigerator.

"I'll get the fryer ready." Nikhil shattered the silence before it turned toxic. But his movements trapped a restlessness as he poured oil into the deep fryer and turned it on.

"Uma, have you forgotten that we're seeing Dr. Stein in a half hour?" Vikram said, looking up from the huge bowl of coconut stuffing Nikhil's *aie* had set aside for him. He had cleaned it out while they stuffed the pastries. "There's no time to do the frying."

Nikhil's *aie* smacked her forehead. "How did I forget?" She put the tray down on the island. "We'll fry these after we come back."

"Mrs. Joshi, I can, I mean, if you don't mind, I can do it. It's just frying, right?" Jess said before she had thought about it. The oil was already heating, and all she wanted was to not leave everything unfinished like this.

"I'll help her, Aie," Nikhil said.

She turned to Jess. "Okay, but on one condition. Stop calling me Mrs. Joshi. I feel like I'm in a classroom. Call me Uma, or then Auntie if you're not comfortable with Uma."

Jess nodded and Nikhil's *aie* pulled her into a quick hug before leaving.

Nikhil checked the temperature on the fryer. Helping his mother fry things before dinner parties had been his favorite childhood chore. It had felt like a science experiment, just like being in a lab but without the pressure of doing well.

"I'm sorry about the inquisition," he said. Jess had looked so overwhelmed when Aie had turned the Aie Treatment on her.

She didn't respond, her mood suddenly mellow as she fidgeted with the tray of *karanjis*.

"Why didn't you tell me Joy's dad is dead?"

Her fingers clenched on the *karangi* in her hand and it split open at the edges like a hapless mouth. She opened it back up and re-folded it as if she had done this all her life. Her fingers so deft, so comfortable with handling food, in the strangest way she reminded him of his *aie*. "Is the oil hot enough?"

He checked the temperature gauge again. "Almost."

"He's not dead." She pursed her lips and gave the edges of the resurrected pastry another squeeze, making sure it was perfect again, and he knew that was all she was going to say about that.

"Why don't you want them to know about the heart?"

She didn't respond, and suddenly he was tired of tiptoeing around all the sinkholes and mines. "Jen's heart?" he pushed.

Jen's heart. There. He was thinking her name, saying it, without wanting to double over. What a hero he was.

Jess responded with cold eyes and more pursed lips. "I thought you were sorry about the inquisition."

He didn't look away. It felt like he was being tested. Does he deserve the truth or doesn't he?

"I don't want them to know." Apparently, he did deserve to be trusted after all.

"Well, obviously," he said.

"Remember how you reacted? They're never going to believe me, and then they're going to dislike me even more."

"Oh, that was dislike. What was going on in this kitchen?"

"I'm sorry. Your mother is very kind. Actually, your family is. I just need to get this done and go home, Nikhil."

She was starting to sound like a broken record. Of course she wanted to get back, and why that made a blast of panic pop in his gut he didn't know.

"What happens when we find the evidence? Do we go to the cops with it?"

"I'm not sure. But I think the police are involved."

"There's a cop, Rahul—can't remember his last name." He pulled his wallet out and dug out a plain white card. "Rahul Savant, he's been investigating this thing for two years." He put it away again. "I think we can trust him. Jen trusted him."

"I know. He's the one Jen was working with." She was measuring her words again. She had this way of stiffening up. It was the most understated thing, like something moving under a layer of sand. The tiniest reconfiguring of particles. She didn't want to talk about the cop. But his need to talk to her about things filled him, scared him, and he couldn't hold it in.

"I think he had some sort of thing for Jen," he said, throwing another piece of himself wide-open in front of her. "Did she ever say anything about him?" Until he asked he didn't even know how much the thought had bothered him. Of another man having been close to Jen in the days before her death. Of his wife putting herself and their child in danger without letting Nikhil in on their little secret.

"I . . . I don't know." She dipped one end of a *karanji* into the hot oil to test it, then pulled it out.

"But what the hell is the point if you don't know? If you don't know, we have nothing." He slammed a fist into the countertop. Jess jumped, and the pastry slipped from her hand and splashed into the fryer. Hot oil splattered up like a fountain. She stumbled back, one outstretched arm pushing him out of the way, her body taking the drops of oil headed his way.

"Shit! Jess!" He grabbed her arm and dragged her to the sink and turned on the faucet, his heart hammering in his chest. He yanked up her sleeve and jabbed her arm under the water. A sprinkling of red splotches dotted her hand. "Where else?" He studied her face, her body. Dark spots stained her sweatshirt.

He scooped ice out of the freezer. "Where else?" he was shouting. "Did you get any on your body? He grabbed her sweatshirt where the spots darkened it and tried to pull it off her.

She stayed his hands. "Nikhil, stop it. I'm fine."

No you aren't. He wanted to yell it. Instead, he took her hand and started rubbing ice on the angry red skin, his hands shaking. He'd hurt her.

He rubbed until the ice was gone. The heat of his anger at himself melting it against her reddened skin. Water dripped into streams from their joint hands and trickled onto their bare toes until it was just his thumb stroking over the translucent skin, tracing the damage he had done.

Her skin was soft, indescribably fine. All of her was so very delicate. He raised his gaze. A mistake. She was watching him. Her wide eyes dry, her lush pink lips moist from having been bitten. Her nose pink from tears she seemed incapable of ever letting out.

His hand lifted to that blush that had a way of streaking across her cheeks and bringing them to life, bringing her to life. He tried to stop himself, but he couldn't. Her lips were impossible not to touch. He traced them. His ears ringing. His body so close to hers.

Breath fanned out of her. Her lips opened an *O* in the center of the plump, soft pink. Those pinprick dimples dipped into her cheeks on either side of her mouth. His mouth opened. Hunger to taste the innocence of those pinpricks rammed hard into the numbness inside him.

He pulled away. The loss of her touch leaving him cold. The guilt of how good it had felt leaving him breathless.

It had felt so good. To have her in his arms. To have someone in his arms again. Just someone, not her, just someone.

"I'm sorry," he said, his voice too loud in her silence.

When Nikhil pulled away from her, she felt so bereft she knew she was in trouble.

"I'm really fine, Nikhil. The sweatshirt took most of it." She wasn't lying; she had barely felt the three dots of oil. Which was more than she could say about what being touched by him had done.

She, who felt safe with no one, wanted to crawl into his arms again, disappear into his wide, hollow shoulders. For all his emaciated body, the spirit of him was huge and protective, and it had enveloped her so completely that for a few moments she had forgotten to draw breath.

And he wasn't even trying. Not only was he not trying, he was trying hard not to be the person he so obviously was. What would become of her if he found himself again?

What would happen if he stopped fighting that thing that had flared between them like a wickless flame, borne from nothing, yet sustained on something?

She had tried not to face it, to not name it. But what she was feeling for Nikhil—what her body was feeling—was not its usual nothingness.

He opened and shut a few drawers and held up a tube of something, his eyes still dark with concern, bright with wanting. "It'll blister if you don't put something on it."

He held out his hand, but she couldn't let him touch her again. Her entire life, the proximity of any man had brought with it either abject terror or absolute disgust or some combination of both. That sickened feeling was actually her body's default reaction to almost any sort of awareness of itself. Except when she danced. When she was dancing, she ceased being herself. She became her dance. When you were movement and rhythm and music, nothing bad registered on your whirlwind of a body.

When Nikhil touched her, it was like she was dancing. Her body moved and melted and felt different. She felt different. She felt.

"Let me," he said. His gaze touched the patch of skin still cold from the ice he'd rubbed into it, and the strangest vacuum flared in her belly, hungry for something, raw with hope, dizzy with a feeling of safety.

Only it wasn't safety, it was madness. Madness that felt like hope but was a hallucination.

She took the tube from him. He was supposed to be the vulnerable one. But the danger of him being hurt by this twin heat burning in their gazes was next to nothing. "Nikhil, you promised we could go to Jen's apartment and search there." She rubbed ointment into the burns she couldn't even feel.

All the warmth left his gaze. The mention of Jen made anger rise in its place, hard and fast.

She had to fan it. "I wish we had all the time in the world for you to work through your family drama. Much as I'm enjoying stuffing pastries for your cousin's baby shower, for a baby she doesn't even want, I can't stay away from Joy any longer."

Instead of letting the anger she'd fanned blaze, his brows drew together over eyes that tried to gauge what she really wanted.

"I don't know what you're up to," he said, "but could we keep Ria out of it, please?"

She couldn't. Because she needed his anger to push him to act so she could get away from him. "Yes, let's. Let's keep Ria and Jen both out of it, because you were right, I have never been in their shoes. I . . ." She couldn't stutter, she had to do this. "I always wanted my baby."

Her words hit their mark. Shame burned inside her. She'd been looking for anger, and now here it was, hot and potent in his eyes. Still, he took a breath, giving her another second to back away, but she raised her chin, showing him no remorse, and he snapped.

"And what about Joy's dad? Did he want him too? Why is it that you keep lying about him? Why do all those hard-as-nails defenses of yours spike out every time he comes up? Do you even know who the father of your child is?"

She wrapped her arms around herself, pressed her knees together, her thighs, clenched everything to keep herself together. She had hurled rocks at him to instigate him into action. He was just reacting. She deserved this.

But, dear lord, it hurt.

As soon as he said it, all his anger evaporated again. "Jess, I'm—"

She raised her hand to cut him off, to keep him away. She was glad he had said it because it snapped her out of her delusions. It was a good reminder of how he saw her under everything, of the huge distance between them.

"I know how you see me," she said, her voice steady. "An unwed mother. A chorus dancer. A film extra." What an apt name for the profession. For her. It wasn't the first time someone had called her a whore. It wouldn't be the last. She didn't care.

He opened his mouth, but she could not do this any longer. "No. Don't insult me by denying it. Yes, you and Jen and your huge, noble hearts that bleed for the entire world. I admire it. I really do. So you can insult what I do, look down on me, I'm okay with it. The world needs people like you."

He shook his head, but she couldn't stop. "And yes, you too. You might think you will never go back to being who you were. But you can't control it. It's who you are. I can see it coming back. But me? My world is just me and Joy. It doesn't matter who his father is. What matters is that I need to go home to him. And if it means begging you to get your act together so we can end this, I'll do it."

How on earth had the conversation devolved into this? One moment heat had sparkled between their bodies, the next she was talking about him not respecting her? He reached for her, but she winced away from his touch and backed out of the kitchen, taking all the warmth in the air with her.

She stormed up the stairs with him close on her heels and slammed the door shut behind her.

He was about to shove it open. But he stilled his hand. How could she think he respected her after what he had said? All she'd done since they'd met was help him, help Jen, whom she hadn't even known. If he knew anything, he knew that she felt tied to Jen. And for whatever that connection was, she had picked him out of the dirt more times than anyone else in his life ever had. She had spent all this time away from her child for Jen, to do the thing that he should have done, so she, a complete stranger, didn't have to.

How had he let those bastards go? How had he not burned down everyone who had done that to his wife? How had he not destroyed the world to complete the work she had given her life to? How had he let his grief and anger shut him down like that?

He knocked on her door. "Jess, I'm coming in."

She didn't answer. He twisted the doorknob, giving her time before pushing it open. She stood there facing him, her arms folded across her chest, her usual "you can't touch me" mask on. She looked exactly the way he expected her to look.

"You want to grab your bag? In case we don't get through everything today, we might need to stay the night."

She raised an eyebrow at him.

"We're going to Jen's apartment. We're finishing this. So you can stop instigating me and then twisting my words."

Despite her best effort, the relief on her face was so stark his heart folded in on itself.

"And for the record, you have how I see you completely wrong."

29

Dharavi is darker than most any place I've been to.
But its spirit is brighter than all the world put together.
The lotus, they love to say here, is the purest of flowers
and it thrives best in the muddiest of ponds.

—Dr. Jen Joshi

The jagged edges of the Chicago skyline loomed in front of them as they flew down the road. Nikhil's mood had swung from gentle and purposeful all the way back to dark and stormy, but she could do nothing to protect him from what was coming.

"It's beautiful," she said quickly, as he swung onto a curving overpass and the lake came into view, shimmering silver in the late-evening light.

"Yeah. Just beautiful," he said.

Wow. Three entire words. He had been silent since she'd heaved a sigh of relief and settled into the car.

He screeched into another turn and pulled into an underground parking lot in a high-rise building, slamming some numbers into a keypad on a post as they entered.

He didn't even pause to think about the numbers he punched in. She wondered when he'd last been here. He pulled into a parking spot, bouncing to a stop inches from a concrete column with a number painted across it in red. His breath came in gusts, the only proof that his rigid body still breathed.

"Nikhil?"

He spun around so fast she started, and before she could stop it a yelp escaped her.

His face turned livid. "What, now you're afraid of me? What do you think I'm going to do? Now, right now the way I'm feeling . . . you think I'd touch you? You think I'm thinking about touching you?"

He gripped the steering wheel, his knuckles white, his anger crowding her. She slipped out of the car before she reached for him, and sucked in a concrete-laden breath. This need to comfort him had to stop. She reminded herself why they were here.

This was it. They had to find the evidence here.

There were no more places to look.

She had gone over all the things Jess had said in her head, but there was no more help to be had. She closed her eyes and tried to get a hold of her stupid thudding heart that spasmed painfully when Nikhil emerged from the car.

This wasn't the Nikhil who had cried in her arms, twice, who had asked to sleep in the bed meant for her. But this wasn't the Nikhil who had teased her by the river either, who had run a thumb across her lips. The Nikhil emerging from the car was one Nikhil dragging that other Nikhil behind him.

"I'm sorry," he said, coming up to her

She didn't mean to but she snapped at him. "Let's just get this over with, okay?" He looked ready to say something, but then he turned around and started walking.

She fell in step behind him. A glass door led to an elevator lobby. He slammed the door open and it slammed behind him. No matter what had happened between them, he had always been considerate and polite. Something no one else had ever done. Her hand shook as she started to push the door back open.

Think about Joy. Think about Jen. Think about . . .

Just as she touched it, the door flew open, the way doors between them couldn't seem to stop doing.

He held it open, not meeting her eyes, and waited for her to enter.

She walked past him.

"Jess, I said I'm sor—"

"I know." She slammed her palm into the elevator button.

"This is hard for me, okay?"

"I know." She should have stopped there, but she couldn't. "You don't think I know this is hard for you?" The urge to reach out and touch his face, to comfort him, was so strong she clutched her sleeves in her fist.

"Why are you so kind to me? Why do you take it when I'm a jerk?"

That was it. "No, Nikhil. Don't. Don't be like this. Don't be nice. You know, if every time you are nice to me you have to balance it out with being awful, why even bother?"

"I said I was sorry."

"And I said I know you are."

The elevator arrived, and she stepped in.

He followed her and pressed the number twenty-one. They watched the numbers change in silence.

He ran his fingers over the hair now covering his head in a thick jet-black stubble, the gesture so familiar she wanted to scream. At least he wasn't doing the ring-twirling thing as much nowadays. His thumb went to his ring, her eyes went to his thumb, and he pulled it back.

"What?" he said, his eyes screaming at her to not answer his question. God, they were such a mess. No. He was a mess. She was just far too tangled up in his mess. The elevator door opened, and she stalked out of it only to have her arm gripped behind her.

It was an aggressive gesture, so of course Nikhil pulled it off with the utmost gentleness.

She groaned. An electric spark zinged through her belly as she met his eyes.

"Don't be angry. Please."

"I'm not the one who's angry here, Nikhil. You are, and it's not at me." Shut up. Shut up before you say something you can't take back.

"I don't know what you're talking about," he said, staring at his hand on her arm.

She wanted to yank it back, but he looked so devastated, she placed her fingers on his and tried to peel them off her arm. "It's okay to live again, you know. It's okay to feel things again."

He let her arm go. "Really?"

She stuck out her chin. She was fed up with his innuendos and guilt trips, fed up with having to shut up. "Yes. Really."

"This from a person who hides behind the largest sweatshirts she can find? Who trembles when she sits in a car? You're the queen of moving on, aren't you? No baggage there. None at all." He dug his hands into his pockets.

"This isn't about me."

"Of course not. Nothing is ever about you. Under those loose clothes, under that damn frozen shell, how can anything be? This is about me. I'm the one who's hiding from the world. I'm the one who won't let anyone see anything about me. Won't let anyone so much as touch me without reliving whatever the heck happened to me."

"You don't know anything about me."

"You're right. I don't. Because you answer every question with deflection. God forbid, you let anyone get anywhere near you."

She spun around and faced him. "Now we're getting somewhere. At least you're admitting that you want to get near me. And you can't handle that you do."

Her words echoed in the silence across the long, brightly lit corridor, the kind of silence that follows an explosion.

Nikhil looked like she had slapped him.

She had gone too far. But she was sick of it, sick of his seesaw and what it did to her. "It doesn't matter, Nikhil. You're right. There's nothing here. Nothing that you could—"

He grabbed her, her hair, her face, whatever his fingers could reach, and slammed her body into his. Taking the rest of her words with his lips.

The shock of the contact, her startled intake of breath, the fact that she pushed into him instead of pulling away fried Nikhil's brain. Jolted his circuits as if someone had thrown a hair dryer into his bath. He yanked himself away, shaking. She swayed toward him, her lips following his, as if the thread of his kiss tied them together.

Her eyes, the innocence in them, the trust, the hot molten trust. All the other shit erased for one blessed moment. Gone. His hand went to her cheek. The soft curve of it sank into his palm, filled it, the feel of her filling him. It felt so damn good. To be able to touch someone. To be able to feel something.

She didn't move away, and it made him stupid.

This time when his lips met hers, it was in wonder and greed and hunger. He plucked at her lower lip, fitted his lips around the lush, erotic curve. Endless softness, honey sweetness. He suckled her, tasted her soft, wet response. She melted into him. Her mouth, the skin under his hand, all of it melted and coated him, cool salve on his burning, torn-up self. Without even touching him, she wrapped him up.

He dragged his lips across hers, tasting the edge of her mouth where a pinprick dimple sank into her cheek. He pressed his cheek into hers, soaking her up. Taking all he could.

Her cheeks were wet.

He pulled away.

There was so much pain in her eyes, he knew he had gone too far. He should never have touched her. Not when his heart was supposed to belong to someone else. Did belong to someone else.

She shrank back against the door he'd pushed her up against.

"Did I hurt you?"

She shook her head, leaning forward as though she meant to lay her forehead on his shoulder, but then she pulled away as though she'd given too much away again.

"Then why are you crying?"

She reached up and touched his cheek, and held up her fingers. They were his tears, not hers.

He took several steps back, but he couldn't go too far.

Silence stretched and wrapped around them and he had to break it. "You're right," he said, and she looked like he had kicked her. "I can't handle it. Whatever this is between us."

She collected herself. Of course she did. Rolled back into that pristine ball. Only, it didn't look easy anymore. This time he saw what it took each time she gathered herself up like that. He hated it. Hated seeing all that she struggled to hide. Hated how easy it was with her. To see. To show. To forget.

He stepped into the home he had shared with his wife.

He never wanted to forget. Never could forget.

* * *

Jess followed Nikhil into the apartment. It was another snapshot straight out of a Karan Johar film. Even with white sheets covering the furniture it was rich, luxurious, and warm. With high ceilings, exposed brick walls, massive vibrant paintings, and cozily arranged furniture. The kitchen and living room were all one space, separated by a glass-and-concrete breakfast bar. A vision of Jen and Nikhil sitting on those leather bar stools and sharing a married moment splashed across her mind like ice water someone had tossed at her while she was still burning from his touch.

She wanted this over. Please, could this just be over?

Each step Nikhil took looked labored, as though the polished wood floors had suddenly turned into an endless desert under a brutal sun. All sense of self-preservation told her to get as far away from him as she could. He stopped, and she stepped closer. The desire to be needed by him beat like a live thing in her chest.

Her fingers itched to touch her lips, where his lips had touched her. She'd felt the touch everywhere, still felt it. What had that even been? How was she still standing after that?

She waited for the horrible memory of other lips to erase his. But her mind wouldn't allow it. Not yet. One of the posters in Joy's school said TOUCH HEALS. The quote had always annoyed her. One of those lies meant only for posters with pretty pictures. Now she would give anything for one more swab of his touch against her raw self.

How had she allowed this to happen?

He reached for her, his fingers wrapping around her arm. Sensation sparkled up and down her skin. But all he sought was balance, a little grounding, refuge from all the memories that had to be attacking him like locusts. Her shoulders squared. Her spine straightened. A wave of insane protectiveness surged through her, and she pressed closer to him.

They stopped in the doorway of a room filled with boxes. "Vic said all the boxes are in the guest room," he said, so close to her his breath blew her hair. "This is it."

They stood there for an age. She didn't remember moving, didn't remember walking to the boxes or watching Nikhil rip them open.

But the next thing she knew, it was pitch-dark outside and they were sitting amid a carnage of cardboard and packaging in a pool of lamplight, Nikhil's face expressionless.

The boxes were filled mostly with medical textbooks and files. There was one box filled with CDs. They would have to go through each and every one of those CDs. Each and every one of those files.

"Tell me about Joy," Nikhil said next to her. "Tell me how it felt to have him."

She turned to him, wanting again to touch his face, to smooth away the grief. Instead, she gave him what he wanted: her words. "From the moment I knew he was inside me, I had this fullness. As if I was tight with purpose. As if my skin enclosed hope. You know that feeling you have where you wonder why you're here? On this earth? What the point of all this is? Where everything seems like just particles dancing around you, meaningless and purposeless. When Joy was inside me, it all fell into place. It made sense. I made sense. Do you know what I mean?"

He kissed her then. Again. A ragged, soft kiss on a sob.

Just like this, she thought.

He pulled away. "I really should stop doing that. I don't know what's wrong with me. I'm sorry."

He looked so tortured, she had to say it. "I don't think Jen would have wanted you to be miserable, Nikhil."

"If she didn't want me to be miserable, she shouldn't have left me."

"She didn't choose to leave you."

"She chose to go to that godforsaken place. To get involved in something that was dangerous. She chose that, when she had me. When she had our baby."

"You chose that too. You chose to go to those godforsaken places. You put yourself in danger too. You have people who love you, people who would never survive your loss in one piece either." But he wasn't listening to her, his eyes were glazed over with the pain of his memories.

"Once she got pregnant, how did that not change her mind? Why didn't she want to protect our baby?"

"Of course she wanted to protect the baby. Don't you think she was careful?"

"Careful?" Anger sparkled in his eyes again. And indignation. As if he knew something she didn't. As if she didn't understand. "Jen knew what monsters these people were. She knew what they were capable of. Then why? Why? You don't know what they did. You didn't see it. I, I couldn't even . . . How could she?"

"I don't believe you." She shoved away from him. Anger crashed through her, building tenfold from the anger she saw in his eyes. Anger so huge it made her arms and legs unsteady as she pushed off the floor, killing all the warmth inside her. "You think this happened to Jen because she wasn't careful? You think what those monsters did to her was her fault?" She backed away from him. His nearness, so soothing a moment ago, fanned her into an inferno.

Maybe she was shouting, but she couldn't tell. "What could she have done differently, Nikhil? What? Stayed home? Stayed in places where you could have taken care of her, where you could have done with her as you pleased?" Sold her, starved her, told her who could and could not touch her.

She spun around, shaking so hard she could barely manage it. She couldn't stand to be in the same room with him. Her skin felt too tight around her. Her scar felt like it would split at the seams, unable to contain the rage inside her. In all they'd done to her, she'd never questioned the colossal injustice of it. Of walking down the streets of her town and needing to wrap herself in her own arms, behind books, under layers and layers of clothes. She had done every single thing she could. Always.

And she had never, not for one moment, thought it was her fault.

She'd never for one moment not known it was them. The bastards who had taken everything. Her uncle who had taken her home by never giving her one. The man who'd bought her and taken her childhood. Those monsters who had taken her body. She'd never blamed herself. She'd felt only anger. ANGER. Such intense anger it had seared the wounds shut. Cauterized them.

But to hear Nikhil blame Jen for what those bastards did to her, to watch him be what she told herself every day all men couldn't possibly be, someone who shoved all responsibility on women because he could, someone who stood apart and took comfort in not bothering to understand—it made the anger unbearable. Because there was Joy. And he would never be this. Because how could she stand it if he were?

"You okay?" Nikhil said behind her.

She was standing at the kitchen counter. The hard concrete clutched in her fingers. She hadn't noticed herself move. That level of anger was unacceptable. It took away her awareness, her control. She tried to loosen her grip but couldn't.

"I didn't mean it was her fault," he said behind her.

Actually, that's exactly what he had meant.

It was easy to blame Jen. So he did. It wasn't just him. The rest of the world did it too. All the time. Blame those who had been hurt. So they could live in the world that didn't know how to stop those who did heinous things. In a world that let them get away with it.

You should have protected yourself better, the bastard's secretary had said to her when he paid her off and cleaned up his boss's mess. *I'm telling you this for your own good. Be careful, it's a brutal world out there for a woman who's by herself.*

Yes. She'd needed the bastard to tell her that. With her body as torn up as her mind, her womanhood bleeding into the endless supply of sanitary pads she slapped on. Yes, she needed the bastard to tell her to take responsibility for being a woman. For existing with breasts and something they could plunder between her legs.

But for Nikhil to be one of them. It made him common, kicked the pedestal from under him. And that made her want to break something.

"I want you to say what you're thinking."

She laughed. Yes. She should tell him what she was thinking.

Nikhil spun her around. "Tell me what you're thinking. Please."

She yanked her arm away, not wanting to be touched by him. Wanting to burn him with the fire that flared inside her. "I was thinking how you were so right. Of course it was Jen's fault that she wanted to help people who were most in need of her medicine. I mean, a doctor who wanted to serve people who had no one else. A doctor who wanted to stop someone from stealing organs and killing people. What was she thinking? And her walking home from dinner with her husband. How dare she! What those bastards did to her, how didn't she think that was going to happen?"

"I didn't mean it was her fault like that."

"Yes, you did." She shoved him away and walked to the wall of windows.

He followed her, looking distraught, horrified at what he'd said, what he'd believed, but she didn't care anymore.

She turned on him. "Look at you. You're angry with her for leaving. Angry. You're angry, Nikhil. So much so, that you don't even want to catch those bastards. You don't care who's really at fault. Because this is easier. Blaming someone who has no voice is easier. And it makes you as much of a bastard as them. Jen was wrong when she said you were the strongest man she knew. She was wrong when she said no one was more fair. She was wrong to believe—"

"Stop it. Don't tell me what Jen thought. Don't fucking act like you know what was between us. Angry at her? At her? You have no idea what they did to her. Just because she talks to you, you think you know what she went through? You weren't there. I was there. You have no idea what it was like."

"Which part?" The question was so soft. Nikhil wasn't even sure he had heard it. But he knew it was going to change his life.

She was pressed into the windows behind her, her sweatshirt a blot of black against the black outside. The anger inside her, inside them, raged around the dead apartment, like fire charring what was already burned.

He slammed his hand into his hair, surprised to find it scraping his palm. Her eyes, they were in flames. Something horrible moved inside him. He tried to turn away from her, but her voice trapped him in place, slid a plastic bag around his head and cut off his breath.

"Which part do you believe I don't understand?"

Why had he started this? Why couldn't he look away from her eyes? Those eyes. He wanted her to stop, wanted to take back ever wanting to know. But those eyes were so filled with the need to have someone not turn away, to have someone see and not turn away, he couldn't turn away from them.

"Which part, Nikhil?" One sharp, blinding explosion of pain popped in her eyes before the words slipped past barely moving lips. "I was raped."

The ground slipped from under him.

"By two men."

An incoherent sound escaped his lips. But she didn't seem to hear it.

"You know how you accused me of not knowing who Joy's father is? You were right. I don't know. It could be either one of them." Her voice dipped then. Falling from sound to pure pain. "Except he looks exactly like one of them."

"Jess."

She didn't register his voice, and he knew she was somewhere else. Not here with him.

"But you're right. That's the only thing Jen and I had in common."

"Jess. Please." He knew not to touch her. Not to move closer.

"I was seventeen. And no one cared what happened to me. No one crumbled to pieces on my behalf. Oh, and there was one more thing we had in common. We both didn't expect to get pregnant. I didn't even know I was pregnant until six months into the pregnancy. I didn't even know such a thing could result in a baby. How could it?" She looked at him with those seventeen-year-old eyes that had frozen in time, pain fossilized inside amber.

She laughed, a spit bubble forming at the center of her barely parted lips. "Until the moment I found out, I relived it every day. But when I saw my baby on the ultrasound machine, everything changed. Joy, from that instant that I knew he was inside me, took everything away. Everything. The only thing I knew was that he was mine. Mine. I had never expected to live again. But he gave me life. I was never exposing him to my horrors. So they stopped."

Not for the first time, he wanted to go down on his knees in front of her.

Seventeen years old.

How fragile, how delicate, how easily breakable she seemed now. He had seen her slight body under those huge sweatshirts she wore.

Seventeen.

His heart hurt so bad he wanted to hold her, erase what warred inside her, wipe at it until it was gone.

Seventeen.

What kind of monsters walked the earth? He couldn't bring himself to call them animals. Because animals never took what wasn't theirs. Never took something only because it was vulnerable, never destroyed what was beautiful simply because they could.

"Can I touch you?" The words made her blink. As though he'd shaken her.

She didn't move. Didn't move away, so he reached out and his hand hovered over her cheeks, over the rivers that slid down that infinitely delicate skin.

She squeezed her eyes shut and moved into his touch. All of her moved. All of him, the world around them, everything moved until she was in his arms. Their touching so tentative there had to be another word for it. What did you call holding a baby shed from the womb so early she had no hope? And yet she breathed, and you, all you could do was hold her so her skin and all those half-formed organs that caused her to be alive just barely held together. You had to become her shell, grow around her, be her cocoon. Because she had to live. No matter what. She had to live.

Once she had shifted into him, into his hold, letting her go was unthinkable. She was deep inside herself, barely aware of him, inside her pain because she trusted him to keep her safe while she was gone.

Tears streamed from her closed eyes and wet him. Drenched him. Unformed him and then formed him again. Silent sobs vibrated from her and through him. For hours, for eons, she wept in his arms. And all he could do was give her sorrow a place to fall.

Finally, when he scooped her up, she barely moved. Didn't press into him. Didn't pull away. The nothingness of her actions told him what to do. When he took her with him to the guest bedroom, he might have floated there. He didn't know. All he knew was he couldn't do anything other than what he was doing.

He couldn't not lay down with her, couldn't not tuck her against him, couldn't not wrap his body around hers and close his eyes against her hair. And hold her and hold her. Until she drifted away in his arms. Fell out of her pain and into sleep. It was then that he let himself drift away too. His sleep wrapped around hers. Their joint collapse into a nothingness so absolute the morning light had to be rebirth.

30

When I was too young to know better, I dreamed of a white knight. Someone who'd rescue me, protect me, keep me from harm. By the time I found him, all I wanted was for him to know I didn't need protecting.

—Dr. Jen Joshi

She thought the prickly jacket of thorns she wore would keep out the predators.

Ignore them. That's what Aama had always told her.

She did.

When her aunt left all the dishes for her to clean in the washing area in the backyard, and she squatted over the pile and scrubbed and scrubbed in the freezing cold, she ignored that her cousins sat huddled around the fire pit in the kitchen sipping hot milk.

When her mother coughed up blood and smiled at her through her gasps for breath, and her aunt and uncle went about their business as if she were already dead, she ignored them. When the schoolteacher stood too close, and the smoke on his breath made her gag, she ignored him. When that shanty-store owner pushed her up against the side of his shop and tried to shove his fat fingers into her panties, she ignored him. Well, she kicked him in the nuts first, then she ignored him.

But the film set was harder. Everyone seemed to think it was okay to stare at her as if she had no clothes on. Everyone from the fifteen-year-old spot boy to the sixty-five-year-old cameraman leered at all the girls as if they were naked. The rest of the girls didn't seem to mind. But it made her skin crawl and her stomach turn.

She wrapped herself in her *dupatta* and hugged her schoolbooks to her breasts, which just would not stop growing. Her *kurta* was several sizes too large. At least three of her could fit in it with ease. And yet, even when she got out of her dancer's clothes, they watched her as if she were still in them, her belly exposed, her chest spilling out of the obscenely low-cut *choli*.

She had asked them for a larger size, but they'd told her if she wanted a larger one, she could find it on a different film set. And roles for untrained chorus dancers didn't exactly grow on trees, so she put it on and ignored what it didn't cover.

She ignored the looks and the licked lips. But their eyes always knew exactly how to find every inch of skin that her *dupatta* would not cover, no matter how tightly she wrapped it around herself.

She thought about leaving the film. But if she left a film halfway, there would be no more Junior Artist roles, and Sister Mary had pulled a lot of strings to get her this job. And dancing was better than scrubbing utensils in someone's house. At least on set she could study between shots and there were a lot of people here and she wasn't locked up in someone's house all by herself and at their mercy.

But ignoring Rajsir's shamelessly lusty eyes was becoming harder and harder. He was the star of the film. Calcutta's brightest rising star. With his large, brooding eyes and the silky flick of hair falling over one eye, the public was desperately in love with him. Several of the girls on set were too. He had no problem pulling them into his trailer. No one ever talked about it after, which for some reason had scared her more than anything.

For two weeks she had done everything she could to avoid his lecherous gaze. But then they'd moved her to the front of the formation, and she found herself dancing with him, a step where he got to run his hand up and down her waist. When he took fifteen takes to get the shot right, she knew without a doubt that she had to quit the film. Even if it meant finding another way to keep herself fed and in school.

But those fifteen takes, those three hours when he got to touch her as if she were his to touch, changed her life. Destroyed every chance she had at ever being safe again. By the end of those hours, he was panting in her face, his lust glinting like madness in his eyes.

She knew she had to run. Get off the set as soon as she could.

She ran to the bathroom, needing somewhere safe, panic beating in her chest like a drum.

He followed her into the bathroom. She was the only one there, but he didn't even check before backing her against a wall. "I'll make you a heroine," he said. "With those eyes, that body, all of Calcutta will be hard for you. The way I am."

"Please leave me alone." She tried to slip past him. But he moved to block her in. Her heart thundered in her ears. She had to keep her head.

Don't look scared. Don't look angry. Don't show any emotion. It will only excite him.

"Oh, look at the princess's style," he said. "So cool. You really know how to work it, don't you? It's working. You've driven me crazy. My madness, it's your fault." He grabbed her around the waist and thrust his mouth into hers. His breath tasted of alcohol and stale fish. His hips pushed her into the cold, sticky tiles behind her. A horrible pressure jabbed into her belly, and she gagged on the bitter bile that rose up her gullet.

She pushed him away, her hands shaking with the effort to move his bulky frame off her. But it only made him smile. "I like it when they struggle. Or haven't the girls been talking about me?"

She would not cry. Would not cry. "I'll scream." Please, please God. Why won't anyone come into the bathroom?

"I want you to scream. I want to make you scream. I want to make you scream over and over again until you can't scream anymore. I want you to lose your mind like you've made me lose mine." He ground his hips into her again. "See that. See how much I want you. All day, all week, he's been waiting to get inside you."

She started struggling. Pushing him away. Twisting. She raised her knee and kicked him between the legs. He screamed in pain. But she didn't wait to see if he had gone down. She yanked the door open and ran into the corridor. It was deserted. Oh God, where was everyone?

She kept running. The Junior Artists' changing room was empty. She locked the door behind her and pulled her costume off as fast as she could. She tugged her *salwar kurta* on and slung the costume on the hanger. She couldn't afford to pay for it if anything happened to it. Then she grabbed her school bag and ran out. It was the middle of the night. If the Junior Artist's bus was gone, she would not be able to get back to the hostel.

The bus was gone.

She looked around, the frantic beating of her heart making it hard to breathe. All the girls from the group were gone; everyone was gone. At the end of the night shift, it was usual for everyone to hurry home, but today something was very wrong. Raj hadn't followed her. Neither him nor that secretary of his, Rao, nor that hulking bodyguard of his were anywhere in sight.

She ran back to the set. The techs were putting away the last of the equipment. They were all men, one more dangerous looking than the other. She ran to the studio lobby. The parking lot was almost isolated. How was she going to get out of here?

"Did you miss your bus?" Rao, Raj's secretary, was standing too close behind her. She scampered back and found herself outside the building with him blocking the entrance.

He tsked. "I can give you a ride home." He took a step down and looked over her shoulder and off into the dark night. "An unprotected girl all by herself at midnight. It's almost as if you're looking for trouble. Then again, you've been flashing those boulders at everyone all week, so you might just get your wish."

She spun around and looked into the face of Raj's bodyguard.

"We can take care of you," the bodyguard said, inches from her face, and she heard herself sob. Before she could start running, the two men grabbed her arms and pushed her into the Jeep that pulled up next to her. She saw Raj in the driver's seat and she knew that all hope was gone. That her life was over.

Rao slammed the door shut and the bodyguard switched places with Raj and took the wheel.

Raj slid in next to her.

"Please. Please don't do this," she said, his face blurring because her tears were flowing and her throat was closing up. Even before the car sped off, Raj's arms were around her.

He straddled her, his fish breath shoving into her mouth along with his wet tongue, his hands shoving into her breasts. "You want this, whore. You know you do." He pushed her down into the seat. Her head slammed into the door with a crack and her back sagged into the leather. He grabbed her hands and slammed them against the glass over her head.

She struggled, with everything she was worth she struggled. But the weight of his body pinned her in place. Her horror and shame stole her voice. "No." It was the only word she could manage. "No."

But he kept shoving it back into her mouth, with his hand, with his fish-breath mouth.

He tore through her clothes, tore the skin of her breasts with his teeth, tore hair from her scalp as she struggled. Finally, as she struggled for breath through the hand that cut off her breath, he ripped through the flesh between her legs. And the pain was so stunning, for a moment the horror, the shame, all of it was consumed by the intensity of it. A burning ripped through her body as if he had snapped her spine in half, he slammed into the pain, pushing her head into the car door. She heard a crack. Another bolt of pain slashed down her spine. He had to have broken her neck. Her head went numb, her struggling, clawing arms fell away from him, as if the strength from them had disappeared. She tried to move, but she couldn't. She couldn't hear, she couldn't see. But the pain between her legs went on and on.

When she thought it was over, the car pulled to a stop. She tried to sit up, but she couldn't move. Her back, her legs, everything was wet and sticky.

"Your turn, Qasim," his horrible voice said. The door opened. Another door opened. She tried again to sit up but her legs slipped against wet leather. She might have screamed, but huge hands flipped her over and shoved her knees into her belly. She willed herself to die. To not feel the pain that followed. She willed herself to die. But she didn't.

"Fuck, sir, you really tore her up."

"Not my fault I'm hung like a horse."

They kept talking, she kept screaming, the car kept moving. None of it stopped. Nothing stopped. It went on forever.

And then, finally, when she knew it would never, ever end, the door opened and she was shoved out of the car.

She didn't even feel herself hit the earth. Didn't feel her face tear against the gravel. Didn't feel her shoulder pop out of its socket. Didn't feel it when another car pulled up. But she knew it was Rao who wrapped her in a sheet and put her in his car and drove her to his home.

31

I was so angry when Nic got here. I was just burning up with the crap these bastards have been up to. But his calm is so deep he makes it impossible to remember that there are problems in the world that cannot be fixed.

—Dr. Jen Joshi

She should have screamed, but she didn't. Somehow she knew where she was. Even emerging from her bone-deep sleep, she knew it was Nikhil wrapped around her. Knew that all that had flashed and scraped inside her all night had been a dream, long gone.

His limbs were undecipherable from her own except in patches of weight and pressure against her skin. She knew it was him because fear didn't jolt through her body, her heart didn't race, panic didn't lodge in her throat. The need to scream didn't have her gulping for breath.

I'm being touched.

Still nothing. She was a freshly formed scab on an ancient wound, too numb for feeling.

Behind her he was awake. She felt his wakefulness in his breath. In his touch.

The swollen skin around her eyes smarted and turned her view of the room into a slit-shaped window. Her nose and mouth felt raw and salty, at once wet and parched from the tears that had leaked from her all night and even in sleep drained her. She drew into herself, trying to regain possession of the armor she had let slip off her shoulders.

He gave her a moment, and she knew he'd been waiting for her to wake up. He hadn't wanted her to be alone when she awoke.

She would never know how he knew just how to do it, but he let her go and got off the bed without gouging her skin off and dousing her in shame.

"I'll go get coffee," he said into the long, translucent silence.

Something was lodged in her heart. Something like that spiked rubber ball Sweetie used to massage his legs when they ached. Sharp and soft at once. The prongs harsh yet comforting. She nodded without turning. Although she wanted nothing more than to look at him. To see what he saw. To know if he could see what an aftermath she was. An aftermath eight years too late.

She waited to hear the door click shut behind her before she dragged herself to the bathroom, splashed her face, and tried to put herself back together. But the rawness was wrapped too tightly around her, the kind of rawness that followed you when you emerged from a prolonged illness that somehow permanently altered you. Her limbs felt heavy, her chest and belly liquid, her forehead fevered.

When she left the bathroom, he was waiting for her, the offering of a steaming cup in hand. Milky tea, sweet, with no hint of ginger or spice. Exactly the way she liked it. She'd only told him that once.

She tried to thank him, but all she managed was to raise guarded eyes to him, so afraid of what she would find in his gaze. He tucked a loose lock of hair behind her ear, pausing a moment before he actually did it. Giving her a chance to pull back.

Can I touch you?

Those words had undone her yesterday. Today, they made her want to press into his hand again. To relive the unspeakable peace of being held in sleep.

He held out two pills. "The headache pretty bad?"

It was terrible, pressing against her eyelids and scraping her eyeballs with jagged nails. The worst kind of retribution for her tears. Eight years in the making.

"It's not bad," she said and got an eye roll in return.

"Medicine is magic. That's what my grandfather said. He was a medical genius. Take these."

She did.

They watched the sun rise over the lake for a few moments before taking their cups to the box of CDs sitting by the open laptop he had borrowed from his mother, leaving nothing more than a sticky note telling her he'd taken it.

She sank into the chair in front of the laptop. He pulled a dining chair next to her and settled into it. They started with the first CD, opening each folder and scrolling through memory after memory after memory.

Each sip of tea settled her insides a little more until she felt fortified enough to slide him a sideways glance. He studied the pictures, his brows drawn together over intense eyes as he sorted through everything Jen had collected. Pictures, patient records, movies, music. All the little things that had made up the woman he had loved.

Suddenly he turned to her with those intense eyes. "I shouldn't have said what I said yesterday. I was wrong. It wasn't Jen's fault. It wasn't your fault. Not even a little bit. I'm sorry."

He didn't say anything more. Didn't dilute his apology with excuses and explanations of what he had meant. It left his apology absolute and it was everything.

All she could do was nod, and just like that her tears started again. She hadn't realized how badly she had wanted him to say that. She had needed it. He wiped her cheeks, and for a long time they sat like that, their hands touching but not holding. Then he turned back to the files and started clicking through them again.

Jen liked to catalog illness. Pink gashes on swollen, sunbaked skin. Distended bellies. Eyes so sore and infected they looked like the inner flesh peeping through ripped, festered skin. Nikhil seemed to feel none of the punching nausea that sickened Jess's stomach. Every once in a while he explained things, named them: gastroenteritic distention, erythema, edema. Talked about how they had slapped together supplies and components of drugs to create treatments on the fly. They had been warriors, disease the enemy.

On the one hand, his foreign terms stripped off the layers that separated them, gave her glimpses of the profession that was such a part of who he was. On the other hand, it shone a spotlight on the world that separated them. But it didn't matter; right in this moment, nothing could separate them. They were each other's only support. Solace all the more precious because they had found it nowhere else.

Jess listened, not really registering anything but the fact that he was talking about the fight, not about who he had lost to it. He was touching the good things Jen and he had done together.

One of the folders contained not patients or diseases but things. Art, actually. Masks and pottery. Sculpture and paintings. Explosions of color and dancing people painted into walls. Stacks of rocks balanced into precarious towers.

She didn't need to ask why the folder had been labeled *Nic's Knacks*. Jen wasn't the one for art.

"It's amazing how we found art even in the most wretchedly poor hamlets. Carvings, paintings, weavings. People had no food or water, but they took the time to beautify their surroundings, their homes."

She stared at the pictures because staring at him hurt. Her eyes stopped on the picture of Nic holding a red glazed ceramic bowl. Veins of gold etched a cracked web pattern on one side. As if the bowl had broken and been pieced together with gold glue.

She couldn't seem to move on from it. She felt his eyes on her as she tried and failed to pull her gaze away from the golden webbing etched into the vibrant red.

"It's beautiful."

"One of our colleagues, Magali, brought it back for us from Japan. It's called *kintsukuroi*. The art of repairing broken pottery with gold."

Her pulse slowed and sped up all at once. "To emphasize the brokenness."

He reached out and brushed her cheek, his fingers lingering. She met his eyes. She couldn't believe she had told him. Now she would forever be a broken pot in his eyes. And yet, speaking those words last night had been like digging shrapnel out of her flesh. She was sore, but the piercing weight of the deeply lodged shards was gone. The relief was indescribable.

His fingers stroked her skin. "I don't think the point is to emphasize the brokenness." He was silent for a few minutes. "The point is that things can be repaired. That they are even more beautiful for having been repaired."

He watched her in that way he had, where he was looking inside her and inside himself all at once.

"What happened to it? We didn't find it in your things," she asked, drugged by his fingers on her skin.

"I sent it to Ria after our wedding. She left Vic, and she was pretty broken up about it."

"And you believed that the *kintsa* . . ."

"*Kintsukuroi.*"

"You believed the *kintsukuroi* would help her understand that broken things can be fixed and made even more beautiful."

He smiled. "Pretty ironic, huh?"

She wanted so badly to tell him that it wasn't ironic. If she touched his skin, traced those stubble-covered crevices down his cheeks that had forgotten how to dig dimples into his face, she would touch veins of gold. She had watched them form more and more every day. He thought he was broken. She had thought it too, but she couldn't imagine how she'd been so mistaken. He was more whole than anyone she knew. Whole on the inside. His were surface cracks.

The smile slipped off his face when she didn't respond, at least not in words. He clicked over to the next image. Then the next.

It took another four hours to go through all the CDs. But it felt much longer. Like trudging over miles and miles of sand dunes without reaching anywhere. They found nothing that could be construed as evidence. But they had found something else. Something you found when you traveled impossibly difficult paths with someone.

Between the terrible truth she had gouged out of herself and the beautiful realities that had been taken from him, their need to heal threaded together and wrapped around them and held them in place.

Somewhere along the way, their bodies had drawn closer and closer until they touched. Arm against arm, thigh against thigh, comforted and grounded. Every now and again, Nikhil reached for her, his hands over hers on the mouse. His fingers touching her hair, brushing her fingers when he brought her water.

For hours and hours, their only conversation was touch. An entirely new language for her. A vocabulary she hungrily soaked up with every inch of her being.

His fingers, warm and gentle, played a harmony across her skin, a tremble in her heart, a sob of longing she barely held in, terror that she might get used to this, hunger to believe this promise of respite.

Finally, when he spoke, it was to ask her if she wanted to eat. She was ravenous. But she could do little more than nod.

They stood under the backlit menu at the Corner Bakery that really did wrap around a street corner with a black-and-white awning. Something about the tidy tables and dim lighting felt like being outside of her life and inside a movie or a book that had sucked her in. She was living someone else's life, but it felt like her own.

Nikhil had taken her hand when they crossed the street, touching it first with the slightest nudge, as though he couldn't help but touch her, but he wouldn't without giving her a chance to pull away. She didn't pull away. Instead, her fingers chased his, their hands doing a little dance of touching and withdrawing, before their fingers interlaced and he finally wrapped her nervous, tingling hand in his.

Now he stood too close behind her as she studied the menu, his hands on her shoulders. He started to drag his hands down her arms, then seemed to realize what he was doing and stopped. Her body held on to the touch, unaware that he had backed away from it. Heat kissed along her arms where his hands had meant to go.

The warm haze that his nearness had engulfed her in all day and all night grew warmer still. She barely heard herself give the cashier her order. She barely heard herself thank her when she handed Nikhil the black-and-white-striped bag.

As she followed Nikhil out of the darkened restaurant and into the sunshine, the brightness blinded her. It felt like her eyes would never adjust. But a few blinks was all it took.

The city was luminous around them. Great sheets of glass and steel and wet streets trapping light and throwing it back into the sky. Melting ice coated each twig and branch on winter-bare trees where fledgling spring sunshine turned it to crystal. A huge steel sculpture that looked like a kidney bean reflected the entire city on its undulating surface. Just beneath it, a noisy ice rink was jam-packed with skaters of every age, spinning and twirling and sliding by in flashes of color, bright coats and scarfs flying in the wind thick with the sounds of happiness.

Suddenly, she wanted to dance. Wanted to fly down the ice until the wind set her face on fire.

"Do you skate?" Nikhil asked, studying her face, drinking in all she didn't say. She looked up at him, everything inside her ablaze, no longer able to hide all the things she wanted from him.

He took her hand and circled the rink. Before she knew it, he had put their bags of food and their shoes in lockers and rented skates, and they were strapping them on.

"I hope you know how to, because I kinda suck at it," he said.

She hadn't skated since she was seven when they still lived in Kathmandu. But some things you never forgot. He didn't suck. He was just a little shaky on his feet at first. Nothing she couldn't fix. She took his hand and together they found their rhythm, within themselves first, then together, and then with the mass of the more deft skaters that traced the inner circle of the rink, moving as one to the music pumping out of the speakers.

Time spun away from them, lost meaning. Their bodies danced. Gripping and releasing as they moved in each other's arms. Their fingers locked together one moment, his hands circling her waist the next. Her cheeks flamed. Their hearts danced. Dimples slashed down his cheeks and stayed there as they traced the rink in orbit after orbit after orbit.

A few teenagers with chains and links hanging from their clothes, and tattoos and piercings gleaming in the sunlight, started to spin at the center of the swirling orbits. Taking turns, then spinning as one to see who lasted the longest. The entire group started spinning together, going like tops until one by one they dropped out and only one remained. A contest. The rest of the skaters slowed down around them, watching, cheering. In the span of a breath, the mass of strangers turned into a community.

She didn't know how it happened, but she let Nikhil's hand go and found herself spinning. They opened up their circle and took her in. It took a few tries. Balancing on the blade was different from balancing on her toes, but soon she was spinning and spinning, her world thrown wide-open, her axis the center of the universe. Nothing but her and energy and movement. She let it all go. She threw it into the air, letting herself burst into particles, into a tornado.

Her only indication that there was a world around her was the cresting and ebbing applause as one by one the other spinners fell away, and still she spun. She didn't care. She could have gone on forever. The clapping and cheering got deafening, whipping around her with the wind. It felt like the passing of ages, it felt like a held breath, it felt like breaking and forming in an infinitely swirling loop, until finally she found Nikhil's eyes, stars trapped in the deepest chocolate, and she let him take her in his arms as hands thumped her shoulders and hoots followed them off the rink.

She wasn't laughing, but she felt like she had laughed until she could laugh no more.

"That was insane," he said, the stars in his eyes so bright they lit up her insides.

She wanted to tell him it had been the opposite of that. It was all that was sane about her. All that was real.

Just like his hand in hers. Just like his eyes.

His grip on her hand was tight as they walked back to the building, as they rode up the elevator. Not the desperate, clinging tightness from before, but a possessive, comforting lightness that spoke a resolve, a choice made. Their hand holding had turned into a language, and it spoke more than any words between them ever had.

Even as they ate at the glossy-as-glass concrete countertop in that lifeless kitchen with no dirty pots or uncooked food, his fingers sought hers out. *You're still here, right?* they asked. *I'm here,* they reassured as they ate in silence.

When their sandwiches were gone, he moved closer. "Your eyes are looking better, not so swollen anymore," he said, running the pad of his thumb over the skin that no longer felt quite as sore beneath her eyes.

All she could do was blink. But even that involuntary action was a risk, a possibility of breaking the connection those fingers, those eyes, had spoken, of collapsing this pathway she had opened up in that moment of weakness last night. It had grown through the day and nudged them into an alternate world all their own.

His thumb continued to caress her skin. The look in his eyes half concern, half plea.

Without realizing what she was doing, her fingers touched her own lips, the memory of the burning softness of his kisses suddenly fresh on them.

When he had kissed her yesterday, it had been a mindless act. A man desperate for escape. Now his eyes were mindful. A man meditating. Rooted where he stood. Steadying himself on a tightrope. Studying what he was touching, contemplating its meaning.

He reached out and touched the fingers she was pressing against her mouth. "Can I kiss you?" he asked.

She must've looked startled, because his eyes turned kind. Kind and hot eyes that were going to ruin her. Only, in this moment, she felt the opposite of ruined.

Suddenly, all she wanted was to feel that hot, yielding press of his mouth again. Needed it. She nodded quickly.

He leaned forward, his hands trailing to the nape of her neck and cupping her head. Sensation skittered down her spine, vertebra after vertebra tingling.

There was no pressure in his fingers, just a caress and enough time for her to pull away. If the pleasure of his touch wasn't enough, the space he gave her again and again melted her. It wrapped around her and erased all the normal responses of her body. All that remained was the memory of his lips from yesterday, the memory of his body wrapped around her last night, the closeness and comfort of today.

Those memories met the reality of his lips, firm and soft, infinitely gentle. He probed slowly, softly. *So this is you. God, this is you.* He lingered and waited and labored over the whisper-soft touch until she pressed into him. Only then did he part his lips to pluck at her lower lip, tasting her before sucking it in.

She fell, her body boneless. Somewhere on her body his hands tightened and held her up and he stopped being tentative.

His mouth parted her open. Her own hunger scrambled her brains.

The last time he had kissed her, it had been the shock that kept her from pulling away. This time the idea of pulling away elicited a groan from the deepest part of her. She pushed into the kiss, climbed into it, reached into his crazy-making touch. The thick, sharp stubble on his scalp brushed between her fingers. The cords of his neck pushed against her palms, filling her hands and her mouth, filling her entire body with the zinging of a million sparklers.

Another groan mingled with hers. The world spun around her as he stood and swirled her bar stool around, spreading her knees and wedging his hips between her legs. The cold concrete edge pressed into her back for a moment before he pulled her closer and angled her head to better leverage her mouth, plunder her soul. Do things to her that turned her to mist and fire, longing and heat. The sensations of spinning on the ice nothing to this.

She was panting when he pulled away and pressed his face into her hair, his breath blowing a rhythm into her ears.

"I want you. God help me, but I want you so bad."

Her response was a sob. Her brain stopped at the feel of his body against her, at the way he held her up, at how the air cooled the wet his lips left behind. She knew there were terrible things beyond his arms, beyond his breath in her ear. Terrible things that waited for her if she kept going. But this thing she was feeling made her mad with the need to push past it. Because just beyond the madness was something she had to feel. No matter the pain and horror, he made her want to push past it.

With no words at all, his eyes made a promise—yes, she could push past it; he'd push past it with her. Maybe together they could leave it behind.

He cupped her cheeks, and in his magic eyes, she found need and compassion the color of liquid hope. "Please tell me I'm not scaring you. Please tell me I'm not doing something you don't want."

She fisted his shirt and nodded against his chest. Nothing had ever felt so right. But she couldn't speak it; the sound of her own voice would break the spell. Her voice was what made the screams that night.

"Jess."

Jess.

She was Jess. With him she was Jess. And Jess could feel the things he was making her feel without drowning her in screams.

"Hey, look at me."

Again he gave her time to look up and meet his gaze. It took her ages, she did it in steps, and when she fell into the molten brown, she wondered why it had taken her so long. So long as he looked at her with those eyes she could do anything.

"Please tell me that you want this."

She nodded.

"No. Say the words."

"I . . . I want this."

"Thank you, God," he said and scooped her up in his arms.

In the span of one breath, they were on a bed. The same bed where he had held her all night, the smell in the room a mix of the two of them. Sweetness of hope and leftover pain.

His lips dragged kisses across her skin, suckled at her lips, nipped at her jaw. It was like being worshiped. It was like having life infused into her. It was like giving life, because this was not Jen's Nic. This man here was hers. All hers.

Nikhil had never felt anything softer than her skin. He was wrapped up in it. He was breathing. The water filling his lungs had dried, and air—warm, lush, sweet-smelling air—filled him and spread life to every part of his body.

He was alive.

He wanted to go on living.

Sadness singed at the edges of his consciousness. All day he had felt removed from himself. He'd been in a dream. Focused so wholly on the incredibly beautiful woman someone had hurt. Hurt but not broken. The will to make her see it, to gather her against him until she did, had been wanton. Was wanton now.

Nothing else mattered but her. The need to strip away the pain that she bore with strength that brought him to his knees was an inferno in his heart. He hadn't been able to keep his hands off her since she had let him hold her all night, trusting him at her most vulnerable, letting him see what no one else would ever see. Then on that skating rink, she had stolen his breath. With her strength, her fearlessness. Watching her had sewn him up and torn him open all at once. It had made him desperate to hold her, to taste her.

He kissed down her neck. Her sweet taste seeping through him so fast and fierce he had to remind himself to slow down. His hands slipped around her, under that bulky cotton, and touched skin over delicate bone, her waist dipping in, her hips curving outward. A belly that sank under his touch and trembled.

He dragged his hands up toward the softness that pressed against his chest. It sent a spark down his center straight to his dick. It had not stirred for so long, the thickening against her yielding thighs dragged a long, pained moan from him.

Her fingers tightened in his shirt. She pushed into him. Her body, her soft, healing body, was alive with response. It was alive.

In the space of that one thought, all the blood, all that feeling sank to the hardness rising and pushing from him. He was fully erect, turgid from starvation. For the first time in two years his body wanted and his brain wasn't screaming.

He tugged at her pants and pressed her into the thick layer of pillows, heat pumping through him. Then just like that, her pliant body stilled. It was slightest thing, but her sudden quiet turned her brittle. She went silent as a lamb to the slaughter. Silent and shaking. Fuck, she was shaking.

He scooted back and away from her. "Jess, what's wrong?"

She didn't answer. Her eyes were wild, terror filled. Not her eyes at all. Jen's eyes from that day when life had stopped.

Stop, I'm pregnant. Please stop.

He jumped off the bed, his stomach muscles clenching as if he'd been kicked.

She didn't follow him with her eyes. She didn't even know he was in the room. She just trembled and wrapped her arms around herself and squeezed those terrified eyes shut.

The pants he had pulled halfway down her thighs bound her legs together. He had to be back on the ship because the floor did a horrible rocking and pitching. He gulped down the vomit that rose in his throat.

For an endless moment, he forced air down his windpipe and fought to feel his feet pressed against the carpet of the home he had shared with his wife.

This wasn't his wife. This wasn't an alley in Dharavi.

He wasn't them.

And Jess was shaking. Because he had gone full force at her body after swearing he wouldn't hurt her.

"Jess?" He laid the lightest hand on her shoulder. She jumped, her trembling body scampering sideways and away from him. But all those pillows held her in place, trapped her, eyes wild, teeth chattering, as if he had pushed her out into a blizzard with no clothes.

"Jess, it's me, Nikhil. Nikhil." He knelt down next to the bed. "I'm not going to hurt you." He put his hands up as if she were pressing a gun to his belly. "Sweetheart, can you hear me?"

Her eyes hitched on his hands. Then very slowly met his gaze. "Nikhil?" Some of the panic cleared from her eyes.

Relief washed through him. "Yes, sweetheart, it's me. Did I hurt you?"

She squeezed her eyes shut, mortification suffusing her cheeks. She pulled her pants back in place and shook her head. "No."

He sat back onto the bed. It sank beneath his weight, tilting her closer to him.

Instead of scooting away from him again, she continued to lean toward him as if she needed the comfort of his closeness. He expelled the breath trapped in his lungs.

They sat there, their knees touching, their axes tilted toward each other. The silence between them heavy, the intimacy from moments ago diluted but still here.

"Did I?" Her voice was a whisper. That wasn't fear he saw in her eyes but worry. Worry and shame. "Did I do anything to hurt you?" She stared at the fingers she was twisting together in her lap.

He took her hands in his, stopping the wretched twisting and untwisting of those long, delicate fingers and shook his head. Of course she hadn't hurt him.

She closed her eyes again, and the long spikes of her lashes kissed her flushed cheeks. "What did I do?"

"You started shaking, as if I . . . You don't remember any of it?"

Her throat worked. "I remember you kissing me. And carrying me here."

"I'm sorry, I shouldn't have . . ."

She met his eyes. "No. No, Nikhil, when you . . . when you kissed me, I actually . . ." She blushed so deep, her incredibly high cheekbones looked almost bruised. She had to have the most flawless skin he had ever seen; you had to almost touch it to make sure it was real.

"You what?"

"I thought . . . I didn't realize . . . I actually . . ."

"You liked it," he said as gently as he could. No way was he going to smile. This was the absolute wrong time to go all caveman.

She nodded, without meeting his eyes.

"And then I did something you didn't like."

She grabbed the strand she had just pushed behind her ear and tucked it back again, even though it hadn't moved. "No. It wasn't you. It wasn't what you did."

Moisture rose in a sheen across her wide, upturned eyes and gathered into two miniature waterfalls. She batted them away before they spilled onto her cheeks, and stood.

He stood too, instinctively taking a few steps back so he wasn't crowding her. She wrapped her arms around herself in a gesture that was becoming too familiar.

She had fallen back into the horrors that trapped her just as he had.

What a pair they made.

"It was . . ." Her head fell forward, defeated. She wanted to say something, but she didn't know how. He knew the feeling.

He wished he could touch her again. Do something to comfort her. He pushed his hands deep in his pockets and held them there.

"Listen, Jess. I'm . . ." She looked up at him then, and he knew she didn't want him to apologize. But how could he not? After last night. After she'd opened up to him, let him close, how had he pushed her like that? He fisted his hands inside his pockets, squeezing out the insane feel of her on his hands. Touching her had felt just—God, where were the words for how touching her had felt?

She took a trembling breath. She was hurting, and here he was thinking about how good touching her felt. "I should never have done that. I won't touch you like that again. I swear."

Her golden gaze met his. Her lashes were still wet and clumped together into spikes. Relief burned in her eyes.

Yes, that thing burning in her eyes, it had to be relief.

32

I've decided not to be afraid.

—Dr. Jen Joshi

What kind of idiot was she? First, she'd told him. Then, she'd allowed herself to be comforted by him, craved his touch. Then she'd gone mad when he'd touched her. No wonder he never wanted to touch her again. The one time in all her life something had felt so good, so right, and she had ruined it.

How long was it going to tie her up? How long was she going to let those bastards keep her from feeling things? From living.

She wanted to live. She wanted to feel what he made her feel. Even though she knew exactly why he wanted her. Even though she had no delusions. She wanted him. The Nikhil in the pictures at his parents' house, the surgeon who could rattle off the names of diseases as if they were foods he ate every day, the man whose need to comfort others trumped everything, that man was only reaching for her because she was broken and he needed to fix things. At long last, he could bear to fix things.

Whatever it was, it was like nothing she had felt before, and it made her greedy. And she wanted it. Whatever part of him she could have, she wanted.

She watched him pack all those CDs back into their boxes and panic bubbled inside her. They couldn't leave. They hadn't found the evidence.

She followed him and started helping, but what she wanted was to reach for him and take him back to before she had let her past take everything away from her again. To where they still had time.

"You okay?" he asked.

Or maybe he didn't say it, just looked at her as if the question was all he cared about.

His eyes, they hooked into her, and she couldn't look away.

Say something. Please, just tell him you want to try again.

"Nikhil, I—"

"This is it. This is the last of Jen's stuff, our stuff. There's nothing more. Two years of being with her, and in two days we've trudged through it all."

"We'll find it. It has to be somewhere." Somehow she knew they were going to find it. She knew it was close. So close she could feel it.

"What kind of asshole waits two years? What kind of asshole doesn't know where his wife might have hidden something she wanted him to find?"

He picked up a box and turned it over. Then another, then another. Dumping out the CDs they'd just put away, watching them spread across the bed. His hands sweeping through them.

"Nikhil, stop, we've looked in all these boxes and it's not here. Stop."

"I asked her if anything was wrong, and she looked me in the eye and lied to me. And then she was gone and it all felt like a lie. Everything. All those people we had treated. All those places, all our faith and enthusiasm, it all felt like a joke. What kind of man spends two years wallowing in self-pity when he should've been going after the fuckers who did this to her?"

The kind of man who knew he couldn't bring her back. The kind of man who knew nothing could change what had happened. Nothing could reverse it. "You want to now. You can get them now." *For you, it's not too late.*

"Yes, but how, if I can't find it?" He threw a desperate glance at the mess on the bed. "I let them get away with it. I let more people die, because I was too much of a coward."

"Nikhil, you were not a coward."

"Not a coward? The cop told me. He told me they were killing people. And all I could think about was how nothing I did would change anything. I let them go."

At least he hadn't sold his soul to let them go. Sold himself.

She slid closer to him and stroked his dry cheek. They had reversed roles. His tears were gone, leaving only anger. Her anger was gone, leaving only tears.

He grabbed her hand, clung to it as if it were a lifeline. "I should have gone after them. I should have fought for justice."

A laugh escaped her and it stopped him. For the hundredth time, she watched his focus moved outward, away from his own hurt and into hers. "What about you? Didn't you care about catching those men, punishing them?"

She took her hand back. "Justice wasn't a luxury I could afford."

He held her face in both hands and pulled her close, his forehead touching hers.

"Stop calling it that. Don't call it a luxury. Don't."

She hated that her tears spilled into his hands. "You didn't do anything because you were in too much pain. I didn't do anything because they bought me off." She tried to pull away. But he didn't let her go.

"I sold myself. I sold my justice. I took their money and I negotiated for more. For a job in Mumbai. In return for silence."

She had been the girl who kneed that shopkeeper in the balls for feeling her up. She'd been the girl who lured the whore dealer her uncle had sold her to into the bathroom at Siliguri bus station and locked him in there and helped four girls escape. But they had broken her. In every way it was possible to break a person, those two had broken her in that car.

They'd finally turned her into the powerless, spineless whore they saw her as. And here she was, whoring herself again. Selling herself to the bastard who would take away any chance Nikhil had left at retribution.

"Jess. You were alone. You had to take care of yourself."

"Don't, Nikhil. Please don't." She couldn't bear for him to forgive her before he even knew the extent of her crime. To absolve her. To make excuses for her. She pushed herself away from him. Stepped away. Why couldn't she stop shaking? Why did she want to tell him everything? Because she couldn't. Not when they had Joy.

The weight of her secrets swelled in her chest, pushing at the damned scar as if they could rip past it. Escape and set her free.

He stepped closer. "You had the strength to start over. To make a decision to get past what they did."

This time her laugh edged hysteria. It was laced with such self-loathing that she sounded just as insane as she felt. "Strength? Decision?" As if weakness had been a choice. As if anything in her life had ever been a bloody choice. "Yes, so much strength, two men could push me into a car, and it took only one to hold me down." More of that maniacal laughter spilled from her. "One of them drove. Can you believe that? I was so bloody strong that it took one man in a driving car to tear me in half?"

"I'm going to break my promise to you," he said, stepping closer behind her and wrapping his arms around her.

Instead of stepping away she leaned into his touch. Those bastards were closing in around her, and Nikhil touched her, and instead of screaming and kicking at him she sank into him.

Finally, when he spoke, his voice was as gentle as his touch. "Jess, you got past it. Look at you, you're this great mother. You're here fighting for Jen. You didn't even know her."

She slid out of his arms and twisted around. "That, what happened back there." She jabbed a finger at the bed. "How is that being past it?"

His eyes saw so much she wanted to cover up. She wanted to cower. But with her gaze locked with his she couldn't.

"They're everywhere, Nikhil. They're still inside me."

But she didn't want them to be. No more. She couldn't breathe. She wanted to breathe. Just one breath. Please. "I can't even let anyone touch me. I'm twenty-five years old and I'm dead. Unable to feel."

He cupped her cheek. "I know you feel this." He dropped the whisper of a kiss on her lips. "I know you feel this."

She slammed her lips into him.

She grabbed his head, his face, hunted him with her mouth, tried to take it, hoard it, but she couldn't reach what she wanted.

He let her go at it, not pulling away. Finally, the exhaustion of it, the futility, made her stumble back. He kept one hand cupped around the nape of her neck, his fingers on her telling her where she was.

"I don't want to feel them between us. They're still here. I don't want them here."

After she gouged out the words from what had to be the deepest place inside her, she just stood there, her eyes gleaming windows that looked out into nothing but darkness, her gaze pinned to a spot on the floor where she still seemed to see long-ago things.

Pain rolled around inside him, old hard pain, new fresh pain.

She shifted her stare to her hands, but the horrors of what they had done to her moved with her gaze and seemed to dance on her palms. Open, face-up palms, a universal plea.

He squeezed his eyes shut. Before him was Jess's helplessness. Behind his closed lids, Jen lay bleeding beneath the murderous thrusts.

He looked back at Jess. She met his gaze, her effort in meeting his eyes Herculean.

The moment danced before him. Life. He could reach for it, or he could curl back into himself and continue to die.

Then just like that, she was inches from him. Her own pain put away. She took his hand. Movement meant existence. She laid his hand on her chest. On the braided scar that sliced her in half.

The puckered skin nudged into his palm through the cotton of her shirt. The living reminder of Jen that had brought him back to the pain of his existence. Her heartbeat was warm and steady under his touch. Under the dead scar, she was alive. She was here. He could do nothing for Jen. But Jess, her? He could make the life she had survived count, help her take it back. Suddenly, he needed to do that more than anything else.

He pulled her close. Their breaths threaded like insidious mists, magic spells intertwining to soothe what he had never hoped to soothe. Her living breath reverberated in his ears and filled his senses. He dove into it, stealing it with his lips. The taste of her was sweet and hot and new, her gasp of arousal already familiar and all her own.

When he pulled away, her entire coiled-up strength was fierce in her gaze. He threaded the fingers of one hand in her hair, and laid his other hand flat against her scar. His past in one hand, the present in the other.

"Nikhil." His name on her lips was at once an affirmation and a prayer. Deep furrows sank between her brows.

He kissed them away. "I won't hurt you. I swear."

She nodded. A hint of a nod. But all her trust propelled the movement.

He pressed his lips to the delicate shell of her ear. "You tell me to stop and I'll stop."

Her only response was stillness.

"Do you want me to stop?"

Fear trembled in her silence, in her dancer's stillness, wound tight around awareness, her entire being suspended between newborn faith and ancient hopelessness.

He removed his hands from her. She blinked up at him. Her eyes naked. Stripped of every defense. For a moment he thought she would pull away.

But she didn't.

His tigress. His dancer. His healer.

Her hands traced up his chest and wrapped around his jaw. His stubble pricked into his own skin. "What if I can't feel anything?"

Warmth tore at his heart. Tenderness uncoiled in his belly. "Didn't you feel anything just now?"

A blush crested her cheeks. She, like him, had felt too much.

He made his voice light. "So, you don't feel anything. So we'll try again. I'm okay with that."

She smiled. And he realized he was smiling too.

"In fact, even if you do feel something, we'll have to try again, you know, just to make sure."

This time her shoulders shook in an entirely different language. Laughter. She pressed her forehead into his chest and her sweet laughter fell against his heart.

He laid his chin on her head. "Because, you know, I'm a man of science, and you know what they say about hypothesis?" Her shoulders shook a little more. "It's all in how much you test it. We would have to be sure you felt something. We can't just make assumptions."

Her laughter tickled his chest. He never wanted it to stop.

"It's no laughing matter. We have to be very thorough."

She laid the sweetest kiss at the center of his chest. His breastbone. Tentative lips pressed into his heart.

"Yes. Yes, that's the perfect place to start your test."

She looked up at him. "Will you help me? Tell me what to do?"

"No. I want you to do what you want."

She went up on the tips of her toes, and this time she pulled his lips down to hers with such deliberate consciousness he forgot what he wanted. Forgot everything but the raw need in her lips as she gathered the scattered remains of him and pressed them together.

"Like this?" she asked against his lips, as her hand stroked his hair.

Yes.

Her breasts pressed into his chest, her nipples darts aimed straight at his heart but also at the thickening in his pants.

As soon as the insistent hardness jabbed into her, she pulled back.

He wanted to pull her back to him, kiss all that uncertainty off her face. But he fisted his hands at his sides and waited, knowing she would find him again.

Her eyes took in the action, then she looked in his eyes, and he knew she saw something in there that brought her back to him. She reached out and unfisted his hands for him and threaded her fingers through his.

I love you.

That's what she wanted to say to him. She wanted to whisper it into his mouth. For all the razor sharpness of his jaw, for the rough, stubbly dents of his dimples, his lips were so very soft, she couldn't stop wanting to touch them.

I love you.

Just a little bit.

She didn't know in what moment of madness she had let it happen. But there it was wrapped up in her heart. She trapped it there in that tiny space because she could never let it get bigger than that.

He watched her with those molten-chocolate eyes. Love wasn't what this was about for him. It wasn't about lust either, that much she knew. Healing maybe, living maybe, moving on maybe. Just not love. She knew he was done with that.

But for this moment she had him, and it was enough. What she could take of him now she would hold on to forever. With her fingers threaded through his, she led him to the bed. He followed her. His eyes lit with so much she had never expected to see there.

She sat down on the bed. Scooted back. That made him smile, those deep, deep dimples balm on her tattered soul. She tugged at his hand, shyness a nervous spark across her belly. He reached for her, cupping her face. His eyes held hers, beautiful, generous eyes. "We don't have to do this if you're not ready."

She pushed her cheek into his hand. This time felt different. This time there was purpose in them both. She was ready. Her body was definitely ready, the alien tingling between her legs so hot she clenched her inner muscles in response. His thumb caressed her flaming cheek. Her heart was definitely ready.

Maybe he wanted an out. "You don't have to do this if you're not ready either."

He laid a knee on the mattress. It sank under his weight as he came to kneel in front of her. He brought his lips to hers, dropping the lightest kiss there, then stopping as if to savor it. "I never expected to want anyone like this again. But you . . ." The heat in his eyes made her skin sparkle with response. His hands caressed her arms. "You are so damn beautiful."

She squeezed her eyes shut. Her body. It was always her body.

You're built like a whore. This is what whores get.

No. She would not start shaking again. No. Don't tremble. Don't. Nikhil was not them.

Yes, he wanted her body, but he . . . No. She didn't care what he wanted. She wanted him. Him. She reached up and grabbed his face and pressed her lips against his again. Focus on his lips. His amazing lips, soft and warm. For a moment he seemed to sense something and made to pull away, but she pressed her lips into his, sucked on them. Her tongue, her teeth, her entire mouth drinking him in.

Maybe this wasn't the way you were supposed to kiss, she had no idea what she was supposed to do, but this felt so good it made all the noise in her head stop. Warmth burned between her legs and licked up her belly and took everything over. It made her want him to thrust his tongue into her mouth, thrust his hands all over her. Erase everything. She grabbed at his shirt, fisting the cotton, needing purchase, needing to hold on.

He groaned a rough-edged groan and threaded his fingers in her hair, tugging her head back, angling her hungry lips so their positions were reversed. Then he fed her hunger, joined it, opening her mouth wide with his own and entering her with a wet, hot slide that wiped her clean.

She gasped. This time he didn't back away. He pulled her closer, pressed her aching breasts into his hard chest. His tongue stroked hers, the friction so intimate she moaned and thrust her pelvis into the air between them. He slipped a hand between them and cupped her. She almost screamed into his mouth, but it came out a sob. How did he know where to touch her, how to touch her?

How were his hands so hot? One finger pressed through the fabric into the bud that throbbed between her legs, engorged in a way that was entirely unfamiliar. It pulsed under his hand. She pushed away the embarrassment and tightened her grip on his shoulders.

"Nikhil." She spoke his name into his mouth.

"Yes. Say my name," he whispered into the edge of her mouth. "It makes me sane."

"Nikhil." She pressed into his lips. "Nikhil."

"Tell me what you want."

"This. I want this."

He nipped at her lip. "I want to be inside you." He pressed his finger into the wet dent between her legs. "Right here."

She sucked in a breath, and he kissed her again. She nodded.

"Say it."

"I want that too."

"You want what?" His hands slid under the hem of her shirt and stayed there. "You have to say it. You have to tell me what you want."

She couldn't.

He dropped the tiniest kiss on her mouth. "Not going to do any more unless you ask for it."

A sob escaped her. "I can't."

"Do you want me to take off your clothes?"

Sparks flitted down her belly.

His hands started to play with the skin at her waist, the back of his fingers stroking under the elastic waistband. Sensation zinged from his fingers up to her breasts and down to where the imprint of his hands still burned. All these sensations, new and sweeping.

She gulped air, her throat bobbing against his nipping teeth. "Yes."

"Yes, what?" Teeth and tongue, rough and soft, grazed her throat.

"Yes, I want you to take off my—" Another swallow.

"Clothes," he prompted.

"Clothes," she repeated.

He gripped the edge of her shirt and eased it up her body, his hands skimming her as he went. His eyes hitched on hers, picking up every nuance as gooseflesh prickled under his touch. She lifted her arms and lost him for a moment as the black fabric went over her head.

"So beautiful." His whisper jabbed like spikes into her chest. She squeezed her eyes shut in the darkness of the shirt around her head and focused on the burning in her body.

In less than the span of a breath, she broke back into light. But he kept her arms over her head. Before he bent to her breasts, she saw the hunger in his eyes.

He was hypnotized by her body.

He pressed his lips to her breasts, where they rose and pressed together. She always wore sports bras, tried to flatten the too-large globes that had brought her nothing but pain.

The body of a whore.

Tears rose in her eyes. She pushed them back, her body starting to lose heat so fast, she struggled to hold on. He freed her arms and dragged his fingers down their length, his lips and tongue teasing her breasts through the fabric. She hated herself as warmth sparked across her skin again.

Whore. Whore.

Despite the storm in her heart, her nipples peaked and pressed into his mouth. He undid her bra and pulled the tightly stretched fabric over her head with almost desperate speed. Her bra soaked up the tears as it brushed up her cheeks.

"God, Jess," he said as the heavy weight of her breasts popped free. He reached out and touched her. Hot fingers on cold skin. His gaze moved from his hand and met hers.

The glazed look disappeared so fast it was like a magic trick.

He let go of her breast. "Why didn't you ask me to stop?"

"Do you want to stop?" She looked away, too afraid to hear his answer.

It's your whore's body. Who can stop?

"No." He shook his head. "Your body . . . you're just so damn beauti—What's the matter? What did I say?"

She wrapped her arms around his head and tugged him down to her breast again. "I want you to keep going. I don't want to . . ."

"Shhh, sweetheart," he whispered against the breasts she was shoving into his face. He tugged her arms off his head, even as they clutched desperately to keep him in place.

"I don't want you to stop, Nikhil," she sobbed. Her body suddenly filthy, numb, and caked in dirt. What was wrong with her? One moment, she wanted him so badly it raged inside her like a fever. The next moment, she was as cold and hard as marble, cracking and crumbling along the veins that should have made her beautiful.

He clasped her waist and tried to push her away. But she didn't want that either. She didn't want him to stop holding her. Didn't want herself distanced from him, but she wanted her body to have nothing to do with the way he touched her.

His hands slipped around her again and held her for another moment. That spot at the top of her head, where his breath always landed when he held her, tingled. When had that become the most sensitive part of her body?

"You want to talk to me?" he said.

No. She didn't want to talk. There was nothing to talk about.

"I've told you everything. And it's okay if you don't want me after what I've told you." Her heart begged for him to turn away from her body. Instead, he took her hand and placed it where his hot, hard length swelled his jeans. For a moment fear made her weak, but then she didn't know if it was heat again or shame. Everything inside her blurred together.

"You think I don't want you?" he asked, but before another sob escaped her, she saw the wonder in his eyes. Wonder, not lust. "This guy?" he said, calling that hard, engorged thing a guy.

She pressed her lips together. It was completely crazy to want to smile when she had been so close to tears seconds ago.

He grinned down at her. His little-boy smile very hot and adult. "This guy hasn't done this for two years. I had forgotten he even existed. And you think I don't want you?"

She looked up at him, her heart one part misery, two parts hope.

"What is it, sweetheart? Tell me."

I hate my body, she wanted to tell him. *Hate that it turns men into beasts. Hate that it's all you see.* But he needed her body. And maybe this curse of hers could actually give him back something he had lost. "Your guy, he . . . he really hasn't done that in two years?"

The dark, deep chocolate of his eyes turned opaque, his pupils dilating with pain. "I saw it happen."

He softened under her fingers, and without thinking about it she stroked him, making him push up against her hand again. He leaned his head back.

"How do we keep them out? How do we make them leave us alone?" He met her eyes again. "I don't want them here, Nikhil. But they're here."

"No." He pulled her face to his, his mouth suddenly intent on hers, his tongue stroking until those words were gone. "No, they're not." He tugged her head back, sucking at her throat, scouring all thought from her mind, leaving behind only sensation. "No one is here but me." His mouth found one hard nipple. "And you."

Her moan turned into a scream. She arched her back and pressed her aching breast into his mouth. "Nikhil."

"Yes. Nikhil. Just me. Just you."

Her entire being centered on his swirling tongue. Pleas tangled in her throat in moans and gasps. His hands circled her waist and fitted her to him. If he had been hard before, now he raged against her, the friction of his jeans scraping her raw.

Just when she thought she couldn't take it anymore, just when something between her legs felt like it would unhinge and explode, he let the hard nub of one nipple pop from his mouth and turned to the other. Cool air stroked the wetness on one side while the heat of his mouth burned the other. An inferno rose inside her. She was begging, but she didn't know for what. Her spine curved toward it, her breasts reached for it.

She writhed beneath him, mindless as he reached down and tugged at her pants. The loss stymied her for a moment. Another set of hands coming back from the past.

"Jess," he said against her mouth. "It's me. Stay with me." His hand cupped her bare mound, and she forgot everything but his long-fingered touch. He didn't give her a chance to leave him again. Two fingers pressed into her soaking center.

"Nikhil." She cried out his name.

"Again. Say it again." This mouth trailed wetness down her body, lower and lower.

"Nikhil. Nikhil. Nikhil." Sobs. Prayers. "Please."

His tongue dug into her navel. She screamed. He nipped a line from that dent to a lower dent.

No.

Before she knew what he was doing, his mouth was between her legs. His tongue dipping into her. This time her scream bordered on insanity, her mind leaving her. Sensation like she'd never known exploded where his tongue pierced her. Then everywhere. She was a storm. A tornado. Particles scattered in the air. All of her gone, exploded, nothing but sensation and more sensation.

He didn't let her go, moving with her as she thrust and thrashed against his mouth. Not letting up until the sensation became a crescendo. An endless dance of crests and waves. Ages passed before she came back into her body. Her head swimming, dizzy, her belly trembling, all of her slick with sweat. He came up then. His lips glistening with her madness.

"Shh," he said, his face over her, smiling. "Breathe."

She shook her head from side to side. She couldn't breathe, couldn't process what had just happened to her.

"I'm going to enter you now. Do you want that?" he said, reaching into the nightstand drawer and retrieving a condom.

"Yes." It's what she wanted more than anything else.

He slid on the condom and entered her. A careful, deliberate slide. He watched her face as she soaked him up. This pleasure was different, sliding against each sensitized inch still buzzing from before, bringing all that sensation back to life. And it set off another flood as he fit into her, the notching so tight, her already satiated belly cramped around her pleasure.

"It's me. Just me, Jess," he whispered against her ear. But she didn't need to be told anymore. It was him. Just him everywhere.

He moved inside her, starting out controlled, and then his rhythm changed, tipping into her madness, his breath hissed, his eyes lost their center. He threw back his head and shuddered in her arms, mirroring the explosion that had just taken her. She wrapped her legs around his hips, her arms around his shoulders, holding him together. All of him. She wanted all of him.

"God, Jess," he said, his voice a million tiny sparks on her skin.

I know, she wanted to say. *God, I know.* But there were no words. For this. There were no words.

33

I almost told Nikhil the truth today. But the phone is no way to tell someone their wife, who they thought was so smart, was an idiot who had let herself get in over her head.

—Dr. Jen Joshi

The last thing Rahul needed right now was another confrontation with Kimi. He knew she was angry with him. Knew that he deserved it. But he just didn't have the time for this today. Somehow someone above him had decided that he needed to have every single inconsequential, paperwork-heavy case dumped on his head. He'd been working twelve-hour days wading through red tape and then trying to find time to hunt down the Jess Koirala trail. Kirit showed no signs of relenting about the case. Which made sense, since Rahul still had absolutely no hard evidence.

Kimi stormed into his office, her blond-highlighted hair hanging down to her waist, her jeans so tight, he could imagine every *hawaldar* and officer rushing to help her when she walked in, until of course they realized who she was.

His intercom buzzed. "Sir, Kimi-madam's here to see you," his assistant's voice said just as she pulled off her sunglasses and rolled her eyes at Rahul.

"Send her in," Rahul said drily.

She didn't smile.

Her eyes looked tired and he choked back the automatic response of panic that rose up inside him. He reminded himself that she was no longer sick.

"Sit," he said.

But of course she didn't listen. She just jumped right to it. "You need to get Papa off my case. He has God knows how many bodyguards trailing me."

"You told me not to and I'm not. I swear." His fingers almost pinched his throat. Their secret code when they had sworn silence as children. Of course she noticed. Her mercurial eyes widened for a second with such sadness, he almost apologized again.

She held up a hand, cutting him off before he did any such thing. "Actually, I want you to tell him you'll do it. Tell him you'll follow me around and watch me like he wants you to."

"Kimi . . ."

This time her eyes flashed anger. All that sadness gone. "Don't worry, I'm not actually asking you to put up with my presence. I know how abhorrent you find it."

He squeezed his temples, but he couldn't get into how he felt about her again. "I just want you to tell him you're doing it. You don't actually have to do it." Hurt flashed through the anger for a moment, but she set her jaw against it. "He'll trust you. And I won't have to keep dodging all those idiots he's got tailing me."

"I'm not going to lie to Kirit-Sir, Kimi."

She put both hands on her hips. "Oh, I'm sorry, I forgot. I'm the one you save your lies for."

"I never lied to you."

"Whatever." She paced his office, studied the medals. He remembered taking each one of them to show her after he'd won them. Remembered her delight at each and her tears of pride. "What if I try and talk to Papa about your girlfriend's case? I can threaten to do a piece on it to get him to let you go meet with her husband."

Okay, now she was just trying to press his buttons. "Jen was not my girlfriend and you know it. Can you show some respect?"

She rolled her eyes again, but it had none of her usual good humor.

"Please don't interfere in this case, Kimi." Kirit would shut down even more if she got involved.

"Okay. I'll stay out of it. But you know what you need to do."

He groaned.

"Get those bodyguards off me." With that she was gone, leaving nothing but the scent of her perfume behind. Tuberoses and mint. Her two favorite things.

He sank into his chair, not even fighting the sense of loss he felt every time he was subjected to her distant anger. If she had come to him for help, she had to be at her wits' end. Kirit must really have her surrounded.

Question was, why was the minister so terrified for her safety suddenly?

34

I may be stupid in telling you all this, in putting all my secrets inside you. But it's what I've decided to do. Keep them safe.

—Dr. Jen Joshi

Nikhil was fast asleep, but she still turned on the faucet to drown out the sound before taking the phone into the shower stall and dialing.

The text from Naag had been ominous. A fitting punishment for what she'd just let happen.

I have some good news for you.

He wasn't quite as cryptic when she called him on the phone. "You've been there for two weeks. You think I paid for a ticket so you could holiday in America?"

"You have my son under threat in Mumbai, and you think I'm on holiday?" she almost said.

Her tongue might've loosened far more than it needed to with Nikhil, but she hadn't entirely lost her mind yet. The usual silkiness of his voice was stretched tight today, and it twisted into a noose around her neck.

"I texted you. We've been searching through all of Jen's things. I swear."

"Seems to me like you're particularly enjoying searching through one of her things."

Her heart froze. Did he have someone watching her here?

"So I'm right then," he said, recognizing her silence for the admission it was.

"I have no idea what you're talking about. Jen just did a really good job hiding it." *Because she knew bastards like you would go to any lengths to undo her work.*

"Really? And it looks like I did a really bad job in choosing you. I gave you the diary six months ago. You've had a chance to pore over it for six months. Anyone with half a brain would have figured out where Dr. Joshi put the evidence from that alone. You're in her home with her husband, and you want me to believe you can't figure it out?" He sounded unusually desperate today. Something was very wrong. Whatever he had at stake was in danger. She couldn't afford for him to feel threatened. When powerful people felt threatened, people like her got shot down in the crossfire.

"I swear I'm trying. I'm close. I can feel it. Her husband is really looking now. I know it took me long to get him there. But he is now. We'll find it." Nikhil really was searching in earnest now. She wished she didn't know this. She wished she didn't know all she knew about him.

"Then you better get back to healing the good doctor*saab*. I didn't pick you for your brain. That body should pull him right out of his stupor."

Every inch of skin Nikhil had touched burned.

You're so damn beautiful.

She felt sick. Helplessness churned her insides. But Naag hadn't picked her for her body. He'd picked her for her vulnerability. Joy.

"I'm doing everything I can. I swear. If the evidence is here, we'll find it."

"You better make sure that you do. Oh, and I'm off to Calcutta to see an old friend. Maybe I can look up some of your old friends while I'm there?"

She slid down to the floor of the shower stall. The water so loud in her ears, she lost him for a moment.

"What? You're so touched, you lost your voice?"

Not this. Please.

"I told you I'll find it."

"So sensitive about Calcutta. I wonder what that's about." He waited, but she could barely breathe, let alone respond. The idea of Joy ever finding out was unthinkable. She would commit murder to prevent it. Do anything.

"If you even think of double crossing me, remember this—if your son disappears, no one will even bother looking for the little bastard's body. You understand?"

"Why would I double cross you? He's my son."

"So asking your faggot friend to disappear with your son isn't double crossing me?"

All she could manage was another stunned silence. And he read it like a book.

"You think I'd invest all this money in you and not even tap your phone? How stupid do you think I am? I know what's happening with him and that male TV star he's fucking. I'll have them both thrown in jail if he tries anything funny. I personally have nothing against people fucking whomever they wish to fuck, but our law sees these sodomizing bastards as criminals, and I'm more than happy to help our executive branch get them off our roads."

"I told you. I'll find it. Nikhil is cooperating. I've worked him over like you said. Please don't bring Sweetie into this. Please."

"That's better. You have one more week. I'm tired of waiting."

She tamped down on the panic and rose to her feet. His desperation had been a live thing today. She felt it in her gut. If he was really going to Calcutta to track down her past, she was out of time.

When he had taken Joy and explained to her what she needed to do, she hadn't had to think about it for even a moment. She would have done anything to get Joy back. Letting them carve a scar into her chest was nothing. Cheating an innocent man was nothing.

The yearning to speak to her baby boy was so strong, she had to force herself not to call him. It was too late in India and he was probably fast asleep.

Plus, suddenly, she felt dirtier than she had ever felt, and she couldn't speak to him until she found a way to be his mamma again, not this woman who had let her body ruin everything again.

She splashed her face with cold water and tried to towel off her burning neck. Her too-sensitive skin, despite Nikhil's gentleness, was marked where he had kissed her, sucked on her. Between her legs was a soreness that had felt intimate and warm when she'd snuck out of bed, taking care not to wake him, reminding herself not to linger and stare like some desperado. Now it felt dirty. The marks on her skin felt shameful, like tattoos they branded whores with in a bygone era.

What kind of mother had sex when her child was under threat? When her child was alone and unprotected? What kind of mother let hope and dreams seep into her heart when there were monsters with their guns pointed at her child?

She scrubbed her face on the towel, refusing to let tears mingle with the water beaded on her skin. No more tears.

Come on, Jen, please, please help me. Where did you put it? I need to get my baby out of danger. Please.

She'd gone into the bathroom with her heart full. When she let herself out she was a paper doll, a balloon animal, thin membranes filled with nothing but air and space. A prick away from deflating to nothingness.

Nikhil listened for her. His senses tuned in to every little sound that came from the bathroom. But all he heard was the water she had turned on the moment she went in there. Other noises had also started up in his head from the moment she had turned the water on.

He glanced once more at the boxes, at the closed laptop. These were the last remaining places where he could hope to find the evidence. To do right by Jen. To keep his promise to Jess.

Jess.

He could still feel her skin against his, her breath, how she had bared everything, her trust, her courage. The force of her will as she fought to leave her past behind.

With Jen, their lovemaking had been fun. A sport—wild, fast, adventuresome—with Jen always the victor and him a grateful teammate.

With Jess, with this girl in whom his wife's heart lived on, with her, words deserted him. With her touch had been a disturbance so deep it had altered him.

His hands, hands he had prided himself on for their skill, hands he had wanted so badly to use for something that made him matter and then given up on, those hands felt alive again. They craved touching her, feeling all those new and unexplored reactions with her. Craved it with such ferocity, he had to stop himself from knocking on that door she'd been locked up behind for so long.

He had never felt so out of control. Not even as a hormonal teenager. She took his control. She had taken his ability to hold back last night. Stripped him to the bone. No, with her sex was not play, not sport, not banter. It was living, breathing, being. It was pain as much as pleasure. It was a tearing up of all he was and of putting it all together again.

This new him was a strange amalgam of guilt and gratitude, calm one moment, raging with restlessness the next moment.

He started to file through all of Jen's stuff one more time, a horrible awareness of what he had opened himself up to descending on him in a crash. As he touched the many things his wife had touched, he knew with absolute certainty that he didn't have it in him to bear loss again.

By the time he was on the last box filled with useless shit, with the sound of the water in the bathroom booming in his ears, he knew he had to find the damn evidence. He had to find it fast.

The windows overlooking the lake were frosted at the edges, the temperature was falling again today. Jen had loved this view. More than anything else in the condo, she had loved what she saw when she looked out these windows. It was who she was.

And just like that, he knew that the evidence wasn't here. Everything in these boxes really was useless shit. None of it meant anything to Jen, and she wouldn't care if someone threw all of it away. So, where was it?

It was the single worst time for the bell to ring. Nikhil strode to the front door and found the last person he wanted to see right now. Seeing Vic in Jen's condo was such a déjà vu moment that for a beat they were both silent.

"Hey, man," Vic said finally, thumping Nic on the shoulder and pushing past him into the living room.

"What are you doing here?" Nic asked, following him.

"I was at a client in the city so I decided to stop by."

"Or Ria and Aie sent you to check up on me?"

Vic met his eyes. For a moment he looked like he was done

with that tiptoeing thing he'd been doing. "You didn't tell anyone where you were going or how long you'd be." His eyes skimmed the white sheet-covered room and filled with sadness. But only for an instant. God forbid the ever-stoic Vic would break down, even though he was the one who had swathed all that furniture in white sheets. Suddenly, Nic didn't want to be here surrounded by the white sheets.

On the heels of that thought came a blast of guilt.

Vic started thumbing a message on his phone. "Hold on, just letting them know I found you." He didn't make it sound like it was a reprimand. But it was one, and it blew the guilt into a storm.

"While you're at it, let them know I don't need a babysitter, will ya?"

Vic looked up from his phone. "Don't you think you're being just a little bit unfair?"

"Unfair? I'm the one being unfair here? Can't I have some damn space? If I need to do this alone, can't I fucking do it alone?"

"But you're not doing it alone."

And there it was, the real problem. "Perfect. Let's make this about Jess."

"Nic, listen. It's just a little strange, okay? You've come home after two years. You're here for the first time since Jen died. And you've brought someone with you."

"Wow, you can say her name. I thought you had forgotten how to say it."

"You think I've forgotten Jen?" Vic looked so angry, it was like he wanted to punch Nic in the face, and it felt fantastic. He needed Vic to stop dancing around him like he was made of glass.

Vic squeezed his temples and shielded his eyes. "I'm sorry. But for two years you've shut us out. None of us could reach you, and suddenly you show up with some teenager you barely know."

"She's not a teenager, she's twenty-five years old." Shit, that made her ten years younger than him.

"And then you cling to her as if you're a smitten teenager yourself. How the hell aren't we supposed to be worried about you?"

"I what? Are you fucking nuts?" Nikhil ran his fingers through his hair, and anger rose in him at having let it grow out. His family thought he'd moved on. Somehow that felt like betrayal. "You think I'd forget Jen so easily?"

"Nic, there's nothing wrong with moving on. Jen would've—"

"No. Shut up. Don't tell me in one breath that you think I'm cheating on Jen and then act like you understand."

"I never said you were cheating on Jen."

"Yes, yes, you did. It's exactly what you implied. And you know what, fuck you. You're right I'm banging the shit out of her. But it's just about the sex. That's what I am now. Someone who needs to fuck to feel alive."

But Vic wasn't looking at him anymore. His gaze was frozen over Nikhil's shoulder.

He realized with a dull thud of horror that the sound of the water in the bathroom had stopped.

He spun around.

Jess looked like he had stabbed her in the gut with a blunt knife and then done it again, harder. Not even a speck of color on her skin, her palms pressed to her belly, where the knife had pierced.

She didn't meet his eyes.

She looked at Vic instead. "Hi." Her lips did a weird stretching thing, but she couldn't form them into a smile. "Is Ria okay?" A tiny cough that hollowed out Nic's insides escaped her. "Is everything okay?"

Vic went to her and patted her shoulder so kindly she relaxed a little, and suddenly Nikhil didn't know why he had been so angry with him. "Everything's fine. I just wanted to make sure you guys didn't forget about the *dohal jevan*. It's today. Nic wasn't answering his phone."

She gave a hint of a nod. "We were just going to leave. Right?" The question was for Nikhil, but she was still struggling to meet his eyes while gathering up all that damn composure.

He had promised not to hurt her. "Jess, I'm—"

She raised her hand, cutting him off, and finally met his gaze, her eyes begging him not to make her acknowledge the horrible thing he had said, not in front of Vic.

"Please," she mouthed. Or maybe the plea was just in her eyes. "I'm ready to go. We're done here. Right, Nikhil?"

He nodded, swallowing his apology for when they were alone and letting her collect her beloved bag before following her out the door. She was right. They were done here.

35

You find the most important things in life suddenly. And it's almost funny how ordinary those extraordinary moments feel.

—Dr. Jen Joshi

All Nikhil wanted was a few moments alone with her. To go down on his knees and beg forgiveness. But Vic had taken the train into the city—his family took no chances when they were smothering you—and he was driving back with them.

Nikhil knew that acting like she hadn't heard his terrible words was the only way Jess saw to handle the shame he knew she was feeling and hiding beneath all that calm. He had to show her it was him, not her, who deserved to be ashamed. But she didn't want him doing it in front of Vic and so he wouldn't.

Fortunately, Vic kept up a steady stream of conversation, drawing her out with stories about how his company approached children's learning styles. Naturally, as a mother, it was a topic close to her heart and Vic seemed so genuinely interested in her opinion that Nikhil suspected he had jumped down Vic's throat unfairly. Something he'd been doing a lot of with his family lately.

By the time they reached his parents' home, several cars were already parked on the driveway. Of course they would come home right in the middle of Ria's baby shower. Aie's silk flower garland was hanging across the main door as it always did on holidays and ceremonies.

"Breathe, Vic," he said, thumping his cousin on the shoulder as they entered the house and hung up their coats. "I'm not going to break down. I'm actually glad I'm here for Ria's *dohal jevan*."

Vic responded by throwing his arms around Nikhil. "Thanks,

man," he said, and this time Nikhil returned his hug as though he meant it. Vic, who never knew how to quit when he was ahead tried again to take the bag from Jess's hands. "Good luck with that," Nic wanted to say to him. Instead he said, "Is it just the aunties?"

Vic nodded and headed straight to the kitchen and to Ria.

Nikhil stopped outside the archway that led to the kitchen.

Aie and her five closest friends stood around the island threading flowers into long garlands as they oohed and aahed over Vic as he kissed Ria, who was perched on a chair that had been draped in a sari.

The last time Nikhil had seen these women all dressed up like this in his mother's kitchen was at his wedding. He couldn't make himself go in. He stepped back into the foyer.

Jess, who had been avoiding his gaze like it held communicable diseases, studied him with calm eyes. Despite how hurt she was, she was assessing his need for comfort and trying to find the best way to comfort him.

"They're all dressed up," she said, leaning against the wall next to him, hiding away with him. She was wearing her usual black sweatshirt over yoga pants. Only, the ill-fitted clothes no longer hid anything from him. "Maybe I should go upstairs and wait there?"

He reached out and grabbed her hand, hoping she wouldn't pull away, needing her not to.

She didn't. She squeezed back and stayed right where she was.

"I'm sorry," he said. "What I said to Vic. I didn't—"

"I know," she said, understanding softening her eyes. "It was just a manner of speaking." Her smile was sad but real, and he knew she had forgiven him even though he didn't deserve to be forgiven. She understood, even though he himself didn't understand. "Are those your mother's friends?" She wanted him to leave it alone, and he didn't know how not to right now.

He followed her gaze to the archway. "Yes. The Auntie Brigade." That's what Vic had nicknamed them.

As was their way, the aunties were all wearing saris that matched—pink and blue—very clever.

"They're wearing matching saris," she said, indicating the archway he had backed away from like a thief in his own home. "Is that traditional for *dohal jevan?*"

"Actually, it's an American tradition. In America, pink is for a baby girl and blue is for a baby boy."

"Really? So girls can't wear blue?" she asked.

"God forbid," he said. "And boys most certainly can't wear pink."

"Oh. Joy looks adorable in pink."

From the look on her face, he had no doubt Joy looked adorable no matter what. A hunger to meet her baby, to know him, washed through him. "I'm sure he does. We just like getting our gender roles assigned bright and early here in America."

"And everyone wears pink and blue for baby showers in America?"

"No. The aunties always match their clothes. They call one another and discuss 'the dress code' before each gathering."

"Really? That's so sweet." She smiled up at him.

What was sweet was Jess when she smiled like that. Her eyes disappearing as if she were smiling into the sun.

It was gone too fast, possibly because he had stared at it like some psycho and made her conscious of it.

His thumb stroked the soft skin of her hand. "Do you really want to go upstairs?"

"No," she said as though he didn't know why she was staying. "It's not like I'm family or anything. I'm sure no one will notice that I'm not dressed up. Do you want to go inside?"

He nodded and led her into the kitchen, his hand pressed into the small of her back. All five aunties turned to them in unison. Their eyes darted in awkward little dances between Jess and him, varying degrees of sympathy shooting at him in lieu of words, the silence coming up abrupt and sudden after the animated chatter they had interrupted.

"Hello, Auntie*jis*, I hope we didn't hold everyone up."

That's all it took. They rushed at him. "Of course you're not holding anything up, *beta!*" "We only just got here." They patted his face, pulled him into hugs. They were smiling, but each face carried a diluted version of his mother's worry. Suddenly, they went silent again. There were just too many topics to avoid. His weight, his clothes, his two-year absence, a strange woman by his side. Finally, after all these years, he'd struck his mother's friends speechless. Crazy as it was, he smiled.

Aie stepped in. "You're here just in time. We were just about to do a quick blessing for Ria. That's all. Nothing elaborate," she said, in the voice she used when she wasn't quite sure how to approach a conversation but saw no way out of it.

A silver platter with an oil lamp, some vermillion, turmeric, and rice, and some sweets sat on the island. The silver platter had been in their family for at least three generations, and his mother had used it to say a blessing for him and to ward off the evil eye at every birthday and Diwali. He had explained the ritual to Jen the first time he brought her home, and Aie had totally embarrassed him by lighting the lamp and twirling the platter around his head three times and then doing the same to Jen.

One of the aunties leaned over the oil lamp with a lighter.

"Come, come, Jen, you come too," someone said to Jess.

The oxygen seemed to disappear from the room, leaving behind so much silence it echoed around the high ceiling.

He didn't know exactly which one of the aunties had made the error, but they all stared at the floor as though it had suddenly turned into the most interesting thing in the room.

Amazingly enough, the mention of Jen didn't tear his heart out. It was funny, in a sick sort of way, that one of them had made the one slip they had all been avoiding with such focus.

"You meant Jess," his mother said, yet again stepping up and lifting the boulder of awkwardness off their collective shoulders.

He should have stepped up and eased things, but he felt removed from the scene, seeing each expression, each little scuffle being fought inside all the players from a distance. The only calm in the room was Jess, her face a peaceful pond with elephants stampeding at the banks, and it grounded him.

Aie held the prayer platter out to Jess. She looked away from him and at the platter Aie was offering her and stepped away from it. "I can't."

His mother looked stricken. "Jess, *beta*, we don't believe in such things. Come, it's okay."

Jess didn't move, her face carefully blank, her jaw set. He recognized the look. For some reason, she believed that she couldn't offer a blessing. Based on the sadness on Aie's face, she seemed to think it had something to do with her being a widow.

Sometimes he hated all the superstition, all the precarious intricacies of his culture. Some days he wished he could throw it all off, un-know everything that Aie had worked so hard to code into him, but that still sometimes felt just as foreign as it felt familiar.

"Aie . . ." he said, "let her be."

His mother put the platter down. "That's fine. Everything's fine. We already have five women here to offer the blessing, so we're fine. Let's do the gender game first. Ria, you ready to pick out the baby's gender?"

Everyone smiled, or pretended to, and surrounded Ria. They offered her a platter of sweet treats and asked her to choose what she had a hankering for. Apparently, the treat that she picked would predict whether the baby was a boy or a girl. There was always a fifty-percent chance that they were right.

The first thing he had wanted to know when he found out Jen was pregnant was the gender. He'd hated not knowing whether to think of their baby as a she or a he. It had made him feel too distanced from his child, and he'd wanted no distance.

Yet again the stab of pain made his eyes seek out Jess, but she was gone. She must've slipped out while Ria chose between a *laddoo* and a *karanji*. The urge to seek her out was strong, but leaving here felt like leaving something precious behind. It felt like cheating. This absence of grief felt like cheating.

He dragged himself to the stairs and sat down on the bottom step, wanting to go up but unable to. He listened to the laughter and the teasing in the kitchen. All that normalcy sat like a weight on his chest, even as it made him feel lighter than he had in ages.

"Where did Jess go?" Ria said, waddling up to him and lowering herself down next to him, an act that took considerable effort, given the size of her belly combined with the fact that she was wrapped up in a sari and had flower garlands draped around her wrists and neck.

"I was just going to go find out."

She threw him one of those looks that tried to gauge what she could or could not say around him, and he wanted to shake her.

"Did you, you know, find what you were looking for?"

He shook his head. No, he hadn't, he hadn't found what he should have been looking for two years ago.

"Nikhil, is everything okay?"

Nothing was okay, except Ria was pregnant and healthy and worried about him. And maybe he needed to stop the tiptoeing first.

"I'm sorry, Ria, but I had to do this by myself." He put a hand up when she was about to interrupt. "And I know I wasn't by myself. But Jess—she's really helped me, okay? And it was the only way I could do it. Can you understand that? Please?"

Ria raised an eyebrow at him, all indignant. Classic Ria. "I can see that."

Then she really looked at him. Not her deer-in-the-headlights look, but a look from before everything had gone to hell. "I'm glad. I really am. And Jess was right that day, we shouldn't have left you alone on that ship for so long."

"You tried. I know how hard you tried. I'm sorry I shut you out. And I'm sorry you felt like you couldn't tell me about the baby. I'm sorry I wasn't here for you."

She wrapped her arms around him. She had to do it sideways, navigating her belly and the fact that they were sitting down. It was a weird, contorted hug, but it wrapped him up exactly right. He tightened his arms around her shoulders, and all that was skewed between them seemed to slide closer to its right place.

"You're here now, baby," she said. "I'm so glad you're here now. I should have told you. You were the first person I wanted to tell. I was terrified."

"I know. I know"

"Viky was terrified . . . is terrified. I thought he'd be all jubilant, but he's been freaking out the entire time. Not that he'll admit it." She took a breath, and met his eyes more squarely than she had in a very long time. "Nikhil, if it happens, if I lose my mind, you have to take care of him, okay?"

He pulled her close again and spoke into her hair. "Lose your mind even more, you mean?"

She smiled against his shoulder. He pulled away a little and made sure she could see his face. "We're going to watch you like a hawk, Ria. We'll medicate you to death if we have to. You're going to be fine."

She squeezed him harder, and they sat there like that forever.

"I think I know why Jess didn't want to do the blessing," she said finally, letting him go. Twisting with that belly couldn't be easy. "Do you mind if I go get her?"

He knew how Jess felt about Ria. He'd seen the way she watched her. He really should be the one to go up there and set things right.

"Please, Nikhil. Trust me." She stood, or tried to. He gave her a push to help her along and they both laughed. Then she turned and waddled up the stairs before he could stop her.

Maybe Ria was the right person to go get Jess and not him. What could he say to her anyway, when he was feeling the way he was feeling? Nothing was clear anymore. Why hadn't he leaned on his family instead of leaning on some stranger? But she didn't feel like a stranger. What did she even feel like? What did you call what he was feeling?

Was there a word for this suspension between fear and hope, lies and truth, relief and regret? What felt like an abomination one moment, violently selfish and irrevocably damaging, felt like a ray of sunshine the next, like plastic wrap being peeled off his face, fluid being sucked out of his lungs, like a brace coming off a broken leg when it still hurt.

He hadn't realized how much solace there had been in the pain. It had become his armor. He didn't think he could give it up. He couldn't be the person who left pain like that behind.

Please, not Ria Parkar. The last person Jess wanted to see right now was the blessed star. As in really blessed. Seriously, was there anything the woman did not have?

"Do you mind if I come in?" the star said, standing outside the room as though she was really waiting to be let in.

Jess could have prayed for mercy. But she needed to save that for later when she was going to have to pay for all she had done. It was the star's room, after all; she was just mooching off it.

She shrugged. "Should you be running up and down stairs?"

"I'm fine. Please, I'm tired of everyone getting on my case. I'm pregnant, not sick."

Okay. "Nikhil said there were complications. It's . . . it's a gift to have so many people worry about you." Great, she was letting her mouth run all over the place again. "I'm sorry," she said quickly.

Amazingly, instead of shooting her one of her patented icy-hot looks, the star seemed embarrassed. "No. You're right. I'm sorry. I didn't mean to sound spoiled. But I did, didn't I? I don't have the best communication skills."

"You?" Jess wanted to say. But Ria smiled, or tried to smile and failed. Which actually worked better than one of her camera-ready smiles.

"Can we start over?" The star held out some folded-up clothing. "I think these should fit you. I know you didn't know we had a ceremony, so you probably didn't bring something. It's brand-new. I've never used it."

Jess stared at the offering of clothes like an openmouthed idiot, taken completely by surprise.

"Take it, please, and come back down. I want you to do the *aarti* for the blessing. Everyone's waiting."

Jess stepped back. "I can't. I . . . I don't know how to." This was a lie, of course. Aama had insisted on *aarti* blessings at every birthday and every festival.

"I can never remember the details of how it's done either. Uma Atya will help you." She smiled another tentative smile. "Actually, with the aunties, you'll have more help than you need. They love telling people how to do things."

Jess wanted to smile at that, but she couldn't. "I'm sorry. I really can't."

"Jess, I know I haven't exactly been nice, but may I say something?"

She paused and waited for Jess to nod. "It's not true. What you're thinking. What they've told you. It's a lie. It's not us but our circumstances that are cursed." She tugged at Jess's hand and put the *salwar kurta* into her hand.

"Giving birth to me triggered my mother's psychosis and ruined my parents' lives. I believed myself to be a curse on everyone around me my entire life. I know now how stupid that was. And don't bother to deny it. Of course I recognize it in your face. It's what you believe. But you're wrong."

"Ria, listen . . ."

"No. Let me finish. When you were talking about your son that day. Something about that, it changed how I saw my pregnancy. You made me want to be a mother. Everyone's tried from the moment I got pregnant, but what you said that day when you talked about Joy, I don't know why, but it changed everything. And then what I saw in Nikhil's face today . . . Please, Jess, please be part of my ceremony. It won't feel right if you're not."

She gave Jess's hand a squeeze and turned around and headed for the door. "They're all waiting downstairs. I'm not doing the ceremony without you." With that she was gone.

From the very first time Nikhil had met Jess, the one thing that had struck him was that quality about her that defied happiness. As though she wore a raincoat and happiness were raindrops that try as they might couldn't permeate. It was how he had felt too, and recognizing it in someone else had somehow made it easy to accept it in himself.

Over the past two weeks, he'd seen every shade of pain cross her face. He'd seen pleasure too, when she was in the throes of ecstasy she'd had to fight so hard for. But never happiness. He'd seen her reach for it over and over and then draw back as though it were too hot to touch. When she had spun on the ice she had stretched herself toward it with everything she was, a tornado of wanting. But it had stayed just outside her reach. When she talked about Joy, he saw glimpses, but they kept getting lost behind worry.

The glaze of moisture in her eyes as she moved the *aarti* platter in circles around Ria's face wasn't happiness either. But it was the closest he had seen her let it get.

"How pretty you look in that color," one of the aunties said, and he realized that he had never before this seen a speck of color on Jess.

Her *kurta* was a soft beige with splashes of darker pink. The exact color of her cheeks when she blushed.

She caught him staring, and the slow glow of happiness she had been fighting flashed harsh and bright. But only for a second. Yet again he had no idea what to do with it. It sat in his chest all evening, even as it waxed and waned in her face as she let the tide of his family carry her along in its celebratory spirit without letting herself drown in it.

When the aunties started to leave, everyone hugged and kissed him as though he had magically turned into someone other than the man who had come home mere days ago. Her gaze lingered on him being coddled and loved, unreadable and yet too readable for him to go on doing nothing about it. When was the last time someone had taken care of her? Shown her she was precious enough to be taken care of?

He found his feet running up the stairs, hungry to see her. Hungry for something, and he slipped into her room with no more than a cursory knock. She was standing there, her own clothes clutched in her hands, ready to go back to her all black. Her gaze crashed into his. So much in her eyes he couldn't interpret, so much he didn't want to. He walked to her and his hands grabbed her face.

Her eyes. God, how did her eyes mirror everything inside him?

He devoured her mouth, falling into her, falling back into himself. He kept on going until the rough edges of his wanting smoothed and then furled again and again because she wouldn't let him go.

"Why did you leave?" he asked against the tiny dancing dimples at the edge of her mouth.

She didn't answer.

He pulled away. "Why didn't you do the *aarti* blessing for Ria when Aie asked first?"

She looked indignant, her eyes punishing him for asking the question. "I did it, didn't I?"

"After Ria made you. But before that. Why didn't you? Tell me."

She shook her head. No.

"You never refuse to do a blessing; why did you refuse?" He had to know what had stopped her with such force, what had made all that heartbreaking happiness seep into her eyes when she'd actually done it, and what made her so afraid now?

"It's nothing. I just don't believe in it."

"Bullshit. What was it?"

"Ria's pregnant."

"So?"

Fear spiked in her eyes. "Accursed people don't bless anyone, Nikhil. What if something happens to Ria or her baby?"

"Don't say that." He studied her face. "Who says you're cursed? Who even believes in this superstitious crap anymore?"

She pushed away from him and turned away.

But when he went to her, his arms going around her, she leaned back into him.

"What did Ria say to change your mind? Tell me."

"No. You should be downstairs. Everyone will wonder where you are."

He didn't care. This was where he wanted to be. With the mix of emotions warring inside him, the one thing he knew was that he couldn't bear to let her go. "I don't want to go down. I want to be with you. Come with me."

"Okay."

But he couldn't move, and she didn't either. "I'm lying. I don't want to go down there." There was a storm in his heart. Of longing, of everything he wanted, of everything he couldn't bear to let go of.

"Okay," she said, her voice as still as the most placid waters, not a ripple of demand. It made him crazy.

"Jess, back at the apartment. I should never have said that. I lost my temper at Vikram. I didn't mean it. Not one word of it."

She twisted in his arms, the strangest energy propelling her, and went straight for his lips, taking his words with a desperation he recognized only too well. Taking the apology that would acknowledge how low he had fallen and reaching past it to the thing between them that set their world the right side up.

Nikhil's skin was silk. No, not silk. Silk was too cold. He was like some sort of living, breathing fabric that emanated such warmth, such strength, she couldn't stop touching it. This skin on skin, this intimate right to touch someone as if he belonged to her, she'd never had this before, and it brought her into herself exactly the way holding Joy in her arms had. It unlocked a part of her she had never dared to let out.

She skimmed her fingers over the *devanagri* script tattooed onto his chest. Two tiny squiggles with a line holding them together. "Gain." She knew that wasn't what the letters were supposed to spell. Even if Nikhil hadn't told her how the tattoo artist had misspelled Jen's name, she would have known that he wouldn't let any other word permanently stain his skin.

The letters were beautiful. Sharp edged and sure. So much like Jen. She pressed her cheek against his chest, sinewy muscle stretched over ribs. "Thanks," she whispered into the name of the person she had taken so much from. And then, "Sorry." She said it soundlessly, terrified of waking him.

He had pulled her leg across his thighs, his fingers clutching possessively at the intensely sensitive skin at the back of her knee. Just thinking of where she was warmed her cheeks, but it wasn't embarrassment, it was reverence, a deep fullness that flooded her body. She used every cell, every pore, to draw in the feel of him, to memorize their touching. This was what being alive felt like. What they had just done was what being alive felt like.

"That's what I am now," he had said to Vikram. "Someone who needs to fuck to feel alive." He might have said it in anger and she might have waved it away as a manner of speaking, but it was the truth. Except, if she knew anything at all, she knew this was so much more than that ugly word. This hadn't been fucking.

What he had said was killing him. He kept apologizing. It had torn her heart out to hear him say it, but if she let him open that vault of worms, they would have to examine what they did mean to each other. What was the point of that? She could see him struggle against whatever he was feeling for her. What was the point of that too?

For her, there was no struggle. She knew in the very depths of her being that this—what she was feeling with him—this was never going to happen for her again. What she had already taken from him, what she was sucking up now like a leech, it was all she would ever have.

The scar she had let them cut across her chest, and the leather-bound diary at the bottom of her bag, every word of which she had consumed with such hunger, knowing full well it was theft—those things alone snuffed out any chance they had, no matter what feelings either one of them admitted to.

Even if he made it past the vows he had always believed could be made only once in a lifetime, no one could forgive what she had already done, let alone what she had no choice but to do when they found the evidence.

Warmth prickled behind her eyelids. But if she moved, if she dripped tears onto his chest, he would wake up and this moment would be over and she could not let it go yet.

She tried to push the tears back, begged her body to comply, but the trickle of warmth slid across the bridge of her nose and spilled over. Moisture pooled where her face pressed against his chest. She tried to hold herself still, but her chest hiccupped to hold in the sobs.

"Jess?" He stirred beneath her and lifted his head, emerging from sleep with an unguarded vulnerability that was going to haunt her forever. "Shit, are you hurt? Did I hurt you?"

The question! The way he asked it, the way his voice turned raw over the fear that he might have hurt her. As though she were something precious. As though she mattered. She snuggled close to him, tucking her chin and pressing her forehead into his chest, refusing to let him see what she wasn't strong enough to keep off her face. He tugged her away, trying to get a look at her, but she shook her head and pressed her wet face into his chest.

Please don't pull away from me. She couldn't say it.

She didn't need to.

"It's okay, sweetheart." He gathered her in his arms, pressed his lips to the crown of her head. His warm breath so tender on her scalp it intoxicated her. He rocked her. His breath turned to kisses and slid down her hair, down her face, licked at her tears, traced her jaw, nipped at her throat.

His eyes soaked her up, his gaze gathering hunger. "Do you have any idea how beautiful you are?" His lips consumed her, stealing her breath even as his words stabbed her heart.

A ragged sob burst from her.

"What is it?" He pulled away again, searching her face with eyes too perceptive, too invested. "Shit. You hate it when I call you beautiful." He pulled her close again. "I'm such an ass."

And in that one moment of realization, she knew that he saw everything that word did to her, remembered every time he had used it and ripped her to shreds.

"Sweetheart, look at me. I'm sorry." He sat up, taking her with him, and sat her down, eye to eye. He cupped her face in both palms. "It's not your body, it's not your face. It's you. It's the peace that is you, the strength that is you. You're beautiful the way—" He searched for words. "You know that brand-new skin that grows over wounds, that threads together a surgical incision? It's the most beautiful thing you've ever seen. It looks fresh and delicate, but it's stronger than anything. That's the way you're beautiful. Just like that." His serious eyes crinkled into a smile. "Shit. That was a terrible analogy, wasn't it?"

Despite herself she smiled. "Terrible."

He leaned close. "You're beautiful because you're you." His words were a caress on her lips. His whispered wonder filled her up.

Her body had brought her horrors; now it brought her what she had never hoped to have. It had always felt separate from her, like a cloak. His wonder soaked it into her being, wove it together with who she was. In this moment, in this precious breath of a moment, it gave him to her even as it gave her to herself.

She climbed into his lap, straddling him, her wanting an inferno, not caring about what she was doing, who she was, caring only about this man under her, so open to her, how could she not pour herself into him? How could she not give it all to him? Not just the skin and the limbs that entranced him. Not just the peace and strength that enticed him. She knew that was what he hungered for, his heart unavailable, but she gave him everything else too, everything ugly and scarred and hot and wanting and terrified and hopeful. Ripping past all she hid under, she took him into herself and she gave him everything.

"Jess," he said, panting in her arms, their entangled bodies slick with their joining. "What are you doing to me?" He was breathing as though he had run until his lungs exploded and flown into a leap and found that he could fly. As though there was nothing beneath his feet. There was nothing beneath hers either.

She had no idea what he was doing to her either. But it was like having her body ripped from around her. From the real her that resided inside the shell that held things inside even as it kept them outside. This was being touched. This was coming undone. This was that moment in which you knew you had left everything behind and convinced yourself to go on living.

It was the cracking of an egg.

She saw the exact moment when the full force of it struck him too.

His eyes went wild, the blast of pain in them so violent she couldn't look away. He rolled over, taking her with him. For one second, his body remained suspended over hers on trembling arms, and then he dropped his head into her shoulder.

"It's okay, Nikhil," she wanted to tell him. But she couldn't. All she could do was pull him closer, unable to bear the thought of him pulling himself out of her.

"I need to get up," he said, the moment unraveling inside him and turning him cold. She clamped down on the sob that rose in her throat because she knew that he saw that she couldn't let him go yet, even as he couldn't stand to touch her anymore, couldn't bear to go on feeling what he was feeling.

"Go," she said. "I'm fine."

Still he gave her time. She almost wrapped her arms around him again to beg him to let her have more.

But she couldn't. She had to let him go.

He went, leaving her slowly, for all the agony in his eyes, withdrawing from her gently. Separating from her as though she were worthy of tenderness. Placing her aside as though she were precious but suffocating, a scarf of silk that was choking the breath out of him.

36

The peon who worked at the clinic was found dead of alcohol poisoning. Rahul believes he was the one who leaked the registry. Another clue wiped away.

—Dr. Jen Joshi

Sometimes you had to chase your destiny, and sometimes it walked right at you and knocked on your window with its pink-painted nails.

Asif hit the button and lowered the window. The bastard politician's daughter had been glaring at the black-tinted windows, but all that rich-girl attitude disappeared as soon as she got a look at his ugly mug. Worked every time. "How can I help you, miss?" he said in English and then looked at his computer genius in the passenger seat. "Correct?"

"Perfect, Bhai."

As soon as she'd seen him, she sensed danger and tried to back away. Smart girl. But he snapped his fingers, and his men were behind her in the time it took for him to grab her blouse and hold her in place. "I said, how can I help you?"

She was about to scream, but Laloo pressed the butt of his gun into her side with a "shhh," whispered in her ear, and she thought better of it.

"I'm sorry, I thought you were someone else."

He laughed. "Yes, all the bitches say that when they see my face. But I know exactly who you are." The idiotic bitch had probably noticed his SUV trailing her for the past week and thought it was Daddy's bodyguards and thought she'd tell them to get lost. God save us from spoiled brats who felt invincible!

Given that she had two ugly bastards with guns behind her and

Asif had her by her collar, she didn't look quite as terrified as he would have liked. Pale as a *roomali* roti. But other than that, no hysterics. He grabbed the two sides of her collar and yanked her blouse apart. The buttons popped and scattered. She yelped, but Laloo's handy *ghoda* at her back did the trick and she shut up.

A dark red scar ran down the middle of her chest, between her breasts, which were too small for his taste. But if her bastard father didn't stop fingering his arse, they'd have to do.

"You know where that came from?" he asked.

"What?"

He ran his finger up and down the thin, puckered line. "That thing that's beating in there. You think your life is more important than the person that belonged to before you?"

"Who are you?"

"Asif Khan. You should Googole it." His computer genius laughed next to him. "Or even better, ask your daddy."

"You know my father?"

"The question is, do you know your father?"

Finally, two men came running up behind her. What kind of *chutiya* bodyguards had her Daddy found her? It had taken them all this time to notice that she was being attacked in broad daylight? They were the ones he was interested in anyway. At least today. Right now, finding the red-haired bitch was more important than using this one to teach her father a lesson.

He snapped his fingers, and his men turned the guns on the two idiots, disarming them in under five seconds. She almost screamed again, but he yanked her close and spoke into her ear. "You make a sound and you'll watch them die."

His men stuffed the two men in the back of the car. He licked her cheek; she even tasted fancy, and she started shaking. "A girl like you shouldn't walk up to stranger's cars. Didn't your Daddy teach you anything?" He gave her a shove, and she fell back in the dirt. Another snap of his fingers and they left her sitting there on her bum, her eyes so terrified, she would be waking up with nightmares for a good, long time.

37

I know Nikhil will never forgive me for the secrets I'm keeping from him. I used to think it was to keep him from talking me out of this. But it's more than that. He sees knowing as loving. Thinks honesty is connection, and now that I've lied to him I can't bear to see the disappointment in his eyes.

—Dr. Jen Joshi

Nikhil rubbed his chest, his arms. Everything felt tight. It felt alien. He felt alien. As though something had invaded his body. As though despite what he wanted, what he wanted had changed.

In the mirror his grown-out hair stood in spikes on his head. Spikey. The memory of the name didn't rip his gut out. Instead of making him angry, the realization made him sad.

He lifted the razor from the cup on the sink and grabbed a chunk of hair at his temple. He touched the razor to his scalp. But his hands wouldn't do it. The fingers in his hair weren't a memory from long ago. The fingers now clutching at the strands needed purchase, needed him. And he couldn't take a blade to them.

He tossed the razor across the restroom and it broke apart, separating blade from handle, the disjointing making both pieces useless. In the mirror that witnessed his coming apart, Jen's misspelled name flashed across his chest and he rubbed at it, making it appear and disappear.

He had told Jess last night how he had spelled the name in English and the tattoo artist had translated a *J* for a *G* in Sanskrit and turned Jen's name to Gain.

Jen had loved that. Had declared it a more apt name for herself anyway.

She had told him he deserved being stuck with the error for not listening to her. She had asked him not to do it.

Nothing is permanent, Spikey. Except a tattoo.

How I feel about you is permanent.

And it was.

It was.

Even dead she was still his wife. Even spelled wrong it was still her name. He rubbed at it. Not to erase, but to stroke, and stoke. To touch the word that had been her because he'd never touch her again.

Because he couldn't stop thinking about how touching another woman felt.

"I'm sorry," he said to the empty bathroom, his whispered guilt echoing inside him.

He had sworn never to forget her. She was right: Nothing was permanent. He couldn't do this again, couldn't bear the pain of another impermanent thing.

Couldn't bear the pain of letting her go. *I won't ever let you go.* He wished he could say the words to her. Needed to say the words to her.

I'm a cheating bastard.

He had never had anything to say that he couldn't say to Jen. It had baffled him how much she had hated that. Finally, something he could have put in that stupid diary she'd given him.

Shit.

Her diary.

Holy. Shit.

How could he have forgotten about the diary?

He stormed out of the bathroom.

Jess sat up, Ria's pink sheets clutched beneath her chin.

"What's wrong? Nikhil?"

"We didn't find it in our things because those aren't our things."

She glanced around, her eyes seeking out the clothes he had ripped off her last night. "Not your things?"

"What we went through in her apartment. That was just stuff, and stuff didn't mean anything to Jen."

He went back into the bathroom and out the other door into his room and started scanning a bookcase.

Behind him he heard Jess get out of bed and scramble to pull on the clothes strewn around the room.

"Why didn't I figure this out sooner? You said she told you it was hidden in something that meant a lot to me, right?" He turned around to find her behind him, her hair tucked inside Ria's *kurta* because she'd pulled it on so fast. She had pulled on the *salwar* pants too. God forbid he saw her out of bed in just a *kurta*.

Jen would've followed him stark-naked. Jess was covered from head to toe, and disheveled. For the first time since they'd met, her perfect shell was gone. She was in complete disarray. She didn't seem to have any idea who she was, where she was, what he was talking about, and she didn't even realize that she was letting him see it. She was more naked than anyone he'd ever seen.

For all of Jen's comfort with physical nakedness, there had been so many things she hadn't been able to share with him. With anyone.

Jess watched him for answers with those naked eyes. His hand hovered over the row of books before he pulled out a leather-bound diary.

A moment of absolute horror flashed in Jess's eyes when she saw it in his hands. Then she collected herself just as he started to come apart.

The diary Nikhil was holding up looked almost exactly like another one she knew so well. Her heart started to beat hard and fast, and it had nothing to do with how restless he looked. Or how he had spared no more than a glance for her, but it had been enough.

He held the book up to her, a strange distance in his eyes. "I know where Jen hid the evidence."

The face staring back at him had to be dripping guilt, but he didn't see it. Because his belief in her lies was absolute. In every ugly one of them.

She took the diary he was holding out and flipped it over, studied it, opened it, her hands desperate to do something. Her body was so used to being a liar, it moved on its own accord. A few pages had horrible handwriting scrawled across them.

"It's not in this one," he said, mistaking her silence for confusion. "Jen kept a diary. She'd had it since before I met her. But she only started writing in it seriously after we met. Her mother gave it to her before she died and told her it could be a way for her to tell her things even after she was gone. Until we met, Jen said she didn't have anything to tell her mother.

"When we first met, I asked all the time to see it. I begged, but she wouldn't let me see it. When I wouldn't let it go, she gave me this one." He took the diary back from her and studied the blank pages as though they weren't blank at all. "'Keep your own diary,' she told me. 'Maybe if you can write something in it that you can't say to me, I'll let you read mine.'

"I kept writing shit in it. Making stuff up. Because I didn't have any secrets from her. But she wouldn't cave. She said that if anyone read her diary, she wouldn't be able to write in it. I realized she really needed to keep it private and I let it go. And I forgot all about it. Shit. How could I have forgotten about it? She had to have thought it would be the first thing I'd go after if something happened to her. And me, I . . . I forgot." He took the diary back and stared at it like it was going to disappear before his eyes. "How could I have been so stupid?"

How could she have been so stupid? How had she not realized Jen would put the evidence in the diary?

"That's where it is," he said. "That's where the evidence is."

What she should've done was ask him where her diary was. Because that would be the logical thing for her to ask. Instead, she stared at him, unable to say another word. Unable to add another lie to the pile of lies she was buried under.

He turned sad eyes on her and answered her question nonetheless. "It's not here. All these days of searching and it was never here. The cops have it. It had to have been in the handbag she was carrying. She kept it with her all the time. They took that bag as evidence."

She thought of her own bag where her deception was zipped into a secret compartment. She had to get to it.

He stroked the brown leather in his hands. Those hands that spoke a language she wished she had never learned. "What kind of man forgets something like that about his wife?"

The kind of man who forgot himself when he lost her.

He looked so angry with himself, she wanted to pull him close.

But she was part of his guilt, and she removed the hand she found resting on his shoulder.

What they had done last night rose between them like a monster they had spawned, all their combined regret and guilt struggling to dismember it before it destroyed them.

"Jess," he said, and that one word held all the words she knew would follow. "I can't forget her. I can't move on. I swore never to let her go. This . . . Last night . . . I should never have let it happen." He looked at the diary in his hand. "I can't do this again."

She couldn't believe she didn't fold over. He waited for a response, but staying upright was all she could manage.

He was having no trouble saying the words. He had decided where they went from here. She should have been grateful. Because it made things so much easier for her. Since she had no choice where she went from here. The floor beneath her feet had suddenly turned to quicksand. She was sinking, but she couldn't show it, couldn't acknowledge that it was rising around her.

"I'm sorry," he said. "I never meant to hurt you."

"I know." And she did. "You didn't hurt me. You . . . you . . . healed me."

A pained sound escaped him. Or maybe it was her. She stepped back, away from him, her hand shoving her hair behind her ear. She wanted to press it against her chest, where her scar tugged and smarted, wishing for her sweatshirt instead of Ria's *kurta* hugging her body.

Her body that for the first time in her life felt like her own. *You're beautiful because you're you.*

So much he'd given her. This pain tearing her insides couldn't take away any of it. He'd given her back to herself. Taught her the pleasure she could feel. Taught her how to go after what she wanted, demand it.

God, she'd let him take her standing up against the bathroom sink last night with his family in the house.

You're a whore with a whore's body.

No, she wasn't. No, she wasn't. No. She wasn't.

Now she knew she wasn't. He had taught her that.

And she had done nothing but lie to him.

If shame were a color, she had to be swathed in it right now.

"Jess . . ."

"No. I mean it, Nikhil. We needed this. You and I. That's all it was." She had the evidence. She'd had it all along. Finally, her baby was going to be safe. "Thanks." Her eyes were dry, all of her felt tinder-dry. There was a God after all. Because if she cried, if he saw how she was feeling inside, the shame engulfing her would consume her whole.

She turned around to look at the bathroom and Ria's room beyond it. They'd made love three times here, or was it four? "I'll pack. It's great. That you figured the diary out."

"Jess . . ."

Jess, Jess, Jess. His lips had whispered her name into her breasts, between her legs. He'd whispered her name into her heart. A name that wasn't even hers. Now, spilling from his lips, it stabbed her with her own betrayal.

"I'm sure the police will find it. I can go home." Her baby, she'd left her baby alone. Now she could make sure he was safe. No one was ever going to touch him again. Because Joy was the only thing that mattered. Not the impossible dreams, not the man who had awakened them, awakened her.

He stepped close to her. But she scrambled back. She couldn't let him touch her.

"Don't be like this." The guilt on his face was a mask of pain. He hated himself.

She couldn't bear that.

She turned, but couldn't walk away. She turned back to him, his beloved face, those sad, noble eyes that could turn so hot and molten one second, playful as a child the next, those eyes that had given her more than she'd ever hoped to have. She couldn't just walk away leaving that much pain in those eyes. She went to him and touched his face. He grabbed her hand, another heart-wrenching sound escaping his lips.

The lump in her throat choked out all breath. She wanted to push her words through it, the way he had made her push through all her horrors.

She wanted to tell him not to fight so hard. She wanted to tell him it was okay. She knew how firmly he had believed that there would never be anyone else to fit him like Jen. She knew his heart had felt so consumed by what he felt for Jen that the idea of anyone else ever finding an inch in there turned everything into a lie. She knew all of that, understood it, because that's how she felt about him.

He was her Jen.

Her hand was still grasped in his. He pulled it to his lips. He didn't even know it, but he was memorizing the feel of her against his skin. He was saying good-bye. Or maybe she was just projecting her own feelings onto him.

She tugged her hand away, and he opened his eyes. There was pity in them now, and his damn need to comfort her, comfort the whole blasted world.

"Jess, this isn't good-bye." He dug his hands into his pockets to keep from touching her again. "I will always be grateful for what you've done for me. Your friendship means everything. It always will."

Friendship? Is that what you called what they had done to each other last night? His eyes darkened with pain again, and she knew she had touched her throat, where his lips, his tongue, his teeth would forever be branded.

"Don't do that. Don't make this about sex."

Her hand fell away from her throat. Of all the things he could have said, nothing could possibly have hurt more. They hadn't had sex, they had made love.

Again she tried to walk away. She needed to find what she had come here to find. Now that she knew where the evidence was, she needed to have it in her hands and get away. For all the lies she needed to get to, she couldn't leave this lie between them. "I'm not the one who's making this about sex."

She had no idea what she'd hoped to achieve by saying that, but she should have expected the anger that flared in his eyes. It was just cover for his pain. Anger and guilt were easier, they gave you power. Pain made you helpless. "I love Jen. I can never stop loving Jen. I don't know how."

"I'm not asking you to stop loving Jen. God, Nikhil, how can you accuse me of such a thing? Of course you will always love her. This is not about Jen. This thing between us. It has nothing to do with Jen."

He looked horrified at what she had said, but not half as horrified as she felt for having let it slip out.

He had backed so far away from her, he was all the way across the room now. "I don't feel the same way."

And that's what she got for losing control. Her shoulders hurt from holding them up. Her spine wanted to curl around the pain. Who would have thought love could hurt like this? She wanted to turn into a snail, roll up, and squeeze into a shell. But then nothing would be able to bring her out. And her life wasn't hers alone. "I know," she said.

"I can't give you what you want, Jess."

My name's not Jess. That's what she wanted to tell him. Once, just once, she wanted him to call her by her real name. Then again, she never wanted to be called by her name again.

"I don't want anything from you, Nikhil. This is not me asking for something. I don't have space in my life for you. Joy will never accept anyone else into our life. He's really possessive of me." It was a lie. But what did another one matter?

After that stupid outburst of truth, the only thing she could think of was more lies to obliterate it so something as useless as truth wouldn't ruin everything she had to do.

The ease with which Nikhil had walked away from her after telling her she was nothing to him, the ease with which he had let her convince him that they had no hope for a future, it was like a black veil someone had thrown over her head before thrusting the key to her escape in her hand. She had to feel her way around it, navigate the darkness that also meant freedom.

Ria was alone in the house, and Nikhil had gone down to check up on her, leaving Jess alone to her stealth. She wondered how Ria was feeling and pushed away the urge to go downstairs and check up on Ria herself. Instead, she picked up her duffel bag and zipped open the false bottom. Sitting there under Joy's smiling face was the thick leather-bound diary crammed with words. Crammed with all of Jen's words.

Aama loved to say that two souls that fit exactly right stay together for seven lifetimes. She had felt that way about Baba. Jess had always believed it was just something Aama told herself to make her widowhood bearable.

But now she didn't know. She had lived with her uncle and his family for seven years, but they had always felt like strangers. Her schoolmates, her teachers, people she had worked with for years—everyone had always felt like a stranger. Everyone except Aama, Joy, and from the first time she had met him, Nikhil. Her soul recognized him. It always had.

"This is not our first lifetime together, Jen," she whispered to the diary in her hands. "And I know this won't be our last. I know he was yours when you had him. But before I met him, my soul was nothing, and without him it will be nothing again."

She remembered with so much clarity the day the person in a burka had thrust the diary into her hands, it was as though it was happening now. The person to actually put Jen's diary in her hands was just a hired thug, of course. She had never actually laid eyes on the man who had stolen her life and turned her into a thief. She had no idea what he looked like. For all she knew, he could be her neighbor in Mumbai who skulked about and never responded when she said hello.

All she knew of the man who had stolen her son on his way home from school and kept him for two days so she would agree to whatever he demanded of her was his voice. That cultured, kind, silken voice that could modulate his intent with the skill of the most seasoned actor, it was a sound that would haunt her nightmares for as long as she lived. The person in the burka had handed her the diary and the cell phone and disappeared, and from then on that voice had told her what to do, held her strings, kept the noose around her neck.

Go to this clinic and the doctor will carve the scar into your chest.

Go to this beauty parlor and they will put extensions in your hair and color it.

Board this flight.

Board this ship.

Read every word in the diary.

Remember I didn't hurt your son this time. But next time, who knows?

She sank back into Ria's bed and pulled the diary close to her chest.

"I am so sorry," she said. "I wish there was another way."

But there wasn't. That's how life worked. When you were in a corner, you either got dug into the walls or you had to sell what you could to barter yourself out of it.

She stroked the thick leather. It seemed to respond to her touch. Jen had taught her so much. How pathetic was she that a dead woman was the best friend she'd ever had?

And here she was ready to gouge out the skin off her back. She still couldn't believe she hadn't thought of checking the diary for the evidence. She pressed into the padded cover with her fingers but felt nothing. Jen had done a great job of concealing it. Nikhil had said that the diary was with the police. That meant even the police hadn't realized that something so vital was hidden in there. Suddenly, her hands on the diary started to shake. If Naag had stolen the diary from police custody, that meant he was even more powerful than she thought.

She flipped the cover open and traced the seam of the paper stuck to the inside cover. She used her nail to work the corner of the seam until the paper curled, then pinching it between her fingers she pulled. The thick card stock peeled off. Taped to the inside of the paper was a thin piece of plastic. A storage device. She stared at the minuscule thing that held within it secrets Jen had died for, her hunger for justice larger than everything else.

Jess, on the other hand, was going to be the end of the road for justice. The end of any chance at redemption for Nikhil. For Jen. She slipped the card into her bra and pressed the edge of the paper back into the leather seam, sealing the evidence of her crime. Her entire body was encased in an icy numbness. Jen was dead. Jess wasn't responsible for her death. She was responsible only for Joy. For her baby. For making sure he was safe. It was the only thing that mattered. Then why didn't it feel that way?

"Ria's water just broke and it's stained with meconium." She spun around. Nikhil stood there, slightly winded from having run up the stairs. She thought she had locked the door. "I just called the ambulance. I have to go to the hospital with her. Everyone else is meeting us there. We can discuss calling the police about her diary when I—"

She tried to slip the diary back into the bag, but his gaze froze on her hands. "What is that?"

Everything slid into slow motion. Nikhil walked to her and took the diary from her hands. His eyes took in the worn leather, the well-used pages, then at the speed of a lethal, slow-moving snake, his gaze found her, pierced her, and started to riffle through her thoughts.

Ching ching ching.

"I can explain . . ." Only she couldn't.

Nikhil's forehead crunched up, his jaw tightened, all of him tightened. He reached for her. She almost took his hand, but he hooked a finger into the neck of her shirt.

"Nikhil—"

He pulled the neckline down, his eyes so focused, so destroyed, she cringed. "Is it real?"

He didn't wait for an answer.

"It isn't. Shit." His hand pressed against the puckered skin. "It's fresh. It's what, six months old? Why would you . . . ? Shit." He looked up at her, eyes dilated with anger so hot she stepped away from it, backing herself against the bedpost.

"Nikhil, I—"

"The evidence. Shit. It was always the evidence. You were here for the evidence." She watched his brain unravel the knot one snag at a time. "You were paid to find the evidence. You were paid to sleep with me."

She pushed off his hand. That's the first conclusion he jumped to? That she was a whore? That what they had experienced together was premeditated and dirty? Suddenly, she was sick. Sick of all the feelings she had let herself feel. Sick of her own stupidity.

What had she expected would happen? Yes, she was a liar and a cheat, and so incredibly stupid to think this would end any differently. She didn't know what she had expected from him, but he was no different from anyone else. She couldn't afford the guilt that she had let bloom inside her. It had never been a choice. And she didn't care that he would never understand.

"Why?" he asked.

She could have dealt with the judgment he'd thrown at her, but the relief in his face destroyed everything. The fact that she'd had no recourse, no choice, didn't even strike him.

She wanted to push him away, leave without answering. But he had her boxed in. "Because I had to." *Because if you had done what you should have, they wouldn't have made me.*

"I don't believe it!" He turned away from her, even the sight of her disgusting him. "You've been scamming me this whole time and you're justifying it? Don't tell me you had to. You *chose* to."

She sagged into the post. "Choice?" How could she not laugh at that?

He spun on her. "Don't laugh. You always have a choice," he said, throwing at her what had to be the stupidest platitude in all the world.

He believed it too. He wasn't interested in what she had to say. But she didn't care. She was sick of her own silence.

"You're right. Of course you always have a choice." She pushed past him and started to gather her things, but he grabbed her arm.

She yanked it away. "You want to talk about choice? Okay, let's talk about choice. I was fourteen the first time my uncle's neighbor cornered me in the street on my way home from school and told me he knew how I could make some money to help my aunt feed her five daughters. I carried a knife to school every day after that. That was my choice.

"But after I turned fifteen and my mother died, he didn't come to me, he went to my uncle, who told me I had to go to Calcutta with him and work as a maid so he'd have money for my dowry. Even at fifteen I knew he was lying. Even at fifteen I had no faith, none of your bloody innocence and belief in humanity. I knew it wasn't a maid's job that was waiting for me in Calcutta. But I had to go. That was my choice.

"Still I fought. I lured the bastard into a bathroom at Siliguri bus station, stole his money, and locked him in there. Then I split the money between the other four girls he was taking to Calcutta and sent them back home. Me? I had no home to go back to.

"You want choice? I chose to go to Calcutta and work. But you already know what was waiting for me there. I was seventeen, Nikhil. Do you remember being seventeen? When you were living in this beautiful house being taught lessons about justice by your parents, I was picked up like a scrap of meat and dumped into a car, where two men took turns tearing up my body. Simply because they could. You're right. I should have chosen to not let them do that to me, to my childhood.

"But I chose it. And you know what else I chose? I chose to let that bastard go on living in his big house, I chose to let him get paid millions of rupees to appear on magazines and in ads. Yes, I chose that, because of course, you always have a choice."

"Jess." Now he was listening to her. Now what she said mattered. But it was too late. He reached for her again, but she'd rather die than let him touch her.

"And yes, I chose to let someone pay me to screw you." They had paid her by letting her son live, but she could never tell him that. "And you're right to call me a whore. Just like they were right to think I was one."

He was breathing hard. Or maybe she was projecting again. "I never called you a whore."

He had. Or maybe he hadn't. She didn't care. All she cared about now was getting out of here before he handed her over to the authorities.

Because of all the choices she'd made, getting thrown in jail was one choice she could not make. She had to get back to Joy.

"Nikhil!" Ria's scream followed a loud crashing sound.

Jess pushed him out of the way and raced down the stairs, a horrible sense of foreboding slamming inside her. Ria was rolled up on the den floor next to the bed, the tall floor lamp lying broken next to her.

She went down on her knees next to Ria, using her hands to sweep the broken glass away from Ria's body. "It's okay, Ria. It's okay." She sat down on the floor and slid Ria's head onto her lap.

Ria grabbed her hand. "Viky . . . someone needs to call Viky."

Nikhil was already on the phone. "Vic and Aie and Dad are on their way to the hospital. The ambulance is almost here."

Nikhil squatted down next to them and took Ria's wrist. He checked her pulse, then her eyes. "Try to breathe. The ambulance is almost here. How bad is the pain?"

"It's not too bad. I was going to come up to get you, but I fell and the stupid lamp . . ."

"It's okay. You're going to be okay." Jess squeezed her hand, wiping the sweat off her forehead. She looked white as a sheet and she was having a hard time breathing. Why had Jess let her talk her into doing the blessing?

"What happened?" Ria asked, breathing through the pain, studying Jess's face then Nikhil's.

Jess waited for Nikhil to say something. But the doorbell rang, and he let the paramedics in. Before Jess knew what was happening, they had Ria on a gurney and in the ambulance. Ria wouldn't let her hand go.

"I'm sorry," she said to Ria as the paramedics took her vitals and started an IV. She slipped Ria's hand into Nikhil's as he climbed into the ambulance and she got off. "Is she going to be okay?" Jess asked, moving away before he could touch her.

He nodded. "The baby's coming. That's all. They're both going to be fine."

Her relief was so strong her entire body sagged.

"This isn't about the blessing. It would have happened anyway. It's just time."

She tried to nod, but some things defied explanation. She turned and started to walk away.

"Jess," he called after her, and despite herself she faced him again. "I'm sorry. I shouldn't have accused you like that. I should have asked," he said, but she didn't care, she just needed him to leave so she could get away like the thief she was.

That's when it happened, the moment that ruined everything. His eyes widened with panic. The paramedics pushed her out of the way.

"Is he safe?" Nikhil said over their heads, everything but terror gone from his eyes. "Is Joy safe?"

She stared at him, unable to respond, unable to bear the pain pooling in her heart.

"Please don't leave. Please be here when I get back." It was the last thing he said before the paramedics slammed the doors in place and the ambulance drove off, leaving her standing there, taking with it the anger that had been so much easier than what she was left holding.

38

I feel responsible for every one of the deaths. I typed those names into the registry. I pinned those targets on each of those people.

I've saved lives too. But somehow I don't feel as responsible for those.

Why is it easier to claim those we lost while forgetting those we rescued?

—Dr. Jen Joshi

Maybe she shouldn't have run. Maybe she should have listened to her heart and trusted Nikhil to come back from the hospital and help her take care of things. Maybe she should have trusted that look in his eyes when he had figured out about Joy being in danger.

Or maybe she needed to stop wishing she had seen him just one more time before letting him go forever.

The autorickshaw pulled to a stop outside Joy's school, and she led him to the door. He squeezed her hard, his arms a vise around her waist. He hadn't stopped doing that ever since she came home yesterday and Sweetie had handed Joy to her at the airport before taking off for London.

Sweetie's boyfriend, Armaan, had hidden Joy and Sweetie in the back of his car and brought them to the airport so they wouldn't be followed. And then taken Joy back so she could take a taxi. She wished she could take Joy and run away to London with Sweetie. But Joy didn't even have a passport.

"One call and I'll be back," Sweetie had told her. "I really don't want to leave you alone."

But she couldn't worry about Sweetie being thrown in jail. She had to focus all her energy on carrying out her plan.

"I'll bring you back a red double-decker bus," Sweetie had said to Joy, fighting tears. "You be good for Mamma, even if she's not as awesome as Sweetie-mamu."

"No one's as awesome as Sweetie-mamu," Joy had said, and Sweetie had lost the fight against his tears when he turned away.

Joy hadn't asked once why Sweetie had to leave. Or why she had been gone for three weeks. He had just refused to let her get too far, sitting as close to her as he could, sleeping tightly wedged into her, clutching her hand all day as he brushed his teeth and changed his clothes. He'd even eaten all his meals on her lap.

She could have told him a million times that she would never leave him again. Instead, she had stuck close and clung to him in return, because words meant nothing in the face of actions.

"I'll pick you up as soon as school gets out, Joyboy. And we'll go to Birdies and get ice cream."

"Chocolate with chocolate brownie and chocolate sauce?"

"Of course."

He let her go slowly and dragged his feet up the steps. Naag had made it clear that she couldn't keep him home from school until the evidence was in his hands. She was lucky yesterday was a Sunday and she had got to spend at least that one day at home with Joy.

Naturally, Naag had been livid when she had told him that she had come home without the evidence. But she had told him that she knew where it was. She had agreed to take him to it this afternoon, so she had to act soon before she lost the nerve to carry out her plan.

Handing over the evidence was out of the question. She had tried. She had tried to talk herself into handing over the little piece of plastic Jen had died for, that Nikhil had crawled out of hell for, but she hadn't been able to. Not with everything those two had given her.

It wasn't just about doing the right thing either. She knew that there really was no way out. As soon as she gave Naag the evidence, he would have no reason to keep her or Joy alive. Her plan was the only chance she had. This wasn't the time to think about the fact that her entire plan rested on Nikhil's ability to judge people. Given how wrong he had been to trust her, there was no comfort in that thought.

She slid her sunglasses off her head and over her eyes. She crossed the street to the BEST bus stop and pretended to wait for a bus, although she hadn't made up her mind where she would be going. She studied the surroundings, trying to spot the bastards who were no doubt watching her and would watch for Joy the entire time he was in school.

The thought made her want to throw up, but she was taking care of it, and she had to focus on that. She used the cell phone Sweetie had handed her at the airport and dialed the number she had stolen from Nikhil.

She remembered sliding the card out of Nikhil's wallet when he was in the bathroom and writing it down, and felt a stab of shame. Which was hilarious, really. Of all the things she had stolen from him, this was one he had offered up. But the irony of her guilt would have made him break into that badly timed laughter of his.

She had to trust Nikhil's and Jen's judgment and trust the police officer.

The phone had been ringing for a while now. Just as she was beginning to believe he wouldn't answer, he did. "Yes?" he said with the impatience of someone who was being interrupted.

"I need to speak with Rahul Savant, please." Out of the corner of her eye, she spotted a black SUV parked across the street.

"Speaking."

"I need to meet you. About a case." She recognized the man in the driver's seat of the SUV. He had been tailing Joy and her.

"Ma'am, this is a private number. You can come into the police station and someone will help you."

"No. Not the police station. It's important."

"Okay. What's it about?"

"I . . . I can't . . . Can you come to the Punjab National Bank in Lokhandwala Complex? Today. At noon."

"Ma'am, I'm going to need more than that."

She took a deep breath. "Nikhil Joshi gave me your number. He said I could trust you."

A full minute of silence seemed to follow. Maybe he was trying to track her number. Maybe this was a mistake.

"Okay."

Relief and panic swept through her like twin currents. She clamped down on both. She had made her choice and this was it. "Just you. Please."

He must have heard the desperation in her voice, because his stern tone softened. "Yes. I'll be there."

The number 141 bus to Lokhandwala arrived, and she climbed aboard the dusty red double-decker, making her way up the stairs to the upper deck. She had just about an hour to get there.

She twisted around to catch another glimpse of the black SUV through the bus window, but her eyes caught another SUV on the other side of the intersection across the street from the one she had noticed earlier. She lifted her sunglasses and studied the car. She didn't recognize the bearded man in a *kurta* with his feet up on the dashboard, but there was something off about him. For all his languor, the other two men in the car had a strange alertness about them. All three wore sunglasses. But they were parked in the shade. She looked back at the other one. Why were there *two* SUVs keeping watch on Joy's school?

Nikhil watched the expression on Rahul's face. Complete, deliberate blankness.

"Who was that?"

"I have no idea. But I need to head out for a while. Feel free to stay and look through the catalogs." Rahul stood and grabbed his keys and then instead of leaving he walked back to Nikhil and peered over his shoulder at the albums with pictures of women in various dance poses that Nikhil had spent the past two hours poring over. "Tell me again, Dr. Joshi, why you said we were looking for this woman?"

"Actually, I didn't say." Nikhil flipped the album shut and waited for the cop to say what he evidently wasn't sure how to say.

"You know you're going to have to trust me," Rahul said.

"Basically, it's like this. If you want my help finding the evidence Jen hid for you, you're going to have to help me find this girl."

"Why?"

"You're going to have to trust me," Nikhil threw back at him.

Rahul studied him for another long moment.

He'd been studying Nikhil like a particularly complex crime scene ever since Nikhil had walked into his office in the middle of the night, straight from the airport. Nikhil had already told him everything he could remember about Jess, which of course didn't even include her real name.

Apparently, all the things Nikhil knew about her were entirely useless when it came to finding a missing person. There were literally thousands of chorus dancers who worked in Bollywood and not a single one was called Jess Koirala.

Rahul had told him that he had been searching for a girl by that name ever since he had found out that she was the recipient of Jen's heart over a week ago. Without any luck. But the elaborate effort that had gone into falsifying the donor records meant some very powerful people were involved.

Rahul had acquired portfolios from as many dance troupes as he could. They were laid out in front of Nikhil. Thirty-odd albums. He'd been through them a dozen times already. Even with all that face paint, he should've been able to pick her out. Shouldn't he? There was no way anyone else had eyes like that or that mouth. His eyes kept searching for that presence of hers. But could it even be captured on camera? That stillness? That calm-as-a-pond, disrupting-yet-soothing feeling of her that fluttered at the edge of his consciousness. Constantly.

I don't feel the same way about you.

If she had looked wounded before, that had killed her. All the courage it had taken for her to lay her feelings out in front of him despite her hopelessness, and he had been too much of a coward. Nothing in her face had moved. But her eyes . . . that look in her eyes had chased him endlessly. He wasn't just a coward, he was a liar.

Of course he felt it.

This thing between you and me, it has nothing to do with Jen.

He felt it in every beat of his heart, in every part of his body she had touched. In every part of *him* she had touched. It had terrified him. He had thought denying it meant he wouldn't have to bear the pain of loss again.

What an idiot he had been.

When he came home from the hospital and saw that diary sitting on Ria's perfectly made bed, he had known it was too late to never love again.

She had known it too; before he had even admitted it to himself, she had known how he felt about her. Still, she had run from him. And that meant she was in danger. That Joy was in danger.

"The only way I will give you any cooperation is if you find the girl." For all his trying to be a hard-ass, he really wanted to beg. "Please, we have to find her."

"Did you give my number to anyone?" the cop said finally.

"What?"

"Did you give my number to someone and ask her to trust me?"

Nikhil stood up so fast the chair toppled over behind him and crashed into the ceramic floor.

Jess.

Rahul gave him a look. "I think we might've found your girl."

39

Nikhil, if you're reading this, I'm sorry. I believe you would have done exactly what I did.

—Dr. Jen Joshi

Of course she knew she was being followed. All these years of being hyperaware of her surroundings might have something to do with it. But mostly it was because the monster had told her in plain words that he was watching her. If he got even a whiff of what she was contemplating, it was over. She had no idea if Rahul Savant would help her or even how. But being out of options had one advantage. You didn't have to waste time on weighing them.

The blast of the AC hit her as she entered the bank. She'd picked this one because it was large and crowded. She spent a moment studying the poster of the latest home loans scheme. The man in the poster was clean-cut with a dimple running through his cheek as he smiled at his family in that overly loving way of ads. Of course he would look like Nikhil. She didn't bother to tamp down on the longing that squeezed her heart at the thought of him. No one had followed her into the bank. But she couldn't take any chances. She would have to be quick.

Her eyes started to search the crowd. She had no idea what the police officer looked like.

"Ma'am. You're here for the home loan scheme?" A man in a blue shirt looked at her with a completely bored expression. There were dark stains at his armpits, but he didn't look nervous. Just like someone who was running an errand and wanted to move on to something else.

She didn't respond.

"The manager you called earlier is ready for your meeting in office twelve." He pointed to the back of the lobby. "Go down that corridor and turn left. It's the second room to your right."

"Thanks." She pulled her purse closer to herself and walked as casually as she could to the door and knocked.

A man in a bright white shirt pulled the door open. *Rahul Savant.* She thought of the way the name rolled off Nikhil's American tongue. He wasn't wearing a uniform, but she would bet her dancing legs this was him.

"DCP Savant." He flashed the ID badge hanging from his neck on a lanyard at her and gestured for her to come in.

She surveyed the room as the door clicked shut behind her. There was another door all the way across the room. Not that she would make it there if he didn't want her to, but knowing her escape route gave her an illusion of control. If Nikhil and Jen had been wrong about DCP Savant, she was dead. Then again, if her plan didn't work she was dead anyway. If they wanted to hurt Joy they would have to kill her first.

"Thanks for agreeing to meet me," she said without moving toward the chair he was pointing to.

"How can I help you, ma'am?"

Where did she start? "You're working on Jen Joshi's case? I'm, um . . ." Despite the overactive air-conditioning, sweat beaded over her scalp and trickled down her neck.

"Here, sit down," he said and poured her a glass of water. "What do you know about Jen Joshi?"

She cleared her throat and searched the room again. They were alone. "Nikhil . . . Dr. Joshi's husband, he said I could trust you."

He nodded but didn't push, and she knew he was adept at gleaning information from unwilling sources. One way or another she was doing this. There was no getting out of it now. "I'm being blackmailed. They . . . They've been threatening to hurt my son. He's . . ." Her voice cracked and she cleared it again. "He's just seven years old. And . . ." She hadn't expected to start shaking. But Joy's face when he had waved good-bye was stuck in her head. And Naag's laugh.

If you double cross me, no one is going to even look for the little bastard's body.

She stood, the chair shrieking against the tile behind her. "I'm sorry, I don't think I can do this." She should never have left Joy by himself.

The cop was next to her in a second.

"Listen, relax. If you don't tell me what's going on I can't help you." He held out a bottle of water. "Someone's threatening your son. Do you know who the person is?"

She shook her head. Even though she had never seen Naag, she could identify his voice in her sleep. But she wouldn't tell Rahul Savant that. There was no way of knowing that he wasn't already in Naag's pocket. If she were being realistic, how could he not be?

"I can't tell you anything until you get me and my son to a safe location. A new name, a new life. I'll go anywhere. Leave everything behind. But I won't tell you anything until you take care of this. Today."

"Listen, ma'am. You need to breathe. I can't help you if you don't tell me what this is about and who it is that's threatening you."

"I already told you it's about the Jen Joshi murder."

"Do you have information about the murderers?"

"I'm not telling you anything more, until you get us to a safe place. Where no one can find us."

"Okay. Where's your son right now? You're going to have to trust me."

She laughed. "I'll trust you when you get us to a safe place."

"How about me? Would you trust me?" The voice came from behind her. She spun around. Not that she needed to see him to know it was him, but there he was. His shoulders a little wider than when she'd first seen him, his face a little less gaunt. The spasm in her heart was a bolt of electricity. Her hand went to the scar, but she pulled it back.

"Nikhil." The name left her mouth before she could hold it back.

His eyes rested on her. Both hard and soft, filled with questions and accusations and relief, so much relief. "You left," he said, not stopping until he was so close she could smell his fresh Nikhil smell. "And now you want to leave again?" That tone, so possessive and intimate, she closed her eyes.

Why had she prayed to see him one more time? Now he was here, and everything was going to be ruined.

She turned to the officer. "They're outside. If I'm in here too long they'll know something is wrong. Please." She turned to Nikhil. "Nikhil, please. They're outside Joy's school."

He didn't touch her, but it felt like he had. "Rahul, get someone to Joy's school right now."

Rahul pulled out his phone and spoke into it.

"He goes to St. Teresa's Primary School," she said.

When he had repeated the information on the phone, the cop crossed his arms across his chest. "Now I'm going to need some details before I can do anything more."

"Tell him," Nikhil said, watching her in that way he had as though he were checking her for injuries. "We have no choice but to trust him."

We.

She turned back to DCP Savant. "Six months ago, he stole my son out of school and took him away for two days. He didn't hurt him. Just made him sit in a hospital waiting room telling him I was hurt. Joy, my son, he's seven years old. He was terrified when I picked him up. Two days after that someone crashed into him when he was riding his bike." She ran her finger across her forehead, just above her brow. "He had to get five stitches. And his arms were all scratched up. The man . . . I've never seen him . . . he said the next time Joy wouldn't get off so easy. Next time they took him I wouldn't see him again. Unless . . . If I didn't . . ." She looked at Nikhil. "If I didn't do as he said. If I didn't get the evidence Jen had hidden."

She pulled the neck of the T-shirt she was wearing down until the tip of her scar was visible. "He sent me to a hospital to get the scar. It's fake . . . well, it's real. But it's just cut into my skin."

Breath hissed from Nikhil, but there was more rage in his eyes than she had ever seen.

"He gave me Jen's diary and made me study it so I could pretend that she was telling me these things."

She was about to say sorry to Nikhil, to reach out and wipe the torment off his face, but he reached out and stroked her cheek instead, his eyes fierce.

"Did you find the evidence?" Rahul Savant was looking at her completely differently now.

She nodded. "I did find it."

Nikhil looked like she had stabbed him, but he didn't take his hand off her cheek.

"It was in the diary," she said directly to Nikhil. "But I haven't given it to him. And if he finds out, he'll . . . If something happens to Joy . . ."

"He knows you're back?" Nikhil spun around to face Rahul, panic in his voice. "We have to get Joy out of school right now." He took her hand and headed for the door.

Rahul followed them. "Where is the evidence?" he asked as they broke into the sunshine and got into the car that was waiting right outside the bank.

She snapped on her seat belt in the backseat next to Nikhil. "I have it. But I won't give it to you until Joy is safe." She couldn't get the SUV outside Joy's school out of her mind. "You have no idea what this man is capable of." What had that second SUV been doing there?

Something about that second SUV was very wrong. Why hadn't she gotten off the bus when she'd seen the second SUV?

Nikhil looked at her face. "Rahul, can we step on it?"

40

Why is evil so layered? When someone is good, it's for one of two reasons: 1) it makes them feel good, and 2) it makes them look good. But with evil the roots are as deep and branched as the oldest tree. The motivations are such a spiderweb of nature and nurture and choice and anger and greed and hatred all woven into a sticky mess. These bastards will stop at nothing.

—Dr. Jen Joshi

Asif Khan loved children. Who would believe that? People thought that just because you could blow someone's brains out and enjoy the red blast so much you wanted to smear the warm red all over your body and roll around in the sensation, that you couldn't appreciate what lovable creatures children were.

Small and delicate and so fucking helpless you could crush them with your bare hands like flowers. *Arrey wah*, he was a fucking poet and everything.

This one was an extra-soft specimen. Pale-skinned and gray-eyed and nothing but skin over bone. He kept tugging his pants up as though he knew someone was watching him and he wanted to protect his butt crack.

Finding him had been too easy. One bullet in one of the two bodyguard's heads and the other one had sung like a nightingale. Nothing like watching your friend die to get you to love life.

His own life was getting too fucking easy. He had almost enjoyed the home minister's games. At least the man was fighting him. He had to hand it to the bastard—he had taken all that trouble to find a girl who looked all chinky and had a son he could threaten and then trained her to fuck with the doctor bitch's husband's head. All so the minister could get his hands on whatever the bitch had hidden that could put Asif Khan in jail. All so the minister could stop

Asif Khan from blackmailing him to let him keep his very lucrative business going. Asif would give anything to know how the politician had gotten the girl to find out enough about the doctor to fool her husband. Definitely a good plan, and it would have been a great plan if Asif weren't such an unbeatable adversary.

The only way to beat him would be if the doctor bitch had connected the transplants that happened in the Gulf with the dead fuckers in Dharavi before he had silenced her. He didn't put it past the bitch. She had been so cool when he had pushed the gun into her belly and told her to back off.

He hadn't known then that there was a child percolating in there. He'd only found that out from the papers, when his men had taken life sentences without selling him out. The bastards should have killed both the husband and the wife and left. But they had let their dicks get involved. Filthy bastards. He was the filthiest bastard, and he wouldn't fuck a pregnant woman he'd been paid to kill.

He'd provide for their wives and kids until the bastards died. If they had sold him out, they'd come back to dead bodies when they walked out of jail.

Hey, they didn't call it the filthy underworld for nothing. If he wanted a clean business he'd have become a priest. Then again, he couldn't remember the last time he'd seen a clean priest.

Everyone in this shit pot of a world had to protect his own arse.

The bastard politician was protecting his own arse too.

Asif almost didn't want the game to end. But money was power, and of course, once you promised the fuckers in Dubai the goods, it became a matter of life and death.

As for the politician, no matter how smart his plan in theory, he had been an idiot in underestimating Asif Khan. Asif leaned into the plush seat of his Pajero. He liked his cars big, like him. That made him smile. He was big and his car was big and they could both drive into anything they bloody wanted to drive into.

Two poetic thoughts in two minutes. He should write a book.

"Bring me the child," he said to Laloo, who was contemplating whether or not to smile because Bhai was smiling.

"But, Bhai, the school security is totally tight, like."

One of these days he was going to kill the useless bastard. He had more doubts than a fucking philosopher. Is life this? Or is life that? The fuckers could contemplate life to shit and do nothing of consequence their entire life.

"Stay here," he ordered before he jumped out of the car himself and crossed the street to the tiny square of dirt that passed for a playground at the supposedly fancy school and zipped down his pants.

The best part of being a man was being able to take a piss anywhere. He let his arc water the lone tree at the edge of the "playground."

The kids started to point and laugh at his performance. The bitch with her hair in a ponytail who looked just like she was playing a schoolteacher in a TV serial ran up to him. "*Arrey*, what are you doing?" she said in Hindi, as though the first thought that had struck her fancy arse when she saw him was that he wouldn't understand her bastard English.

He reached out and grabbed her arm, his fly still open, and before she could scream he flashed his *ghoda* at her—the metal one stashed in his pocket, not the flesh one hanging out of his pants. "You make a sound and all those kids will be dead."

She started trembling. But she didn't make a sound.

"Good. Now you see that wet patch on the tree where I just watered it? Don't take your eyes off it until I tell you to. Understood?" She nodded.

He zipped his fly and walked to the kids on the lawn.

41

I went to med school to fight nature's violence against us. But in the end, all of nature's brutality fades before our own.

—Dr. Jen Joshi

When Rahul's phone rang and he hit a button on the dashboard setting off the police siren on the car, Jess knew something was very wrong.

Joy.

She wanted to fold over.

"There's been some sort of attack on Joy's school," Rahul said. The officer who was driving sped up. Rahul pulled out his gun and snapped and unsnapped something into it.

They started speeding through traffic with the siren screaming above them and screeched to a stop outside the playground.

"Stay down," Rahul said, and both police officers got out of the car to the sound of gunshots.

Nikhil threw himself on top of her. As soon as the gunshots stopped, she scrambled up to look out of the window.

There were five children huddled on the steps of the school behind Joy's Sheila-teacher, but Jess's eyes sought only Joy. He wasn't with the children. He was in the arms of a bearded man in a red *kurta.* Rahul had his gun pointed at the man, and the man had a gun pointed at Rahul with the arm that wasn't carrying her son.

"I'm coming out," she screamed. "I have what you need. I have the evidence." She pushed the door open and stumbled out, Nikhil close behind her.

"No funny business." The madman carrying her baby pointed the gun at Joy's head. She nodded, meeting his eyes.

Three men and the officer who had been driving their car lay on the muddy ground in pools of blood. All of it had taken under one minute.

Joy found her eyes. She shut her own. *Close your eyes*, babu, *Mamma's here.*

Her baby squeezed his eyes shut.

"Put the child down," Nikhil said, and the madman swung his gun between Rahul and Nikhil, his eyes entirely too calm.

"There's no way out of this, Asif Khan. It's over," Rahul said.

"I have what you want in my hand. It's not over, *chutiya*." He jerked the gun he was pointing at Joy.

"Let the other children go back inside," Nikhil said, and Asif pointed the gun at his head.

Rahul's gun hadn't moved from Asif, but the bastard was using Joy as a shield.

Nikhil's hands were in the air, his gaze steady on Asif. "The other children. You don't need them." He looked at the group of children huddled behind their teacher. "They're going to go inside."

Rahul didn't take his eyes off Asif. "The entire police force will be here in two minutes. There's nowhere to go." He looked at the teacher. "Take them inside."

The teacher started herding the children into the building, and Asif turned the gun on Joy again.

She pulled the SD card out of her bra and held it up. "I have what you want in my hand. Put him down. Please." She met Asif's eyes. "Please."

"You're the bitch he sent to America. Where's your red hair?" The bastard actually smiled. He was calm. So incredibly calm.

"Yes. I dyed my hair. I have Jen's evidence against you here. Right here."

He pointed the gun at Rahul's head, then back at Joy's. "Bring it here."

"Jess, no," Nikhil said, but she was already next to Asif. "Put him down, you can take me. DCP Savant will let you go if you take me."

Within the blink of an eye, Asif had the gun pressed to her head and his arm locked around her throat, squeezing her windpipe. But Joy was on the ground. Joy was on the ground.

Nikhil squatted down, his eyes steady as they met Joy's. He held out his hand. "Come here, *beta*."

"Go, *babu*," she said, and Joy was in Nikhil's arms and Asif was dragging her across the field. Rahul was trying to get a clear shot. She met Rahul's eyes and shoved her elbow with all the anger collected inside her into the soft center between Asif's ribs. The breath whooshed out of him, giving her a chance to spin around and kick with all her strength between his legs.

He folded over. But just for a moment before straightening again just in time to catch Rahul's bullet in his shoulder. He stumbled back, swung his gun at Joy, and fired. Nikhil spun Joy away from him, and Jess took a flying leap at Nikhil.

42

The real reason to have this baby is to see Nic being a father. I fully expect it to be spectacular.

—Dr. Jen Joshi

She had been in and out of consciousness for two days now, and the mad panic that had taken up residence in Nikhil's heart since the bullet sliced right through her and nicked his shoulder had finally calmed somewhat. He had been part of the team that operated on her. And since he'd sewn up the torn muscle and tissue himself, he knew that the only organ the bullet had hit was one corner of her lung.

Nic had operated on a lot of bullet wounds, and the damage a bullet did was one of those infinite possibilities things. In the complex mosaic that was the human body, you could never predict the extent of the damage until you opened the patient up. This bullet had blessedly missed every major organ and blood vessel.

He squeezed his eyes shut, reliving one more time that moment when she had slammed against him with the impact of the bullet meant for him.

"Are you okay, Dr. Nic?" Joy asked, tucked in next to him on the couch across from her hospital bed. He studied Nikhil with those eyes that were so different from his mother's in color and shape and yet exactly the same in what they held.

"As okay as one can be right now. You?" He wasn't a fan of lying to children, and Joy seemed to respect that.

"I'm fine. Just waiting for my mamma to wake up," he said, rewarding Nic's honesty with some of his own. Nic's heart squeezed.

Joy was so tiny, so frail. The way Nikhil had always felt as a child. On the inside. On the outside he'd been a gargantuan ball of fat.

"Me too, buddy."

Joy patted his arm, and they watched her for a few moments in silence. Then Joy turned to him again. "Dr. Nic, do you like my mamma?" But his face held the real question. How can anyone not love someone as amazing as her?

Nikhil knew exactly how he felt. "Very much." And then, because this child was not one for shallow platitudes, he added, "She's one of the strongest people I've ever met."

Joy brightened, sitting up straight. "Yes! Did you know she can pick up all our shopping bags by herself when we go to the market? And she can spin forever. And she can reach the loft cupboard without a ladder because she can jump so high. And she can hold up Sweetie-mamu all by herself and take him to his room when he gets sad and drinks too much and comes home."

Nikhil ruffled his hair. "Yes. But she's also very strong on the inside. You know how she helps your Sweetie-mamu? She did the same thing to me when she first met me. But with her heart."

Joy smiled his mother's two-pinprick-dimples smile. "And you know something? She's the best mamma in the world."

Nikhil smiled too. "I imagine she would be."

Joy looked disappointed.

"What?" Nikhil asked.

"When I tell her that, she always says everyone thinks their mamma is the best." Then he frowned. "She thinks her *aama* was the best, can you believe that?"

"Actually, I can. Mine is pretty awesome too."

He sat up even straighter. Apparently this was an argument he really enjoyed having. "But I *know* why mine is the best. Like, I have a *reason*."

"What's your reason?"

"My mummy always asks me one question." He held one finger up. Why did kids do that? Indicate numbers with their fingers. He wanted to kiss the child's finger, but instead he asked him what that one question was.

"She always asks me if I could have anything in the whole world, what that would be? And she always gets me what I ask for."

"Come on! Really? Nobody can give you anything you want. I'll bet you make it easy on her."

"Nope." He shook his head vigorously. "I don't."

"Tell me the last thing you asked for."

He didn't miss a beat. "Chocolate-chip ice cream."

Nikhil made a face. "Lame."

He held his hand up. "With extra chocolate chips." He shook his hand when Nic tried to interrupt him again. "Chocolate brownie." More hand shaking in Nikhil's disbelieving face. "And chocolate sauce on top."

"She let you have all that?"

Joy lifted his eyebrows and nodded.

"How bad was the tummy ache?"

He pinched his thumb against his forefinger.

"So, she's never said no to anything?"

He shook his head. Then he sat up again. All alert, as he tended to do when he had an idea or a thought struck him. "It's only one thing." Again, he held up that finger.

"And that one thing is?"

He studied Nikhil, gauging if he was worthy of sharing his mother's one failure without feeling like a traitor. "She won't get me a doggie."

"No way."

"Yup." He sighed. "She says she'll get me whatever I want as long as it doesn't have a heartbeat."

"Yup, that definitely rules out a dog."

"Yup. A big no-no."

"You know, my mommy got me a dog when I was five."

Joy's little mouth opened in awe. "How lucky." Longing spilled from his eyes. And envy. Lots of envy.

"Well, I thought I was. I even called the dog Luckster."

"Luckster?" His lips twisted as if Nikhil's choice of dog names were something of an embarrassment.

"We used to do that in America when I was a little boy. Add a '-ster' to everything."

"So you'd be Nicster?"

"And you'd be Joyster."

He giggled, his soft cheeks pushing his eyes into slits. Something he didn't do nearly enough of.

"Must have been so much fun, *na?*"

"It was. He was a golden retriever, and he and I were inseparable. He slept in my bed. I sat next to his bowl and ate with him. I even took him into school for show-and-tell."

"Wow. Is he with your mamma now?"

"Actually, a few weeks after I got him he got sick."

"Oh no. What happened? Did he die?"

Nic must've looked surprised because Joy lowered his voice. "I could tell from your face. You were like this." His lips dragged down at the edges as he made a sad face. "Did she get you another one after that?"

"No. I couldn't. I couldn't ever even pet anyone else's dog after that."

Joy hopped off the couch and climbed on Nic's lap.

"Can I tell you something?"

Nic adjusted himself so Joy was perched comfortably on his lap.

"What are you two doing?"

They both turned around at the sound of her voice.

"Mamma!" Joy hopped off Nikhil's lap, ran to her, and wrapped his arms around her. Yesterday Nikhil had explained to him exactly how to do it without touching her wound, and even in his excitement he did a perfect job. The strangest sense of pride swelled in Nikhil's chest.

"Joyboy, my baby boy." She tried to wrap her arms around Joy, navigating the IV line and the monitor wires. Nikhil adjusted the wires so they weren't in her way. She held Joy and turned those eyes on Nic.

"Hi."

"Hi yourself. How are you feeling?"

"Awake." Her eyes were tired, her lips chapped, but an awake her was the most beautiful thing he'd ever seen.

"That's good."

"Mamma." Joy straightened up. "You know how you say you will never buy me a dog?"

"Really, Joy, that's the first thing you say to Mamma when she wakes up?"

"No. I'm not going to ask you for one again. I know it has a heartbeat. I know you won't get me one. But can we get one for Dr. Nic?"

Nic's heart did another awful squeeze in his chest.

Jess looked at Nic, her shadow-rimmed eyes weary.

He looked away from her and at this amazing child she had raised and widened his eyes. *Not now, buddy.*

Joy widened his eyes back. *I got this. Trust me.* Then he turned back to his mother. "Dr. Nic needs to learn to love another dog. He's still too sad about his old one who died."

The lump in Nic's throat was large and painful, but it was also so damn funny his shoulders started to shake.

"Nikhil?" she asked, looking at him as though she feared that he had finally lost it.

"What? The metaphor is hilarious." He was all-out laughing now. "But also brilliant."

"Really?" she said, and she started to laugh too.

"So, are you going to tell me your real name?" Nikhil asked after he had laid Joy on the couch and tucked him in. Joy had fallen asleep on his lap.

She tried not to think about how he had held her baby. How Joy had melted against him in complete trust. "You already know what my name is," she said, looking at her hands because now that she was sitting up, now that the world wasn't a blur, she couldn't meet his eyes. "You've seen it on the hospital paperwork."

He picked up the sheet of paper laying on the nightstand. "Come on! That's not your real name."

She narrowed her eyes at him. Or tried to, because what she really wanted was to touch him. After watching him almost take that bullet meant for Joy, she wanted to shake him, wanted to kill him, wanted to thank him, wanted to hold him and never let him go.

"You want me to believe you're a chorus dancer who's called Kitty Sinha? Come on! That's like something out of those seventies Bollywood movies Aie made us watch."

She tried to look angry, but it was funny. "And you're an Indian American called 'Nic Joshi.'"

He smiled. Those glorious dimples sinking deep into his stubbly cheeks. "True. We're stereotypes, both of us."

Only nothing about him was a typical anything.

He took her hand. "Stereotypes are supposed to be predictable. Nothing about you is predictable. Nothing." He squeezed his eyes shut. "Nothing is predictable about how you make me feel."

"Please, Nikhil. Please don't. Please don't do this to me."

"But I want to. I know I said before that I couldn't. But I was lying. Because look at me. I don't even know how not to. I want to do everything to you, with you."

The shaking started somewhere deep inside her, her shoulders vibrating because the air was sticking and unsticking in her lungs. Sobs, but not sobs, laughter but not laughter. An inner vibrating dance too effusive to be contained on the inside.

He moved his hand to cup her face in that too-intimate, too-familiar way. She pressed her cheek into his palm, two involuntary motions, without instruction, without logic, without fear that should've been learned by now but wasn't.

He smiled again, and she knew he wasn't done turning her world upside down. "At least tell me what to call you. So I don't feel like an idiot when I tell you how I feel."

"Kitty," she said, wanting to torture him.

His grin widened. "You would do that to me?"

"It's my name."

"No, it isn't." His laughing eyes got serious again. Dancing between joy and sincerity, the two halves of him that she was trapped between.

"How do you know? Did you ask Joy?"

"I knew it! And no, I didn't."

"My name is"—she took a breath—"Nikita, Nikita Sinha. Everyone calls me Kitty or Nikita here. But everyone at home always called me Nikki."

"No way." He was laughing again, his perfect untimely laughter. "Nic and Nikki? Really? That sounds like the title of a really bad Bollywood film."

It sounded lovely. But she couldn't say it.

"Nikki," he said, and God above, something heavy and liquid rushed through her. Bloodletting. This had to have been what bloodletting felt like. Like disease and impurity and pain flowing from you, taking your life, but also taking what was killing you. Aama was the last person who had called her by that name.

"Hey," he said as her grip on his hand tightened, the shaking inside her deciding to go with sobs. Very carefully, he wrapped his arms around her and held her close, his breath falling on that spot on her head.

He whispered her name. "Nikki. I think that might just work." She closed her eyes and drowned in the sensation, soaked up his words. "I love you, Nikki. Please don't ever leave me again. I don't think I could take it."

43

The greatest gift Nikhil ever gave me was family.

—Dr. Jen Joshi

"Vic and Ria are making a huge donation to the new surgery wing at Holy Spirit Hospital and they're naming it the Jennifer Joshi wing. They're all flying down next month for the dedication ceremony," Nikhil announced, turning off the phone.

"That's wonderful," Nikki said, although Ria had already told her yesterday. But Vikram and Ria had wanted to tell Nikhil themselves.

"Ria had already told you, hadn't she?" Nikhil asked, shaking his head at her across the dining table where takeout containers of *biryani* sat wiped clean.

"I heard them talk about it on the phone yesterday," Joy said, hopping off Nikhil's lap. In a matter of three weeks the boy had turned into a complete traitor.

"Jenna's coming too," her little traitor said excitedly. Ria and Vikram had named their baby girl Jenna in honor of Jen. Nikhil had told Joy that she was his little cousin and Joy could talk of little else.

He took Rahul's hand and tried to pull him off the chair. Rahul had taken to coming around to the flat ever since she'd come home from the hospital a week ago. At first it was because he was trying to find answers, but then it was like Nikhil and he had suddenly become long-lost friends. "That's Ria Parkar's daughter. You know Ria Parkar?" Joy, her little name-dropper, said to Rahul. "She's a big film star. She's Dr. Nic's sister. She told me I can come see Jenna anytime. You want to see Jenna's pictures?"

"Go pull them up on your computer, Joy. I'm going to help Dr. Nic clean up," Rahul said to Joy, and Joy skipped off.

Sweetie rolled his eyes and stood. "Dr. Nic and cleanup! Evidently, DCP Savant hasn't spent too much time with Dr. Joshi." Sweetie had returned from London two days ago, and over the past two days Nikhil's inability to pick up after himself had him in a state of shock. "Almost makes me want to go back into hiding," he had said to Nikki that morning.

But she was glad that he was home safe.

It still felt a bit strange to believe that they were safe.

Asif Khan was in a coma in police custody. Even five bullets hadn't killed him. Rahul was waiting for him to wake up from his many bullet wounds so he could make sure he went straight to the electric chair from there. Jen's evidence documented the horrific list of all the organs that had been stolen and transplanted into recipients across the Gulf. Nikhil's friend Omar was working with Rahul on tracking down the other side of the ring.

Naag had sent Nikki one last text telling her he would not be contacting her again unless she tried to find him. True to form, his last text had been a threat. If she tried to find him or talk to the police about him, he would be back, otherwise she was free. Naturally, his phone number had been entirely untraceable. Rahul was still trying. She had told Rahul every detail she could remember. She was determined to do all she could to bring him to justice. Never again would she let any bastard get away with turning her into a victim. But she wasn't going to let it consume her life.

That was Rahul's job, and he was doing it.

"I need Asif Khan to get out of that coma," Rahul said. "Until that happens, we can't track down the man who sent you after Nikhil. The home minister's office won't authorize that search until Asif wakes up and makes a statement. At least we've worked with the UAE authorities to cut off the ring. I'm sorry that's still all I have."

"Don't be," Nikki said. "We'll get him. How's your friend who got attacked by Asif Khan?"

Rahul's face turned dark and stormy and so tormented she was reminded of Nikhil when she had first met him. Evidently, there was history with this friend.

"She must be fine. She won't see me. Won't speak to anyone." Nikhil patted his shoulder, and Rahul stiffened some more. The man took the strong-and-silent type to a whole different level. "Oh, and Nikhil, everything is sorted out with the clinic. You can start on Monday."

Joy hollered from the bedroom, and Rahul went off to find him.

Nikhil picked up a few glasses from the dining table. "Please tell Sweetie I can clean up." He took them into the kitchen where she could hear Sweetie rinsing things out.

"You want me to lie to Sweetie?" she called after him and then yelped when he came back out and scooped her up from her chair.

"Funny. But you know what I *can* do?"

She giggled. "I'm about to find out, am I not?"

He pressed a kiss into her ear before putting her on the couch and then tucking a blanket around her. "I can take care of people." And then softer: "And I can really take care of you."

She stroked his face where the dimples sank deep beneath her palm. "That I do know. Thank you."

He dropped a quick kiss on her lips.

"What was Rahul saying about the clinic?"

He sank down on his knees on the floor next to her. "I have a job. At Jen's clinic in Dharavi."

She wasn't sure how to react to that. "If that's what you want to do, it's wonderful."

"It is what I want to do." He dug her hand out from under her blanket. "I want to make sure the clinic starts up again and make sure the organ transplant registry is fixed."

"I know. I thought you were considering the job Holy Spirit offered you after you operated on me there."

He played with her fingers as though they were endlessly fascinating things. "Do you want me to take that instead?"

She shook her head. "No. That's not you. The clinic in Dharavi is perfect for you."

"Yes it is, for now," he said. "You sure you're okay with that?"

"Of course."

"Because if you don't feel safe staying in Mumbai—"

She pulled their joined hands to her lips. "I've never felt this safe in my life." He was here, and she couldn't explain it, but it was like having armor. Maybe not so much armor as a shield at her back. Like if she looked away from Joy, from her life, like if she lay down and fell asleep for a bit, there was someone who could step in for her as the world spun, someone to take over until she was ready again.

"You are safe. I will do all I can to keep you safe." It took an effort for him to say it, but he believed it. He believed that he could make that promise again, and that made everything in her heart expand and fill her up.

"Forever." He dropped one of those feather-quick kisses on her lips, and she held his face and kissed him back. Forever.

"Ice cream?" Sweetie walked in with a tub of ice cream, cups, and spoons.

"Yay, ice cream!" Joy ran up and climbed onto Nikhil's lap as he sat cross-legged on the floor. Rahul sank into a chair.

Sweetie handed everyone bowls. Chocolate on chocolate on chocolate, of course.

Nikhil fed her a spoonful. Joy fed Nikhil a spoonful.

"Holy wow! You were right, Joyboy. This is the best ice cream in the world," Nikhil said as Joy pushed another spoonful into his mouth without waiting for him to complete his sentence.

She stared at the two of them. Hope no longer felt like a splinter in her heart but like chocolate on her tongue. Suddenly, it struck her, Nikhil and she could both taste food just fine now.

And it was the most amazing thing.

Dear Jen,

You thought I'd never be able to write something in this diary that I couldn't say to you. But you were wrong. And here it is:

I don't know how it happened, but she found a way to navigate her way around all the broken pieces of me you left behind. And somehow she grew each one until it filled in the cracks.

You know that look on the faces of patients when they wake up after the critical twelve hours we give them after lifesaving surgery? That's how I feel sometimes, like an illness that should have killed me passed me by and decided to let me go.

You're still here. You'll always be. Sometimes I think about it and I still can't believe you're gone. But you left a little piece of something inside Nikki—like a starter cell in a petri dish. Yes, I know she doesn't really have your heart, but somehow, she does.

I think you managed to save us both. Thank you.

—Dr. Nikhil Joshi

Acknowledgments

With each new book, the number of people I am indebted to grows, and this in itself is the thing for which I am most grateful. I have to start with my best friend, Rupali Mehta, who has been my first companion on this and most paths. Thanks, my darling, for agonizing over my stories with me from the very moment they spark up in my head and then sticking it out no matter how long and hard the labor of bringing them into the world becomes.

My beta readers, Tamar Bihari, Heather Marshall, Joanna Shupe, Robin Kuss, Clara Kensie, Savannah Reynard, Kalpana Thatte, Nishaad Navkal, and Mohanish Hatwar, for asking all the right questions and then for helping dig for answers.

My idols, Kristan Higgins, Nalini Singh, and Susan Elizabeth Philips, for their shining example and their precious support.

My beloved niece, Rutvika Charegaonkar, for traipsing across the slums of Dharavi with me, and the incredibly generous Christa Desir, for her work with Rape Victim Advocates (www.rapevictim advocates.org), who do so much to heal and empower sexual assault survivors.

Senior Inspector Ravindra Bhide, for patiently and fastidiously answering my questions about the Mumbai Police Force, my friend Smitha Shetty, for her compassionate insights into the world of organ donation, and Advocate Pallavi Divekar, for her trusty legal eye. This book would not be possible without their knowledge and experience. Any errors in authenticity are entirely my own.

My editor, Martin Biro, for his excitement about this story ever since it was just an idea and for his sharp eye, unerring kindness, and faith. My agent, Claudia Cross, for her wise, always even-keeled counsel. My publicist, Vida Engstrand, for her wellspring of inventive ideas and monumental support. And for every single person at Kensington Publishing who has made this such a great experience for me.

Mama, Papa, and Aie, for bearing neglect and easing the weight of my familial responsibilities so I can do this thing I love. Manoj, Mihir, and Annika, for navigating this path with me. Your patience makes this possible, your pride makes it all the more precious.

Finally, my deepest thanks to you, my readers, for taking this journey with me one more time. I could never, ever thank you enough.